Firebrand

RED HORIZON
STEFAN COLEMAN

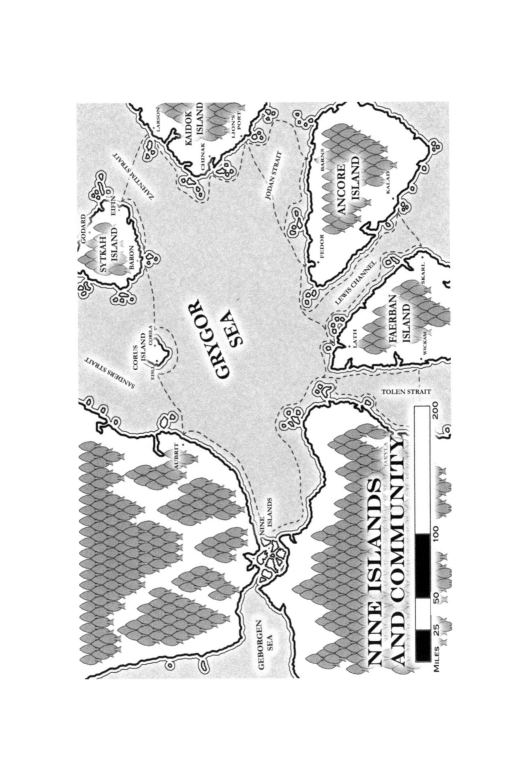

NINE ISLANDS
AND COMMUNITY

MILES 25 50 100 200

LARSON
KAIDOK
ISLAND
CHINAK
LIONS
PORT

ZAHNTINI STRAIT

GODARD
EIFEN
SYTKAH
ISLAND
BARON

BARNS
ANCORE
ISLAND
KALAD
FEDOR

JODAN STRAIT

GRYGOR
SEA

LEWIS CHANNEL

SKARL
FAERBAN
ISLAND
LATH
WICKAM

CORUS
ISLAND
COBLA
EISLA

SANDERS STRAIT

TOLEN STRAIT

ALLBRIT

NINE
ISLANDS

JAKYLA

GEBORGEN
SEA

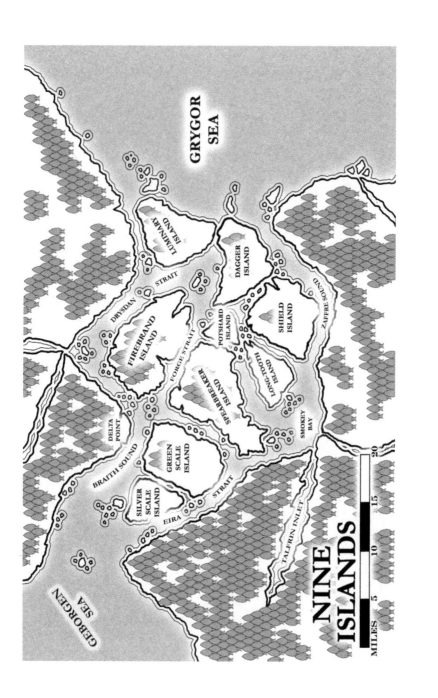

NINE ISLANDS

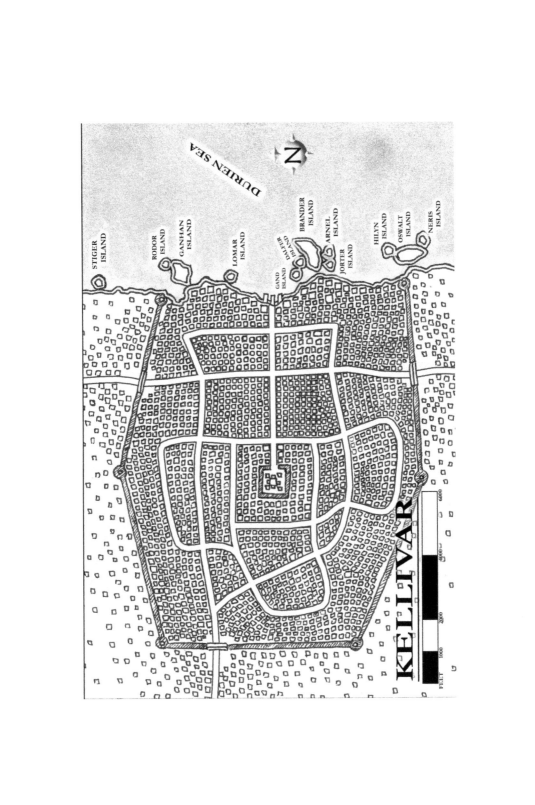

DURIEN SEA

STIGER
ISLAND

RODOR
ISLAND

GANHAN
ISLAND

LOMAR
ISLAND

BRANDER
ISLAND

GAND
ISLAND

DALFER
ISLAND

ARNEL
ISLAND

JORTER
ISLAND

HILYN
ISLAND

OSWALT
ISLAND

NERIS
ISLAND

KELLVAR

FEET   1000   2000   4000   6000

Table of Contents

Chapter 1 1

Chapter 2 33

Chapter 3 49

Chapter 4 61

Chapter 5 73

Chapter 6 87

Chapter 7 99

Chapter 8 119

Chapter 9 137

Chapter 10 155

Chapter 11 165

Chapter 12 171

Chapter 13 193

Chapter 14 207

Chapter 15 223

Chapter 16 243

Chapter 17 261

Chapter 18 279

Chapter 19 295

Chapter 20 309

Chapter 21 321

Chapter 22 341

Chapter 23 363

About the Author 381

Chapter 1

A cold, leather hand clamped hard over Maer's mouth, pinching his jaw, and jolting him awake from his dreams. He struggled to rise, but the hand held him down, and cold fear seized him. He took a breath through his nose, then another, the icy air stinging his nostrils as his eyes shot open, but the world was dark. The world was empty.

Is this what death feels like?

He closed his eyes, and opened hands that were clenched and shaking, and forced his breath to steady. He forced his mind to focus, for now was not the time to be paralyzed, he told himself. Here was not the place to be paralyzed.

He opened his eyes once more to the darkened world that was cloudy and blurred, but soon his mind gave him clarity, and he remembered where he was. Chilled air watered his eyes, so he blinked to clear them, then focused his gaze further towards the hooded figure silhouetted against the haze. One of the figure's hands was pressed over Maer's mouth, but as he looked downward, he saw that the other clutched a long, shining blade.

The figure stared down at him, the billowing of his cloak the only part of him that moved, but then he flicked his wrist and the knife disappeared, dancing across a loose cloth before being silently sheathed. He brought a finger to his lips, and then the hand covering Maer's mouth withdrew, and Maer felt some of his tension leave.

Maer sat up and looked around, barely making out the line that separated the rocky landscape from the heavens and took a minute to massage his tired muscles. A low moan whispered along the tops of the peaks, and he shivered, pulling his own cloak tight around himself to block out the icy tendrils that always managed to find a crack. Behind him a horse stamped, its hooves making a dull clamp, and then another, to signal at the least their horses had not abandoned them yet.

"Rise, but use caution," the figure whispered. "We are not alone."

"What do you mean, Onesh?" Maer asked, feeling a warmth spread through his body that quickly turned into a cold knot as the words settled.

"A shadow stirs," Onesh answered. "The wind is… troubled. We must ride quickly."

"What's out there?" Maer asked through a tight jaw, taking care to pack his bedding as quietly as he could. He thought back to the night before when Onesh called him away from the group, saying too many bodies would cause too much unwanted attention.

"We're too far west," Onesh said, almost to himself. "I may have made a mistake, allowing you to accompany me, but my options were limited, you understand. Time is short. The others…" He trailed off, and the knot in Maer's stomach tightened further.

"Onesh, what am I not seeing?"

Onesh stayed silent. His head turned steadily, searching, but whether it was searching for the right words or something else, Maer could not say. He could hardly hear even his breathing, but when he finally spoke, his voice was grim, and Maer almost wished he hadn't.

"Darkness returns to Ildice. The Shadow moves against Learsi."

Onesh pressed hard as they rode along the peaks of the Truvona Mountains, trusting their steeds to understand the meaning of haste. The horses complied with the flight. Indeed, to Maer, the horses appeared to desire the speed even more than their riders, and it amazed him how Onesh was able to compel them so. Only when they crested a ridge some miles further and the silver moon broke through the haze did Onesh slow the horses' gait, but even then, their pace was still quick. Maer did not mind.

They continued eastward for a mile or so more, but due to the light, Maer could barely discern any landmarks or path, and so couldn't quite identify how far they'd traveled. His gaze darted around, occasionally glancing behind, but the gray horizon had long been playing with his sense of distance, and he couldn't even be sure how far they had gone from their main camp. The landscape changed little, save for the stones varying their shades of gray or height by a few meters, but otherwise there was nothing. Fortunately, it seemed to be enough for his partner.

When they reached one ridge, they saw the faint puffs of smoke of their main scouting party's camp rising above the fog, casting an orangey glow that stood out like a beacon, so they turned their horses towards it and continued on. An outer guard nodded to them as they passed through the camp's perimeter, and once safe within the heated glow, Maer tried to relax.

"Oi, where've you been?" one of the men around the fire called out. "Disappeared the other night, rode off into the fog…"

Onesh raised his hand. "Silence, young one. Not all the stones are without ears."

"Not all the stones are without ears?" the man snapped back. "What the blazes…"

"Arlen, enough!" another voice growled, and Arlen went silent. "Welcome back."

Onesh dismounted and approached the speaker, a grizzled lieutenant who sported a patch over his eye.

"Thank you, Treel," Onesh greeted, clasping hands with him. "Alas, we have no time for pleasantries. I have a need to speak with you."

"So, how'd the ride go with him?" Arlen greeted Maer, gesturing to an open spot by their small fire and extending to him a steaming cup of coffee after the two older soldiers went off on their own. "Was he all doom and gloom, or did he actually smile for once? Did he keep talking about hunting the shadow? I see he still speaks in his lame…"

"He smiles enough," another soldier, Bardor, interjected. "At least I think so behind that mask. He may take things more seriously than most, and he can be a little strange at times, but aren't we all?"

"He seemed concerned," Maer answered, accepting the cup with shaky hands, and as he took a seat, he tried not to stare off towards where his partner disappeared. He thought about mentioning the knife, which truth be told, he had thought about a lot on the ride back, but Onesh had given no explanation, only rode harder, so he had no opportunity to ask. The thought came back more so, now, and he could feel his heart start to race, but the thought of mentioning it to the men felt awkward, and strangely pointless. Maer leaned in close to the warm flames. "So, um, what do you guys know about him?"

"Not much is known about Onesh," Bardor shrugged, poking the fire. "He showed up one day, before I was assigned here. Arlen would know more. He was his old partner."

"Not much worth knowing," Arlen grumbled. "The man's crazy."

"What do you mean?" Maer asked. Arlen shook his head, and then gestured around him.

"Look around you!" Arlen answered. "There is nothing but rocks, and sky, and cold. There is nothing here, but that fool of a man keeps insisting there is. Even has the lieutenant believing his ways. The only thing of weight out here is us. There's never been anything more."

"No life at all?" Maer asked. "Are you sure?"

"Have you seen anything?" Arlen countered, laughing into the darkness. "And when you rode out with him, did you see anything? Gotta say, when you came in to our patrol, I was very glad to be reassigned, and I'll just leave it at that."

"What does he say is out here?" Maer asked, looking around for fear of the noise. "Or out there, or out…"

"It doesn't matter, alright," Arlen snapped. "Just let it go."

"When you've seen as much as I have, you'll understand."

They all jumped at Onesh's words, no one having heard his approach.

"Seen as much as you?" Arlen scoffed. "How much could you have seen that I haven't? I know this land and the lands beyond far beyond what anyone has seen, even you."

"If you say so," Onesh chuckled, though not dismissively, gesturing his hand downward that, surprisingly, made Arlen hold back his next comment. He beckoned to Maer. "Come, join me for a little walk, and stretch your legs after that ride. Let us talk."

Maer stepped away from the comfort of the fire to join his partner, unsure of his thoughts. Still, he followed, and felt an odd sense of peace he didn't feel around the others. They didn't seem to go anywhere specific, but once they had put a little distance between themselves and the group, Onesh stopped and put a hand on his shoulder.

"Forgive me if I startled you earlier," Onesh said lightly, his voice gentle and soothing. "People tend to wake loudly, and I don't like to take chances I don't have to."

"What was out there?" Maer asked, feeling the tightness of his muscles leaving. "What had you nervous?"

"Nervous?" Onesh began, and then chuckled. "No, not nervous, though I see how you could see it as such. Excited would describe it better. I sense one of my old foes has returned after many years, and with his return marks the return of something far greater, far more wonderful, far more fantastic... I am sorry, old memories have a way of resurfacing, especially as of late. I was hoping we could have a moment to speak of other things. There are answers I must have. Your name is Maer, and you're a sergeant, correct?"

"Yes, sir," Maer answered. "Fifth year in the service."

Onesh paused, his hands momentarily closing as his shoulders slumped. He looked out across the mountains, his eyes glazing over, and he let out a slow breath through a thin smile before turning back to Maer.

"Ah, wonderful," Onesh said. "Though you may drop the 'sir' with me. I abandoned my titles years ago, as they are not of any use to me here, and I haven't been that person for a while.... There are not many of us here, mind, and there's only so much work you can give a private before it becomes faster to do it yourself, so we've learned to deal."

"I... see," Maer said, smiling at Onesh's easy speech and less than stoic demeanor. He studied the man, who had pulled down his traditional hood and scarf, and noted hard lines marking leathery skin as the light gave the man's hair a silver shine. "Begging your pardon, then, but what rank did you hold, if I may ask?"

"I was once a captain," he answered, softly. "A leader of thousands, but like I said, that was a long time ago, when I was a different person, a different role. But on the note of role, what brought you up here?"

"Requested transfer," Maer answered, shrugging, and Onesh nodded. "I started off in Asard as a part of the city guard, though I requested escort duty often, so I got to travel a lot. I even made it to Kellivar for a time. I've seen the cities, country, rivers, forest, coastland, and flatland of Ildice, and I got to know some small towns and villages, too. But then I had a crazy idea of wanting to be up in the mountains." Maer paused, grinning sheepishly. "Actually, I was kind-of fascinated by everything in the stories, all the legends of the mountain guardians and the riches to be found. Reality, though, it's not what I hoped."

"So, tell me about your dreams."

"My... dreams?" Maer asked, taken aback. He felt his hands start to shake, and a burning in his cheeks despite the cold.

"Yes, your dreams," Onesh continued. "Or perhaps tell me the whole truth. There is more to your story than just wanting a change. Something happened, didn't it?"

"Well, yes."

"Who were they?"

"Who was who?"

"The person you couldn't save."

"How..."

"I've seen too much over the years," Onesh answered softly, laying a strong hand on Maer's shoulder. "Some of it was wonderful, but far more was not. I do not know everyone's experiences, but one thing I have seen in everyone is pain, and with that pain always comes a story, especially with the nightmare I heard you haunted by. So now I ask, why have you come up here?"

"It's a long story," Maer sighed, dismissively, hoping to end conversation there.

"My story is already long," Onesh chuckled, but gestured openly for Maer to continue. "I have time to add a few more pages to it."

"Why do you care about what I have to say?" Maer asked, raising his eyebrows and cocking his head to the side. "You barely know me. Besides, it's not a happy story to tell."

"I care because it's real," Onesh replied. "And I care because a person's life is always worth caring about. You're right, though. I don't know you, so I understand why you don't trust me. But, if we're to ride together, I'd like to know who I'm partnered with."

"Alright, well, I'll make it short," Maer said, crossing his arms and shaking his head. "Because the long version is, well…

"I had a partner, once. His name was Gethin, and he was the sergeant in command of my squad. At first, we were stationed in Maltis, but reports of brigands outside of Gangburg required the two of us to be transferred. Gangburg was nice. It was small but people were always coming and going so something was always happening, and most of the people were fine and gave no trouble. Once in a while a few would try, but they were stopped without much of an issue.

"Well, um, on that day, I was watching the gate when a group from outside approached. I followed procedure and called for reinforcements, but when they rushed and breached the gates, I froze. I couldn't draw my sword and they took advantage."

Maer went quiet as old thoughts flooded back. He turned away, and whether it was so Onesh couldn't see his eyes, or he couldn't see Onesh's, he wasn't sure. His chest tightened, and his stomach suddenly disagreed with the coffee he was drinking, but in his head, the accusations started to come.

"People were running," he said quietly, forcing the words out. "Screaming, but I… I couldn't move. Before my sword cleared my scabbard, they were in the city. The other guards fought well, and the brigands were killed, but Gethin...

"I transferred to Kellivar a couple of weeks later to join the city guard, but nothing felt right. As one of the few survivors, I was branded a hero, but it ate at me constantly. I couldn't connect with anyone and couldn't get my failure out of my head, so I transferred here. I figured that out here, I wouldn't be able to let anyone down. People say I'm crazy for wanting to come out to this cold, barren place, but the way I see it, it's nothing less than I deserve."

Onesh nodded, the hard lines of his face softening. "The loss of a comrade is never easy," Onesh said gently. "I've seen many people fall through my years. Some fell as the result of my failure. It is not easy to live with, I know, but we live because our time has not yet come, so neither has yours. Also," he added, almost as an afterthought. "I wouldn't dismiss the stories."

"Oh, was that what brought you up here?" Maer asked, grateful to turn the conversation away from himself.

"A long time ago," Onesh answered. "You could say that, in a manner of speaking."

"But you believe in the stories?" Maer pressed.

"Not the stories as they are told now," Onesh replied. "But the original stories, oh yes, I believe in them completely."

Maer bit his lip. "Is... is that why Arlen calls you crazy?"

Onesh gave a long, slow nod as a smile tugged at his mouth, and his eyes glittered with a silver gleam. "That's one of the reasons, but allow me to explain. Arlen sees what is before him and believes that is what is. He does not question it and has no imagination for what could be. To him, the stories are just that, stories, but to me... they are history, not fiction, and the people in them… all existing, all real. I look at the stories and see them also as what people can be, for good or bad."

"Not a bad way to think," Maer acknowledged. "At least they ended well. Good endings are not overrated."

"Have they ended well, though?" Onesh probed. "Because there is one part that is never in any story, though everyone seems to think it is."

"I can't think of one," Maer said. "The last great battle ended a thousand years ago when the Dark Lord was stopped, further north near the northern edge of Ebaven. The war was long, resulting in more casualties than the sum of any other wars combined, but it ended. Alliances were made that have held since then, with trade maintained between Ildice and Ebaven, and we've enjoyed peace with the exception of ordinary conflicts. What was left out?"

"At no point was the Dark Lord killed."

Maer shook his head and brought his hand up to massage his neck. He thought through all the lore and stories he had read, thought through all the logic, and found himself coming up empty.

"He had to have been," Maer concluded after a moment. "After the last battle, his tale ends. History goes on without any mention of him. He was finished."

"The absence of evidence is not evidence of absence, young one," Onesh stated. "We know he was stopped, but while there's no mention if his continued existence, there's no mention of his death or demise either. Arlen believes that when the Dark Lord was stopped, he was likewise destroyed, and that not being mentioned in the history books since is the proof of that."

"Which makes sense," Maer said, nodding. "But continue."

"I know… otherwise," Onesh answered. "But let me ask you, since we're away from the others… what do you believe?"

"To be honest, I'm not sure, now," Maer answered, shaking his head. "I mean, historically, I know the Dark One came from the west, which people say is just wasteland and desert, though that never made sense to me. We have outposts, after all, and our past lords had their reasons for establishing them and keeping them. I know Ildice and Ebaven have had trouble with others who reportedly came from beyond the mountain, but they're men like you and I, not creatures of darkness. If I must take a side, however, I'm sorry, but along with the Adonari, they had to have all died."

"Ah, the Adonari," Onesh said approvingly with no sign of discomfort at Maer's differing opinion, which Maer respected him for. If anything, there seemed a definite affection coming from the speaking of that name. "I wondered if they would be mentioned. If I may, I must ask… what are they to you?"

"Heroes," Maer said, feeling his heart start to race and chills go down his back. "The war ended because of them. They fought with the strength of ten men, and could fight on with dozens of arrows sticking out of them at once. They were wise, as well as intelligent, and taught the people of Learsi to fight the dark. They died for us, too…" Maer trailed off, but Onesh waited for him to finish. "They died for us, but their sacrifices brought about the Dark Lord's defeat. I have mixed feelings about all that if you know what I mean."

"I do know," Onesh said, laying a hand across his chest. "There were many names listed among the fallen, many very fine names among the Grey Wardens, the Hunters, the Black Company, the Nathairians… Well, I am pleased to see that you have a respect for the histories, which is more than can be said of some of the others. At the least, I feel comfortable riding at your side, and look forward to our time together. I shall let you go now, lest the others think you have become as crazy as I am, for I must tend to my horse. Take care."

"Hold a moment," Maer said, breaking free from what almost felt like a trance. He stared hard into Onesh's face. "You asked all your questions. Do I not get any?"

Onesh laughed, his warmth dissolving the cold knot of uncertainty in Maer's stomach.

"That is fair," Onesh replied, bowing his head. "I apologize. What would you like to know?"

"Well, uh," Maer began, stumbling over his words. "I don't really know much about you, and neither does anyone else, for that matter."

"Few care to learn," Onesh answered. "I'm not secretive, but I don't always need to tell everyone everything about my life."

"Well, uh, you've probably figured I don't have anyone significant in my life," Maer said. "Do you have anyone?"

"I used to," Onesh said, his smile gentle and warm, yet his eyes glistened in a way that caused Maer's throat to tighten. "A long time ago. She died… well, she was killed, actually."

"Oh, I'm sorry," Maer replied.

"It's alright," Onesh assured him. "She lived a good life, an honorable life. I will see her again, in this world or the next."

"I'm confused," Maer said.

"If you believe the stories," Onesh began. "Then remember the stories. If you believe Emyran conquered before, because the stories say, then believe he will again, because the stories say."

"Hold a moment more, if you will," Maer asked. Onesh paused. For a moment, Maer thought he saw a glimpse of the commander he used to be. *No*, Maer said to himself, quickly. *The soldier the man still was.* "Something's been giving me pause. You call me 'young one,' as if I were a child, and though I'm only three years past my twentieth, I'm not that young. Also, you speak of your time as 'long ago,' but frankly, you don't look much older than the lieutenant, who's only in his mid-forties. My question, then, if you don't mind, of course… how old are you?"

Onesh chuckled. "I don't like to talk about my age. I am youthful enough to keep going, old enough to know my going may end soon, and while I'll call myself an old soul, I refuse to call myself old. Will that suffice?"

"Not at all," Maer answered back, but then with the strength given from his conversation, he dared to speak more. "But I suppose it will do for now. I'd like a straight answer to this next question, though. Something was out there today, wasn't it… something more than just shadows?"

"Yes," Onesh answered. His tone was not dismissive, but there was a severity that concerned Maer.

"Will you tell me what?" Maer asked, after a moment passed enough for Maer to know Onesh wasn't going to continue.

"You already know," Onesh said.

Maer bit his lip. "What about the Adonari?" he asked. "You reacted to that name. What are they to you?"

Onesh's smile twitched at the corners, and in the old man's eyes, Maer could see pain, but also a joy indescribable.

"They are… special," Onesh said after a time. "And ones I owe my life to."

Maer averted his eyes from the figure taking form before him. As before, he was alone in a world of darkness and silver fog, no landmarks, no light, save that the fog appeared to make its own light. Even his own form was shadowy, though it was difficult to feel he was even there.

"Their blood is on you."

The words echoed around him as the fog swirled and dispersed. Maer watched it collect again, and then it started taking on multiple forms. He recognized people, buildings, a sword, a banner, a generic soldier, a wall…

"His blood is on you."

The fog took on one more form, the one he hated the most, who stared at him with eyes empty yet with tears.

"What good was your sword?" the voice said again, speaking through the familiar figure. "What good was the soldier when the soldier failed? What good will the soldier be, now? Why are you here?"

Maer closed his eyes, fighting the pain, but the grief was too strong, even in this world. He was tired, so very tired. He was tired of fighting his memories, tired of fighting his past, tired of fighting the hopeless walk of looking for hope in a world of darkness… he knew the truth. It would always return. And he was done.

"I'm here for one reason," he answered. "I am here to die."

"Oi, soldier, on your feet."

A rough kick to Maer's side snapped his eyes open from where he lay by the dead, but still smoking, fire. His eyes widened as he looked up at the hazy figure that stared down at him with an eye that seemed to shine like molten amber. His hand leapt for his sword, but it was regrettably just out of reach. Horse's hooves stamped outside of his vision, and a low whistling around him brought back memories and the feelings of the mountains. When the dream world finally cleared, he was able to recognize Lieutenant Treel as he stood holding his large double-edged sword casually across his shoulders... and gulped.

"Yes, sir," Maer answered crisply, taking care to keep his voice lowered. He rubbed his side, debating whether he preferred the rude awakening to the gloved hand from the night before and decided that regardless he'd be wearing his armor to sleep with him the next night. Thankfully, standard armor out here meant leather, for although it was not as strong as the chain or plate he usually wore in the cities, its weight gave it greater ease of movement. It retained more warmth, too, and it was quieter, and on the days that he was sure a voice whispered in the wind, the silence gave him comfort.

He tried to don his gear quickly, but fumbled at the straps with fingers that were already stiffening from the chill wind, and once done, cast his cloak over it all to trap in as much warmth as possible. The sky was clear and pitch black, and stars covered the expanse, but a silver fog rolled along the ground, distorting the landscape below knee-level. The effect unnerved him, but he stayed silent.

"You don't complain about the dark," Lieutenant Treel growled, extending a hand to pull Maer to his feet. He gave him a quick nod. "Good. I hate whiners."

"It's dark in the cities, sir," Maer answered simply. "At least here you can see the stars. The cold may prove to be a problem though."

Treel let out a grunt. "The cold is always a problem. It's the only thing you can count on. Winter's almost here, too. We'll be getting snow soon. So, congratulations, you're just catching the last of the warm season."

"Comforting; thank you, sir," Maer said.

Treel shrugged. "You get used to it. You hate it, but you get used to it."

"How long have you been stationed here, sir?" Maer asked, rubbing his hands together and breathing into them to get some feeling back.

"Long enough," Treel chuckled. "Nine months between Tilgal and Posmor. I'll put in a transfer to Chanost one of these days, where I'll have some days of warmth and real sun, but for now, I'll pass the time keeping you all out of trouble."

"Do you see any trouble up here, sir?" Maer asked.

"Just the usual kind," Treel replied. "A soldier forgets to pack enough rations and has to go without for a day, or a private doesn't have warm enough gear and has to be sent back to the outpost. Once in a while, you get someone who just can't handle it out here, which is why you came in."

"Do people have to be transferred out often?" Maer asked.

"Often enough," Treel sighed. "I've not known any who have stayed a full deployment, save for Onesh, and he's been here longer than I."

"Do you think there's something out here, like Onesh?" Maer asked hesitantly.

"There are many mysteries still out there," Treel replied, staring out towards the west. "But enough small talk. Get the men up; we ride back to Tilgal once everyone is saddled. Report to Onesh when you're done. You're riding with him again."

After Maer had roused the others, he looked around and found Onesh was missing. Remembering the comment made the previous night about the horses, he went to the little outcropping their mounts were tucked into and found Onesh standing alone. When he crept closer, he could hear the man muttering. There would be a pause, but then the muttering would continue, as if he were talking to some silent companion. Maer inched closer and looked around, but oddly, no one else was around save their steeds.

"Onesh," Maer said hesitantly. The man looked up. "Treel wants everyone mounted. He said to report to you, too."

"As I thought," Onesh replied. "Good. I spoke with him earlier. Since you appreciate the stories, I hoped you would accompany me on a small side trip on the way back."

"Of course," Maer said. He wanted to say something about the man's muttering, but wasn't sure how to phrase it, so he let it stay, especially when Onesh smiled.

"Perfect," Onesh said warmly. "Thank you."

"You're… welcome," Maer said curiously, shaking his head as he walked away. He rejoined the main group, finding his swords where he had left them and buckled them on. Onesh came leading his horse, and then spoke with Treel as the others went to collect their mounts. Treel nodded and the two clasped hands, then he turned and gave the order to ride. Within minutes, the company set forth, leaving behind nothing but a charred firepit.

Though the sky had colored from inky black to blue, the darkness still saturated its expanse as they rode back to Tilgal, galloping through a sea of fog that swirled at their feet. The wind stilled its whispers, leaving the air quiet save for the steady rumbling of the horses' progress, and no-one saw it necessary to interject their voices into it. As they rode further, the sky lightened to a steel blue, and then, abruptly, Onesh reigned his horse next to Maer's.

"We turn west, here," Onesh stated, breaking off from the group. Maer turned his horse to follow.

It was hardly even a path they were on, Maer thought, realizing he could barely see anything even with his partner leading the way, but Onesh seemed sure, and if anything, his pace quickened. They rode through a rolling plateau of stony hills and came to a stop at the base of a small ledge.

"We're here," Onesh said as he dismounted, and walked to the unnaturally flat ledge. "Come, look here."

The ledge was the same color grey as the landscape, but when Maer dismounted, he noticed the floor had been laid, as with brick, not flattened by weather or some other natural occurrence. He bent down to study the stones, and saw intricate detail, but of a style he hadn't seen before. It was graceful and elegant artisanship, but still practical, a perfect blend of beauty and practicality. He looked up across the stonework, and then he saw a small tree standing by itself, surrounded by raised stones.

"What am I looking at?" Maer whispered, his eyes transfixed on the small plant with white flowers and dark green leaves. He studied the flowers closely, noting how they had six teardrop shaped petals that were also maroon and gold close to the base. He noted, too, the way the leaves were the same shape, yet slightly larger, and felt oddly thick. He took a deep breath, and the aroma of grass in a morning dew, cedar, and garden lilies assailed his senses all at once. "And how is this possible?"

"It's not so much what you see," Onesh answered. "But more what it represents. This tree, the gracelis tree, is one of the few of its kind that exist beyond Adonar. They are hardy and are said to grow far greater when the conditions are right, but they are said to survive anywhere.

"I've heard of it," Maer nodded. "I read a story about how one of these was brought over to turn the tide in the war… but I never understood how a tree could do that. Is this that tree?"

"No, that tree is elsewhere," Onesh replied. "However, stand up, and look at the rocks. On each of the stones at the base, you can still see the impression of names carved here. Furthermore, if you step back, you can see…"

"A speared dragon!" Maer exclaimed. "The mark of Adonar, the symbol they carried upon their banners!"

"Caution with too much noise," Onesh said in a low voice "But you are right. This place was once a guard post used during the last war. Some of us still keep it."

"To think," Maer remarked, bending closer to the engraved stones and touching their surface gently. "Almost a thousand years old and I can still see…"

"Wait," Onesh whispered sharply, causing Maer to tense and turn quickly. From seemingly nowhere, an ornate bow had materialized in Onesh's hand, and an arrow already sat knocked, though it remained undrawn. Onesh rose to his full height, his coloring almost as gray as the stone, and Maer found his limbs unable to move. Onesh turned slowly, looking in Maer's direction, and now his face was chiseled in hard intensity with lips grim and eyes blazing. Then, as Maer tried to move his hands to the hilts of his swords, Onesh raised the bow, pulled back on the string... and aimed straight at Maer.

"There you are, my old foe," Onesh whispered with glee. "Let us dance."

"O – Onesh," Maer choked, his voice cracking as a new unknown fear struck him. "Onesh, it's me. It's Maer, your... your partner." Arlen's words echoed in his mind, and the revelation that they were right pounded in his head. "Just put the bow down..."

"Do not fear," Onesh said calmly. "Now you shall see."

"Onesh..." Maer began, and then Onesh burst forward.

"Laehenarado!" Onesh roared as his arrow jumped free, passing inches to the side of Maer's throat, and a guttural yelp rose from just behind him. He turned, but a dark mass fell upon him, sending him to the stones below, and the hot stench of rotting flesh and wet fur filled his head. His senses dulled, but he vaguely sensed a pack of some animals descend upon them, and from seemingly far off, he heard a terrified scream.

Then he saw a gray figure leap among the beasts. Their knives flashed and danced, seeming to glow from their own inner light. Another figure appeared in the fray, also gray-clad and indistinguishable, but this one had a pair of swords in his hands...

The weight grew heavier as another body fell upon him, and he struggled to breathe. Pushing hard, he barely managed to shift them to the side, and then it was another struggle to free his legs. After a few more heavy breaths, his vision cleared.

"What...?"

"Kythraul!" a voice not Onesh's hissed. Maer turned quickly and saw a man dressed in shining plate mail with a pair of broad, curved swords strapped to his back. The man appeared normal, despite not being there a few minutes ago, but there was a strange power and authority that radiated from his being. When Maer looked into his eyes, he froze again, for the man's eyes glowed with a golden light.

A sudden hard smack across the head cleared his daze.

"Who are you?" Maer asked, recovering from Onesh's blow and taking care not to stare too much.

"I am Laehenarado," the man said grimly, but not unkindly, inclining his head. "But we have too little time for proper introductions, so listen carefully. Malgalon is ready, or very close to, if we see his more vicious servants. It is possible that his boldness is premature, but I would not put too much trust in that, for he is crafty and knows well how to sow the seeds of chaos, destruction, and war."

"Malgalon?" Maer asked, his mind racking itself over for recognition.

"You call him the Dark One," Laehenarado replied.

"But who are you?" Maer asked once more. "And where…?"

"His kind go by many names, through many legends," Onesh interrupted, rising from where he was inspecting the tree. "But they are the Vigel. Though they protect us and fight the shadow, this one has also been my friend for many years, and, on this trip, has taken the form of my horse. You know the stories, so remember what you know."

"Remember quickly," Laehenarado commanded. "We were lucky, but I suspect your friends are in trouble. They are, unfortunately, only human. Prepare yourself, then, for they may already be gone."

"He's right," Onesh said as Laehenarado's form took that of a horse once more. He swung into the saddle that materialized with the form. "Hurry, mount up!"

"But…" Maer protested.

"Now!" Onesh ordered, and Maer found himself compelled to obey. They thundered off in the direction of the other men, riding against biting wind, and Maer's eyes stung. The landscape was nothing but a blue-gray blur, the sun not yet touching rising above the horizon, and the moon failed to cast much light, but it was enough.

Roars of carnage and cries of pain began to rise in the distance, and Onesh spurred them on harder. An icy chill seized Maer's stomach, almost causing him to reign in his horse, but somehow he made himself follow Onesh. He hated it, but he knew his duty.

The last ridge rose before them, one final barrier between him and his patrol, but in his heart, Maer knew what he would see. In his mind, he was back at the city gate, back on the bloodstained ground. His sword cleared its scabbard, but then the darkness took him.

Arrows whistled forth from Onesh's bow. Laehenarado, in human form once more, had his swords drawn, and danced through the crowd of beasts that had been previously devouring the last of the men in Maer's patrol. Roars of victory cried out from the beasts as Arlen was cut down and his body ravaged along with the others. Bardor held on a little longer, but then his sword arm was hacked off, and then his legs. He looked over at Maer, pleading, yet try as he would, Maer could not move. Once again, he could only watch, and as he stood lifeless, his sword fell from his hand.

One still remained, looking little more than a blur of silver. His blade swung swiftly and wildly, shining bright and unstained as it cut through the blackened terrors. The man was a storm, yet the wielder remained calm.

"Treel!" Maer choked out, feeling some hope, but in that moment, Treel's blade faltered, and a black blade slipped past his defenses to plunge into his side. He roared in pain, swinging backward to cleave the beast's head, but then he, too, dropped his sword and fell to his knees.

Laehenarado was by his side in an instant, defending his fallen body, and then quickly, so quickly Maer thought visions had clouded his sight, Laehenarado was not. In his place, a creature, beautiful yet terrifying, rose on long clawed legs and let out its own roar of challenge. The creature reared its massive head attached to a long, muscular neck, snapping hard against black steel, and proving the stronger. Its tail lashed out, sending black figures flying, and its front claws ripped across flesh as easily as if it were water. Great wings opened on its back, two pairs of majestic, feathered beauties, though the creature would not take flight.

Onesh strode towards Treel, calmly loosening arrows into the angry beasts that were more focused on the other creature and causing one after another to drop. Maer tried again to move, but a dark figure crashed into him, sending him to the ground again. He met Onesh's eyes, seeing a man more terrifying than the beasts, and then when Onesh shot two more arrows his way, he closed his eyes. Two dull thuds and dying growls sounded just behind him, and when he looked back, he saw two more dark forms laying still. He closed his eyes again, biting back the tears of shame, and after a few more moments, everything went quiet.

"They're all dead now," Onesh said gently. Maer heard him approach, and then strong hands lifted him to his feet. Laehenarado was in his human form once more, and he was moving through the bodies to check for survivors.

"I couldn't do anything," Maer managed. "Again."

"No," Onesh said, shaking his head. "But very few can even stand in their presence, let alone draw a sword against them, for it takes more than courage to stand in their presence. You felt it before, on the ledge, and then you felt it before cresting that ridge. They exude terror. It's over, now, regardless."

"You should have let them kill me," Maer said. "You should have let me die. Look at me, I'm nothing! I let Gethin die. I let these men die. I should have done something, but I didn't! What good is my life to anyone?"

Onesh bowed his head, and Maer saw his eyes water. "One of the worst tragedies I've seen in all my years is a man who feels he has no more worth, because when they feel that way, they decide their life is done, and so choose to end it themselves. We are in this world for only a fleeting time, some longer than others, but every life has a purpose! Every action, every situation, creates the person we are, and if we let the moment break us, then we lose every good that can come from it."

Maer looked up at Onesh, but the man had his gaze downward, and his fists were clenched. His mouth was drawn into a grimace, and then his shoulders sagged.

"What's done is done," Onesh spoke quietly. "We cannot change it. All we can do now is decide how to go forward. Come. There's one you must speak with."

"Who?" Maer asked hesitantly. "Not one of the creatures…"

"Maer," Treel choked.

"Lieutenant, sir," Maer said, collapsing next to him. Warm tears flowed, and a wave of giddiness spread through him. "You're still alive. Not all is lost…"

"Maer, my body is broken," Treel said, his eyes closing and a small grin lighting his face. "My battle is done. This is it for me."

"Treel, lieutenant, I'm so sorry…"

"I don't have time for apologies," Treel coughed. "I need you to listen. Our deepest fears have come to light, and word must reach the High Lord's ears that the darkness has taken form once again. He must know what to prepare for… if any preparations can be made."

Treel took a deep labored breath.

"Our men deserve a proper burial," he continued. "And their families deserve to learn of their fate from one of their own. You're their voice now. Maer, you are our voice now."

"Sir, you're going to make it…"

"Be quiet and let me finish," Treel growled before coughing up a mouthful of blood. "The dead have no use for their weapons, so my sword I leave to you. It's spilled more blood than I can measure, but I foresee that there is much more that will need to be shed before it can be laid to rest."

"I can't," Maer choked. "Sir, I don't deserve this. I couldn't do anything…"

"Then do something now," Treel whispered. "And if you should fall, pass it to someone you call worthy." Treel looked over at Onesh. "Farewell, Master Onesh. It has been an honor serving, far more than one like me deserves."

"Treel," Maer cried as the man's eyes closed, and he felt a hand upon his shoulder.

"Treel is dead," Onesh said gently. "And we've lingered here for too long. Laehenarado, please help us with the bodies."

"They grow bold," Laehenarado growled as he worked, his hands tightening into stony fists when they didn't hold one of the patrolmen. "They've been given permission to pass."

"Indeed," Onesh replied. "This is far more than the few daring individuals I've disposed of before. This was planned, coordinated, between multiple packs. I counted eight bodies earlier at the grave, and I see maybe twenty here."

"Could any have escaped?" Maer asked, wiping tears, and regaining his composure. "Are… are there more out there?"

"There are many more out there," Laehenarado answered as Onesh went among the men, bending down to study Bardor curiously. "But a fatal flaw of Kythraul is they will not retreat, but that works in our favor. They are relentless; they keep attacking until either there is no one left to attack, or they're all dead. Great praise I give to Lieutenant Treel, the Shadowbane, for if he had fallen before our arrival, the beasts would have invaded Ildice, and eliminating them would have been far more difficult. Even worse, had they made it past the mountains, I would have been unable to follow."

"But you're one of the Vigel," Maer exclaimed. "You fight the shadow. Surely you would have been able to find them again."

"Find, but not fight, not in Learsi," Onesh said. "Emyran granted them charge of the borders, but only there. They were not to set foot in the lands to the west, Mahlen, nor were they allowed to draw arms in the east. Yes, even they are not without rules, but if you can believe it, those rules are for our benefit as much as for theirs. Now come, we have tarried here too long. We have work to do now, and then more to do later. We will pile the kythraul in one place to burn, but we will build a mound over our friends, for we cannot carry them out. Treel will be buried in a grave of his own; he will be laid to rest with the weapons of his fallen foes, like the heroes of old. He's earned that…"

Maer's hands shook as he worked. His limbs had grown numb, though not from the cold, and a haze seemed to cloud his vision. His new sword weighed him down, its charge more burdensome than its mass, and the stench of the bodies threatened to make his stomach wretch. When he could focus, every face seemed to stare at him, either with accusations or hatred, so he closed the eyes of the men. When he approached the kythraul, though, and looked down at them, their dead eyes threatened to devour his very will. He tried to focus elsewhere, but their yellow fangs seemed to wish for his throat, and their long black claws threatened to close around an arm or a leg and rip into fragile flesh. He settled for closing his own eyes, but even that barely let him work.

Stones were placed reverently over the bodies of the scouting party. They built the mound high, taking care to place each rock so as to not mangle the corpses further, and then Onesh took out a wine skin and poured the contents over them. Treel's body was placed in a crick in the rock, a collection of blackened swords forming a base, and when they completed their tasks, they poured oil and the last of their dry wood on the mound of black beasts and set it ablaze. The smoke rose high, tainting the clouds.

"That is it, then," Laehenarado said with a nod. "I must tell Maikahael quickly so we can prepare."

"And my ride goes with you, at least for a time," Onesh gestured. "The Remnant will want to know. We have waited too long for this day... let us take the paths through Posmor. I have business to deal with there before we continue."

"Wait," Maer said, his heart racing at the words as he realized he would be alone. He opened his mouth to speak, then swallowed quickly to relieve the dryness. "I need you to come back, to explain to the captain what happened..."

"No, you do not," Laehenarado said, cutting him off. "We all have our tasks, and Treel gave you yours."

"I can't do this alone," Maer choked, feeling his head go light.

"Take one of the severed claws and collect a few of their blades," Onesh added. "They will give weight to your testimony."

"And do not be afraid," Laehenarado concluded. "We don't always choose our tasks, but we can choose how to respond to them. This one is given to you, for the race of men."

"But Onesh..." Maer trailed off and realization finally dawned. Chills went down his spine, down his arms and legs. "Sir, you're not..."

"It should be obvious by now," Onesh laughed, and then it struck Maer that the silver gleam in Onesh's eye was not just the moon's reflection. "After all, you know the stories."

"But... I thought... you all were dead..." Maer gasped, feeling the warmth growing in intensity. "After the great war, when you fought..."

"As you can see, we're clearly not," Onesh smiled. "I am not the only one, either, and I am not the last."

"So, when you speak of the stories..."

"I speak of me and mine."

"I won't see you again, will I?" Maer asked after a pause. The feeling of warmth remained, but there was a new pain, yet one that felt manageable. Onesh shook his head.

"This will likely be the last time we speak," Onesh confirmed. "At least while you are alive. Whether things happen beyond that, I cannot say. These last words I give to you, and I pray you remember them; though your life has been filled with pain and with tragedy, you still live. As long as you live there is a purpose to your life, and whether you know it or not it is your task to find it. If I knew it, I would tell you, but for now, Sergeant, I order you, live.

"Now, ride!" Onesh said, his voice strong. "You may know of the stories, but now is the time to truly know them, for the stories will soon be the only thing to save us. Ride for the race of men, and be the voice that carries the stories of these men as far as they need to go. Ride now for hope. Ride now for life. Ride, in the name of Emyran! Up the sails!"

Onesh pulled free a ram's horn and let fly a lingering blast of passion and fury that echoed across the mountains and left Maer speechless. Before the echoes faded, he was mounted and gone, disappearing towards Posmor. Maer lingered a moment longer, and when the spell left his limbs, he turned in the other direction.

Onesh and Laehenarado were gone, out of sight and out of sound, though firmly in memory. The lieutenant's sword was on his back, his own swords were at his side, and a few of the black blades were secured in his bags. War would soon come. Death would become common. Fear would grip the hearts of everyone. The enemy would be on the lips of even children. All this he knew, yet, as he rode, he knew something else, something he had not known for a while. He knew hope, he knew life, because new words echoed in his mind.

The Adonari still live. The stories are real.

Chapter 2

Thousands of miles away to the east, beyond the shadows and cliffs of the Truvona Mountains, across the grassy plains of Ebaven and the Great Western Road, and near a spit of land at the edge of the Geborgen Sea, a lone vessel made its way home. Unaware of the distant troubles, it minded its own on the gentle waves of the fjord, bobbing casually as its captain and most of the crew remained asleep under its sturdy decks.

At ten paces across and eight times that long, she was considered moderately sized. Three towering masts held aloft torn and yellowed canvas sails that showed almost as much patchwork as there was original sail, and chipped letters painted across the soft gray bow spelled out *Dawn's Embrace.*

It was a little past sunrise, enough so that the sky was still dark off to the west, and a sliver of orange flame rose above the horizon, reflecting off the water, but only a few eyes on this ship were awake to witness its glory. The first was the night watchman from the last shift, a short but burly man who went by Eiran. He had fair but tanned skin, hair as black as coal that he kept neatly trimmed, and dark grey eyes that could pierce a moonless sky. The second was a younger man who had joined him part way through, and he went by Joshian. Like Eiran, he had fair tanned skin, but he was taller and more toned, strong, but considerably smaller. His eyes were bright and blue, like an evening sky during a storm, and the way his dirty blonde hair sat could make one think he had challenged said storm. Both had slept well, despite the gale from the night before, but for a third, stumbling up to the deck, the morning appeared anything but glorious.

"Good morning, Dayved," Joshian called to the half-asleep crewman with a mirthful tone. There was a lightness to him, an air of freedom and peace, but also purpose, intent, and a willingness to leap into action at a moment's notice that gave the newcomer a pause. "You had a full night's sleep, yet you look like you were awake for most of it."

"Yes, sir, sorry sir," Dayved replied, rubbing sleep out of his eyes and fighting back a yawn. Younger than Joshian by five years and Eiran by ten, Dayved was the youngest crewman on *Dawn's Embrace*, but he pulled his own. Muscular but lanky, he kept his dark hair cut short and his face clean, save for a small patch on his chin, and his brown eyes had a silver glint many girls considered attractive. He opened his mouth, but before he could speak again, Joshian cut him off.

"Dayved, for the last time, I'm still just Joshian," he said laughing. "I'm the captain's son, but I'm not the captain, so no special bowing or anything for me."

"Ah, give him some slack," Eiran said from his position on the mast. "If he wants to bow to the future lord of the seas, commander of storms, slayer of death…"

"Don't you start, Eiran," Joshian laughed. "I rue the day I ever showed a personality in front of you."

"Meh, I like my ocean masters springy," Eiran joked, dropping down. "Come to think of it, your pa's been pushing the captain bit pretty hard for a while now, hasn't he?"

"More than I would prefer," Joshian answered somberly, shaking his head. "But not just him, either; I've heard comments like that through the village from time to time. 'There's Joshian, he'll be a captain one day.' 'Hey Joshian, when are you going to follow your father's footsteps?' 'Hey Joshian, you'll be perfect for my daughter.' Did you know the Stormwinds threatened to sign on as soon as I gained my captainship? The Rockthornes, too, said when I got a ship, they'd keep her together, so I guess that means they'd back me. And don't even let my brother start talking. Calian will get anyone to follow him…"

"You don't want to be a captain?" Dayved asked. "When we talked, I always thought…"

"One day, I do," Joshian said, nonchalantly, though he turned to look out over the waves. His hand closed around one of the mast lines and he stretched himself taller, the light of the rising sun illuminating his face.

"One day, I'll push to be a captain," he added softly, "but right now, I just like being one of the crew. I like a simple hard day's work, the feel of the wind or the salty spray on tired muscles, and having a drink as I talk about the day's catch. I like climbing the ropes and keeping a sail together during a storm, knowing I had a direct hand in making it happen and keeping her together. But more than anything, I like sailing with my old man."

"Even with his conditions?" Eiran asked with a knowing grin.

"Yes, even with them," Joshian continued, taking the comment in stride, but then paused, turning slowly with his mouth twisting into a half frown. "Wait, how did you know about them?"

"Everyone knows about them," Eiran scoffed. "Think about it, a person like you disappears for about half the day, only showing up in the morning when it's absolutely necessary."

"Honestly, I wondered about that myself at first," Dayved confessed.

"We all did," Eiran continued. "Well, naturally, we asked questions, and some speculated further. Our current theory is that one day he's going to make you first mate until you're ready to push for your own ship, which right now seems pretty likely. After all, he did make you navigator this trip, which, might I add, it's been a good one so far."

"Well, thank you for that," Joshian said. "And I mean that, honestly. At least I won't be able to say I'm not prepared… wait a minute. Dayved, why are you up right now?"

"I lost the game last night," he said with a shrug. "I have to pull anchor." Joshian and Eiran shared knowing looks.

"Happens to the best of us," Joshian said lightly, slapping Dayved's arm. "Give me a bit and I'll give you a hand. As for you, Eiran, you should have time to get a decent breakfast."

"What happens in a bit?" Dayved asked. On cue, the sound of heavy boot steps carried up on deck. Dayved and Eiran excused themselves as the owner of those steps appeared.

Although Joshian was taller than most, the captain of *Dawn's Embrace* dwarfed him in more than just height. With rich, dark brown hair and a thick, curly beard that covered his face, his eyes had a steely gaze that could crack stone or stop a bear in its tracks.

"The sea looks good today," the captain announced, his voice deep and strong, as he stared out across the water. He took a deep breath, letting it out casually as his eyes closed.

These are the moments, Joshian thought, with the wind blowing casually, and the salty air filling his nose and tongue. *These are the moments I live for, the peace, the life, the joy.*

"It does indeed. Good morning, Father."

"Yes, it is a good morning," his father, Captain Ralshian, answered. "Though on this ship, it seems you've forgotten that it's 'Captain.'"

"I haven't forgotten, sir," Joshian answered calmly, though respectfully. "But as I recall, it's only 'Captain' around the crew, and, as you can see, there aren't any of the crew around."

"A fair point that I'll concede," his father said, laughing. "As I like to say, rules, they're like the sea. Some days they're harsh, other days they're mild…"

"Sometimes they're rigid, and other times they're flexible. But whatever their condition, you can either fight them and struggle, or go with them and make your life better," Joshian finished to his father's knowing nod. "I know them well."

"Good that you've finally been listening," his father said, scratching the mane of a beard that nearly covered his warm and wild grin. "So, navigator, where are we now?"

"Eastern end of Zaffre Sound," Joshian answered. "I looked over the maps last night, and I put us about two days from home, assuming all goes well, and assuming we don't have another storm delay."

"Two days sounds right," Ralshian agreed. "And your numbers sound accurate. Shame we can't cut that down to less."

"I know," Joshian said, nodding. "It'd be nice to get back for Calian, but we ran according to schedule, everything has worked as planned, everyone is still well, and the one way to make it faster isn't worth the risk to the crew."

"Yes, I agree," Ralshian said, mirroring his son's affirmation. "Well, we best get started, then. What are you up so early for... wait, you didn't lose last night, did you?"

"No, sir, I didn't lose," Joshian answered. "I wasn't in the competition last night, anyway, since I had first watch. I'm up to help whoever did lose pull anchor, though, figured I'd get in a bit of exercise before having to sit below deck. Besides, you know Norvik, how he hauls the last man up to pull kitchen duty. If I do any job on this ship, it's not going to be as punishment."

"Spoken as a true Farstrid," his father said, proudly, slapping him on the shoulder. "And spoken as a good crewman. You've got the makings of a good captain in there."

"Well, I am your son," Joshian answered, putting a hand on his father's. "I learned from the best. But I have a few years to go yet."

"Ah, there's where you're wrong," Ralshian sighed, turning his head as the first crew members were making their way on deck. "Knowledge. Experience. Loyalty. Commitment. Those are what makes a captain, not the years. For some, it does take many years, true, but for others it will only take a few. You have the makings of greatness in you. When you choose to acknowledge them, though, only you can answer.

"You already know the first rule. Do what needs to be done. The second rule, though, if only by a bare margin, is trust the men and they'll trust you in return. Mainlanders all seem to think that rank determines the wealth and worth of a man, but what good is rank if the people aren't willing to follow? Rank may get you finery and things, and titles will give you prestige in others' eyes, but trust will give you true respect, and true respect will give you true followers… brothers.

"You do what needs to be done, you always have, and that's one thing I'll always be proud of you for. Keep to those principles, and you'll do fine. Now go on, get about your work."

The rest of the crew came up from below deck, rubbing sleep from tired eyes, or holding cups of hot coffee. Joshian tapped his hand to his forehead in a salute and stepped away as Will, his father's first officer walked up. After dodging around barrels and nearly tripping over a coil of rope that had been left at the base of the center mast, he came up to Dayved, who was preparing to raise the anchor.

"Took you long enough, mate," Dayved said, once Joshian had moved near to him. Joshian tossed his shirt to the deck and took a position on the anchor line.

"That's better," Joshian laughed, getting a solid grip on the rope. The two pulled in tandem, seasoned fishing muscles straining against the massive weight until they brought the awkward mass up to the edge. Joshian held the rope steady, bracing his foot against the ship's rail, and once he felt certain of his grip, Dayved leaned over and brought it the rest of the way up. After tying the anchor where it would be out of the way, the two slumped against the deck and basked in the sunlight that was winning over the darkness, smiling at the bit of blue that had saturated the sky. On either side of the fjord they were anchored, mountains rose, decorated either by dark green forest or steep, gray-streaked cliffs.

"Thanks mate," Dayved said cheerfully. "I could have done it by myself, you know, but since you insisted on helping, I couldn't say no."

"Uh huh, sure," Joshian answered, closing his eyes for a moment as he leaned back and let the sun warm his skin. "I'll let you solo it next time, then. Or, better yet, let's just drop it over the side right now and you can show me yourself."

"Pass, thank you," Dayved answered, grabbing Joshian's shirt and throwing it at his head. Joshian caught it easily and tucked it behind him. After a bit, Dayved added, "How soon do you think we're getting home then?"

"About two days," Joshian answered, sitting up and using his shirt to wipe his brow. He stood up and turned to offer his hand to Dayved, who, after taking it, pulled himself to his feet. "That was one of the things I had to speak with the captain about."

"Well, we're on schedule, at least," Dayved said, his voice carrying a tone of disappointment. He knuckled his back and stretched. "I mean, don't get me wrong. Seeing other ports was amazing and all, really gave an idea of how much bigger our community is, and I really had fun at Spearbreaker and Stalwart, but there's something to be said about being home with family… and Cierra. Plus, everywhere has their own rules and customs we must follow while we're there, due to those oaths… never really thought about what they meant until now."

"So, Cierra does hold your heart, then," Joshian said, grinning. "Rumors get passed around all the time, and it's amazing how words get twisted."

"True, but this rumor is correct. I've only been seriously interested in her for a few months, but I think she'll be my bride one day, you know, assuming her da's fine with it and all."

"If I know him at all," Joshian assured him. "He will be more than happy knowing you're interested in her. That being said, I fear for anyone who voices interest in my sis, having to go through my father."

"I kinda want to see that," Dayved said.

"I kinda want to, too," Joshian agreed, laughing. "But speaking of fathers, it looks like it's time to heed the words of mine and get to my own work. Take care of yourself, mate."

Joshian left Dayved and went below deck to the cabin he shared with his father. Closing the door, he shut away the sounds of the deck and prepared for another few hours of study. He started by stacking a small pile of old maps and logbooks on a side table, and then went to the boarded-up cupboard to pull down some worn volumes. The sounds still drifted through, though, and then he felt a lurch as the ship began to start off. Settling the longing in his feet that had started to build, he grudgingly sat down at the cabin's desk to study.

Sailing filled him with joy and purpose, especially sailing with his father, and the open sea always felt free. There were times, though, that he regretted the agreement he had made with the older sea captain. His father had long been regarded as one of the best sea traders on Firebrand Island, possibly among the Nine Islands, and his crews were never left wanting for hands. When any voyage came about, he had his choice of crew.

Though anyone strong enough, once reaching the age of ten, earned the right to sail on the fishing ships, only those who had come of age were allowed on the deep-sea ships and trading vessels, with no exceptions. Prior to coming of age, Joshian dreamed of the day he would sail by his father's side, possibly as first mate, but when the day of his first trip arrived, he learned that not only being his son didn't carry the weight he had hoped, but he also didn't have the skills to truly deserve to be on his father's crew.

His father had other thoughts, though, for when Joshian told him of his concerns, he presented his own terms. Put simply, Joshian would be allowed to sail every route his father sailed, provided that from the time the crew awoke to the mid-day meal, Joshian would devote himself to studying. *Ordinary people don't sail on my ships,* he heard his father's words echo in his mind. *And they never have. If you want to be ordinary, then you can take the ordinary routes. But if you want the best, if you want to sail the whole of the Nine Islands and beyond, then being average won't cut it. You must be much more.* He knew exactly what his father had in mind. He knew his father's intentions. However, he wanted to sail more, so he swore to himself to endure.

Some of the lessons he did enjoy, though, such as studying the maps. Maps were always fascinating, and when he was younger, he used to dream of what the other islands, or distant lands, even looked like. He had already seen most of the islands he had wanted to see, but every new place only made him want to see more, see further.

He learned to write and read through daily log entries, which a condition placed upon him even earlier on when he was just a cabin boy. *Day's wage for a day's entry,* his father had said. *That's how you'll be paid, and I will require full sentences.* After discovering words, however, he discovered history, and then his dreams were given substance and wings. Far off lands and battles could now be painted in his mind, but also, he could finally understand what all his father and the other captains really did. He discovered the joys of astronomy when stories told of how past ships used to use the sky to navigate, and mathematics helped turn general distances and speed into actual calculable numbers. Everything had value, he concluded. He just wasn't sure if he was ready for what it all meant.

Sometime in the middle of his reading of *History of the Adonari War,* he put the book down and leaned back, closing his eyes. In this glorious war, the last of the great Adonari fleet had come to the aid of the mainland before being lost to history. This was the war that drove back the Dark One, whose name no one knew even now, away from the free people of Learsi. It had also helped unite the people together and ushered in the thousand years of peace. Nations allied together where once they had been at war. Heroes grew up from ordinary people and were turned into legends.

The battles played around in his mind, filling him with a longing to have been a part of their world. He saw the ships of the Last Fleet arrive on the mainland; their white sails trimmed in golden thread that caught fire in the sunset. He saw the moonlight reflect off the blades of the Grey Wardens as they danced through mobs of the enemy, clearly outnumbered but never faltering in their strides. He heard the thunder of hooves as Ebaven Lancers joined other Sanatian Cavalry on the open plains, mowing down the forces of Mahlen…

In his heart, he felt pain at what the people must have suffered and endured, yet excitement that people were capable of such feats. He knew many called the words 'story,' and it was a story, the story of origins and endings, but he also believed it to be true. Or, rather, he wanted to believe it was true, because if it was true, then people could do what was described, and people could be fantastic.

He heard commotion on the deck before footsteps sounded in the hall, and then Dayved came bursting into the cabin.

"Captain's calling you up, mate. Says there's trouble."

"What kind of trouble?" Joshian asked, putting down the book and following Dayved.

"Captain didn't say much," Dayved answered. "Just that there's a shipwreck off our starboard bow, well, not much of a ship now, and I'm not sure how many there are. But Captain says you should be up there."

Joshian emerged onto the deck with Dayved, which was full of energy as crewmen rushed around the deck and others worked to lower a small dingy into the water. A second boat had already left, their crew rowing toward the ship, which Joshian agreed didn't look like much of a ship at all anymore.

"Captain," he asked, walking up to his father. "What do you need?"

"Take a look," the captain answered, handing him a spyglass. "See that little patch of white, off by the rocks?"

"I see it, sir," he answered. "Poor thing looks torn to pieces. I'm counting five, no wait, six bodies, and there's one man waving. Ship's so bad, though, I don't even know where they're from."

"They're in bad shape," his father agreed. "Take Dayved and prepare some beds down below. You two will be on medical care duties for the rest of the trip."

"Aye, Captain," Joshian answered, subdued. "Dayved, let's get started."

"Aye, sir," he said, but stopped short. "Sorry, forgot."

By the time they had finished their preparations, making do the best they could despite not having much in the way of medicine or space, the rescue boats had returned. One man, a worn out, frail individual with long white hair and beard, whom Joshian recognized as the one waving, wept openly. He watched as bodies were pulled carefully from the boat and laid out on the deck, where other crewmen would check for signs of life.

Joshian bent down to one body, a middle-aged man from his looks, who was dressed in raggedy blue clothing, and felt for a pulse. The body felt cold and stiff, though, and he sighed, looking at the old man with sympathy as all around him the crewmen were having similar luck, and the body count far exceeded the original amount he had seen through the glass. But then, one man, Jayne, got excited.

"Captain," he said. "This one, I don't know how, but this kid's still got life in him!"

"He's alive?" the old man asked, ceasing his weeping and Joshian felt a hopeful smile cross his face. "The boy is alive?"

"He's weak, real weak," Jayne answered. "But he's fighting. Doesn't have long, though, maybe a few days at best."

"It'll take a couple days to get home," Will, the first officer, added.

"And even that's pushing it, by the looks of him," the captain said, bending down to lay a hand gently across his forehead.

"How much time do you think he has?" the old man asked.

The captain sighed, then wiped his hand on his pant leg. "Maybe a day."

"Then we'll have to make time."

All heads turned toward Joshian, and movement stopped as eyes fell upon him. The air seemed to grow thicker and colder as everyone, including the old man and the captain, looked his way. Will cleared his throat.

"How can we make time?" Will asked. "You know the routes, and you said yourself two days."

"Aye, I know the routes," Joshian answered, thinking to himself the odds of the boy's survival. "I know all the routes we take, can take, and if I may be so bold, I know the one that will get us home in time... with a bit to spare. It's not easy, and I wouldn't suggest it if there was another route, but the Sword Strait lies not even a mile from here. Time wise, we'll gain a day and a half."

"You are right, it's not easy," the captain agreed. "But you are also right that we would make it in time."

"You up for it again, Captain?" Will asked.

"Not me," the captain said, shaking his head. "Only ever go once."

"But does anyone know another way?" Joshian asked, after feeling a heavy silence fall. He looked around, catching glances and head scratching, but no one had suggestions. Others looked at him with a strange curiosity, but Joshian brushed it off. "Because I see no other way, and if that's what it takes... then I'll take it."

If there were any eyes not looking at him before, all eyes fell upon him now. He resisted the urge to massage his neck and forced himself not to look around, for fear of falling under the weight of people's expectations.

"Joshian," Will began, in a tone that, though quiet, resonated in Joshian's stomach. "Are you sure you know what you're asking?"

"Two men are still alive and need help, one of them barely clinging to life. With time now as his enemy, we can't afford to waste any. I see only two options here, and one involves a man losing his life for certain. I refuse to accept that. Captain…"

"Are you willing to risk this ship?" the captain asked, almost in warning but also almost challenging. "Are you willing to risk this ship, my ship, to save these men? Are you willing to risk this crew, all for one man?"

"I know this ship," Joshian answered, looking his father in the eye. "And I know this crew. I also know that if a chance to save a man's life exists, then it should be taken over accepting the certainty of his death. It needs to be done."

"Then do it," the captain ordered. None of the crew moved now.

"Captain," Joshian began, but his father cut him off.

"It needs to be done," the captain agreed. "I agree. And you made the claim. So, do it. Take the helm, son. Will you be the Captain now?"

Joshian looked around again, this time looking intently at the rest of the crew. Some were openly grinning. He looked back at the bodies lying on the deck, seeing Jayne hunched over the body of the boy. He looked into the old man's eyes and saw the pleading. Finally, he looked back at his father.

"Aye, sir," Joshian answered, feeling a warmth rise from his core and travel through the rest of his body. He stood up tall, straight, feeling a new strength he hadn't known before and clenched his fists. He looked his father evenly in the eyes, and the captain looked back. Many emotions crossed the captain's face at that moment, with joy and excitement at the forefront. But beyond all of them, pride. The weight of that pride settled, and Joshian swallowed.

"Joshian Farstrid," the captain said. "The ship is yours."

Chapter 3

Joshian's head swam as the words echoed in his mind and consumed his thoughts. Never had words created in him such a sense of authority and terror as those four simple words. *The ship is yours.* He had heard those words uttered only a few times before, but never to him, and never on his father's ship, a fact he knew most of the crew was aware of. He had spoken more than he intended, but he knew he had to keep going. He knew the response.

"Aye, Captain," Joshian answered, taking his position at the helm. He rested his hands on the mighty captain's wheel, a wheel that once guided his father's previous ship, and had been darkened and smoothed with age. The wood felt soft but solid, polished, having stood the test of time and weather that all manner of storms had thrown against it. He had gripped the wheel many times in the past, sometimes even having control of the helm while his father walked among the crew, but for the first time he felt the weight of its power.

I couldn't have said no, Joshian assured himself, staring at the wood. *Not when a claim is offered. If the claim is denied, the captain loses face, and the captain can't lose face… Dad can't lose face, not here or now and certainly not by me. Whatever happens from here…*

"We're taking the Sword," Joshian announced. "Onward, then."

The sea is not the same anymore. The thought settled in Joshian's mind. *It feels… bigger, while at the same time so much smaller, tamer but more dangerous.* He felt responsible for it, or to it, like he had a say in what it did. It was powerful, that thought, uplifting, but so humbling, and it created a knot that settled deep into his stomach. The knot grew heavier the further they traveled, and when they finally reached the mouth of the strait, Joshian felt nauseous.

He looked up at the mouth, and the walls of stone stared back. Their cliffs, which stretched higher than the masts of the ship, cast long shadows that turned the water before it into inky darkness, and plunged the ship into a cold sheet of bleakness. The cliffs themselves were various shades of blue and gray, devoid of life, but the mouth of the strait, lined with teeth of jagged rock and opening to a chasm of plunging darkness, echoed with a crashing whisper. Joshian swallowed. The maw grinned.

"Steady as she goes," Joshian called out as chilling dread closed around him when the cliff's shadow engulfed the rest of the ship. The warm-toned wood took on a ghastly shade that only darkened, and the old sails snapped. The old ship drifted forward, its creaks and groans echoed off the cliff walls, and when combined with the passage's own whispers, it became a haunting moan.

"We're good on this side," a crew member called out. "We've got a good ten meters off the starboard side."

"Only five on port, though," another called out.

"Changing course five degrees, starboard," Joshian called, turning the wheel in response. The ship accepted the course correction, and Joshian breathed. A loud screech turned his eyes up to the granite cliffs, but now his eyes could perceive hundreds of nests of gulls and cormorants. *I won't fear your song now.*

The crew was tense but alert. Every available man had a hand on a rope or had eyes watching the cliffs, and all were waiting to act as needed. Joshian knew them all, had learned under them all, and though he trusted them, seeing them focused on their individual part made him realize how much they trusted him… and he smiled. His hands tightened harder on the wheel, and the knot in his stomach dissolved.

The ship lurched to port, so he spun the wheel quickly, straining as the ship fought back. He wasn't fast enough to prevent it from grazing the wall, but still managed to keep it on track. He gritted his teeth, regretting the damage, but then jumped when a hand fell upon his shoulder. He let the warmth of the hand course through him, steeled his feet, and then brought his father's words back to his mind. *On edge, a person won't act the way they know they should. Be calm. Think. You're almost done. You're almost through.*

Nodding, he opened up his senses more. He could distinguish the sounds coming from the cliffs. He could see traces of light reflecting off the sea-moistened stone. He could feel the rumblings of the ship, knew which ones were with which parts, which ropes. He also remembered all the numbers he had run when contemplating this path before.

We're almost there.

His grip tightened more, but he forced his hand to relax, and pried his fingers from the wheel. The ship moved faster, lurching suddenly again as it caught a pocket of current, and he threw his weight into the wheel, but still struck the side again. This time, splinters and chunks of wood flew off in a shower from the impact, and the ship shuddered. Joshian cringed, but kept his feet, if only barely. The walls bent around, twisted, and narrowed, and the top slanted inward, seeking to engulf them.

Then there was light. Rounding one of the corners a spark of light appeared, and the ship welcomed it and rushed towards it. Faster it flew, now, swept up in the mercy of the current toward the opening a hundred meters away, and Joshian fought to keep her on track, but the wheel was stiff. *I can't turn. She's on her own. The current is her master, not me, but I can do what I can. If something happens...* the wheel strained even harder in his hands, gaining ground on him, but he braced himself harder. The hand on his shoulder tightened and he pushed against it, using their strength with his. The wheel stopped moving, and the cliff wall drifted in the ship's bow. At the last moment, he smiled. He set his feet, and then released the wheel.

The wheel spun freely for a few rotations before he thrust his hands forward, and the handles slapped hard against his hands. Let free temporarily, the ship shifted toward the opening before Joshian straightened her, pointing her forward, and then she raced. *Just a little more, girl. Come on, girl, just a little more.* The opening neared. The walls closed in tighter so now no more than three meters separated the ship from the cliffs. Joshian narrowed his focus. Then the light engulfed them.

The light shown out beautifully, radiant, and pure. Shadows were cast back, and the ship was bathed in a white and yellow glow that appeared as brilliantly as gold and silver. The ship slowed, drifting casually in the deeper, wider water, and the crew cheered. Joshian, feeling an immense sense of relief, sighed.

"Well done," his father said from behind him, squeezing his shoulder once more before removing his hand. "Very well done."

Without the hand, his shoulder felt light, almost empty. A few deep breaths stilled his pulse, and a few more after that made him realize he still gripped the wheel, so letting the wheel go reluctantly, he almost felt a part of him drain away into the ship. He looked up at the sky, blinking, the light feeling brighter than usual, and saw that though the trip had felt like eternity, the sun showed only minutes had passed.

When his eyes adjusted, he turned and looked back at the way they had come. The strait was now almost hidden, due to the way the sun shined on the exit, and if he hadn't known it was exactly there, it would have been easy to mistake for just another niche in the wall. He turned back around, taking in the crew celebrating, but then his eyes focused on the chunks of wood that had splintered onto the deck. He turned back to his father.

"Captain," he said. "The ship…"

"Is still sailable," his father finished with a knowing smile. "At least enough to get her home. You felt it, didn't you? You understood the ship when it spoke to you, didn't you?"

"Aye," Joshian answered, though his mouth was dry.

"Some go years without that feeling," his father continued. "To some, a ship is just that, but to me… it's like a part of my being. I'm connected to it, to the sea, to the crew. When it hurts…"

"I feel it," Joshian finished, nodding. "I don't…"

"I know," his father said, nodding. "Now, down to the cabin with you. I won't hear your protests; rest up for a few hours and join us when you're awake. You won't admit it, not even to yourself, but I see the weariness, and I remember it from my time. When you can trust yourself, though, come back up, and you can help bring her home."

"Aye, sir," Joshian said, smiling tiredly. Not denying his father's claims, he disappeared below deck.

"You've got yourself a fine son, there," Will said, walking up after Joshian had gone below. "A good son by anyone's standards, but an honorable man as well. Might even be good enough to let him court my daughter, but you never heard that from me, else people get any ideas about her."

"He is a fine son," Ralshian answered his first officer, smiling proudly. "As fine as any father can be proud of, and then some, and if he continues along this path, he will be a very great man. Still, I wondered about him. It's one thing for a father to see greatness in a child, but such another to see it fulfilled."

"He has skill matched by few," Will agreed, but Ralshian shook his head.

"Skill can be learned," Ralshian sighed, turning the wheel slightly to steer the ship more towards the center of the wide channel. "But my pride is in his heart. You saw how he sailed, true, but with life on the line, something else came out, something you can't teach. His compassion became conviction, his knowledge became faith. He had no doubt in his mind when he spoke to me. He wasn't just telling me things I already knew. He spoke his heart.

"I used to wonder what it would take to push him to the point of being ready to go further, what it would take to bring out his... passion. For all his talk, I wondered if even his potential wasn't just a father's wishful thinking."

"Not just you," Will consoled, smiling. "He seemed to want the life of a crewman more, but then, you can hardly blame him. He may be your son, but he's still young."

"Yes, he is young," Ralshian answered. "Young enough that a father's pride can be surpassed by surprise. It's never happened before, being done by someone so young, but regardless, the claim of one has been made... and fulfilled."

"You always did say your son wasn't ordinary," Will laughed, and Ralshian laughed with him. "But speaking of surprise, I may be able to add a little more to your plate."

"I doubted I could be surprised anymore," Ralshian answered. "Today proved otherwise. Go on."

"Those shipwrecked fellows earlier," Will said. "When I saw their ship from here, something felt off. It didn't look like one of ours, nor one from any of the other islands. At first, I wondered if it was a mind block on my part, but when I saw their clothes, I knew that wasn't the case at all. Also, Jayne recovered this bag from the wreckage. Recognize that symbol?"

"Oh, I recognize that one," Ralshian grumbled, sighing deeply. "I know that one very well."

"I thought you might," Will said, subdued. "Well, here's the summary. The old man has a broken leg, but otherwise he just needs some food and decent sleep before he should be healthy enough to talk much. The boy on the other hand fares far worse. Physically, he looks unbroken, but he's barely awake, has a really bad fever, and I could almost see his strength fading. Two days would have been too long, true, but I don't even know if the time we've given him will be enough."

"Whether it's enough or not, there's nothing more we can do other than what we can do," Ralshian sighed. "Mistress Leanne has worked wonders before, so if any hope can be found, it will be in her. But, on to my ship; she feels alright, but how is she?"

"She's fine, Captain," Will said, giving a half grin. "It's only cosmetic damage, but I know it felt like more to him. We'll make it back without any problems, well, problems from the ship at least."

"Good," Ralshian said, gripping the wheel. "All hands, make for home before the light sets. Let's fly!"

The flame from the pile of corpses and the smoke of its burning permeated Maer's thoughts as he rode. The icy wind made his eyes water, but his horse knew the way, so he allowed his mind and thoughts to drift. The heavy sword strapped to his back comforted him in a strange way, but it still felt wrong. The weight was too great, its length was too long and too awkward, yet carrying it did give him strength. With it, for the first time in a long time, his direction was clear and not leading toward a grave.

He knew hours had passed by the time his horse brought him back to Tilgal, but he couldn't say where the hours had gone or even how many. He passed other soldiers who looked at him strangely, but they asked him no questions so he offered no explanation. His eyes felt raw, but they were clear now, and he could only imagine the thoughts the soldiers directed his way. He approached the captain, and the man looked at him with sympathy.

"Welcome to the ranks of the burdened soldiers," the captain said in a grave, somber tone. "What is the mission tasked to you?"

"Kellivar," Maer answered. "I ride for Kellivar. Darkness takes new form, and the shadow rises."

"And you have proof?" the captain asked, yet in a tone that conveyed no sense of doubt. Maer appreciated it, and he nodded. He pulled forth the claw and dagger, and unwrapped them from their cloths, then held them out. The captain stared at them for a long moment but chose not to take them.

"So, Treel and Onesh are dead," he said at last, raising a hand in a closed fist against his heart. Maer stopped him.

"Onesh still lives," he said. "He said something about a hunt, heading north through Posmor, the Remnant wanting to know and something else about Emyran."

"Did he, now?" the captain asked, smiling. A dreamy look crossing his face as his eyes glazed over. "Hope now rides into the heart of darkness. Dressed like the dawn, he carries the light, igniting the flames of those he sees. His blades are swift, and his bow is steady, yet his heart burns with the flame that would consume all who would set fear into others. A true hero, a true firebrand…

"Ride, Maer, in the name of Emyran, and may He guide your task, as we set about to complete others."

"Captain, what is happening?" Maer asked. "In plain speak, if you will. And who is Emyran?"

"The Darkness gains strength, and returns again," the captain said, smiling a deadly grin. "It comes to consume us, much like it did long ago. It seeks to enslave us, to control this world, and drive us to despair."

"Then why are you smiling?" Maer asked, laying a hand on his sword.

The captain's smile broadened, reaching his eyes, making gray eyes Maer hadn't noticed earlier shine brightly.

"Because Emyran returns. He is, well, he is the light in the darkness, and the sun during the day. He is hope when hope cannot be found. He is strength when all strength is gone. He is patient, yet firm, loving yet deadly. He is, well, you'll see if you seek Him. Now fly, Maer, and should our paths cross again, I'll be glad, but I know not when that would be."

Maer turned to go, but before he reached his horse he turned back. "You're the kinsman that he spoke of, aren't you?"

"One of many. If you look, you will find us. Happy hunting."

Maer bid farewell to his horse, and the gentle beast nuzzled him affectionately. He turned to collect a fresh mount, but the horse nudged him in the back, and he heard some of the men laugh. "Rest, my friend," Maer said to him, but the horse refused to leave his side, so Maer laughed in turn. "Very well. But if you ride with me, then I shall have to give you a name…"

Mounted once more on his horse, Solas, Maer flew down the mountain paths. Cold gave way to warmer autumn and gray stone turned to brown trunks and red and gold leaves. Flowers began to appear; patches of small, light green kandaceas and daisies, and three-petaled blue melindais accented by the emerald-green grass. Along his path, bright orange cimorellis rose up, their petals catching the sun like tongues of flame. Wolves howled on either side as he passed, and birds flew overhead, and he smiled that life had returned. At the bottom of the mountain, other animals made themselves known, with squirrels chittering in the trees and rabbits running through the undergrowth. He rode on.

In Chanost, he took as long a rest as he could afford before continuing, riding through the passes of the Beorlang Range towards Asard. Weeks went by, as strange days became strange nights. Some nights a pack of wolves would circle, staying far enough away to not spook the horse, as if they were guarding the camp, or else tracking him and unwilling to let go of their prey. During the day, though, he caught glimpses of them running alongside, but never threatening. Birds would stay overhead, almost spurring his horse on, and the squirrels sprinting through the trees lifted his spirit.

He rode as far as the Great Western Road and turned east towards Asard. At the crossroads that diverged towards Maltis, he directed a rider to the coastal city, but continued the ride for Asard himself. More days passed, the journey wearing him down, but when he finally rode into the walled stronghold of the city, he stayed only long enough to sleep the night. A messenger offered to take the charge from him to let him rest, but Maer refused.

"Do you really want to bear the news of our impending doom to the High Lord?" Maer asked the messenger through a wild laugh. The messenger swallowed, stared at the trinkets, and hung his shoulders.

"No, I don't," the messenger sighed. "But I would carry it anyway, if it was my duty."

"You are a good man," Maer replied, feeling nothing but compassion and sympathy for the man. "Your time may come, but this is mine. Watch and be ready until then."

"Be well, then, soldier," the messenger said. "And may your road be clear."

Spurring Solas to a gallop, Maer rode off to Kellivar.

Chapter 4

The sky glowed with the flaming tongues of evening light as the sun descended on the island of Firebrand and upon the people finishing their day, at least, it did to Calian. Gray clouds took on a sliver of gold edge, and far into the east, just above the horizon, the Sailor's Star had begun its ascent to guide the last ships home. Looking out at that star, Calian let out a sigh.

Calian, the younger son of the captain of *Dawn's Embrace,* Ralshian, looked very much like his brother, Joshian, in most respects. His face had the same shape, but with less definition around the cheeks. His hair was shorter but had the same coloring. His body, too, though clearly muscular, was much leaner and shorter, needing a good four inches to match his brother's height.

His companion lounging next to him on the docks, Seth, who was using a pile of coiled ropes and nets as a pillow, was a couple of years older, but a couple inches shorter. He had the build of a man used to long treks through the woods, but also of one who liked to climb on a regular basis. He had dark sandy hair cut short and manageable, and his eyes, which always seemed to stare off beyond the present, were a gray-green mix, like the sea in a tide pool.

"Are you sure you want to wait longer?" he asked Calian, yawning. He stretched, then sprung lithely to his feet and crossed his arms over his chest.

"Absolutely," Calian replied, continuing to stare out. "Mum said they'd be back today, and I dare you to name one time that things didn't go the way she said."

"We both know I can't," Seth said shrugging. "Now, I'll admit, she's one of the few who can tell anyone to do anything and have them actually listen, but no one can tell time what to do. I know you were hoping otherwise. I was too, but your old man's like clockwork, always dependable but taking risks only when necessary."

"You sure about that?" Calian asked, grinning, and pointing out across the water. "Because I see evidence to the contrary. Well, not the dependable part. Just that."

"Are you…" Seth began, turning around to stare across the sea. He threw his hands up in resignation. "I give up. No way your mum could have predicted that, absolutely no way. Too many circumstances, way too many things to deal with… Well, they would have had to have taken a different route, or maybe just pushed harder in other places… oh, what if they took the sword…"

"A lot of what-ifs, but they don't matter," Calian agreed, but when he saw Seth turn and walk off, he added, "wait, where are you off to?"

"We're going to need a few more hands to get things unloaded and tied up," Seth answered, walking backwards. "And there's no way you're missing tonight, not by a long shot."

"Then I'll see you tonight," Calian called to Seth's already turned back. *One person certain, then,* he thought, *and Joshian will no doubt be there. I wonder who else.*

As Seth walked off, he tossed a salute over his shoulder and Calian turned back to watch the ship come in. He always enjoyed watching the ships come in, especially his father's, and especially now, because he knew the next time that ship left harbor, he could be on it.

"Welcome back!" Calian called from the dock as *Dawn's Embrace* sailed up. A few of the boys Seth had gathered shouted to their fathers who waved in turn, and older youths set themselves to receive the ropes soon to be tied off. "Mom said you'd be back, despite being a day early, but I'm still surprised. Not that I mind, but what happened?"

"We had a change of course," his father called back. "We took the Sword just a few hours ago. And thank you for the welcome; I'm glad we don't have to unload all of this ourselves."

"Who took it?" Calian asked as he tied down the rope tossed to him.

"Your brother took it," his father answered cheerfully. "Or more like he demanded it."

He walked down the gangplank and met Calian in a tight embrace before holding him back at arm's length. "Well, now," he declared after a moment. "I left you a boy, but you look more like you're finally a man. And a happy names day as well. Your brother commented often about wanting to be back for it, and I am glad to be as well."

"I am too," Calian said. "To think, I'll be one of the few to celebrate on my actual twentieth. Which reminds me... brother," he added, seeing Joshian appear on the deck, looking tired but otherwise well. "I claim the next trip; I've been shore bound for too long and I need an adventure."

"And you'll have it, little brother," Joshian said, embracing Calian tighter than usual. "Dad keeps a hard bargain, though, so I hope you've kept up your end."

"Of course, I have," Calian replied. "After all, you've got five years and a few inches on me, so I can't be letting you get too far ahead... Wait, you didn't risk the ship just so you could get home for me, did you? I know the risks..."

"Believe me, I do too," Joshian interrupted. "I tried to find ways to shave as much time as I could afford, but the best would bring us in sometime tomorrow. The shipwrecked travelers that we found stranded, however, made us reevaluate, though. We'll have to have Mistress Leanne take a look at them, but it looks like the older just needs his leg set, some food and then something for the pain. As for the younger... Oh, hey, check out this symbol on the bag."

"Blazes! That's..."

"Yep," Joshian nodded. "They're definitely not from around here."

"I can see that," Calian answered, his eyes wide. He turned to address both his father and brother. "Well, we have a few here to help with the unloading and all. Should we send for someone to come look at the patients, or just bring them to Mistress Leanne now?"

"Send a runner to let her know they'll be coming," Joshian answered. Calian looked over at his father who shared an amused grin with the first officer, but at his nod, Calian turned back to his brother. "But otherwise, they should be fine to move. Now, you wouldn't know what's for supper tonight, would you?"

"Uncle Talum brought a marlin in," Calian continued, and when Joshian smiled in response, the old Joshian was back. "He just caught it the other day. Marianne brought back enough clams for a stew, and we've got apple pie for dessert. Mum baked some bread, too. Also, and these are her words, not mine, but she'll be 'most displeased if you are late'."

"That's mum for ya," Joshian agreed, shaking his head, chuckling. "Then we best work fast."

"Go on, get out of here, Captain," Will called from the deck. "You too, Joshian. We've got things more than covered so we'll take it from here. It's not every day you can be present for a twentieth. You've earned it."

"Will Treker, you're as good a man as I've ever known, and I will gladly take your offer," Ralshian answered him. "I'll see you tomorrow."

Calian picked up his brother's and father's bags and threw them over his shoulder.

"Good to see the old place is still holding together," Ralshian said, looking around the village once he stepped off the dock onto the gravel road.

Confused, Calian looked over at his brother, who was shaking his head and hiding a grin.

"Says it every time," Joshian mumbled. "Just go with it."

"Not every time," Ralshian sighed, staring more intently. "But, if the village needs repair, I'm usually the one making the run, and though our nets have been good to us lately, having to spend more for maintenance is never what I have in mind. Fortunately, all looks well; I'm in need of staying shore bound for a while."

They set forth into the village, climbing the gentle slope leading into the center of town, and were greeted by a few watchers at the main gate. Here, harder-packed gravel mud, stained light gray from the ocean's salt, made up their path, but with very few carts using it, and the majority of the traffic occurring between the dock and the town gate, nothing more was ever needed. The "main street" passed by the town hall and a few taverns, which were distinguishable only by signs hanging out front, as the buildings had similar construction of darker support beams framing gray planks. There were small shops here and there, but most of the wares were sold from small carts and enthusiastic salesmen.

There were no inns, however, but that was not too unexpected. Visitors of any kind were rare, after all, and most were relatives that stayed with their respective families. When actual strangers did come, however, they were directed to the *Angel Fish* tavern adjacent to the town square. There, either someone would come to offer accommodations, or if there was absolutely no one, they would take the guest room at the top of the stairs.

The construction served them well through the years. Although much of the village's business occurred on the coast, most of the town resided inland where the tides and storms struck with less ferocity. Timber acquired from the larger outer islands took care of most of the buildings and construction projects, but when quarried stone was needed, like for the forge, the town hall, and all the pubs and taverns, it was gathered and shipped from Ancore, or Faerban. Except for general maintenance and repairs and the occasional rebuilding of foundations, most of the buildings stood where they had been first placed.

As the three moved through town, they were greeted with enthused hellos and warm handshakes. Ralshian always had time for a few words and a laugh before passing by. Once though greeting one individual, though, another hand would soon be there to take the last one's place, and thus the cycle continued. The walk wasn't far, but it was definitely slow. Calian didn't mind. He always liked seeing how respected his father was, and the conversations were at least interesting.

Conversations mostly centered mostly on business, either with trades that had happened on the trip, or with runs soon to come. In all cases, his father could assure the inquirers that all trades had transpired without trouble, and they would leave contentedly with formal nods or smiles. Some were purely social, and those were usually nothing more than a friendly handshake or a few kind words before passing by. Master Torkral Rockthorne, the town blacksmith, just waved from his forge before going back to his hammering. After most of the crowd had gotten in their greetings, two captains, Captain Lanamir and Captain Aleon, joined them for a few moments to discuss coordinating a tuna run for the next week before moving off to their own homes for dinner. Calian took it all in stride.

"The three new ships are finally finished," Calian said, continuing his news once the two captains had left. "I'm not sure if you noticed them coming in, but they are quite impressive. A few tried making claims, but none more so than Balam Perch, at least, he was the loudest. He tried saying that since his father was 'the greatest captain around,' and his uncle was one of the best spears this side of the mainland, then it was, and I quote, 'only right that he should be promoted.' Ha! And he's barely a couple years shy of thirty, too. Of course, things got a bit... heated... when I said the only reason that his claims held any weight was because the best were currently sailing, and, well, long story short... I got a few good licks in, but when mum found out it took me a few days to sit down again."

Ralshian laughed. "Don't ever tell your mother I said this, but yeah, you're my son alright, and you did good. Don't ever be afraid to stand up for your beliefs, so long as you're willing to accept what comes. I'm not too proud to say that his elder bloods are some of the best sailors I've known, but he still comes a few leagues shy of matching them, yet. It's good to see you remembered the first rule of fighting."

"Of course, I remember it," Calian began with a grin. "I remember them all. Don't pick a fight with the brother of a girl you like, or her father, because that never ends well. If you pick a fight against a stronger opponent, don't back down and accept whatever beating you get because you'll be respected for it. Make sure your fight matters if you're the one who starts it, since you'll have to defend it. And finally, whatever you do, don't be stupid by getting yourself killed, or else mom will bring you back to punish you herself."

"That's more than a few," Ralshian said with a chuckle, but Calian interjected.

"Hey, not my fault you name more 'number one rules to fighting' than just the one."

"He's right," Joshian said. "You told me a few more, too. For example, all men can fall when tripped. A crewman you fight with will still be a crewman for the rest of the voyage. You only lose when you accept defeat... That's all I can think of right now."

"Alright, then here's another one," Ralshian conceded. "Don't judge a man by his age. Some of the oldest can be complete fools, while some of the youngest can be greater than you can imagine. Age is just a number. The person is the one to judge. But anyway, moving on."

"Yes, moving on," Calian said. "Mayor Pinard spoke about opening negotiations with the mainland for rights to other fishing runs, especially the tuna by the northern end of Grygor Sea, and he said something about opening the village further to outsiders during the summer months, maybe hire on some additional ships and crews. Naturally, this would mean more housing, more supplies, more a lot of things, but he asked me to let you know as soon as I could so you could discuss it more. Those are all the details I know, though."

"No, that's good," his father replied, nodding. "I'll bring it up at the next captain's meeting. Thank you. Anything else happen while we've been away?"

"No, that's about it," Calian finished. "I feel I'm forgetting something, though... oh, that's right, Marianne's got a couple suitors."

"Wait, what?" Joshian asked, turning from his private conversation with the Stormwind brothers to the one between his father and brother. "Marianne's got what? Alright, who do I need to visit?"

"Relax, brother," Calian said, holding up his hands. "Taylor Mayson, barely nineteen, came to me and made his intentions clear. He spoke of how he had grown to care about her and how he'd be able to make her happy, so I told him no one who couldn't work the entirety of the herring run would be worthy of approaching you, father."

"Calian, *we* can barely work the entirety of the herring run," Joshian laughed. "We did it maybe once, when the run was the slowest it had been in decades and even then, we were nearly dead by the end. Seriously, had it been any other crew and if we weren't at each other's side, we probably wouldn't have made it ourselves."

"Still," Calian continued. "In the couple of weeks since I told him, I've noticed him pushing himself harder than I've seen in a long time. When he does come of age, he might make a serious contender. At the least, father, he'd be worth considering as a crewman."

"He's a decent kid," Ralshian agreed, stroking his beard. "Not as hard a worker as some, true, but a decent mind when he works to use it. I'll see what he's like in a few years and keep an eye out in the meantime. Alright, anyone else?"

"Davis Tanner," Calian said with a laugh. "I think he's more interested in being in the family of a Farstrid, though. Some people seem to think it'll help gain some standing. I told him only a captain would be a suitable man for you."

"Simple, I like it," Ralshian laughed. "Nicely done. How did he take it, and how does she feel about them?"

"He hasn't done much in response," Calian said, shrugging as much as the baggage would let him. "He looked dejected. As for her, she said she was more interested in the attention than with the suitors themselves. Besides, it's Marianne we're talking about; I don't think you need to worry about her just yet. If anything," he added, laughing. "It's really Joshian who should be the most worried."

"Why me?" Joshian asked.

"Marianne's been talking with some of the girls, and apparently you have a few interested in you as well. I've been listening to some of the other men, and your name has come up as a possible match for their daughters. Contrary to your outward desires, mate, you're popular."

"Ugh," Joshian groaned, and Ralshian laughed. "Marriage will come later, in a few years, after I have my adventures. I'm not ready to settle down yet."

"It's not so bad," Ralshian chuckled, nudging Joshian. "You'll know her when you see her, and if you don't, well, she'll make herself known eventually. Don't stress about it. Now, as for worrying about Marianne," he continued, his voice taking on a gruff tone. "I'll decide that when the time comes."

Joshian chuckled, but stayed subdued for the rest of the walk, which brought them from the town center and down a side road to their home. Built by Ralshian's grandfather and kept well, the two-story wooden home stood at the edge of a stand of trees and a rocky beach. A small vegetable garden grew off to the side, and the smells of cooking dishes leaked out from the front door to welcome them. Before entering, Ralshian held them up and spoke in a low voice.

"Now, about tonight…"

"Father, if I may," Joshian interrupted, clearing his throat. "I've been preparing for a while, and I believe I have the rights." Ralshian sighed and Calian grinned.

"Yes, son, you do," Ralshian agreed. "I was just going to say, I'll get your mother to sleep early, but you are to be as careful and quiet as possible when you get back, because if you wake her, stumbling in drunk, you'll wish the sea demon had found you first."

"We know, father," the two of them answered. "I remember the stories of when Dayved got in trouble with that."

"Good, good. Now, Joshian, go on ahead and say hello to your mother. Calian and I will be along shortly."

Joshian took his bags from Calian and went inside the house.

Chapter 5

Joshian opened the front door quietly, taking a moment to breathe in the aromas of his mother's cooking. Baking bread, stew, seasoned fish, and the tangy-sweet smell of baked apples filled his nose and made his mouth water, giving him pause before putting his bags down. He looked around, taking note of a few things, like the way some of the pictures had been rearranged, or how some of the chairs had been moved to accommodate for the season's changed lighting, but his father's chair was where it had always been, in the back corner where the sun wouldn't get in his eyes, and the potted pink nerlissas were still in bloom, like always.

Setting his things in a corner, he rummaged around in his pack until he found the two wrapped items he bought earlier and tucked them into his jacket pocket. At the last moment he remembered his boots, knowing his mother would have words if he dirtied the, evidently, recently cleaned floor.

Sneaking up behind his mother as she stood over a pot, stirring, he gave her and gentle squeeze and a peck on the cheek. "Hello mum, we're back."

"Welcome home, sweetie," his mother, Emylie, said as she put down her spoon to hug him. Her dark hair that normally fell well past her shoulders in waves was tied up in the back and dusted lightly with stray flour. She was a small and slender woman, but those who knew her well knew her presence commanded respect, and though Joshian towered almost a foot above her, he always felt a little smaller around her. "You're right on time. How was your trip?"

"It was good," he said, reaching into his pocket and pulling out one of the packages. "But very eventful. Also, I got you something. Here, open it."

"Aww," she said, her mouth falling into a quivering smile as she held up the silver necklace inlaid with pearls he had brought. "They're beautiful. Help me put it on?"

"Um, well," he said, fidgeting, and wearing a sheepish grin. "I, uh, I don't really know how."

His mother laughed. "You can work rope into impossible knots and un-work impossible ones again, you can rig patches or repair on any size ship, yet in these matters, you've always struggled. I have a feeling you'll be doing this a few times in your life, for some girl who stirs your heart, so you had best practice now. Now, first you undo that clasp..."

"Mother, that's beautiful," a girl's voice said from the doorway to the dining area. "Did Father get that for you?"

"This one came from your brother," their mother said. "Joshian has good taste."

"But he's doing it wrong," Marianne said, her laugh conveying a joyful sound that always put him at ease. "Welcome back, brother."

"Glad to be back, Marianne," he said, kissing her forehead. She had the same long brown hair as her mother, but he saw she kept it in a tight braid, now, wrapped almost like a crown around her head. Her eyes were more like her brothers' eyes, though, of a darker blue, while their mother's eyes were grayer. Smiling, he added, "You can clearly see I'm doing something wrong, so tell me how to make it work."

"Well, like mum said, you have to open the clasp first, and then keep it open," she said, working the metal with dainty, precise fingers. "Then you slide the loop through, and just make sure the hair doesn't get caught. Then, that's it, you're done. Got it?"

"Perfect," he said, reaching into his pocket again. "Now I can get it right for you. Here you go."

"Oh!" she exclaimed, opening the wooden lid. "Blue topaz, right?"

"Correct," he answered as she hugged him. "I remembered you mentioning you liked Auntie's ring, so I kept my eye out. And yes, I know I'm early for your name day, but I figured you wouldn't mind your present early."

"They are so pretty," she said again.

"Well, you're worth it."

"Ah, the silver tongue of a Farstrid," Ralshian announced, coming into the kitchen. "As well as my eye for value. Had you not been my son, I might be inclined to feel threatened."

"Father, we both know when it comes to flowery words that you have no equal," Joshian laughed. "How else would mom have agreed to marry you?"

"That's right," Ralshian agreed, walking over to kiss his wife and daughter. "And don't you boys forget it, either. Sorry, you men." He paused, looking between both of his sons. "I can still hardly believe that my two boys are grown men now. After all those years raising you, you've become your own men. It does a father proud, it does."

"Now, now, dear," their mother said, looking into his eyes. "We can spend time with pleasantries later. For now, you all look starved, but we have a twentieth that needs celebrating first, so, Calian, into the main room with you. The rest of you, go get your things. Quickly now."

When the family gathered again, various parcels of different sizes and shapes were set before Calian, which he enthusiastically opened. Some gifts were practical; from his mother he received a nice set of dress clothes, finery proper for traveling to other ports and markets. From his sister, a dark blue hooded cloak stitched to be waterproof. From his father he received a new belt knife, "for real men's work," and from both parents, a set of leather-bound books. One book was a collection of maps and history. Another was a set of stories written by Lord Alexander Grichmal from his time during the Adonarian War. The third, though, was completely blank. "Your own story will have its place," their mother said. "And someone will want to know it, though you may forget it."

Joshian's gift was a silver-worked flute, polished to catch the light and make it seem to glow with an internal flame. "This is the instrument to entertain kings," Joshian said after Calian blew on it, producing a note clear and purer than one from the wooden ones. "I'm not sure where you'll find a king, mind, but a talented musician needs an instrument worthy of his skill."

Calian's final gift was presented by their father. It was a three-pronged bladed spear about as long as he was tall, with the head of pure steel and the shaft of polished cedar. Calian's eyes danced around the metal head, following the design carved around the handle, which appeared to be a snake spurting flame. When the realization finally struck, his breath caught.

"I'm charged with Leviathan?" Calian asked in a whisper. Ralshian smiled proudly, and Joshian leaned forward, intently.

"When I went to Torkral," Ralshian said from his position in his chair. "I told him the design for the spearhead, but he chose the etching. His words were that you have a fire inside you that spreads to others, a passion that strengthens those around you, you're independent without being closed off, and strong without being boastful. I know great things are in store for your life."

"This symbol hasn't been given in years," Calian commented. "Not since Captain Kathar fell, and decades have passed since then."

"And now the charge falls to you," Joshian said, solemnly, looking at his brother with a new respect. "To think, my own brother... wait till the guys see this tonight, ideally in a few hours, provided that supper is done now?" He looked over at their mother, hopefully.

"Yes, supper is ready," she said, getting up and walking over to hug Calian. "And if you come help set the table, we can get to eating."

"And while we eat," Calian said as he set his spear in the corner next to his father's and brother's, which had etched a marlin and a wolf, respectively. "You can tell me all about the trip, especially those two castaways you found."

"Work first," their mother ordered, casually. "Talk later. Now hurry up. How do you think we feel, cooking all day and not able to eat any of this, eh?"

"Yes mum," Joshian and Calian said, at the same time their father answered, "yes dear." The three of them looked at each other, shared an amused grin, and then set about their tasks. When they were seated, and the food spread across the table, Ralshian prayed a blessing and then they were silent as, for the next few minutes, everyone savored the various dishes, followed quickly by a round of enthusiastic compliments, praising many times over the work, skill and love that went into the meal. Then Ralshian and Joshian told the tale of their trip, ending with how Joshian navigated and sailed the Sword, resulting in how they were able to come home as quickly as they did.

"Joshian was brilliant," Ralshian praised, and Joshian bowed his head at the adoration. "Not just with him taking the Sword, either, but with how he did it. He truly read the ship, in a way that can't be explained.

"Unfortunately, the people we rescued could present another problem. The clothes were enough to cause surprise, but the symbol on the bag, as you've both noticed, that's the symbol of Ildice, which means there's no doubt that they are under the authority of Ildice. They may even be nobility themselves. The old man appears friendly, and though worn out, he spoke freely. Once he's rested, I'll talk with him more. A good night's rest can do wonders."

"Where will they stay tonight?" their mother asked.

"The boy was taken to Miss Leanne's," their father answered. "The old man insisted on staying by his side, and his leg needed tending to, anyway, so they'll stay there tonight."

"Very good," their mother said, wiping her mouth. "And speaking of night, you two had best be heading out, assuming you still plan on going tonight. Just, don't get into any trouble you can't get out of, alright? You're my sons, and I worry."

"Don't worry, mum," Joshian assured her. "We won't. It'll be a good group around us, and we'll keep things under control."

"And don't spend what you don't have," Ralshian added. "I will not be bailing you out."

"Again, not to worry," Joshian said, patting a bag at his side that jingled with coins. "I have it covered."

"Good," Ralshian said with a nod. "Now, go on and get out of here; I'll help your mother and sister with the cleaning."

"Thank you," the two said, taking their plates to the wash area. They kissed their mother farewell and went off into the night, taking their spears with them.

"Are you expecting trouble, Joshian?" Calian asked, the two walking briskly through the warm night down towards the town square.

"Hopefully not," Joshian laughed. "But you never know. Why do you ask?"

"Well, you had me bring my spear," Calian answered. "I thought they don't let them in?"

"You're right, they don't," Joshian said. "But there's a tradition we follow tonight, and this is a tradition that goes back long before we even had a village, so it's pretty important. It can be a bit painful, but you'll understand when you get through it. Therefore, Calian, let me first tell you a story.

"Long ago, when the Adonari War was fought, Ebaven, Ildice, and Sanasis joined with Adonar to fight the nation of Mahlen, which was ruled by the Dark Lord. Legends say that Adonar was once part of the mainland, and there were good relations between the four nations, but over time, people changed, and not for the better. The war raged on for years, and many fell, though mostly from Ebaven and Sanasis. Ildice was further from the fighting, so they suffered less, and the Adonari are, well, Adonari, but Ebaven and Sanasis started to resent them, and a divide was created.

"Now, at first only the men could serve in the army, while the women and children were left to wait at home, and with the combined power of four nations, no one expected the war to last more than a few skirmishes. Unfortunately, it went far longer than that, and people were dying too quickly, but the Adonari youth didn't want to stand by and do nothing. They wanted to stand by their fathers and were willing to go to battle, so they pleaded with their elders. The elders' verdict was clear, however, that no youth would go to battle. They declared that it wasn't safe for their people, as future generations depended on their survival.

"The youth wouldn't stand for it, though, so one night a group of the boys, armed with their spears, went to the local tavern while the elders there had drunk enough to lose their wits. They declared loudly, "Name us the men we are so we may fight!" and the elders weren't thinking, so they said it was so. These youth then pressed the elders to allow everyone to go to battle if they so desired, and the elders agreed, so it was so. They tried to deny it the next day and retract their words on the grounds that they weren't in their right mind, but the fire had already been ignited, and once lit, it's hard to extinguish. The war changed greatly that day to their favor."

"Wait, hold on," Calian said. "I noticed you said Adonari youth. I'm assuming the other nations didn't follow suit?"

"Correct," Joshian answered. "Ildice, Ebaven, and Sanasis continued to fight their way, and train their way. Their youth were content to sit back, but the Adonar youth were the ones who stepped up. We follow their example in honor of them.

"A lot of things changed after that," Joshian continued. "For example, it was decided that elders had to come to a unanimous decision for matters of that nature, and if an elder was deemed not of sound mind, then his vote was considered void. Weapons were barred in taverns, too, officially, not just as a general rule, and even knives had to be declared. The actions and courage of the youth did prove to the elders that their voices were meant to be listened to, though. As a result, the age that a person could choose to go to war at was lowered from thirty to twenty. From there, they just figured if you were old enough to make that decision then you were old enough to be recognized, and here we are."

"I always wondered about that," Calian shrugged. "The age thing, I mean, like, what makes twenty more special than nineteen?"

"Tradition runs deep in our village," Joshian smiled. The two approached the town center. "Oh, hey, Dayved and Seth are here already."

Dayved and Seth sat near the stone pillar in the middle of town square, opposite the entrance of the *Flaming Gut* tavern, and their spears were propped up. Calian could see the light reflecting off their metal heads, which appeared freshly polished and sharpened. When Calian got closer, he saw that the etched budding tree on Seth's spear and the etched bear on Dayved's had been cleaned out, as well, defining their design. The two stood up when Calian and Joshian entered the square and waited as the two approached the pillar.

"Glad you could both make it," Joshian said, clasping hands with his friends.

"Glad that I could," Dayved said. "Who else are we waiting on?"

"I spoke to Andrius and Petorius," Seth added. "They both wanted to come, but they had to wait until the forge didn't need them anymore for the night. Also, Jemas and Jhonas wanted in."

"Yeah, they talked to me too, earlier," Joshian confirmed, laughing. "Man, I love those Stormwinds, and if they want in on this then this should be a pretty interesting night."

"Do you hear that, brother," a voice asked from the darkness. "Looks like our years at sea have given us a nice reputation. Or maybe our years at land too… still, I've never seen a storm we couldn't sail through."

"Right you are, Jhonas, right you are," the other said as the pair walked up. "But this one has got a nice reputation building already. Look at that spear."

"I'll be," Seth said, peering close as Joshian greeted the two warmly. Jemas and Jhonas Boanerges, despite having two years between them, were together more often than they were apart. When you spoke of one, the other would often be included, especially where trouble came in, thus earning their titles of 'Stormwinds' or 'Stormwind Brothers.' As they grew, and their trouble became less, their intensity remained, so now their group used those names fondly.

Both were fairly tall, with rich chestnut-red hair, bright blue-green eyes, and chiseled jaws. Jemas, the elder and equal to Joshian in age and height, styled his hair neatly parted on the side, but kept a bit of scruff for his beard. Jhonas, however, wore his hair short and messy, but was clean shaven. On Jemas' larger spear was etched an eagle with spread wings, and on Jhonas', there was a hawk in flight.

"There's still debate about those storms," Joshian joked, throwing some mock jabs at Jemas. "Between the two of you, we all know you cause them."

"That's right," Jemas agreed, throwing a few good-natured jabs back. "Why, without us, the seas would be calm and trips boring and nothing would happen…"

"Oh good, you're still here," a new voice announced from the direction of the forge, at the same time another said, "I hope you weren't waiting on us."

"Yes, we're still here," Joshian called out, turning away to greet the two newcomers who towered over him by a good half a foot. "And yes, we were waiting on you, but you're worth waiting for."

The two, Petorius and Andrius, were also brothers, and were the sons of the blacksmith Torkral Rockthorne. At six and a half feet tall each, they towered everyone their age, as well as most of the men in the village. Due to their time in the forge, their thick arms and heavy chests were ripped and solid, with every inch of them covered in muscle. Dark brown, curly hair nestled on their heads, and while Petorius, the elder, sported a short beard, Andrius had grown his out. Their eyes were unique like their father's, gray blue but with a touch of gold. Their spears were like them, large and weighty, and Petorius' spear bore a hammerhead shark while Andrius' had a saw shark.

"Well, thank you for waiting," Petorius said, engulfing Joshian's hand in greeting. "Pa's been working on this spear for a while, now, and I knew I didn't want to miss this ceremony."

"An honor guard of seven, too," Andrius said, taking a quick survey of the gathered group. "I'm impressed."

"Calian's going to be a legend," Jemas laughed. "I mean, he'd have to be with friends like us! Besides, I sailed on some of his first runs, and Joshian, he's got the same heart as you. I wouldn't be surprised if he surpasses us all. But enough talk. Let's get to the party!"

"Before we do, there's one thing that still confuses me," Calian said, causing the group to pause. "I get that the spears are a part of history, but why do we even have them at all?"

"I thought you would have told him already?" Jemas chided Joshian. "Slacker."

"Sorry, there was a lot to cover," Joshian answered. "I told him the history of the age and Adonari going to war, but then got distracted by everyone."

"I'll take this one," Petorius said. "Assuming you don't mind?"

"Go ahead, mate," Joshian answered. "You would know better than any of us."

"Alright, so Calian," Petorius began, rubbing his hands together. "The spears are of the sea and were the chosen weapons of the Adonari during the war. The three prongs of the spear represent the nations of Ildice, Ebaven, and Sanasis, the nations the Adonari youths went out to defend. The metal is always iron, symbolizing strength and resolution, but the wood is taken from here, as a piece of home. We choose the spear to remember the Adonar, to remember their sacrifices, despite being rejected by the mainland, like how we were rejected."

"That… still doesn't quite answer the question," Calian said, shaking his head. "I mean, it's cool history, and the spears are neat looking, but I don't quite get the necessity, I guess you could say."

"I've got this," Jemas said, becoming uncharacteristically serious. "Spears were assigned to Adonari warriors because a spear was more than just a tool of war. It was a tool of provision. You've been chosen to be a protector of the village, but you've also been chosen to provide for the village. Taking the spear means accepting that charge, and carrying that spear signifies your readiness to carry out that charge, wherever you go."

"Did you mention how each spear is individually made?" Dayved asked.

"I was going to save that to the end," Joshian replied. "Which looks like is now. Alright, Calian, so the last part is that yes, every spear is unique, and no two individuals will have the same crest at any given time, making your spear uniquely yours. Now that you've received the charge, protect it with your life, for a Firebrand without their spear is like a ship without a sail or a hunter without their bow. There have only been a few points in our history where a Firebrand was stripped of their spear, for when the spear is taken, so is their standing in the village."

"I think I understand it better," Calian said, nodding to the group's eager looks. "That also explains why you're so attached to yours, and refused to let me handle it," Calian added to Joshian. "And all this time, I thought you were just being selfish."

"In a way I was," Joshian admitted. "I mean, the spear is me."

"And with that, now I think we covered all the history," Jemas said, turning to the others.

"Can't think of anything else," Petorius agreed. "Joshian, anything you need to add?"

"No, I think that's about it," Joshian answered.

"Perfect," Jemas said, slapping his hands together. "Now we can get to the ceremony. It's going to be interesting what's in store for Calian's new future."

"I couldn't agree more," Joshian said, taking point. The others crowded around in anticipation, making seven standing in a circle around Calian. Seven, Joshian thought. Rule of seven… He shook his head and focused on his brother. "Alright, mate, so, now it's your time. We had to keep quiet about your part, but now that you're ready, here's what you should expect, and here's what you need to do…"

Chapter 6

The *Flaming Gut* tavern was one of the few buildings that had been around since the founding of the village, in one way or another. Stone floors held up wood walls supported by pillars of worn tree trunks and heavy beams, giving the place a rustic but warm feel. Low-burning candles illuminated the room with a shifting, orange glow that caught the spear heads and turned them to flame. Darker wood furniture, which looked to have been there since the day it was first built, were scattered in no noticeable pattern, with a few benched tables lining the walls, smaller tables dotting the center of the room, and an empty platform set against the back wall.

Only a few patrons sat at this hour, though, scattered around in small bunches. Some were deep in thought and subdued, while others were engaged in serious conversation, but a few looked up when the group entered.

"Leave your spears at the door," the tavern-keep said gruffly, glancing up a fraction to level dark eyes at them before going back to clean the glass in his hand. He wiped his forehead with the sleeve of the simple shirt he wore under his apron and scratched at his shaggy gray beard. "You all know the rules."

"I'll leave my spear," Calian answered, standing his spear upright and slamming the butt of it into the floor. "Once you acknowledge me a Firebrand."

"Boy! You think you're ready?" The tavern-keep answered, laughing a rich, throaty laugh, and a few of the other patrons laughed with him. "Why, I seem to remember not too long ago you getting switched for letting Mistress Myra's chickens get loose, due to, what was it... incompetence, or was it just laziness?"

"There was also the time you failed to secure Master Troyer's place around the time of that winter hurricane," another voice called from the back. "Poor man took nearly a week to get everything in order again, not including the papers and documents scattered everywhere. A lot of people were held up for days after that."

"Aye," a gravelly voice added from the corner. "What about th' time ye failed to secure my ship in the middle of skrei season, wasting more hours than I would care to fixin' a problem that never should'a happened in th' first place?"

Calian simply inclined his head. "I'll admit, I've made mistakes," he answered, steady but subdued. "I acted the boy, thought as a boy, talked as a boy, but there comes a time where I must put those ways behind me, and take responsibility for myself. That day is this day. That time is now. I stand before you as a man who has done wrong in the past, and who will no doubt make other mistakes, but everyone knows that the man who is afraid of failure will never succeed. I am not afraid." A few quiet chuckles were heard in response, and a twinge of a smile touched the corners of the tavern-keep's mouth before he subdued it. Joshian, though, allowed himself a small smile. With the approval of the elders, the rest would be simple ceremony. Calian continued.

"However, in presence of you all today, I apologize again for anything I have done to wrong you, and hope that with your forgiveness, I may move on to do everything I need to do. I offer to everyone, right here, right now, that if I have committed any other acts that have caused offense or trouble, speak now! And if I have not already paid recompense then I shall settle up now."

"You've paid your debt," one patron said, and another murmured in ascent, and then another. Calian accepted their acceptance with humility, simply bowing his head to each person who spoke. Joshian squeezed his brother's shoulder. *Your debts to us have been forgiven, my brother,* he thought. *You've grown a lot those last few years. You are not the boy you once were.*

"Alright, so you made your pledge, I'll acknowledge that," the tavern-keep chuckled. "But what's to hold you to it? What oath could you swear that will hold you to your claim?"

"The blood I've shed should be oath enough," Calian said, keeping to tradition. "The blood that will continue to be shed as I do what needs to be done will prove it, but the blood I shed now will bind my claim." Hefting his spear, he drew the bladed part across his forearm, slicing a clear line. "By my honor and my blood, I pledge myself to the wellbeing of this village. I pledge to serve faithfully under anyone with the title of captain, to respect and honor those who have come before me, and to respect and guide those who come after me."

The tavern-keep kept silent only a moment longer before nodding and pulling out a bottle of golden-colored wine, setting it on the counter. He grabbed two glasses and poured one for himself and the other for Calian, then slid one towards him. "You've earned your place, Calian Farstrid. I'm honored to have a drink with you."

"And you as well, Master Gayre," Calian said, tipping back his glass.

"Yes, I'm honored to share a drink, even if I share one with you alone," Master Gayre continued, but Joshian stepped forward and slapped a piece of silver on the counter.

"Not alone," Joshian said, taking up Calian's spear and slicing his palm until a small line appeared. "As this one has shed his blood for me, so I'll shed mine for him. I, too, would like the honor of drinking with him." Master Gayre nodded, pouring two glasses, and Joshian and Calian drank, and then the rest of the honor guard followed, repeating the oath. As if a wall had broken, rounds of laughter and cheering burst from the room, and Calian looked a little dizzy, but happy.

Once the last escort had done their part, Dayved and Seth went into the back room and pulled out some instruments. One of the men called for a "proper jig," so, taking up a pair of fiddles the two began to play while the others fell to tables and decks of cards. Joshian and Calian remained at the bar, where Master Gayre produced some cloth to bind up Calian's arm.

Two men rose from their seats and approached the two of them. The first, Captain Lanamir, had his black hair tied in the back with a leather cord and a short gray beard. His eyes were dark gray with a hint of blue, giving them a metallic edge, and his leathery, wrinkled, and tanned skin carried with him his time at sea. The other, Captain Aleon, had most of the color left in his brown hair and full-length beard, and his warm, rich brown eyes had a touch of gray that made them look earthy. His skin was a little softer looking, but not much so. Both tossed their coins on the counter.

"I remember that hurricane well," Captain Lanamir said, taking up Calian's spear and slicing his hand with it. "I also remember how after that hurricane, you worked to fix everything that got ruined, and even figured out a system to make his work more efficient and effective. I look forward to the day you sail on the main ships, but for now, I'll share a drink with you."

"And I remember the little chicken incident in full, as well," the other, Captain Aleon, laughed, taking the spear from his friend. "Four others were with you, but you took the punishment for them all. After your beating you brought everyone together, collected the pesky foul, and repaired the fence. The more interesting part, though, was how after the other four learned of your punishment, they went to Mistress Myra and requested the same. It takes a special man to earn that loyalty, and with that man I'll share a drink."

"And I wish you, Captain Lanamir, Captain Aleon," Calian said, raising a glass to the two of them, slurring his speech. The two captains laughed, donned their hats, and stepped outside, but as they passed Joshian, both men whispered words of thanks, which he returned with gratitude. Joshian rose from his chair and slapped his brother on the back.

"How ya feelin', little bro?" he asked with a knowing grin. "Ten drinks would put most people on their back, but you seem to be managing alright."

"Yesh," Calian said, rubbing his temples and closing his eyes. "But much more may be too much."

"Ten drinks," declared a balding man from the corner. "Ha, when I was your age, I could down twice that."

"I never said I was done, yet," Calian shot back, his eyes opening with the light of challenge to them. "I've got sense enough to know when to be done, but I ain't done yet."

"Ha-ha, that's the fire of the Farstrids for ya," the old man said, walking up to the counter to toss down a coin. He picked up the spear as well. "I sailed on that ship the time you messed with the rope work, and I've never seen anyone push themselves so hard after. Ye earned your respect, and if I was still sailin', I'd be proud havin' you on m' crew."

"And I on yours, Captain Pinek," Calian said in turn. Captain Pinek stepped outside.

Midnight rolled around and some of the more sober patrons helped out those who were less so. Two others had bought drinks and Calian had managed to get them down, but now looked a little disoriented. Dayved and Seth packed up their instruments and collected the coins dropped in the bowl, leaving a portion to the bar as tradition dictated. Jemas and Jhonas, to Joshian's surprise, had kept their drinking to a minimum. Petorius and Andrius, however, had been cornered early by a couple of the other men, and were finishing questions concerning some other spear designs.

Calian rose from his chair but staggered a couple of steps into Joshian who leaned him against the counter before sitting him back down in his seat. Master Gayre slid him a glass of dark, murky liquid as Joshian held him steady. "Drink this," Gayre said, chuckling. "It'll help with your head now, and in the morning."

"Mugsch oblig... obig... obli... thanksh," Calian mumbled, taking the drink.

"Nothing to be ashamed of," Gayre said with a deeper laugh. "You downed thirteen tonight, so we'll see if it's lucky for you or not. I've seen bigger men fall from less, and some who went for more when they should have stopped."

"So have I," Joshian agreed. "Shoot, come to think about it, I've heard stories of some who have had to have their honor guard restrain them. I never thought about the kind of drunk Calian would be. I'm just glad it's the loopy kind."

"Whadayamean, loopy?" Calian declared, half awake. "I'm not loopy, I'm not, I'm really really not."

"Keep drinking," the two said, laughing again.

"Oh, speaking of stories," Gayre added. "Rumor says it was you who took the Sword this morning. Any truth to that?"

"Lots of truth," Joshian said, his cheeks reddening. "There were two that had crashed and needed immediate care, and there was no other way to get here fast enough, so I took it."

"Did I hear that correctly?" a gruff voice asked from the back shadows. "Some lad barely old enough to taste the sea's wrath has taken the Sword?"

"Aye, that be the case, sir," Joshian answered back, surprised to have not noticed the man when they first entered, but knowing he had not entered since they'd been there. "And if you care to join me for a drink, I'll tell you the tale, for what it's worth."

"No one says no to a free drink," the man said, rising from the shadows. "Regardless of the tale's truth or not. Still, a story is always good if told right."

"Fair enough." Joshian said, dropping coins on the counter. "Then hear my story and decide from there."

The man walked up, steadily. His large form sported a deceiving gut, and his hair and beard, while still full, were granite gray. His dark gray eyes glowed brightly and youthful, despite him appearing at least thirty to forty years older than Joshian's own father, and his weathered face seemed carved from a log of oak.

"Captain Malrig," Gayre said, setting down a glass and filling it. "Good to see you about. Your usual?"

"Ha, nay, I'm just a retired old man, but that drink will do nicely," the old captain laughed, taking the glass. "My captain days are long past, now, my days of honor seeking far behind me." He stared wistfully into one of the candle's flames, the light reflecting like a pair of torches in his eyes, but then came to and turned his body toward Joshian. "But you, lad, you're the son of a Farstrid, Ralshian Farstrid. Good man, that one; served on my crew when he was younger. Seeing as you're the older and sober one now, I guess that makes you Joshian."

"Aye, sir," Joshian said, tapping his glass before taking a drink. "And I know you, though by reputation only, unfortunately."

"Ah, but at least you've heard of me," the old man said.

"More than heard of you," Joshian replied. "My dad used to tell me stories about your trips, how you were with your crew, and how you made decisions concerning your crew. He's used your captainship as a model for his own ship, and it's through studying your routes through the outer islands that I've made a name as a navigator. Seth, when he tells his stories, puts you up there with Adonari warriors. Why, sir, if I may be so bold, next to Lord Alexander Grichmal, you're the closest thing we have to a legend, and easily one we would call a hero."

"So, I haven't been forgotten by the younger generation," Malrig sighed, leaning back in his chair. "And Seth speaks well of me, that's nice. He always was a good grandson. How is he out on the sea with you?"

"One of the best," Joshian answered, leaning back as well. "One of the best watchmen I've sailed with, he could read weather miles off better than anyone, and I've not heard of a storm he's had to leave his post for. My dad always took his word, too, even if other crew countered it, but he always proved right."

Malrig smiled, draining his glass, and then tapped the rim and nodded towards Gayre for a refill. "He always had a good head on him. Nice to hear he's using it well. Now, then, tell me your story."

Joshian spoke, intending to cover only the main points, but the old man probed deeper, asking questions about all the events leading up to it, seeking Joshian's thoughts on the crew, asking thoughts on individual members, or just asking about his overall feelings.

"You're an interesting man," the captain said simply. "A rare one at that, so I'm going to give you a bit of an old captain's wisdom. See, from my experience, there are three types of captains. You've got your shoreliners, those who travel the same routes because they know those routes, and don't branch out. You have your planners, those who think about what they want to do and then map out how to make it work. Finally, you have your whirlwinds, your brash, hero type captains, who jump headlong into everything. If they succeed, the whirlwinds become heroes, but if they fail, they become nobodies, either because people try to forget them, or there's no crew left to remember them. You, though, you're a category of your own, and that is a rare breed, for the best captains are a combination of all three.

"Thanks for the drink, lad," Malrig said, getting up. "Remember one thing if you remember nothing else from me. The rules of captainship, no doubt explained by your father already, are superseded by one; bring the crew home. Bring them home, and no matter what else happens, you can make a situation right. A wife will forgive you for dropping her entire shipment of grain overboard if you bring her husband home. Trust me, I've done it."

"I appreciate the advice, sir," Joshian said. "But I'm no captain, not yet, not for a while."

"Boy," Malrig said, shaking his head. "The term 'Captain' has nothing to do with title or position. It's who you are! Some are and some aren't, that won't change, but… remember my words, lad." Captain Malrig left, tipping his hat towards them once he put it on. The door closed, and then Gayre looked down at the counter and laughed.

"Well, now, that's interesting."

"What's interesting?" Joshian asked, turning back to Gayre, who shrugged.

"I don't think Malrig is coming back. He didn't pay."

"But, sir," Joshian said, looking confused. "There's no reason he should. I offered."

"Yes, you did," Gayre said, scratching his head. "But he doesn't let people buy for him, save for a very few. Though people have often invited his company, most have left with him treating. Some have been allowed to pay for theirs, but tonight… Your brother looks to be a little steadier, so you had best get him home while he can still walk. He did good tonight, so no shame there, and he kept himself under control, so that's even better. I look forward to when your father comes by to hear how things went for himself, and I have no doubt your drink with Malrig will have him thinking. Take care of yourself, and have a good rest of the night, Joshian."

"You as well, sir," Joshian said, hefting his spear. "Come on, Calian, let's go. Pete, Andrius, thanks for coming. Seth, Dayved, always a pleasure. Jemas, Jhonas," he added, winking. "Thanks for not causing trouble."

"Us, trouble?" Jhonas said with a laugh. "I do think I'm a little hurt by that."

"Brother, you'd be offended if he didn't think we'd cause trouble," Jemas said, shoving him over.

"Ah, I guess you're right," Jhonas said, getting up. "You take care of yourselves, Farstrids. Have a good night."

Chapter 7

When Joshian woke up the next morning, the sky was still dark, but a sliver of sun peaked above the horizon. He glanced over at his brother, still asleep, the snores suggesting he'd still be out a few more hours yet, and he chuckled quietly. *You earned it,* he thought. He threw on his pants and shirt but held his boots in hand as he crept down the stairs.

"Good morning," his father said from the kitchen table with a mug of steaming coffee in his hand. The stoic man reclined in a loose shirt and worn wool pants that he would not leave the house in, but from the looks of it, leaving the house was not on his mind that morning. He gestured to the stove where the small flames were keeping a coffee pot warm. "I made a full pot, and this is first cup. Help yourself."

"Thanks, Dad," Joshian said, pouring a cup, and adding some milk and honey. "Hey, do you mind if we talk, and I mean, not tell Mom? It's nothing bad, I just, I'm trying to figure out some stuff."

"Always," his father said, sitting up a bit. "What's on your mind?"

"Yesterday," Joshian answered, sitting down. He cupped his hands around the mug, soaking in the heat, and stared into the tan liquid before drinking. "Everything was crazy. I mean, by almost this time yesterday I was reading about history and stories, and then a few hours later we have the two and I'm sailing through the Sword. Later that night I'm drinking with Calian and then Captain Malrig comes up and shares a drink with me. Me, of all people. I mean, I know I'm your son and all, but I'm no one too special. I don't get it, all that's been happening, and…"

"I know," his father said, smiling. He took a drink of his own, then cleared his throat. "I remember the day I took the Sword, fulfilling my claim of one. It was special, true, but overwhelming, and any captain you talk to is going to say the same. Most of us go into a trip knowing we're going to take it, but you're one of the few who took it out of necessity; for most captains, the taking is usually planned beforehand, or a trip is even made special to do it."

"I don't know what made me do it," Joshian confessed, taking a drink. "I mean, it worked, and everyone is alive and all, but I don't know if I was ready."

"I can't convince you that you were," his father said. "Only you can do that. And maybe you weren't ready. Maybe you became ready when the time came. You saw what happened, and you saw the result. A lot of other people did as well, though, and they know what it means, so just be aware. People are going to look at you differently from now on. They're going to be expecting things. They're going to believe you are ready, despite your protests. What's worse, you can't protest anymore."

"I'm protesting to you."

"Yes, but I'm your father," the old captain laughed. "And in this act, we're also equals. I remember the conversation I had with my father and uncle over this same thing. When we spoke, I was just into my thirties, and his words were along the lines of, 'about time you finally took it. I was afraid you would put it off another few years yet.'"

"Wait, you're telling me you were nervous?"

"Nervous? I was terrified!"

"Then, why did you do it?"

"One of the same reasons I asked your mother to marry me. Nothing good happens in this life by doing nothing. To do anything worthwhile, you must reach out and take it. And if we don't, someone else will beat us to it."

"Why haven't I heard this part of the story before?" Joshian asked, looking at his father in a new light.

"It wasn't necessary," his father answered. "You're in a different place now, and you can understand things differently. Now, you're ready."

"So, um, what now?" Joshian asked, sighing. "Do I start looking for my crew?"

"Ha-ha, no, not at all," his father laughed. "You just keep living. Every experience is an opportunity for something amazing to happen, so just look at things that way. Just have courage, and know you've got people behind you who have already walked the path.

"However, if you want my advice for the time being… go take a walk. You just got back from a major trip, and you just finished celebrating your brother's twentieth. Life isn't just about the exciting moments. Sometimes, you just need the quiet ones too."

"Well, I could take a walk down to the docks," Joshian agreed. "I can see if the ship is unloaded and then stop by to check on the shipwrecked people…"

"Tomorrow," his father agreed. "Tomorrow you can do that, but don't forget, I know you. I know how you think. Take some time to yourself. Will should have gotten the ship unloaded last night, and as the two are in Mistress Leanne's care, they are in the best place they can be. Walk through town, walk along the beach, go back into the forests a bit, it doesn't matter. Just take the day to make sure your head is on straight."

"I just want to take it back," Joshian sighed. "Or at the least, just take away the knowing from people."

"No, you don't," his father replied, smiling knowingly. "You just don't want the expectation. You want to exist like you're simple, like you're average, but I told you before… average isn't going to cut it, especially because I know you're more."

Joshian finished his coffee and then rose to pour more. "I don't know what I want," he confessed. "I just… I feel like I'm not me anymore. I just want to be me."

"You're who you've always been," his father said, getting up to pour himself another as well. "You're just discovering more of what that means. When I became your dad, I didn't change. I just discovered another side of myself. I'm me. I'm just more of me."

"I don't like change."

"Doesn't matter. It's going to happen. But don't let it worry you."

"Yeah, too late for that."

"Then start over," his father said, smiling. "Start from this position, and then keep going. The thing that's interesting about life is that a path will open the more you walk. You might not be able to see it immediately, you might not be able to see far, but when it comes time to take a step, you'll find your footing.

"Now, finish your coffee and get out of here. I have no problem with you clearing your head, but sitting leads to wallowing, and I'll not have that. Just remember that you're my son and I'm proud of who you are and where you're going."

"I know," Joshian said, giving a small smile in return. "But thinking a little more, I need to run, not walk. Outside, I mean, not run through life and all, just physical, yeah, physically run. You're right, the ship can wait, and knowing Will, it's probably all done anyway, and the two others are in good hands, so I won't worry. No, I won't worry at all. I'm not sure where I'll go, but the woods sound good, so I'll just do that."

"Good, then do that," his father said, smiling, though only partially paying attention. "Stop talking and start doing."

Joshian put away his cup and pulled on his boots, grabbing a light jacket before stepping outside. He started up the road, away from town, and ran. Reaching the end of the road, he continued, through the trees and up the hills, not caring where he went.

He dodged pine and spruce trees, stepped nimbly over bent roots that lay across his path, and ran until he reached a clearing at the edge of a cliff. Looking around at the small camp sight, he laughed, realizing he was not surprised he had found his way here, as more of his thinking journeys brought him here than anywhere else. He looked warmly at the rough canvas hut built into the trees, and at the downed logs bracketing a stone fire pit blackened from old use, and remembered the times he sat with his friends around the fire. He inspected the charred remains in the pit, but lamented that they were old, showing a lack of use, and so he collected a few sticks together and built himself a fire.

As he built up the flames, he let his mind drift back, reliving old times. He remembered years ago when he, Petorius, and Jemas liked to run off out here, just sitting around the fire, laughing. They were barely old enough for the ships, and knew virtually nothing of the world, but if you asked either of them, they'd assure you they knew everything. Petorius had given them each a knife he had made himself – he still kept it in a box in his room – and of course they started whittling, but being kids, and blades being sharp, none of them left without a few new scars.

He remembered, once, when Jhonas had insisted on coming, and something happened to result in the two of them getting into a fistfight, though he couldn't remember what anymore. He did remember the black eyes, split lips, and how it had taken years to reconcile.

He remembered when Andrius had first come out here, how along with his tools he had brought a ridiculous amount of string. Everyone had laughed at that. He had a plan, he had said, and it would be good, but we would just have to wait. Sure enough, Andrius started gathering branches and logs together, lashed them into a fort, and then the whole group came together to physically build the camp. Looking around now, he noted there were still a few pieces of the old string hanging in the branches, but everything had been rebuilt over the years, some multiple times.

He remembered the time when he first brought Calian out here, just the two of them, when Calian was ten and himself fifteen. Though they had gotten into a lot trouble upon returning home due to not telling their mother where they had gone, this was also one of his fondest memories. He had taught Calian how to build a fire that day, then roast some fish over the coals. They burned the fish, but it was good because that was one of the first times he had really been able to see Calian as a friend, and not just his brother.

He remembered, finally, the first time Calian had gone off with just Seth, Dayved and Sailis. They were able to take care of themselves, but it was one of the first times Calian hadn't needed him, which was both encouraging and somewhat lonely. Calian was grown up now. Calian was a man, and though Joshian was proud of him, it was hard to stop thinking of him as anything but his younger brother who needed his protection and guidance, but he knew that that was no longer his decision to make. Calian, now, would choose who would guide him…

"Hey."

Joshian spun around, startled, but when he saw Jemas appear from the trees, he relaxed.

"Jemas, hey, what are you doing here?"

"I came by to check on you," he said, looking up into the trees. "Seth wanted to get in some hunting with Jhonas, and his dad said he'd be able to take us to Haeden Island. I thought I'd see if you wanted to come. When your dad said you were clearing your head, I figured I'd look for you here. Need someone to talk to, or you want to be alone?"

"I don't know," Joshian said. "But if I talk it'll take longer than they'll like to wait, so you should probably head out."

"Yeah, I figured it'd take a while," Jemas said. "Which is why I told them to head out if I wasn't back sooner. So, what's on your mind? You know, now that I think about it, we don't really come out here anymore except to think. We should, though. Remember when Seth built that perch up there, how he used to pretend he was keeping us safe from raiders?"

"He was eleven," Joshian smiled. "And the smallest of us at the time… wait, he still is, come to think of it. He loved to climb."

"Pete and Andy could really build," Jemas continued. "They turned that canvas bit and a few logs into a pretty sturdy tent."

"Yeah, tell me again how you got that canvas?" Joshian joked, and Jemas laughed.

"Bought and paid for," Jemas smiled, shaking his head. "Eventually. After Jhonas and I… procured it. Yeah, we didn't sit well until we told pa, and then we really didn't sit well for a while after."

"How times have changed," Joshian sighed.

"And how some things stay the same," Jemas agreed. "So, is this one of those conversations we talk about understanding girls again?"

"Ha-ha, no, just life this time," Joshian said. "You've probably heard I took the Sword."

"Heard you and Captain Malrig talking about that firsthand, actually. Didn't get a chance to talk to you after, and I just have to say, that's awesome mate."

"Awesome, yeah, except in the minds of others, like my dad, his crew, and Captain Malrig, I'm a Captain in all but name."

"And that's bad?"

"I don't know, honestly" Joshian said. "I don't really know what to think."

"Do you want to be a captain, though?"

"Yeah, one day."

"Have you ever considered that 'one day' might be closer than you planned?"

"Yeah, I've considered it," Joshian said, sitting at one of the logs. "I just… I thought I'd be different. You've seen the other captains, how they act, how they stand…"

"Maybe it makes them different," Jemas said after Joshian trailed off. "Maybe they're different because they became captains. I don't know, or maybe people are born to be captain or not and you were just born to be one."

"Captain Malrig said something like that," Joshian said.

Jemas shrugged. "Still, think about it this way. At least you know what direction your life is supposed to take. You and Pete, I kind of envy in that sense, I mean, Pete's going to inherit the forge as the next blacksmith, maybe even expand it. Andrius, I wouldn't be surprised if he gets into ship building, but me, I've got no clue."

"Well, if I'm a captain, you can sail with me," Joshian smiled. "Captains get to pick their own crew, from what I know, though how they pick them, I don't know."

"Good," Jemas answered, smiling slightly. "Someone's got to look after you. You'd get into too much trouble without me."

"No, I think I get into too much trouble with you," Joshian finished. "At least you keep things exciting."

Jemas stared off, going quiet in a way that was unnatural for him. Joshian wondered if his comment had caused offense, despite the lines being often passed.

"Since we're, um, talking like this," Jemas said, interrupting Joshian's concern. "Between you and me, mate, I'm not doing too good right now."

"You're doing fine," Joshian said, casually, though taken aback.

"No, I mean, I'm not doing… good, you know, I'm stuck, mate. I don't know what I'm doing anymore, not sure where I'm going. It really hit me the other day… I don't know if I belong anywhere anymore."

"That's, um, that's not like you," Joshian said, not sure what to say.

"It was just, I was hearing people talking about all of us," Jemas answered. "And I've never disliked you, mate, so don't think it's like that, but when people talk about you, it's good. Your brother, too, but any time me or my brother come up, it's along the lines of 'look how much better they are,' or 'remember how they used to be.' I'm always known as that 'troubled kid,' and, I don't want that."

"Was that why you were more subdued last night?" Joshian asked.

Jemas nodded.

"You've got a real place here, though," Joshian answered.

Jemas shook his head. "I've got a place on my old man's boat," Jemas corrected. "Beyond that…" He paused, staring out across the water. "I sometimes think, maybe it'll be easier for everyone if I wasn't, here."

"Don't say that," Joshian said, quietly.

"Sorry," Jemas replied, lowering his gaze. "Sorry to lay that on you… I'll keep quiet…"

"No, don't," Joshian interrupted. Taking a deep breath, he added, "don't keep quiet. Thanks."

Both went silent for a while, just looking over the water. A lot of thoughts went through Joshian's head, thoughts he couldn't wrap his mind around, and he didn't like them.

"Were you serious, you and your brother, about signing on as soon as I got my ship?" Joshian said, breaking the silence.

"Yeah, I'm serious," Jemas answered.

"Why?"

"Frankly, you're one of the best people I know," Jemas answered. "You ain't perfect, so don't go thinking too much of yourself, but you've got this uncanny ability to just know where a person can be used best, and when we're around you, it just feels like you've got a place for us. And don't think me too weird or anything, but... you just feel right, like, I can't explain it. There are some I'm around that just feel wrong, or like it's wrong to be around, but... I don't know," Jemas added, standing up and pacing. "You're one I'd jump in after if you went overboard or something."

"Appreciate the sentiment," Joshian said with a smile that Jemas mirrored. "Same goes for you."

"We've had each other's backs for a while now," Jemas added. "And knowing I've got your back, let's talk about the Sword for a second, and I'm going to be blunt with you, because I think you need it. Was there another way to save those guys other than going through it?"

"Sure," Joshian said. "Well, someone else..."

"Not what I asked," Jemas interrupted. "Other than sailing through the strait, was there another way to get home in time to save them?"

"No," Joshian said.

"So, the ship is going through no matter what," Jemas said, and Joshian nodded. "Give me one reason you couldn't do it. Not *shouldn't* do it but *couldn't*."

"I… can't," Joshian said, surprised.

"Good," Jemas said, continuing. "Then, finally, even though I know your answer already, do you regret saving the two men?"

"No," Joshian sighed. "I don't regret saving their lives."

"Then don't regret the how," Jemas said. Joshian sighed.

"If only it was that simple," Joshian said. He stood up and stretched. "It's good talking with you. For what it's worth, you're probably one of the few I feel I can be real with, not someone without some other kind of… agenda, I guess, so…"

"Thanks," Jemas said, forestalling Joshian's words, but not rudely. "I get it. You too. And, about the other thing, you're welcome."

Later that afternoon, Joshian and Jemas went back to the village, neither talking, but neither needed to. Jemas headed to his home, saying he had some nets to help his pa mend, and Joshian went back to his, where upon arriving, he found Calian groggy but awake and nursing a sore head.

"Ugh," Calian groaned when Joshian asked him how he was feeling. "I am never drinking like that again."

"Part of the point," Joshian said, forcing a laugh, but keeping his voice down for Calian's sake. "How's your stomach?"

"Odd," Calian sighed. "But I don't know if I want to eat anything."

"Keep it light, but definitely eat something, maybe some eggs or a bit of broth. Have you seen dad?"

"Not today. He was gone when I woke up… around noon."

"Slacker," Joshian joked. Calian groaned again.

"I'm too sore to argue," Calian managed to smile. "Knowing him, he's at the *Flaming Gut* talking about last night. Flaming Gut. They should call it Flaming Head, or Death in a Cup."

"Just get some rest, and eat something," Joshian chuckled. "I'm stepping out for a bit more. I want to go see about the two; I just can't get them out of my head."

Calian mumbled something that sounded affirmative, so Joshian stepped out and headed towards the center of town. Late afternoon and early evening meant most people would be heading towards home or finishing work, and tonight was no exception. He passed a group of young women, recognizing a few of his sister's friends, and a couple of them waved. He hesitantly waved back, making them laugh and talk quietly amongst themselves, and quickly hurried on, his ears reddening by the second.

He passed by Dayved, who was talking and laughing with Cierra, a cheery-eyed girl with short blonde hair and hazy-green eyes but declined an invitation to stop. *Having a girl was all well and good for him*, he thought, *but there was too much to think about and worry about first before he could let girls add to his troubles.*

When he approached Mistress Leanne's door and knocked, the girl tidying up and making lists of the inventory, Lizzi, said that the old man had gone out walking in the village, and the boy was still asleep. Lizzi smiled shyly, and Joshian thanked her warmly as Leanne poked her head in.

"When you find him," she said. "Would you kindly tell him to get back here and that he shouldn't exert himself yet? Just because he has the heart of a warrior does not mean he has the body. Say nothing of that last statement, mind, for I believe he's stubborn enough to try."

Setting off with a new mission, he first went towards the shops and taverns near the square, and inquired about the man's location as entered each establishment. Most had not seen him, so he left those quickly, but a couple directed him down the road towards the docks, so after thanking them, continued his search there.

Taking a quick look before deciding on the tavern at the edge of the harbor and walking inside, the pleasant aroma of pipe smoke mixed with oil lamps and wine greeted his nose. The tables here were of lighter colored wood than in *Flaming Gut*, but with more lamps set in the walls and open windows letting in the sun, the walls of the *Pipe Dream* were brighter, which made the furnishings darker by comparison.

Near the center of the room, many of the smaller tables had been pulled together, and a large group of men sat around it, talking, and laughing loudly. One of the men was the old man from the ship, and though he appeared weary, the smile on his face was genuine. A voice called Joshian over, so he took a seat at the table with the rest of them.

"And here's the man who made it possible," his father's voice boomed. Looking around, Joshian recognized a few of the men of *Dawn's Embrace*, as well as a few other captains. "Had it not been for him, things may have ended differently."

"Us," Joshian spoke, nodding towards his father but including the other men in the smile he added. "I may have taken the Sword, but we all made it possible."

"I never properly thanked you," the old man said graciously, rising and giving an awkward bow with his fist across his heart. "Isaiah, at your service, and on behalf of myself and the boy, Timothy, thank you. If anything can be done, please let me know, for I am in your debt."

"No debt to be repaid," Joshian answered, rising in turn. "At least, none I would accept. And Joshian at yours."

"Spoken like a true Adonari captain," Isaiah said, bowing his head. "Like the stories of old were made flesh."

"Ah, if only," Joshian said, chuckling. "About the Adonari part, I mean. The captain part, not yet, but one day."

"Oh, forgive me," Isaiah smiled. "Given how your father is, and listening to the way he spoke of you, I just assumed you were as well."

"He's on his way," Joshian's father added, proudly, seeing Joshian hesitate. "Well on his way."

"I'm glad to see you on your feet, at least," Joshian said to Isaiah, who winced.

"One foot, for now," Isaiah said. "The other, hopefully soon. I'm generally a quick heal, but this one is taking a bit longer."

"One of the problems of getting old," Captain Pinek said. "We're not what we once were."

"Fortunately, and unfortunately," Isaiah replied.

"Isaiah's been speaking with us for a while, about the topic we've all been curious about, so let me fill you in as well," Joshian's father said. "Yes, he does come from Ildice, and he's sailing on behalf of the high lord. The high lord's son, Timothy, was on his way to Vandor to address the growing problem of safety concerning the Great Western Road connecting Ebaven to Ildice when they crashed where we found them."

"Lucky you crashed there, then," Joshian said, nodding.

"Why do you say that?" Isaiah asked, confused.

"I'm assuming you came down Luminary?" Joshian asked, looking around at them all. His father nodded. "If you had crashed further north, we wouldn't have had enough time to get you here, and if you had tried going by Potshard, well, there's a reason it has that name. I'm actually surprised you crashed at all... wait... you got caught in that storm, didn't you?"

"Aye, we did," Isaiah replied.

"Yeah, the winds are bad by those cliffs generally," Joshian said. "The other night must have been terrible."

"As I'm sure you can imagine," Isaiah agreed. "So, what do you do when you're not saving lost souls?"

"Joshian was our navigator," Eiran said, grinning. "One who's sailed every route of the Nine Islands and then some, too, but I wager that if you gave him a map to anywhere, he'd be able to sail it."

"Only thanks to Dad," Joshian smiled. "Sorry, Captain. Only thanks to Captain, his ship, and these guys here."

"No need for 'Captain' at this table," Joshian's father laughed.

"But we are around crew," Joshian shot back. "And it was 'Captain' around the crew. Make up your mind already." The group laughed.

"I like this village," Isaiah chuckled. "I haven't laughed like this... for a long time. It seems everyone is always laughing."

"You're welcome to stay," Joshian's father said, but Isaiah shook his head, sadly.

"I would love to," Isaiah began. "It feels like a home, but I have my duties. Speaking of, though this meal and drink were just what I needed, I must get back to Timothy. I'm glad to meet you, Joshian."

"I am as well," Joshian said, inclining his head. "But that reminds me as well... Leanne asked that I tell you not to exert yourself too much, and to get back. Apparently, there is more healing for you or something. I believe I was meant to tell you that as soon as I found you, though."

"For your sake, I'll say nothing of the timing, only that you informed me," Isaiah chuckled. "Nothing against her care, of course, but I believe I have found more healing just being with people, talking, and laughing again."

"The healing of our souls often helps the healing of our bodies," Joshian's father added.

"Yes, yes it does," Isaiah agreed, rising from the table, but then quickly steadied himself. "And sometimes, though, physical rest is really required, as it appears my body is telling me."

"Still, you look better," Joshian said. "I wager you'll be fit to travel soon."

"I wager I could travel now," Isaiah answered. After a moment of silence, he added, "if need be."

"Too late in the day to travel now, regardless," Joshian's father said, rising in turn, and as if it was the signal they were waiting on, the rest of the table rose as well and started to clear out. "Not when there's dinner to be had at least. Would you like some assistance getting back?"

"Thank you, but that won't be necessary," Isaiah chuckled. "Is what I want to say, but now, I think I will take you up on that. Besides, your drink is a bit stronger than what they brew in Ildice, and I think it may be getting to my head."

"We'll walk with you," Joshian's father said, moving for the door and Isaiah followed, with Joshian taking up the rear. Bidding farewell to the other crew, the three stepped out into the street.

"Speaking of heads," Joshian's father said, turning back. "How is yours?"

"Oh," Isaiah said, turning to Joshian. "I beg your pardon; I wasn't aware of any problem."

"No ailment of the body," Joshian answered. "Just the spirit, using your term. Sailing that narrow channel meant more than just getting home sooner and rescuing you. It is one of the tasks prospecting captains must undertake, so now…"

"Now that path is laid before you," Isaiah finished, and Joshian nodded. "And with that comes the decision to walk or run from it."

"Exactly," Joshian replied. "But in answer to both of you, my head is better. I'm still processing, but Jemas found me, we talked… and I accept it. More so, I accept that I did it, and though I know it means the village will see me differently, I'll deal with that when the time comes. For now, it's better to have a future all but determined in others' minds than not having any future at all. That's my decision for now."

"A good decision," his father said, but then shook his head and chuckled. "Still, I can't say I didn't wish you had decided to put in a formal claim. You're a solid leader among the younger ones. People look up to you. I believe you have the strength to be greater than I one day, but that's probably just father's pride talking."

"Not just father's pride," Isaiah commented. "If I may be so bold, I saw something there as well." They continued on past a few more buildings in silence, and when they reached Leanne's place, Isaiah stopped. "Here is my final destination for the evening. Thank you both, and I wish you a good night."

"You as well," they replied, and when the door closed, they made for their own home.

"Hey Dad," Joshian said after a bit. "I'm sorry for not. I'm sorry for letting you down."

"You aren't letting me down," his father said. "Son, I'm proud of you and your accomplishments, but accepting the responsibility of being a captain is huge, and if you aren't ready, having it forced on you isn't going to help in the end. Now, in some things a little push is fine, but with the lives of others under your control, I'm proud you aren't giving in to the pressure. Whatever you do, whether it be a captain or crewman, I know you're going to do it with everything you have. Still, it's a father's job to encourage. I only want the best for you, nothing more."

"I know, I know," Joshian laughed. "You've been saying that for years."

"Well believe it," his father said, throwing an arm around his shoulders. "You may be a man, but you'll always be my boy."

Chapter 8

The sun was already above the horizon when Joshian woke in the morning. The night's sleep had settled his head, so now his thoughts felt more his own. He looked over and saw Calian's blankets in an empty crumpled mess, so he turned back and stared at the ceiling, letting his mind collect itself, but keeping an ear out for anyone's approach.

He wasn't sure what he felt, he confessed to himself, with his role in everything, the village, his future, his friends. But he had to admit, there was a peace in knowing he had a role. And maybe that was his role, being what people needed, but maybe that was only part of it… he shook his head, then pulled himself up. He threw on his clothes, and went down the stairs, where his brother was at the kitchen table eating a bowl of porridge. His mother smiled at him from over by the stove and fixed him a bowl as he poured a cup of coffee for himself. She set it at the table, and he took a seat next to Calian after kissing her cheek.

"You don't look dead this morning," Joshian greeted Calian before digging into his bowl. "How are you feeling?"

"I find defying the odds entertaining," Calian said stoically through a mouthful. "As well as cheating death. I defy death. Muahaha."

"Oh good, so normal," Joshian smiled. "Any good plans today?"

"None specifically. Probably going to hang out with Seth and Sailis, maybe see if Dayved wants to do something if he's not occupied with Cierra. Haven't planned much beyond waking up and getting dressed."

"Slacker."

"And what about you?" their mother asked. "Are you going to be a slacker as well, or are you going to set a good example?"

"I'm going to check on the boy when I'm done eating," he said. "The old man is doing well, though. I had a chance to meet him yesterday, but the boy hadn't been up, so I'll see if he's up to talking, and see if he needs anything."

"Why?" Calian asked. Joshian put down his spoon and paused.

"I don't know," he said. "Maybe it's because he's still a kid. I guess I feel responsible for him."

"Well, have fun being productive, then," Calian said through another mouthful. "Way to make me look bad, even though there's nothing I could really do anyway."

"I could find you something to do," Joshian said. "Or you could come with me, if you want."

"Your father's there already," their mother said.

"Ah, then I'll wait," Calian answered. "That place is too small as it is, and too many would be too crowded. I'll try to meet him another time."

"Say hi to the guys for me, then," Joshian said, draining his cup and then putting his dishes in the sink. He grabbed a jacket and stepped outside.

Fluffy white clouds bathed in soft gray and pale-yellow light blanketed the morning sky. The wind picked at his clothes almost playfully, not cold enough to be nippy, but enough to make him think his jacket would be necessary later.

He walked up to Mistress Leanne's place and knocked on the weathered door. Heavy bootsteps thudded their way towards him, and then the door opened to reveal his father, and further in, Joshian saw Isaiah seated next to Mistress Leanne.

Mistress Leanne Thomas, a distinguished woman with silver grey hair that matched her eyes, sat in one of the rocking chairs next to a soft fire. She was one of the oldest in the village, some saying she was old enough to have founded the village, but she was known far more as a healer. Her knowledge of herbs and medicines had served many among the island community, not just Firebrand, and she had personally created a few ointments and elixirs .

"Joshian, good morning," she greeted him from her chair, her wrinkled face smiling warmly. "Thank you for bringing Isaiah back last night."

"Good morning, ma'am," Joshian replied, inclining his head. "I hope I'm not interrupting."

"Not at all," Isaiah said, rising to shake his hand. "We have merely been talking and enjoying her rather invigorating tea… actually, though it is a bit random, perhaps you would care to share an opinion to a question we were discussing."

"I'm intrigued," Joshian replied.

"Excellent," Isaiah replied. "Now then, what are your views on kingship and lordships?"

"Random indeed," Joshian said with a pause. "But that is a curious question. May I ask the context?"

"There is no lord in this land, thus it's a topic I've been curious about... when I haven't been worrying about Timothy, that is," Isaiah said. "Your father has given his view and a bit of history, a history I would love to study in depth, mind, and hope one day to get the chance, but I'm curious as to the thoughts of the younger generations, specifically yours."

"Well, kingship," Joshian said, thinking, looking around Leanne's place. "Honestly, that's tricky. There's not much need for a king or a nobleman here since we govern and take care of ourselves. I know there hasn't been a king in Ildice, let alone Learsi for a thousand years, and people have survived, so I would argue they aren't needed. I know that the stories speak of the king who fought the Dark One, and he was a great ruler. The stories also hint at the king coming back when the dark one rises again, but, as the dark one isn't here, there isn't much need for the king. Also, I hate the idea that someone should be treated differently because of who they were born to. A person is right to lead, or they aren't."

"I'm impressed," Isaiah said, turning to Joshian's father, and Joshian felt his cheeks redden. "Simple, straightforward, has a good understanding of how things run but also knows the stories. You'll forgive me if I don't hold to the same view, but I can hardly fault you an opinion if I ask it."

"Master Isaiah," Joshian said quickly. "I apologize if I offended you, and mean no disrespect to..."

"No need to apologize," Isaiah laughed. "Timothy would take offense at any appeared slight against him, to be sure, but a person is entitled to their opinion if asked."

"Thank you," Joshian said. "Now, if I may ask, curiosity and all, what's your role in all this? You said the boy, Timothy, is the son of a high lord, but who exactly are you?"

"I am a simple servant," Isaiah answered. Joshian laughed.

"You are far more than a simple servant," he said. "I can see that, but you can keep your secrets. I won't pry beyond what I should. Timothy has been weighing on me far more, anyway. How is he?"

"Not good at all," Mistress Leanne said, shaking her head. "I was hoping his fever was the only issue to worry about, but it's gotten worse. He barely wakes, he burns and sweats a fit. Isaiah spends half the night trying to cool his head. When he wakes, he won't eat, and the body won't heal with sustenance, so he can't gain strength. I'll do what I can, but I don't see any reasonable hope."

Joshian hung his head.

"May I see him?" he asked. "I know it won't make a difference…"

"He's at the top of the stairs," Leanne answered, just as a cry came from above them. Isaiah rose, but Leanne put a hand on his arm, drawing him down. "I don't expect him to be much as far as conversation goes."

Joshian went upstairs as the others talked, careful not to make much noise. When he got to Timothy's door, a pain gripped his chest as he looked at the boy's pale, sweat drenched face, and at once a strange passion overtook him. He marched down the stairs, and the conversation ceased.

"What about unreasonable hope?" Joshian asked. "Forgive me for interrupting, but you said no reasonable hope, so, what about an unreasonable one?"

"Just like your father," Mistress Leanne chuckled. She sighed, rose from her chair, and went to her bookshelf, where she pulled down a dusty leather journal. The pages were old and torn, sometimes coming out completely, and she set it down on a table and flipped through them, muttering occasionally.

"Here is one," she said, gesturing to the drawing of a plant with teardrop shaped leaves and small yellow flowers. "It's called *truvonastil*. It used to grow plentiful on this island, but over time we've cleared it to make room for other crops. It has an odd smell, not quite unpleasant when it's fresh, but with the flowers so small it looks more like a weed than anything. An interesting thing about it, though, is that it naturally thrives in baren, rocky, conditions, such as mountain ranges. When it's in bloom, it turns whole mountains golden."

"I know that flower," Joshian's father said, coming up.

"I think I do, too," Joshian echoed. "Back in… Chinak, wasn't it?"

"Yes, Chinak. I thought that peddler wasn't quite right in the head, though."

"I'm glad I'm not the only one," Joshian sighed. Isaiah cleared his throat. "My apologies. We met a man who sold bunches of it, but by a different name. He claimed that it could cure any disease, heal cuts and burns in a day, mend broken bones, and more other uses than I can remember. Don't tell me he was, in fact, right?"

"No, not at all," Mistress Leanne replied. "But in many ways, its effects come off like that. When boiled in a tea it can relieve pain in the head or body or ease sleep. The vapors can make breathing easier or help a fever to break. When placed in a compress around a cut or a burn, the juice eases pain, but as for the mending of bones, regrowing limbs, bringing people back from the dead – yes, I've heard them all – it has yet to show that power."

"That's much better than an unreasonable hope," Joshian declared.

"It is now," Isaiah said warmly.

"How soon would you like it?" Joshian's father asked. Mistress Leanne grunted.

"As soon as he arrived would have been the desired time," she said simply, though not unkindly. "He needs it now, but to be honest, I don't know what time he has left, so any trip may be in vain."

"We can leave now," Joshian's father said.

"Then go now, please," she said. "This may be his last hope."

Isaiah rose as the two men collected their things. "I already owe you everything," he said, shaking their hands. "One day, I hope to be able to tell you why."

"Always a fan of stories," Joshian replied. "Here's hoping you get to tell it."

"I'll be here," Isaiah said.

Joshian and his father stepped outside.

"I'll make the ship ready," Joshian's father said to him, once the door closed behind them. Joshian stood at attention as he listened to his father's instructions. "We sail hard and fast, but we sail as soon as there's enough of a crew. Gather as many as you can find. It doesn't matter if they're not of age yet; if they can sail the fishers then they'll do. I'll choose from what you bring. Understood?"

"Perfectly," Joshian answered. "Are we going straight through the night?"

"I don't know," his father told him. "I know some men who can do it, but it depends on the crew we end up with. I'll find Will and the rest of *Dawn's Embrace* who are available, and you use your best judgement for the rest. We leave within the hour. Go."

"Done," Joshian said simply, running off towards the center of town as his father went off towards the docks. As he ran, he thought through names for crewmen. One name came to mind immediately.

He ran to Seth's home and found him there, along with Calian and Sailis. Sailis, a year older than Seth, wore a perpetual boyish grin that made him appear younger, and the thick head of dirty-blonde hair disguised his actual height, which made for a running joke among the group. His blue-gray eyes always seemed to glow, either with joy or mischief.

"Hey, Joshian!" Sailis said when Joshian came up. "Mate, I'm so sorry for missing Calian's night. We were held up in Aubrit longer than planned, and we got in early morning yesterday."

"It's all good," Joshian assured him. "We had a full group, but you were missed."

"Thanks," Sailis said. "So, hey, what's up?"

"Medicine run," Joshian answered, smiling inwardly at the choice of words Sailis had picked up in his year of traveling. "We're heading for Chinak, and we leave in an hour if all goes as planned. Are you three interested?"

"Heck, yeah," Sailis said, his grin growing wider. "Sailing with your old man?"

"Yes, we are," Joshian said with a nod. "And if you're coming, get your things."

"I'm in," Seth said nodding.

"Same," Calian said. "Assuming Dad's fine with both of us going at once."

"He said to use my best judgement," Joshian said. "I want you to come."

"Then I'm in," Calian smiled.

"Good," Joshian stated. He looked off into the distance, scratching his chin. "Then here's the plan. Seth, when you're ready, can you talk to Pete and Andy... oh, and Dayved's place is on the way. Can you get them?"

"Without trouble," Seth answered. Seth disappeared into his house and Joshian addressed Sailis. "Sailis, go find Paul and see if Jase can come as well. Then run by Tommas and Chase's place."

"On it," Sailis said, and then took off.

"What about me?" Calian asked. "What should I do?"

"First, I need you to get home and get our things," Joshian told him. "Dad's getting the ship ready, and I still need to get over to Jemas and Jhonas' place. On your way, try to find Nicch and Owhen."

"Perfect," Calian said gleefully. "I'll see you at the ship."

That's three more people at least, Joshian thought, moving through the village to Jemas and Jhonas' place. *Seth will grab three if he can, Sailis might get four. Calian might get two, and I'm looking for two of my own. That's fifteen if everyone comes, plus whoever dad gets. By the*

time they can get back, it should be time to leave. That plan should work...
Let's go with that.

Lost in his thoughts, it took him a moment to realize he wasn't alone. Turning, he found Jemas walking beside him.

"You following me?" Joshian grinned. Jemas laughed.

"You looked to be going somewhere in a hurry," Jemas said.

"We're saving the shipwrecked kid," Joshian said, not breaking his stride. "Sailing for Chinak to pick up a few things. Are you in?"

"Do you even need to ask?" Jemas asked. "When do we leave?"

"Within an hour," Joshian said. "You going to be ready?" Jemas nodded.

"You alright, now?" Jemas asked. Joshian laughed.

"I don't have time to be otherwise," Joshian said, and Jemas smiled. "But yeah, I'm good. You alright now?"

"I'm better," Jemas said, moving off. "I'll see you down there, and I'll bring Jhonas."

Leaving Jemas to get his brother, Joshian continued to the docks, still lost in his own planning. The village passed him by in a daze, and he barely acknowledged those who greeted him. When he arrived at the dock, a crowd had already gathered around his father's ship. He stopped, taking in the scene, and realized it was far busier than he expected. As he approached the ship, he found the men frantic.

"Change of plans," his father growled when Joshian reached him. The man shouted orders at his crew before turning back to him. "*Evening Star* caught the shallows off Potshard, ran aground. Don't know the details, the bird we received didn't have anything other than that most of the crew was injured. We don't have time to wait for anyone else; enough of them are here and can sail. Get on board as soon as you can."

"Begging your pardon," Joshian said, moving with his father. "The medicine is needed too. Time is running out as is."

"I know that," his father growled softer. "And if there was another option, I would take it; *Evening Star* had almost a full crew, and Dawn's the only ship large enough to handle them all that's not pulled up for repairs. I don't have a choice in this one, not when the village's problems outweigh the needs of one."

"I know," Joshian said, nodding. "But I'm not a fan of giving up on anything. I'll stay here, I'll find a captain, and we'll get the medicine. If anything Mistress Leanne said was true, then the medicine may be necessary for *Evening Star's* men as well. I'm sorry, but I can't go with you this time."

"I see that," his father said, smiling proudly. Activity slowed around them, so much that he had to shout orders to get the crew moving again before he could turn back to Joshian. "You've got your course."

"Clear skies, then," Joshian said. "And calm seas."

"And may the wind be in your favor," his father responded, inclining his head.

Stepping off *Dawn's Embrace*, the gravity of it all struck him. He had a mission, an important one, but the means was gone, and he was on his own. *Well, not quite*, he thought to himself. *I have a crew. He chuckled. I just have no captain, or a ship. I need a plan, a new plan. I need a ship.*

"Talk to me, Joshian," Jemas' words cut through his thoughts. "What's the plan?"

"We don't have a ship, or a captain," he told him as Jhonas walked up. "*Evening Star* is in trouble so dad's going off to help them. It's only on Potshard, but it'll likely be a couple of days before they can sail again. I don't want to spend more time waiting than I have to."

"No ship?" Sailis said, running up. "That's not cool. I wanted to sail."

"We're sailing," Joshian said, looking up as Seth came running up with Dayved and the two blacksmiths. Joshian could hear the clanking of tools from the oversized bags the two carried. Paul stood with Sailis, stoic and thoughtful, with a curious expression on his face. Calian moved through the crowd and handed him his travel bag.

"Would that be wise?" Paul asked, looking around the group. Paul, a year Joshian's senior, was tall and lanky, with dark brown hair trimmed around his ears, and he wore enough of a beard to cover the narrow part of his chin. His dark eyes could often be called hard, but those willing to spend time around him knew it for thoughtfulness and depth.

"Wise, maybe, maybe not," Joshian said. "Before anything else, though, we need a ship. Jemas, how's your father's ship? I know it's a fishing boat, but you go out for sword fish and shark, so it should be able to make the journey."

"No good," Jemas said with a shake of his head.

"He's got it pulled up for repairs," Jhonas added, quickly. "The pitch is being reapplied, and with sword season done, he figured it the best time."

"Shame," Joshian said, nodding. "Most of the other boats are four- or five-man crews, and with the storms out there, it's unlikely they'll be able to make the trip."

"What about Captain Aleon?" Dayved asked.

"We're fixing the chains and some of the fittings on his," Petorius said. "It'll be a few more days at least; chains are tricky."

"Captain Lanamir's, then?" Calian asked. "He's got a trade ship."

"And when the mast is repaired, it'll be fine," Andrius said, shaking his head. "We're still waiting on a barge shipment from Sytkah."

"And we should seriously consider banding it better, too," Petorius added to Andrius. "Another ring where it broke should have prevented that."

"And at least a few more ropes holding her in place," Andrius continued, scratching his chin. "I had some thoughts about a new system for rigging…"

"Guys, on point," Joshian interrupted. "Captain Zebahd, Captain Aleon, Captain Lanamir, they're out. Who else is here? I need anybody at this point."

"Anybody?" Seth asked from the side. "Should we consider retired captains?"

"Never thought about that," Joshian said, grinning. "But, yes, retired captains will work as well. What are you thinking?"

"I was thinking of Captain Malrig," Seth said. "Grandpa can hardly go a week without saying, 'if I was still sailing, I would do,' and then he would go into some cool story or another."

"That still leaves the problem of a ship," Paul said. "He doesn't have a ship, anymore. Besides, he rarely comes down to the village anymore, let alone go out to sea."

"His old ship is *White Crest*," Seth said. "The same ship that we keep stocked for emergencies. It's smaller than *Evening Star* or *Dawn's Embrace*, so it makes sense it wasn't taken out, but it was a trading ship in its time, and it can make the larger islands without trouble. And he comes down plenty, at the least to visit me from time to time."

"He would know how to handle *White Crest* properly," Joshian affirmed. "And I won't deny I've always wished to sail with him."

"I haven't known captains to come out of retirement," Paul commented. "Will he be capable, still? Come to think of it, how long has he been retired?"

"Time is no issue for him," Seth laughed. "Joshian, he's ready. He'll jump at the chance."

"Go," Joshian acknowledged. "Alright, then," he continued as Seth ran off. "Dad's crew is gone, so we can't count on them, but there are others in the village. A crew is needed, so let's prepare one for whichever captain is able to come. Dayved, you can run. Go after Seth and when Seth is talking to Captain Malrig, ask him who else he should have for a crew. You'll pass the word back to everyone else."

"And us?" Paul asked. "What should we do?"

"Wait here," Joshian answered. "I'll look into the ship, see what all needs to be done to get it ready, and then I'll get back to you. I guess, hang out here and wait for Dayved to get back? Sorry, I wish I had more for you, but we're stuck until a few other things happen."

"You do your thing," Jemas said. "We'll wait."

Head swimming, Joshian went to look for Captain Vincent, the harbormaster who retired from necessity due to a broken, mangled leg. He found the man in the main dock house, pouring over shipping reports, but he looked up and grinned when Joshian knocked on the door frame.

"Joshian Farstrid," the old man said. "I'd have thought ye would go wit yer father. Shame about the Star. But what can I do fer ya today?"

"Captain Vincent," Joshian began. "I, we, need a ship. I was told *White Crest* is ready to sail, and I wished to see if that was the case."

"Of course, she's fit," Captain Vincent laughed. "What's th' point in havin a ship for need if we don't keep her ready? But what sort of emergency could ye be havin? Don't tell me *Dawn's* got a leak in her? Mighty fine ship, that."

"No, no trouble with dad's ship," Joshian answered. "But I'm sure you've heard about the two shipwrecked people we picked up earlier?"

"Aye, the poor souls," Captain Vincent confirmed, so Joshian continued.

"We need to sail for Chinak, for an herb that's supposed to heal them," Joshian finished. "Dad's ship was supposed to make the trip, but *Evening Star* made for a change of plans."

"Amazing how plans change," the old captain agreed. "Well, the ship's ready, but I'm no fit for sailin anymore, so I'm sorry to say I can't help ye."

"That shouldn't be necessary," Joshian assured him. "If all works out, Captain Malrig will be making this journey."

"Malrig," Captain Vincent laughed. "Most men look forward to retirement, but that man has fought it harder than a drowning man fights for the surface. It'll be good for him to get back out, maybe break his leg in the process. See," he added, seeing Joshian concerned expression. "There is nothing worse for us than leavin' the sea when we feel there's more to do. At least for me, I had my leg, so now I'm done. For others, well... this may finally quiet his mind, give him peace. Oh yes, young Farstrid, you'll have your ship, and if you manage to get him out on the water, all's the better."

"Oh, he'll be going alright," a gruff voice growled.

Joshian turned to see a large, barrel-chested man, with short hair and shaggy beard the same granite gray color as his eyes, which were as hard as stone. His skin had tanned to an oak-colored brown, leathery but still smooth.

"Ryken, my old friend," Captain Vincent said, grinning. "I thought you were done years ago, too?"

"So did I," Captain Ryken growled, though not unfriendly. "But when that old man's grandson came running up to us asking him if he'd be able to captain his old ship again, the old geezer asked for a first officer, and something in me couldn't say no. How ya doing, Farstrid?"

"I'm well, Captain Ryken," Joshian answered, inclining his head.

"Good," Captain Ryken said, acknowledging Joshian's nod. "Now, what are you doing here? This ain't your job."

"Forgive me, sir," Joshian said quickly. "Originally this was my father's mission, and when he was needed elsewhere it became my responsibility, so I figured looking into getting a ship fell on me."

"Most would look into the ship before rousing a captain," the old man chuckled. "But you Farstrids seem to have a fair amount of luck to you. Don't look so admonished, all is well. Malrig sent me to look into it anyway, so it's good to see we have a ship. Now, Seth wasn't too clear on the details, but I'll have you fill the captain and me in later. He did mention Kaidok, though."

"Chinak, specifically," Joshian confirmed, and the old captain nodded.

"Always knew my last run wasn't my last."

"I'm sorry…" Joshian apologized, but Captain Ryken raised a hand to forestall other comments.

"No captain ever knows which run will be his last, but we all know it'll happen. For some, they run it, and that's it. For others, they run it, but another doesn't come. We all hope for that 'one last run,' every captain. Maybe today is that one."

"Why'd you retire, then?" Joshian asked. Captain Ryken turned and started walking out.

"There are some things we just have to do when we have to do them."

It took Joshian only a moment to move after the captain left, but clearing the door, he still had to quicken his step to keep pace with the man. When they joined the rest of the crew at the docks, Captain Ryken walked up to Captain Malrig, who had arrived and was surveying the group.

"Farstrid's made sure the ship's set," Captain Ryken said. Captain Malrig nodded.

"My old ship," the man said, a hint of a smile cracking his face. "Well, not the crew I usually sail with, but under the circumstances, it'll have to do. At least they're of age. So why aren't you with your old man? *Evening Star* has a lot of good men on it."

"That's why my father went," Joshian countered. "And from what it sounds like, some of the medicine we get now will be necessary for that crew as well."

"I see that," Captain Malrig said, walking off. "Ryken, sort through those who are here, and finish making my crew. Make it fast."

About ten minutes later, Joshian stood on the deck, looking up at the sky. The sky made for a strange canvas, with patches of blue dispersed between patches of gray cloud, and whiter wisps reflected the evening sun's golden color. The breeze blew light, neither warm nor nippy. It simply… was.

"You're thinking along the same lines as me, I'm willing to guess," Calian said, walking up from behind him. The ship had cleared harbor and now the crew stood ready, hands lightly holding ropes, ready for any command. Most of those Joshian recruited were there on board, and a few others hearing Seth's yelling through the village had turned up as well. Joshian turned his head. "You're thinking it could rain, or it could be clear, or it could be cold, or warm, but in the end the weather has no idea what it will decide."

"The stories were always much simpler," Joshian sighed. "At least there, good weather meant nothing bad would happen, or ominous weather meant trouble on the horizon. This…"

"With this, anything could happen," Calian said, shrugging. "Good or bad." Joshian smiled, nodded, and turned back to the horizon.

Chapter 9

By the end of the first day, the clouds had cleared, and a warm wind had risen to carry the ship through the islands. They moved steadily, and Joshian found himself amazed at the skill of the aged captain, the way he knew how to coax as much speed from the sails and the inexperienced crew as could be. They had sailed hard, too, stopping only for sundown, and from what Joshian could gather had already made it halfway to Lath. The crew was in good spirits, but Joshian knew the weight of this journey would likely only be felt by him. Those thoughts filled his mind as he walked around on deck on first watch.

So consumed was he with those thoughts, he barely heard Captain Malrig join him on deck.

"Nothing to report so far, Captain," he said, once he registered the man standing there, but the old captain waved him off.

"You would have yelled if there was something," Captain Malrig said, taking a deep breath. "Nice night, it's looking to be. Nice trip. Good crew."

"I'm glad you think so," Joshian said, distracted, though the captain took it for hesitation.

"What do you mean, boy?" he asked. "Did you doubt they would succeed?"

"No, not really," Joshian began. "Well, I don't know, I mean..." Malrig's finger struck Joshian squarely in the middle of his forehead. Stars crossed his vision and things went hazy, and when his vision cleared, he picked himself up, not remembering a fall. Rage and confusion hit him when he rose, his cheeks reddening, and as he advanced towards Malrig, his hands clenched, ready for another strike. "What in the..."

"What's wrong with you, boy?" Malrig growled, though almost gently. Joshian rubbed his brow.

"What's wrong with me?" Joshian countered. "What the blazes..."

"You're going to get people killed like that," Malrig continued. "If you doubt your men, they doubt their lives."

"These men are your men," Joshian answered. "You're the captain."

"They came because of you," Malrig growled slowly. "They came to follow you."

"I never..."

"Yes, you did, and you know it," Malrig admonished. "You summoned them, you told them to gather. Now you owe them."

"I can't," Joshian sighed, turning away. Malrig grabbed him by the collar and pinned him against the mast.

"What did you say?"

"I said I can't," Joshian answered, his cheeks red and burning as rage built again. "I'm not a captain, and you know it."

"As you keep saying," Malrig said. "But the question I want answered is why."

"I don't know," Joshian answered. "I don't!"

"Yes, you do, boy," Malrig growled, his face looming above Joshian's.

"You know something I don't then," Joshian shot.

"You can lie to me, but don't you dare lie to yourself," Malrig said. "Now answer me!"

"Fine. I'm not right for it…"

"Wrong!"

"I'm not ready, yet…"

"Keep going."

"I can't…"

"Joshian!"

"I'm terrified!" Joshian yelled. "You happy? I'm terrified, alright. I'm my father's son, but I'm terrified… I've always been terrified of leading others. I've heard the stories my dad told, amazing stories about how he led men through some of the worst things imaginable, stories about having to rally a crew against near impossible odds, and stories about taking care of the shipments of everyone… but he also told me stories about how men lost their lives under his care. I can't handle that, alright!" Joshian slid down to the deck as Malrig released his collar. "I can't."

"You are your father's son," Malrig said, surprisingly soothing. His voice, still a growl, was a low rumble, not carrying much heat. "But you are your own man, too. If the world needed two of your father, then we would have it, so stop living under the assumption that you need to be. I do not accept you not being right for it, because one only needs people willing to follow for them to be right for it. I do not accept you not being ready for it, nor that you can't, because you demonstrated you were and can by taking the Sword. However, it is good you are terrified. Yes, I am glad to hear it because it means you understand what it means. You understand the weight of the position, and a person that does not will not lead well. But none of that matters, now, because all that does matter is what you will do about it."

"I don't know," Joshian said, looking up at him. "I don't know why people follow me or how I took the sword. I don't know what I am right now."

"Yes, you do," Captain Malrig said, chuckling. "Well, you might right now, but back in the tavern, I met the man who knew exactly who he was and what he did. I hope to meet that man again, and I look forward to that day with anticipation."

"What are you talking about, Captain?" Joshian asked. In answer, the man laughed harder.

"Are you a Firebrand or not?"

"Where did that come from?" Joshian asked.

"We'll speak again when you understand," Malrig said, walking off. "But think hard on what we've said tonight. Have a good rest of the watch and sleep well."

Joshian watched the captain go, feeling the flush of his cheeks fade, and sighed. From hardened and gruff to wise and compassionate, the man was all the mystery rumored, and as hard to figure out as Joshian heard. He knew people, though, Joshian admitted, which made him all the more confused.

The rest of the watch passed without incident, and Seth came up a short time later to relieve him. Joshian went down to his bunk, but sleep evaded him as his mind remained restless. *Are you a Firebrand?* Of course, he was a Firebrand. That happened, officially, when one underwent the ceremony. What was Malrig talking about, then? And why was he making him think at this crazy hour of the night anyways? It took a few more hours before his mind could slow down and settle itself enough to allow sleep, and once it did, it felt only a few moments before Ryken was moving up and down the rows of bunks, waking the crew for the morning's journey.

The first morning was cool, but comfortable, and clouds streaked the sky in bands of color from billowy white to pale or vibrant blue with darker streaks stretching behind them to the opposite horizon. Water dampened the deck, bringing out the dark color of the *Crest's* wooden planks, and the sails flapped loosely, spraying drops of water on the unfortunate targets below. Gulls screeched above Joshian's head, and Captain Malrig's orders rang through the air. They set forth at once, and by the time the sun had risen above their heads for mid-day, they had cleared the Marble Sound and were within sight of Faerban Island.

A few hours later, they pulled into Lath for the night, and with the choice of going into town, most took the opportunity. Darker clouds rolled in around them and the wind grew chillier, but though a few drops fell, the weather never went beyond a light drizzle. After a few hours, holes opened, so by second watch, the clouds parted far enough to expose star-lit sky. The night passed in peace.

For their second morning, the clouds from the previous night still lingered, so the air was fresh and clean. Malrig stood alert and ready, with a fire in his eyes and a radiance in his face. The change was interesting, Joshian noted, the difference between the man in the bar and the man on deck. The sea brought out a different side, a different kind of life, and it was easy to believe the legends he had long heard about the aged captain.

Ryken strode about the deck, slapping hands and backs, but Malrig's energy was contagious enough. Excitement had spread, and the crew was alive in a way Joshian hadn't seen before.

Joshian moved with everyone else, tying ropes of hoisted sails and boosting Seth to scamper up one of the lines. It felt good working a morning rather than studying, and he hadn't thought about how much he had missed it, but it… well, it felt different, though he couldn't place it. It didn't feel like he thought it would. He passed by Malrig, who stood calmly staring out over the water.

"How far do you want to push it today, Captain?" he asked him.

Malrig scratched his beard as he stared between the harbor of Lath and the open ocean. "We left in good time, so I plan to make Fedor by nightfall."

"Is that's all, Captain?" Joshian asked. Malrig turned to stare at Joshian. "With the wind behind us, we could make Chinak a few hours after sundown."

"That's nearly two hundred miles," Malrig said. "Over open sea, for that matter."

"We would save a couple of days, though," Joshian pressed, and Malrig nodded.

"That we would," Malrig confirmed. "But the risk and potential cost are too great, to this ship and everyone on it. We'll make Fedor tonight, and then it'll be a day to get to Lion's Port. We'll stay there the night, sail on to Chinak and finish our business, and then be back in Lion's Port that evening. I want it faster, too, but I count nine days, maybe eight, and most good ones will tell you the same."

"What will the not so good ones say?" Joshian asked. Malrig smiled.

"Two weeks at best," he said, chuckling. "Don't you worry, we'll make it."

"My Stormwinds would make shorter, too," Joshian said to himself, and then Malrig's hand closed around his shoulder, letting him know his words were accidentally spoken aloud.

"You were right, Captain," Joshian said louder, though not loud enough to be heard by any of the other crew. "Last night, about what you about the crew. They're some of the best I've sailed with, and I picked them because we sail well together. I know how they work, how they are together, and I know we would make it. I trust them all with my life. That's why I chose the crew I did. I just don't want to lose any of them."

The sun was still a few degrees above the horizon when they pulled their ship into Fedor. Though bright golden light still warmed the sky, the harbor was quiet and full of ships that had either come in or were being worked on. A few men standing around were able to catch the ropes tossed to them, tying up the ship, but Malrig signaled Seth and Sailis to check the work once the men had moved off, which resulted in more than a couple knots to be retied. After the two confirmed the work, Malrig nodded and turned to Ryken.

"I need a drink," Malrig said. "You coming old mate?"

"Aye, that I am," Ryken said. "Good with the ropes, you two. We leave at first light, otherwise, you know what to do."

The two captains left, leaving the rest of the crew standing around deck. They started dispersing, some in groups, and others going off on their own.

"Joshian, Paul, hold up," Balam Perch said, walking up with a couple of others to where Paul had joined Joshian. Balam, just shy of thirty, was tall with long blonde hair and his face was clean shaven save for a small strip above his lip. "We're grabbing a drink, you guys coming?"

"Any pub in particular?" Joshian asked, smiling. "Or do I really need to ask?"

"The *Ale Barrel*, naturally," Balam said chuckling. "Where else? Besides, ever wonder why the captain wanted to stop so long here to begin with?"

"He's not that bad," Paul said in his friendly yet monotone voice.

"Oh, I didn't say bad," Balam corrected, still laughing. "But Malrig, he knows his drink. Notice he didn't go in at Lath? Apparently, he doesn't like their brew."

"Can't say I blame him," Joshian laughed. "Their stuff is too watered down. Not enough flavor."

"Lath used to have a pretty bad drinking problem," Paul said. "Too many would get drunk and drown at night. Wasn't safe to have the stiffer stuff."

"I know," Joshian said. "I don't like thinking about it, though. Too sobering, no pun intended."

"Man, I hear ya," Balam agreed. "Sometimes forgetting the bad is for the best. I do it when I can, otherwise it leads to conversations like this when we could be having fun. Well, you do what you want, but we're going."

"Oh, I'm coming with you," Joshian said quickly. "Paul?"

"Not for long," Paul said. "And only for one, maybe two."

"One hour is hardly enough time for anything," Balam laughed.

"Drinks," Paul corrected. "I'll stay for only one or two drinks."

"Ah, come on," Balam nudged. "Live a little."

"Paul's right," Joshian interjected. "I'll be keeping it light tonight; we've got to be going early."

"Suit yourselves," Balam shrugged. "I just know I have to take advantage while I can."

"We'll be fine," Joshian laughed. "Lead on."

They carried on down the dusty street, but while still a way from the tavern, Balam interrupted the conversation.

"Hey, Joshian, I hope things are good with us, I mean, I'm pretty sure Calian mentioned the fight earlier."

"We're all good," Joshian shrugged. "Calian can stand up for himself, he doesn't need me fighting his battles."

"Ah, good," Balam said. "I mean, you're a fun sailor, and I'd hate any kind of trouble, you know."

"Shouldn't be any trouble here," Joshian laughed.

The tavern was only a short distance from the docks, enough so that their walk down the empty streets was just uncomfortable and not completely eerie, but when they stepped into the old building, they were greeted with rustic architecture, which gave a comforting feeling. Rich-grained planks lined the walls and made up the tables, and the yellow light from flickering wall lamps and chandeliers cast a warm glow. A large three-section bar in the center of the room and clusters of small tables around the outer walls made up most of the furniture, and in one corner, a couple of brewing kegs had been set up to provide open drinks of their generic ale. Finally, amid pushed-back tables, a large group surrounded a drunken boy who was swinging a spear like a mad man.

"What's going on?" Joshian yelled over the noise.

"Age day," a patron yelled back. "Got drunk, started going crazy!"

"How much did he drink?" Paul yelled, backing up as the crowd fell back."

"He didn't make it past the honor guard," another patron answered. "Four shots, four little shots, and he goes off like this."

"You seem to have enough on your hands," Joshian said. "We might try back later."

"Good plan, that," the bartender agreed. "A couple older folk tried stepping in to bring him down. Sad thing was, they took the wrong end of the spear themselves. We've got a few covering them, and we've already sent for a healer."

"Oh blazes," Joshian mumbled.

"Captain," Balam said quickly, rushing over to the downed figures of Malrig and Ryken. "Well, that'll be the end of this trip, it seems."

"It'd be no such thing ya bleedin' water rat," Malrig grumbled, sitting up. "He only got my one leg. Fortunately, I've been blessed with two."

"Technically, Captain," Paul pointed out. "You're the bleeding one, not us…"

"Oi! Pipe down!" Malrig yelled. "Or you'll be bleedin' too, when I'm done with ya!"

"Cap's fine," Joshian nodded, turning to study the swinging boy.

"Of course, I'm fine," Malrig grunted. "I just said so. Now, what are we going to do about my First?"

"How bad did he…" Balam began, but Joshian cut him off.

"Cut through the arm and the leg on the right side," Joshian said with his back still turned, watching. "And a slash down the front that'll become a beautiful scar. He won't be sailing, not any time soon, and if my memory is right, even if someone gets here quickly, Fedor doesn't have much in the way of medicine or supplies."

"Your memory isn't wrong," Malrig grunted. "But you just named the problem. What you lack is a solution…"

"He can't sail," Joshian said, almost absently. "Not for a while, and while I believe he would normally heal fine, he's also not home, so we have to make do. We need to get him out of here, to… first we need to bandage him enough to be able to travel at all. We need to know everything this place has, and to get the healer here faster if possible."

"Balam," Malrig ordered. "Get back to the ship and tell the crew what happened. Send some of them here and others to search the village."

"Yes, sir," Balam answered, darting out the door.

"The swinging spear presents the biggest problem," Joshian continued to himself. "Paul, I need you to run, and I mean really run, back to the ship and get Calian, Seth and Dayved. Tell them to bring some of the smaller coils of rope. Also, I need Sailis. Fly."

"I know what you're thinking," Paul said, grinning broadly before taking off.

"You got a plan, boy?" Malrig grunted. Joshian nodded.

"Oh, I've got a plan," Joshian confirmed. "A good plan, too."

"Those are the best kind," Malrig answered. "Better question, though; will it work?"

"Yep," Joshian nodded. "With one of a few different outcomes, though. It'll make him stop, regardless."

"Any injuries?"

"To us, no. To him, maybe."

"But it'll work?"

"Aye, it'll work."

When Seth, Dayved and Calian came barging through the door moments ahead of Paul and Sailis, carrying lengths of rope along with their spears, heads turned. The bartender took one look and sighed.

"No spears," he said. "You know the rules."

"Leave em," Joshian ordered. "Paul, Dayved, take one rope, loop it on both ends."

"Oh, we're doing that plan," Calian said, grinning. "Seth…"

"Moving tables, I know," Seth said, jumping into motion and staying along the outer edge of the crowd.

"What should we do?" one of the drunk's honor guards asked, the group of them holding their spears around their wild friend. "I feel we're not doing much…"

"You're right, you're not doing much," Joshian answered, shortly. "But you're about to. On my mark."

"Yes, Captain," the boy answered, but Joshian was already focused on his men too much to notice.

"Seth, thank you," he said. "You're my eyes, now, stay alert. Calian, start moving to the left. Paul, Dayved, good, big loops. Alright… now, toss em now! Do it now!" The two ends of the rope looped around the drunkard's limbs, halting his progress, and then Calian darted to the back and pulled his rope, tangling it in the boy's legs. The boy started to fall, and at Joshian's signal, Seth vaulted forward and wrestled the spear from the boy's hands. Paul and Dayved pulled their rope tight to slow his fall, and then Joshian signaled the honor guard who leapt in to restrain their friend completely. Malrig rose to his feet, hobbling on his good leg.

"Sailis, your turn," Joshian said, and Sailis came forward with some supplies from the ship.

"Not bad," Malrig said as Sailis started tying a tourniquet around Malrig's leg, and then went over to Captain Ryken. Joshian nodded.

"Yeah, it was pretty good," Joshian sighed.

"Most people would be more involved, though," Malrig shrugged. "Most would have done it themselves."

"I know," Joshian said. "They're better though. I have no complaints."

"No, you don't, do you," Malrig chuckled to himself, but the words were lost in the noise of Balam rushing in with the two Rockthornes and Stormwinds.

"The first fight of any real interest," Jemas began, looking around at the scattered mess and the people and sighing in mock sadness. "And you didn't send for us immediately? Joshian, I thought we meant more to you than that?"

"You do," Joshian laughed. "I just wanted the place intact when we left."

"It would have been," Jemas laughed when he saw some of the concerned faces around him. "Well, most of it would have. But speaking of intact, how's Captain Ryken?"

"Depends on the news you can give me," Malrig growled.

"Well, then, terrible," Jemas sighed. "This place is pretty empty. I had to bang on a few doors just to scrounge the list together that I did, and it's not good. Apparently, the ship that was supposed to come in has been delayed about a week, and everything from hunting accidents to drunk boys on their name day have sapped things dry. They've got bandages, sure, but even we have that, and they've got nothing for any kind of infection or fever. Our supplies are better, Captain."

"A shot of the stuff that took this kid down will solve the infection," Malrig growled. "One good thing about a drink that'll get someone drunk in four shots. Just find me something to get my First somewhere he can rest."

"We've got a board outside from the ship that'll work," Jhonas said. "And we found the healer who can at least try not to make things worse, unless Sailis has other news he can give."

"Not this time," Sailis said, shaking his head. "Multiple wounds of this nature, I'd need actual medicine if I were to get him seaworthy. As he is…"

Malrig nodded. They rolled Captain Ryken onto the makeshift stretcher despite his groaning and protests and carried him to the healer's house. Though lacking supplies, the old man there showed remarkable skill and care, making do quite well with torn rags for bandaging and a few herbs that had the captain sleeping easily. The old healer spoke with Malrig and Sailis for a while, insisting on taking him as well, but the old captain declined, accepting only the man's help with rebandaging his wounds before he was on his feet.

"You may not be a captain," Malrig said to Joshian. "But you're no boy, either. I'll give you that. You're good with the crew, too, and I'm out Ryken so I'm making you my First Officer until he recovers."

"Aye Captain," Joshian said.

"What's that?" Malrig asked, his lip twitching in a half grin. "You're not going to fight me on this one, not going to protest about not knowing how to Captain or any of that? Not going to tell me you're not ready, that you're not born to it, or any more nonsense?"

"There's no time," Joshian consented. "You were right, I do know these guys better than most, and I know how well they can work together. With Captain Ryken gone, we still need to move fast. Faster, actually."

"Then as my First, I'll ask you plain," Malrig said. "Chinak is a good distance away, and though over open water, straight is the course that could save about a day, maybe two. I don't need to remind you of the troubles surrounding the Jodan Strait because I'm guessing you've already considered them. What are your thoughts?"

"It'll be interesting," Joshian said. "Currents, winds, not to mention storms in this time of year, but we'll find similar between Barns and Lion's Port anyway. Unfortunately, what it really comes down to is we've got two that really need us now, and Captain Ryken's condition seems the worst for the immediate present."

"My thoughts as well," Malrig grumbled. "How soon can we sail, then?"

"They can all sail now," Joshian said. "With the lighter day we had earlier and clear skies and a wind begging to be used now, we can sail through the night."

"If you can ready them, get them sailing and keep them going…" Malrig said, trailing off. "Not many captains can do that."

"Not many will," Joshian agreed, and then laughed. "I've always wondered about my limit. I'm willing to see if you are."

"Then get them moving," Malrig said. Joshian smiled.

"Seth," he said, turning, gesturing him over. "We're doing a herring run."

"Herring run?" Seth asked, confused. "But… oh, okay."

"All of you, head back," Joshian said. "Seth, go straight to the ship, tell everyone there what's happened, and take a count of crew. Paul, get to *Ale Barrel* and see if anyone stuck around. Jemas, Jhonas, Dayved, Calian, do a quick run through the village to see if anyone went elsewhere. Report to Seth and we'll see if we have everyone once we get there. Sailis, wait here with us. Good?"

"Done," they all said, taking off in different directions. Joshian and Malrig stayed back with Sailis to speak with Ryken and the healer a little longer, getting a list of items he would need. When they came back to the ship, every man was moving.

"Everyone's here, Captain," Seth called as the three neared. "Calian was the last one in before you, and you are the last ones, save for Captain Ryken, of course."

"Has everyone been told how we're going?" Malrig asked. Seth nodded.

"We're all ready, Captain," Balam said, coming up. "Whatever you have planned."

"Not my plan this time," Malrig chuckled.

"Who then?" Balam asked.

"Joshian, of course," Seth said, running for the mast. "You're going to need some eyes up top," he added to Joshian, who nodded.

"Are you sure, Captain?" Balam asked.

"We're sure," Jemas said. Malrig roared with laughter.

"I'm sure," Malrig said.

"Let's hope luck's on our side then," Balam sighed.

"We've got two Farstrids," Dayved called. "That's better than luck! Let's do it Captain."

"I've always made my own luck anyway," Malrig said. "Joshian."

The sky was clear, Joshian noted, the setting sun's horizon glowing pink that faded through the spectrum to a deep violet at the other end of the sky. Pale red clouds in washed color spread behind them, soft like the wind at their back. *They all listened,* Joshian thought. *And they accepted without question. They took to the plan because it was mine, and those others called me captain.* He stood silently for a while, staring at the sky, until a rough hand brought him out of his thoughts.

"Joshian," Malrig growled. "Get a hold of yourself."

"I'm here, Captain," Joshian answered. "In fact, I'm more here than I've been before. Let's have some fun."

"I like that sound," Malrig said grinning. "Call it out."

"All hands, listen up!" Joshian yelled out. "Captain Ryken has fallen into trouble. We're going to do what we can to get him out. Chinak is normally two days away, but we're going to make it in one. We sail hard, but we sail smart. You all know your ability, and so do I. If we sail as one, then we will succeed. Yes, it is a dangerous path, but life hangs in the balance so I will risk it. This is our time for action, our time to write our story. Seth, stay as my eyes up top. Dayved, on the anchor. Sailis, on the sails…"

Loud shouts of excitement and the chaos of a crew in a hurry to depart filled the deck. Joshian continued directing the men and sorting through departure tasks, so within minutes they had left the harbor and were sailing across the open waters. The sky grew darker, going from the faded rainbow to an inky blue-blackness until the stars pierced the black and the moon let forth its light to let them see for a mile without trouble. The sea rolled and white capped the choppy waves, but their tailwind grew.

An hour in, Seth called out.

"Captain, clouds rising fast from the south and the east. They'll be on us within the hour!"

"Keep me updated," Malrig called back. "How big?"

"Uncertain at this point," Seth called back. "Depends on where those clouds meet up."

"What's your gut say?" Joshian called up. Seth hesitated.

"My gut says bad," Seth answered.

"Storm was bound to happen at some point," Joshian sighed.

"Can't have a good story at sea without one," Malrig chuckled. "Maybe this is my last one… All hands get ready! We're about to have one amazing storm!"

Chapter 10

Captain Malrig's words echoed across the deck.

"Where's it going to hit us?" Malrig yelled up to Seth. "Behind us? In front of us?"

"Right on top of us!" Seth yelled back. "Sorry Captain, but it ain't going to be pretty."

"Are you sure?" Balam called back. "Are you sure you're not just…"

"Give me one reason to exaggerate this!" Seth yelled back. "Captain…"

"It is what it is," Malrig yelled back. "Keep those eyes alert, and we'll do what we can from down here."

They sailed on, but the clouds continued to rise behind them. Mist rose in their tailwind, and soon the sails were dripping, and their clothes were soaked and cold, but they pushed on, yelling louder as the wind picked up.

Rumbles rose behind them, but the flash of lightning made their heads turn.

"Glad to see your prediction was wrong," Balam called up to Seth, whose face was white.

"Captain!" Seth yelled down in response. "We need more speed, lots more speed. The wind's picked up! This will be one of the biggest storms I've ever heard of, and the worst I've seen firsthand. The clouds are increasing, and I can't see how far back they stretch, but it'll be about a quarter of an hour before they overtake us. Please tell me there's more to be pulled from this ship."

"We're giving you all she's got, Captain!" Dayved called out as a wave splashed over the deck. "There's no more speed to be had, not without more sail."

"Flamin' storm," Malrig growled. "I've never lost a ship before, and I don't intend to now! Not this ship. Unless this is my last trip…"

The clouds rolled in heavier, and thunder roared around them. Lightning crashed down. The storm surrounded the ship.

"Seth, get down!" Malrig ordered. "You'll lose more than can be gained up there."

"Aye, sir," Seth called back, swinging down. He worked his way down the ropes but stumbled as a bolt struck the top of the mast. Wood splintered and rope snapped, showering Seth as he dropped the remaining twenty feet to the deck. He landed hard, and a burning timber fell after him, but before it could hit, Dayved pulled him out of the way.

"Seth, you alright?" Paul yelled, hauling on a rope to try to keep the broken mast mostly in place as Seth and Dayved rose to their feet on shaky legs. A flash of lightning illuminated the deck for a moment, revealing the chaotic mess before plunging it into darkness again.

"I'm fine," Seth yelled back. "Better than that mast, for sure. I'm surprised most of it still stands. And Dayved, thanks."

"Any time, my friend," Dayved said as Sailis ran past them to throw a bucket of water on the burning brand.

"Get those sails trimmed!" Malrig called. "And tighten those lines; we'll have to weather this one out."

"You want us to drop anchor?" Dayved called. "Or are we going to drift?"

"Drop the sea anchor, slow us down," Malrig ordered. "We have to let this one pass us."

"Anchor dropped, Captain," Dayved answered. "And the sails are tied tight."

"You've done good, all of you," Malrig yelled over the thunder. "We've got an hour, still, until daylight, so keep those ropes tight and don't a one of you fall off this ship!"

"We ain't going anywhere, Captain," Joshian laughed, but his mirth was muted by the roar of the thunder around them and other pieces of mast falling to the deck.

One of the ropes snapped, bringing a few timbers down, and Joshian heard Malrig cry out.

"Curse this bloody ship," Malrig roared, throwing aside the tress that had fallen on top of him. Blood poured from the reopened wound in his leg, and when he rose to his feet the leg buckled and he dropped to the deck. Panting, he waved Joshian over.

"This leg won't hold me," he said. "And I won't be awake much longer. Last order I give, now. Forget this trip. Just get her to port if you can, but no matter what just keep these people alive. You picked a good crew. I like them, too. Ryken will last for a while yet, but that won't matter if you don't make it safe. Got it?"

"Captain, we've got too much at stake," Joshian yelled. "Don't you dare give up yet! We're not done!" Malrig stirred but gave no answer as his breathing slowed and he passed out. Joshian's fists clenched, and he rose to find the crew looking expectantly at him.

"So, what now?" Calian asked. "We've got no captain, we're stuck in the middle of a blasted storm, not sure how far we are from…"

"We're about fifty miles from Fedor," Seth interrupted, then shrugged when some looked at him. "I'm good with distances."

"Except that puts us fifty miles from Chinak as well," Joshian said, closing his eyes.

"We can make it," Jemas said, grinning, his voice grim yet excited. "Jhonas and I have handled far worse in the past, and I don't mean to let this one hold me back. We can make it, and you know it."

"I know the stories that were told," Joshian answered. "But the ones you're talking about, those crazy maelstroms, were with your father, one of the best deep-sea fishers I've ever known. We don't have anyone of his skill and daring, let alone even a captain."

"Yeah, but we've got you," Seth pointed out. "And you've got us."

"That's right," Petorius added. "I heard the captain. He told *you* those last details, told *you* to get her to port. Captain trusted his ship to *you*."

"Think about this a moment," Joshian said, holding up his hands. "You all know the laws. The authority granted me as a temporary captain allows me to get her back to port, nothing more, but what you're suggesting is a new captain entirely. Are you two sure you want to?"

"Three," Andrius spoke up. "I'm with my brother on this one, so I make three."

"And I'm with my brother on this," Calian said, smiling. "I'll make the fourth."

"Wait a moment," Balam said, walking forward. "Joshian, you're a good sailor, I will give you that, but I have the years you don't, and I've been waiting for this moment for a long time. If anyone should be captain, it's me."

"We're behind him, also," Balam's companions added. "Nothing personal, you understand, but it's his time."

"That may be so," Joshian said. He closed his eyes, taking a deep breath. When he opened them, he looked at everyone intently. "But maybe that old man was right. I look out at you all, and I see a plan. It's risky, but if everyone does as I know they can, then it will work. I've been running for pretty much my whole life, and up until now it's been fine, but now I'm done. No more running." He brought his hands together, cracking his knuckles. "I make my claim as captain."

"You had my support from the beginning," Jemas said. "I want it on record that I was first, before anyone else."

"And I was second," Jhonas added. "I was there at the time, I remember."

"I claim the spot of the seventh," Dayved said after. "I saw you take the sword; I knew then that you would be in this position eventually, and I hoped I would be able to see it. I'm behind you as captain."

Though the wind ripped around them and the ship still tossed in the waves, everyone paused, and the deck was silent.

Balam's mouth was working but no sound came out, and everyone who made their claim for Joshian stood straighter while those who didn't seemed to slump. When the moment seemed to weigh upon everyone the most, Balam spoke up.

"Hold a moment," Balam said, but one of his companions held up a hand.

"You really took the Sword?" Efrain, one of Balam's companions, asked. He was young, only a few days older than Calian, and had black hair and bright silver green eyes, and he was shorter than Seth by a few inches. Joshian nodded in response, and Efrain smiled. "Alright, then."

"The rule of seven is fulfilled," Joshian acknowledged. "No one that has heard can deny it, but if we're going to do this, then we go together. We go as one unit, one voice, one crew, do I make myself clear?"

"And if we aren't?" Balam asked, crossing his arms. "What then?"

Joshian stared at him, holding a gaze that made the older man flinch back and turn away. "If you aren't," Joshian began. "Then you get below deck, and you stay there until we get to port. Better you let us carry you as dead weight than weigh us down. As for the rest of you, don't you dare be afraid, because today you become legends! Today, we will ride this storm, and we will defeat it.

"Jhonas, I remember those stories well. Get on those sails, do what you feel. The control is yours."

"Aye, Captain," Jhonas said, moving to unfurl the sails. "But Jemas…"

"Dayved, I think you know what I'm going to say," Joshian said, turning to Dayved wearing a grin that he returned.

"You want me on the anchor," Dayved laughed.

"Yes, I want you on anchor," Joshian agreed. "We're going to ride this one out, alright, ride it out for all it's worth, but I need you to keep control just in case. We can't go backwards, and sideways won't do us much good. We can't go up, and we sure aren't going down, so that leaves forward. Get to it."

He turned to Sailis. "Sailis, I need you below deck to take care of Captain Malrig. I don't doubt your skill as a sailor in the slightest," he added, seeing the hurt expression on Sailis' face. "But right now, your skill with healing is something I need far more."

"Aye, Captain," Sailis said, gratefully. His smile returned, lighting up his face. "And Captain, for what it's worth, consider me number eight."

"I will gladly," Joshian affirmed, nodding. "Petorius, Andrius, I need you with Jhonas. Get us as much sail as possible and patch us up as best you can. It won't be perfect, I know, don't give me that look, but you'll do it good.

"Seth," he added, but then hesitated, looking at the mast. A painful feeling hit his gut. "I don't want to ask…"

"Which is why you don't have to," Seth said, looking up. He grabbed a line Andrius tossed to him, tied it around his waist, and scampered up the broken pole. "I told you you'd need eyes up top."

"Calian, I need you and Paul clearing the deck for now," Joshian continued. "Every piece that can be reused, do so. Everything else, keep the paths clear."

"You'll get your sails, Captain," Calian affirmed, moving off. "It'll happen."

"Put me on the sails, Joshian," Jemas said, walking up. "Whatever is on your mind, you've got to know I'm best with my brother."

"No, I need you as first mate," Joshian said, laughing at the curious look Jemas gave him. "Remember the other day when you joined me out on the point? You gave me a lot to think about, and you were right. You've always been there for me, despite whatever we went through. Sometimes you were pushing me into things, sometimes pulling me out, but you've had my back. Will you have my back again?"

"Always," Jemas said, inclining his head. "Let's do this, then."

The wind blew harder, and the waves crashed harder upon the deck leaving everyone drenched. Balam had disappeared below, but his companions did not, and though miserable, everyone fought on with the same purpose. The water reflected the same gray as the sky, but it was foaming now and swirling, brightening as another bolt of lightning crashed through the clouds. The ship creaked and groaned. Ropes stretched and canvas flapped. Joshian stood by the wheel, feeling the shudders run through the ship. He smiled.

A half hour more passed before they broke through the cloud barrier. Black sky pinpricked with white, yellow, red, and blue dotting the expanse greeted them, and the moon shown the brightest of them all. Behind them, the storm continued to rage, but before them their path was clear. They made Chinak as the sun started its climb and pulled into port as the morning crews made their way onto the docks, who stared at the mess of a ship with gaping mouths before they could recover.

At Joshian's nod, Paul went forward with the negotiations for the medicine and Sailis took the lead with arranging care for Malrig while Petorius and Andrius headed up temporary repairs. Paul returned without trouble, and Joshian concluded the trade as his crew secured a few bushels below deck.

After a short stay and a few hours of sleep, they left port and traveled back, reaching Fedor before the sun set completely. Captain Ryken was well, though still weakened, and at the old healer's permission the crew made up a bed for the captain, though they didn't move him there until the next morning. Malrig, however, stayed mostly asleep, waking long enough to see the ship was still mostly together before having a drink and falling back asleep. Everyone slept well and woke up late the next morning. They took things easier, sailing back to Lath, and then arrived back in Firebrand two days later.

Captain Ryken recovered enough to walk around, and Captain Malrig was well enough to captain again. While Malrig accepted his rightful position, Ryken declined, leaving Joshian as first officer once more. Neither spoke to Joshian much, but when they did, there was more of a sense of equality, and even Jemas was risen a little higher. After they pulled into home, however, Malrig pulled Joshian aside.

"I gave you orders to return to port and abandon the mission, boy," he said gruffly, the high sun beating down on them. "I never took you for one to break orders, so give me one good reason why you did."

"With all due respect," Joshian said. "You weren't the captain. I was. You turned the ship over to me, and though I already had reservations about going back, the rest of the crew did as well. When eight spoke for me, I acknowledged them, along with making a claim. The right to continue the mission was mine, but more than that, lives were counting on our actions, and they needed doing. So, sir, if you want one reason why I changed plans and went forth, it's because I had to. I can't sit by when people need help."

Malrig stared at Joshian with a steely glare, and Joshian stared back evenly, equally. Malrig inclined his head, and the corner of his mouth twitched. "There you are," Malrig growled. "Glad to have you back."

"Good to be here," Joshian acknowledged. "But we're not done yet. There's still more for me to do. Hey, Jemas, I need your help."

Chapter 11

When Joshian and Jemas walked into Leanne's place, both she and Isaiah rose from their chairs. Isaiah looked stronger, but still tired. Though visibly worried, a flicker of hope flashed across his face when he saw Joshian enter. Leanne, however, was remarkably calm, rising almost as more a formality rather than an urgency.

"Captain," Isaiah greeted him. "Begging your pardon, I mean Joshian. Are you well?"

"Quite well," Joshian answered, giving an incline of his head. "I trust he's still holding on, ma'am."

"He's stronger than I give him credit for," Leanne said calmly. "The boy wants to live."

"We have the plant," Joshian said, and Jemas handed over a bundle of the herbs. "Whatever assistance you need…"

"Lizzi!" she called sharply, and the shy girl came rushing out. "Elizabeth, please heat the water to a boil, then gather some linens."

"Yes, milady," Lizzi replied, disappearing.

"The herbs need to be handled with care," Leanne said to Joshian and Jemas, pulling back her sleeves. "But it is tedious. Jemas, begin by plucking the leaves. Joshian, I'll need you to mince the stems. You will find the scent to be unpleasant, for while the flowers are sweet and the aroma nice when boiled, raw is quite…"

"Ugh," Joshian groaned, cutting into the first piece. An almost rotten, wet, odor assaulted his senses, and Jemas coughed next to him. Leanne, with a pair of cloths stuffed up her nose, smiled.

"As I was about to say," she said, holding a pair of rolled cloths. "Quite strong and quite terrible. You will want to cover your nose before you begin, and careful not to get any on you."

As predicted, the work was tedious, but they worked steadily, and were rewarded with Leanne's approving smile. Joshian wished Sailis would have been here instead, as he at least had some interest in herbs, but Sailis had Malrig and Ryken as patients already, and he didn't like to put aside a charge under his care. Well, Joshian admitted, Sailis had an interest in everything he didn't understand…

Once Jemas finished plucking the leaves, he took the pestle Leanne passed to him and began mashing the leaves with a bit of water, turning it into a stringy paste. She took Joshian's cut stems and added them to a pot of boiling water that Lizzi brought over, and then removed her nose plugs. Joshian followed suit, and this time when the scent assaulted his nose, while it was very strong, he felt strangely invigorated yet relaxed. Jemas chuckled next to him.

"This is but a taste of what this plant can do," Leanne said. "You shall not experience its full ability, not at the moment at least." She took the pestle from Jemas and set it aside carefully. "But Jemas, how are your hands?"

"A little… warm," he answered, looking at them oddly. "And a little… tingly, I guess."

"This plant is strong," Leanne said. "You're in no danger, do not worry, but it can be unpleasant for some. I figured you two are used to getting your hands battered, so it shouldn't be too noticeable for your calloused skin. Still, it is a bit stronger than I expected.

"I'll put this paste in some bandages to wrap around his head," she continued, moving around the table. "And then some will be placed directly over his chest. You noticed the warmth and the tingly feeling. That's the medicine increasing blood flow while also delivering a mild pain reliever. Lastly, we'll save the water, for when it's consumed, it helps to increase energy, and the sailors of *Evening Star* will be grateful for it. I'd offer you some to try, but after your journey, I believe natural rest will be best."

"We're fine, ma'am," Jemas began, but Joshian stopped him.

"Don't argue, mate," Joshian smiled. "Something tells me she knows us better than we do right now."

"Of course, I do," Leanne answered matter-of-factly. She wiped her hands on her apron and sat down in a chair. "I'm impressed with you two, and your crew. This boy would have perished if not for you, but now, I think he's going to be alright. I will say, though, right now, there is nothing more you can do, if that's what you're waiting for."

"Are you sure, ma'am?" Joshian asked.

"Go, Joshian and Jemas," she replied gently. "Though I believe you have something else that you need to do away from here. I'll tell Isaiah you left when he awakens; the poor man is finally getting sleep. Take care."

Joshian nodded to her before stepping out with Jemas. Though it had been around noon when they arrived back to port, the sun indicated hours had passed since stepping into her place, and the weariness touched him.

"I don't know about you," Jemas said, stretching. "But that was more exhausting than pulling in a deep-sea tuna, and I could use some sleep… or food. That tuna idea has me hungry. Where are you off to? What did Leanne say you had to do?"

"She didn't," Joshian sighed. "But I know what she meant. I'm heading off to the *Pipe Dream* if you want to join me. If I'm not mistaken, the captains should be gathered."

"It's a council meeting, though," Jemas said. "You know the rules, as do I. Are you sure about this?"

"I am," Joshian said. "And I'm going in. You said you'd have my back before…"

"You don't have to ask," Jemas said, taking a deep breath. "Though if this doesn't work…"

"I know," Joshian nodded.

The streets were nearly empty, quiet, with sounds coming from the lit windows along the sides. Joshian walked up to the door to *Pipe Dream* but didn't pause, simply opened the door, and walked in.

The tables were arranged such that every man assembled was gathered around the makeshift island with no outliers, and the lights were lit along the walls with more in the center illuminating the table. On the counter to Joshian's side were the swords of the captains, as was tradition. The captains at the table stopped their conversation, and their faces all looked towards Joshian.

"You all know me," Joshian began. "Nevertheless, my name is Joshian Farstrid, and I stand before you to make my claim as Captain. Weeks ago, I sailed the Sword, and twelve hours ago I returned from a trip to Chinak for the medicine that would heal the boy under Mistress Leanne's care. I just left from there now, and she says he will now live. While my mission was completed, I see now my task is not.

"I set out with Captain Malrig and Captain Ryken," he continued. "And when it became necessary, through the support of the crew, I did my part to ensure the mission was complete. Tradition at that time made me a captain, though I passed the responsibility back when it was time, but I am who I am. I am one of you.

"I hold the claim of one fulfilled, and the support of the seven affirmed. My first officer, Jemas, is a witness to that. I stand before you now, asking for three to affirm me, for I make my claim as Captain. Who will stand with me? Who will stand for me?"

Captain Malrig rose to his feet.

"I stand, Farstrid," he declared without hesitation. "I knew looking at you that you had a destiny, and when I saw your work, my feelings were confirmed. Though retired I may be, I'm proud to stand for another Captain."

Captain Ryken also rose to his feet, despite the bandage around his leg, which he had declined to see Leanne about but that Sailis had tended well.

"I stand," he declared. "You called before, and it felt right to answer, but when you call now, it feels my responsibility to do so. I owe you my life, at least in part, and I'm honored to be a part of your next steps."

"I'm not allowed to stand for you," Joshian's father said from his place. "But I am no less proud."

"Aye, but I can," Captain Zebahd said, rising to his feet. "And I will. My boys speak highly of you, always have, as have any who have served with you. I've seen many Captains with the right skill, as they've pointed out, but few with the loyalty you command. You're far more than just your ability, and I'm proud to stand for that. I'll stand for you."

"Thank you," Joshian said. "What do you need me to do now?"

"Now?" Mayor Pinard laughed. "Jemas, pull up two chairs for you and your Captain and have a seat. We've still got work to do."

Chapter 12

The bed was warm, though scratchy, Timothy thought, and the mattress far too hard for his liking. The birds outside, if they could be called that, were screeching a head-splitting tone. *Curse them*! At least the bed didn't rock, which meant he wasn't at sea anymore, which was a relief. *I swear*, he thought to himself. *If I have to see one more fishing village before I'm able to get some hot food, a warm bath, and a nice feather mattress under me... wait, where am...*

"Ah, good morning, young lad," an older woman's voice said, interrupting his thoughts. "Or rather, good evening, since you've slept through most of the day, as well as much of the past few weeks. Are you hungry yet?"

"Why do I feel so weak?" he demanded, struggling to sit up. "What happened, what did you do to me?"

"Excuse me, boy," the woman said in a tone far too stern for his liking. "A little gratitude would go a long way here, especially considering you would be dead without us. Do you remember crashing into the rocks?"

"Of course, I do, woman," he said curtly. "But you are mistaken, though that can be understood by your age. It has only been a day or two at most. Now, where is Isaiah? He is supposed to be always at my side, and since he's not then he must be sent for. Now, run and get him for me."

"Boy, I will not be spoken to that way," the woman said patiently, though her tone cut like ice and her eyes pierced like daggers. Were he a lesser man, he told himself, he might have been afraid, but he held her gaze.

"And you will stop calling me boy!" he snapped back. "My name is Timothy Ephaestus, son of the High Lord Kevian Ephaestus, ruler of Ildice, so you will listen to me!"

"Oh, I'll listen, child," the woman said, folding her arms under her chest. "But not because of whatever lofty title you claim. We haven't had any kind of lord for as long as we've been a village, and we bow knee to no man save for one. You are not him. Here, we look out for ourselves, we take care of ourselves, and we get by."

"Fine," Timothy said, throwing his hands up. "Then get a ship ready and get me off this bloody island and back to my home." The woman laughed.

"Child, you were lucky to be found at all," the woman chuckled. "This 'bloody island' is the reason you are alive. Besides, we haven't got a ship ready, at least not one you would consider 'worthy' or accept."

"Then go make a ship ready!" Timothy said, fuming. "Get a ship ready and get out of my sight." The woman laughed again, of all things.

"For once, I shall oblige you. As for your ship, well, you may find that harder than you can imagine. By your leave, my young lordship," she added, giving a mock curtsey before leaving. The nerve!

The sound of footsteps in the hall outside heralded an older man, whose head and beard were greyed, yet whose silver eyes were bright and clear. Isaiah looked thin, though, much scrawnier than Timothy remembered, but except for a limp seemed fine.

"I heard voices," the old man said, a smile spreading across his face. "Blessings from above, you're alive. You scared me something terrible."

"What do you mean, Isaiah?" Timothy asked, sitting up. "I'm clearly fine, as you can see, just a little tired."

"But my lord," Isaiah said, dipping his head. "For a little less than a month, you've suffered a terrible fever, and you wouldn't wake, save for minor spells. This is the first day since we've crashed that you've been truly awake."

Timothy shook his head, but then paused when he caught his reflection in a small mirror by his bed, and he shuddered. His face, which he considered ruggedly handsome save for his lack of facial hair, was thin and gaunt, and his normally well-styled hair of deep chestnut brown was messy and unkempt. *The only thing that looks right are my eyes,* he thought, *eyes that are a pure, perfect blue, only right now I wish they weren't. I don't like what I see.*

"What happened," Timothy asked, though the words felt almost pulled from him. "Tell me everything."

"Well, my lord," Isaiah began. "I must confess that my account of everything holds more holes than it does substance. Too many pieces are missing, so your best option, my lord, would be to ask one of the captains responsible for your rescue."

"One of the islanders," Timothy spat. "I believe I shall pass. I would sooner trust a Sanatian trader than I would one of those subservient miscreants. No, I've never questioned your loyalty or your word. Speak."

"My lord is too kind," Isaiah said with a bow of his head. "So, nearly a month ago, we were rescued by a Captain Farstrid of the *Dawn's Embrace*, and they brought us here, to what they call Firebrand Island, or Grichmal Isle as it's known in Ildice, and we've been in this house since. While I've been awake, I've had the pleasure of conversing with the mistress of this house, Mistress Leanne, and she's given me many of the details. When it was first determined that you might not survive your fever, Captain Farstrid took it upon himself to lead the expedition that resulted in the acquisition of the medicine needed to help you. Within a few hours of treatment, your breathing came easier, and shortly after that the fever broke."

"Any chance we can get some food in here?" Timothy grumbled. "And no fish; if I never see another fish again, I won't be disappointed. I want… beef, yes, beef, with a mushroom sauce and some fresh steamed vegetables."

"Begging your pardon, again, my lord," Isaiah said, bowing his head. "But I'm afraid they don't have beef on this island. As it is a fishing village, they have a variety of fish and marine animals, though they do keep some chickens and swine, but the cattle here are for dairy purposes."

"Then have them kill a cow and make me some food," Timothy said, as if that settled things. "Tell them it's for their visiting lord and it would do much to heal the poor first impression he received."

"My lord," Isaiah answered. "These people wouldn't do that. I heard the last part of your conversation earlier, and she told no lie. These people care nothing for titles, but they've been remarkably persistent about the caring for life. It is truly amazing, people coming together to do what they do best on their own, giving their talents as they're able to help everyone else. For example, Mistress Leanne was apprenticed to the previous healer, and the current blacksmith has taken his sons on as apprentices, though they still sail on the ships as needed. They genuinely care about one another. You should see it."

"Who's in charge, then?" Timothy asked. "Or rather, who do I need to talk to?"

"The captains are the ones who make decisions," Isaiah said. "But it's the people who raise up and elect the captains. What's unique is that captains view themselves as servants to everyone, responsible for caring for everyone under them, especially their crews. There is a mayor, but if anything, he's responsible for making sure everyone's efforts are put to the best use, such as directing when shipments go out, determining whether tides and other conditions are ideal for sailing, those sorts of things. If people want things to happen, he helps make them happen.

"Your father will be interested in learning how this village works, with the allowing of the people to govern themselves. He has had problems maintaining control in some of the outer regions, and some of his advisors have persisted with the thought that people will choose anarchy over government if not presented with leadership. Your words will help lend weight to that debate."

"Ordinary people... I won't believe it," Timothy sighed. "Now, how soon can we leave here?"

"Begging your pardon once more," Isaiah said. "But I would advise against that. I don't believe you should be leaving in your condition."

"Are you a loyal servant to my father or not?" Timothy demanded.

"I'm not telling you what to do," Isaiah said, calmly. "I'm merely concerned for your well-being. In all the years I've been with your father, I've only ever been loyal and faithful, and if you insist on leaving right now, I will do everything in my power to make it so." Timothy sighed.

"No, your loyalty has never been in question," Timothy admitted. "You've always been good to us, and you've always done whatever was asked. Very well. Find me a ship willing to sail as quickly as possible; I'll not demand it be ready now. We still have business in Vandor after all... wait, Isaiah, the papers! Where are the documents?"

"I regret to say they've been ruined," Isaiah said, hanging his head. "When we were rescued, the bag holding them was pulled from below, which had filled with water as soon as we crashed. The ink has bled, and even the seals were ruined. I have them here, and I can make out some of the words, but nothing can be said of their content."

"Then we really must leave as quickly as we may," Timothy said alarmed. "More than a month of time lost..."

"We will, my lord," Isaiah assured him. "I have not been idle here. While you've recovered, I've gotten to know the village and some of their captains, and there are many who will be willing to take us."

"But how soon?" Timothy asked.

"A week or two, they told me," Isaiah answered. "But no more than that." Timothy sighed.

"That won't do," Timothy groaned. "That's far too long. We need to leave sooner."

"Unfortunately, nothing can be done about that," Isaiah said, regretfully, and then bowed. "I will, however, see what I can do about supper for now. By your leave, my lord."

"Go ahead," Timothy said, inclining his head in turn. He watched Isaiah leave, and as the old man's footsteps drifted down the hall he lay back down on the bed. Soon sleep overtook him again, and his last thoughts were complaints about the mattress.

Isaiah hobbled down the hallway, grateful that his leg was well on the mend, but his mind was still ill at ease. Speaking with Timothy had taken more out of him than it once would have, and he realized the light and open speech of the village had done far more to his mind, relieving a stress he could see he had carried for a long time. His stomach growled at him, and he winced, thinking about Timothy's demands. He had been around entitlement for too long. Yes, this trip would ruin his facade for a while, if not completely.

"Have you finished speaking with the young prince?" Mistress Leanne asked as he came into the main seating room.

"Only a lord," he answered with a bow of his head. "And yes, for the time at least, milady." She chuckled.

"So, are you finally going to eat something then?" she asked, staring at him knowingly, but smiling. "It's good you care enough to sit by his side this past week, but you have your own self to take care of, too, and Lizzi and I are more than capable of looking after one."

"You are right, of course," Isaiah replied. "Still, in many ways, I hold Ildice to be my responsibility, much as Firebrand is yours."

"We all have our tasks," Leanne agreed. "But sometimes even we cannot do everything on our own. The hardest is knowing when to step aside once our task is done."

"My task will never be done," Isaiah chuckled. "As long as there is an heir to the Ephaestus line, it is my task to protect it."

"Perhaps," Leanne acknowledged. "But even we need rest, and we must trust there is a greater plan beyond ourselves."

Isaiah laughed.

"You speak words I have often given," Isaiah replied. "It is humbling to hear them turned back at me, for I cannot deny the wisdom behind them. But you are right. Perhaps I have taken too much of a burden."

"Or perhaps you've carried the right burden while you've needed to," Leanne commented. "And now is the time to relieve some of it. You are not as alone as you may feel."

A creaking of floorboards caused their heads to turn, and Isaiah sighed. He rose and Leanne rose with him.

"Pardon me," he said, giving a small bow. "But I must see what I can do about finding something for the boy that he will willingly eat. And please forgive him; he's been spoiled, true, but I've grown to care for his family over the years."

"Do not worry," Leanne laughed. "This is not my first stubborn patient. One of the more stubborn, perhaps, but I've had worse, and I'm forgiving."

Timothy woke and opened his eyes some hours later, distressed to see the same room and the same bed, and frustrated to feel the same gnawing hunger. He looked over the room and his eyes settled on the loaf of bread and jug of milk set on the table next to him, and his stomach growled in appreciation. He noted with a wrinkled nose the fillet of fish set on a plate with the other food, yet minutes later, as he reached to rip off a portion of the bread, he discovered that the fish had vanished, and his fingers were sticky with the residue of the salty meat.

He put it out of his mind, and nibbled more on the coarse bread that he decided did not taste terrible, and then drank down the jug of milk, tipping the jug to his mouth to drain the last few drops. He went back for more bread, but stopped himself when he became aware that he was scraping up the rest of the crumbs with his fingers and shoving them without any decency into his mouth, and then grudgingly licked his fingers clean. *This village must be getting to me*, he thought. *More than I wished it ever could.*

He waited a few minutes before concluding that a servant would not be in to collect the tray and decided that stepping outside would be better than staying in the room, anyway. *This place is too small, too stuffy, to… mundane…* He pulled on his clothes that had been folded and dried, and then stumbled down the hall. The main room of the healer's house appeared empty at first, but then he saw the old woman sitting quietly in a chair, sewing, but she looked up as he entered.

"Isaiah went to find you a ship," she said, looking back down at her work. "I trust the food is gone?"

"Yes, thank you," he said, running a hand through his tousled hair, but shaking himself at the thought that he had just exchanged pleasantries with the woman.

"You are welcome," she replied, simply, making him come up short. As he started looking around the room, not sure where to go, she added, "the weather's good right now. Summer still clings to the air, and the breeze carries away all troubles. It would do you well to see our home."

Timothy sighed and left, stepping onto the dirt street. He stood up tall, listening for the cheers and praises, and was greeted with... nothing. There was no cheering, no crowd of people calling his name or even recognizing him. It was like he was nothing special, a commoner... a nobody.

A few people passed by. Some nodded in his direction, some offered a sickeningly cheerful hello, but none would go out of their way to address him, just said hi as he entered their space. Some even had the audacity to insist he be the one to move as their cart passed, dangerously close in his opinion, and he made a note to bring that up to the village's magistrate.

He looked up and down the street but noted nothing of interest, so he decided to head in the direction of the sea. The sea meant docks, he reasoned, and docks meant ships. Ships, therefore, meant a way home, and home meant being free of this place forever. *Isaiah was adequate, even exceptional, for most things*, he admitted, but for other things Timothy knew the only one he could count on was himself.

The road, though mostly hard packed dirt, was strangely clean, and he found himself reluctantly impressed with the distinct lack of dust. If anything, everything looked well cared for, and pleasant. The buildings were constructed from wood, but nothing looked run-down, and all the construction seemed solid. The structures were simple, but now and again he recognized elements that would have belonged back home, and at other times the architecture looked Ebaven.

Small flower boxes or gardens in front of street-side windows drew most of his attention. He recognized the bold red, royal blue, and soft yellow of the evelly, julier, and korena lilies. He recognized the small five-petaled flowers of the blue garinots and the red graisonots from some of his books. He also recognized the bright purple jamipin and shannorose, but then physically stopped when he remembered he had only seen some of these flowers in the gardens of Vandor long ago. That in turn made him look closer at the people.

All of them were tanned, but some were darker skinned while others were lighter. Some had dark black or brown hair, others had lighter blonde or white. Some were tall, almost giant-like, and others were considerably shorter, though from his observation, no one seemed to care. Also, everyone had eyes of different colors. Some had traces of blue, like back home, while others had brown like he remembered from Vandor. Others had green or even darker, and most had touches of gray like Isaiah's. What struck him the most, however, was the air of nobility he could almost physically feel, and the sense of authority everyone seemed to radiate. It wasn't just present in the men, either, but the women and even the children that passed him. He moved along quickly, eager to escape the feeling.

As he approached the docks, he found a large crowd gathered before a large fleet of ships of all sizes and makes. Some ships were three masted, others had two, and still others had only one. Some were quite long while others were wide but shorter.

One stood out more than the others, however, a beautiful three-masted ship of dark stained wood, and sails that looked to have brand new canvas flapping in the wind. It was directly behind a platform on one edge of the crowd, and Timothy noted many pointing at it. *Must be for sale,* he thought with a smile. *I would sure love to own a vessel as magnificent as that one, and it will save us much time to have a ship already able to sail. Isaiah, what was so hard about finding a ship?*

When he got closer, Timothy could feel an air of excitement in the crowd. Spying a young man about his age, Timothy approached and grabbed his attention.

"What is the purpose of this gathering?" Timothy inquired. "And to whom must I speak to about acquiring that ship?"

"Hey, I know you, you're that shipwrecked kid," the young man said, smiling, and though the title of 'kid' irked him, Timothy could sense no malice coming from him. He extended his hand. "Name's Calian, and I'm afraid that request will not find an open ear. A new captain's getting raised today, and when they're raised, they get their first ship. If you want that ship, well, you have a captain to get through first."

"Captain?" Timothy asked, suspicious, looking down at the hand then looking back up. "I wasn't told of raising a navy here. Are you planning a campaign of some kind?" Calian laughed, shaking his head.

"No, not at all," Calian answered, pulling his hand back. "We haven't had war for a long time, now, so not that kind of captain. We're electing a village leader, though."

"I don't understand," Timothy said. "What good is a captain if not to lead men to war?"

"Captains are unique," Calian began. "It's difficult to explain, but I'll try my best. A captain serves two main roles here. They're the lead of their ship, but they're also a voice for the people. When decisions need to be made for the village, they're the ones who gather to make them. They organize trade and communication between villages, are responsible for knowing the currents and tides, and are responsible for knowing the migratory routes of fish and whales. When trouble arises, they're the first to respond, whether it be shipwrecks, storms destroying buildings, or even dealing with village crimes. In short, they're responsible for taking care of us."

"Ah, so captains are like your elite, your privileged," Timothy said nodding, but Calian shook his head.

"Not quite," Calian said. "See, they're just like everyone else. We respect what they do, just as they respect us and what we can do. They are, well, first among equals, you could say."

"So, what does it take to become a captain?" Timothy asked, shaking his head, and not believing what he was hearing. "I assume a trial of some kind must happen."

"Attention, everyone!" a voice called out. Calian held up a hand to silence him, focusing on the speaker who had risen to the platform, and Timothy, annoyed at having been silenced so easily and for not having his question answered, turned to watch the proceedings.

"I have here in my presence one who has put forth his claim to be raised as captain," the speaker announced again. "His reputation precedes him, and his respect has been well earned. There are none of this village who do not know his name, so without further ado, Joshian Farstrid, please come forth."

Timothy sensed movement in the crowd and strained to look, but he couldn't determine who was coming forth, as there were so many bodies. Then one man rose from the masses onto the platform, but when he turned around, Timothy saw the man was young, barely old enough to be one of his father's soldiers, let alone an officer.

"That's the one who's going to be a captain?" Timothy whispered to himself, though louder than he intended. Calian turned towards him, wearing a wide grin.

"Aye, that's the one," he said. "Also, he's my brother."

A young captain, Timothy thought. *I can use that. He'll have less experience, true, but with the fantasy of assisting a lord's son, earning the gratitude of a foreign nation... yes, I can work well with that.*

"Joshian Farstrid," the speaker announced. "You have put forth a claim, yet what right do you have to make it?"

"Three weeks ago," Joshian began, with a voice so strong and powerful Timothy found himself taken aback. "While sailing aboard the *Dawn's Embrace,* we rescued two men who had crashed off the Grygor Sea. When we determined they likely would not survive without immediate care, I petitioned my captain to sail through the Sword Strait, and I was given command. I brought the crew through safely, thus satisfying the Claim of One.

"After complications among the recovered men arose," Joshian continued. "I went out again with a different crew, this time with the purpose of acquiring the medicine necessary to save them. Some will argue about the cost of this trip, sailing so far for so little, but in my mind, saving a man's life is worth any price. However, when both captains sailing with us were injured and prevented from commanding the rest of the trip, I took command again, this time by the voice of the crew, also completing the Claim of Seven.

"Furthermore, we completed our leg of the quest faster than most captains would have normally taken," Joshian said, and Timothy sensed the speech's conclusion. "Both captains recovered well, and the medicine was brought in time. No lives were lost, and that medicine has since been used to care for others in our village, namely the crew of *Evening Star*. I made my declaration that night to the captains themselves and fulfilled the Claim of Three."

So, you're the one who saved me, Timothy thought, looking at the new captain with grudging respect. *Well, I must admit I am grateful for that, but at no point can it ever sound like I owe him anything. I know his kind. He did his duty, after all, and nothing more. Still, Father will likely reward him, and I see nothing unreasonable about that, I suppose.*

"You present a strong and honorable claim," the speaker announced again. "Taking the Sword, saving the lives of stranded sailors and Firebrand captains certainly carries worth as a claim, yet where is this crew you spoke of? Where are these men who stood for you? I see only a crowd of people, yet none willing to stand and -."

"I stand!" a voice called out, and the crowd parted around the man who spoke. "I, Seth Farrin, make my stand that Joshian is a captain, and one whom I will gladly follow."

"I, Dayved Gaulia, also stand," another voice cried. "And I stand as testament that the sword was taken as he claims."

"I, Jemas Boanerges, also stand," a passionate voice roared. "And I'll keep on standing, as long as I can."

"I stand too, Jhonas Boanerges," a grinning boy announced. "I'm with him."

"I, Petorius Rockthorne, make my stand," a larger man announced, shortly before another large man declared, "I, Andrius Rockthorne, also make my stand."

"I, Calian Farstrid," Calian called out from his position in the back. "Gladly pledge my support to raise him as a captain." The crowd fell away from him as it had for the others, and Timothy was pulled back. As he looked at Calian, however, it struck him that this man, although young, was not to be underestimated at all.

"Stop!" the speaker announced. "I hear the voices, and I say the claim of seven has been fulfilled."

"Wait, one more moment," a new speaker cried from the crowd. "I, Balam Perch, formally make my claim as captain..."

"Balam Perch, you have no claim!" a steady voice cried out, causing Timothy to turn reflexively. An excitement rose inside of him and looking around he saw several others mumbling, some chuckling, but almost all grinning. The circle that opened reveled a tall but lanky man.

"You may have age, but I dare you to back your claims with actions beyond that of a normal crewman," another said from the man's side. "Our captain has been through more than most, and he's proven his ability to handle everything that's ever been thrown at him, and then he did it better than any could have even dreamed! Oh yes, Joshian is our captain, and we stand before everyone to say not only that we stand as number eight and number nine, but that you have no claim."

"Sailis, Paul," Joshian called out in a strong yet gentle voice, holding up his hand. "I accept you as number eight and number nine gladly but hear him first. We are not done yet."

"Where is his claim of seven, then?" Sailis asked.

"Sailis Bartolomie is correct," the speaker announced. "Joshian has been acknowledged and his claim accepted. Who now will speak for Balam as well?"

"My friends are all behind me," Balam declared.

Murmurs rose from the crowd as the man named Balam looked around, but no one spoke up.

"You spoke for me on the ship!" Balam cried. "Are you cowards to speak now?"

"Joshian led us," a voice said from the masses. "You abandoned us."

"We can't stand for you," another voice called. "Not yet."

"Traitors!" Balam yelled, turning away, and storming off. "Traitors, all of you!"

"Balam's claim has been denied," the main speaker called. "But Joshian's claim is not complete. The claim of three remains, a claim some give more weight, being the affirmation of a captain by the captains…"

"Joshian is what he is," a booming voice rose up. "I, Captain Malrig, see Captain Farstrid."

"He sails his own path now, and his judgement is sound," another voice growled. "I, Captain Ryken, gladly see Captain Farstrid."

"He's a natural leader, and I accept him," an older, but still strong voice, spoke up. "I, Captain Zebahd, see Captain Farstrid."

"Three captains have spoken aloud," the main speaker announced once more. "Three captains have acknowledged one. The claim of three has been fulfilled.

"One final claim remains," the speaker continued, gravely, and Timothy felt a shift in the crowd. Before, there was excitement, but what fell now was a blanket of severity. The people grew quieter. "As all of you know, a device that serves only the purpose of being a weapon has been discouraged for as long as we can remember. Bows and spears have been used to hunt. Hammers and axes have been used to build. But the sword serves only to kill another, and the charge of carrying one only a few can bear. This charge carries the most weight, though it is a weight only understood by those who do carry it, in the hopes none will have to. Therefore, Captain Farstrid, I extend to you your own sword, that you may bear the weight of defending your own crew. You have taken the Sword, true, but do you accept it?"

"I accept the sword that you charge to me," the new captain declared clearly and without hesitation. "And I am prepared to bear the weight that goes with it."

"I speak before you all," the speaker declared with a note of finality. "I present one who was risen by the seven, accepted by the three, and who shouldered the burden of one. No claim of weight has been raised against him, and no claim has been spoken out against his ability. Therefore I, Captain Pinard, present to you all, Captain Joshian Farstrid. Captain Farstrid, this ship is now yours."

"Thank you everyone," the new captain said as the crowd cheered, and Timothy almost found himself caught up in it all. The man held up his hands to silence everyone, and when the noise had died down, he continued. "Captain Malrig once said that the term 'Captain' isn't a title, it's who you are. I denied that for a long time, believing that a captain was one who was greater than I ever could be, but then I thought more on it, and what a captain represents. A captain is one who leads, but he can't lead unless there are those willing to follow, so really, the strength of a captain is determined by the strength of the crew. My crew is great, and I am honored to lead them.

"For a crew to be great, though, they must be united. They must work together, acknowledging each other's strengths, and work to bring out the best in each other. They must trust one another, depend on each other, and when they stumble, be willing to let the others support them. That bond creates brothers, and brothers will give their lives for each other. But there are some moments where you won't have your brothers. There are some moments where one will have a separate task, one they must do on their own, and those tasks require the utmost courage. Courage and heart, therefore, make a crew great, and so I name this ship *Courageous Heart*, in the hope that it will be a reminder of the demands required of us all. I am humbled to be here, and excited, and I look forward to all we can do together. Thank you."

The gathered crowd cheered, and many went forward to congratulate the new captain. Timothy looked around for the other, Balam, surprised that he didn't try to cause trouble. He saw, though, that those who voiced support for the new captain all gathered to surround him, appearing friendly but also giving the sense of being family. In fact, the whole crowd felt like a large family, and Timothy felt completely a stranger. His attention was drawn from his own thoughts, however, when he felt a solid hand fall on his shoulder.

"Hey there, it looks like you're finally awake," the new captain said warmly, wearing a friendly smile, and Timothy found it odd his steps had carried him to the podium, rather than away. "You certainly gave everyone a good scare, but I'm glad you're doing better. We've never been properly introduced. I am

Captain Farstrid, but my friends have always called me Joshian. What do I call you?"

"You don't know who I am?" Timothy asked, astonished.

"I know you're the shipwrecked boy," Captain Farstrid laughed, and to Timothy's discomfort the others laughed in kind. Try as he might he could sense no air of superiority or insult in their laughter, only joy and friendship, and could find no reason to dislike the man. "But I figured 'shipwrecked boy' would grow old after a while. So, what's your name?"

"I am Lord Timothy Ephaestus, son of the High Lord Kevian Ephaestus, ruler of Ildice," Timothy declared proudly. Joshian smiled.

"That's a bit of a mouthful," Joshian said. "Let's just stick with Timothy and Joshian, then. Well, officially, welcome to our village. Feel free to stay as long as you like."

"I wish to leave as quickly as possible," Timothy declared. "Immediately if possible. How soon will you be able to travel?"

"Well, if my ship were ready, I could take you now, but since it's not, immediately won't be happening. Where do you wish to go?"

"Kellivar," Timothy said. "I wish to sail for Kellivar."

"That's pretty far south," Joshian nodded. "Well outside the islands. I will need a while for preparations to be finalized, at least a day. Why haven't you spoken to the other captains?"

"Other captains, according to my manservant, would not be available for another week," Timothy answered. "I want to leave by tomorrow."

"Tomorrow, eh?" Joshian said, scratching his head. "A trip like that, yeah, I'll need another day to get preparations ready. The crew will have to decide whether they want to come or not, and then I will need to find replacements if needed. Come down here about midday the day after tomorrow and we will see what we can do. Hey, how is Isaiah doing? He has been by your side for the better part of the week if I'm not mistaken. He cares about you greatly. You're lucky to have a man such as him by your side."

"He's fine," Timothy said, moving away. "I'm feeling tired, and I think I've had enough fresh air for one day."

"Sleep well, then, and heal better," Joshian said with a wave. "Until later."

Timothy worked his way back through the crowd and then walked back to the healer's place. He vaguely remembered his way and was grateful to see a sign hanging above her house so he wouldn't have to ask for the assistance of anyone. As he entered the building, he saw this time the main room was empty, and went to his room, laying down on the mattress and closing his eyes. He intended merely to think, namely over the idea of a place where titles and lordships had little meaning, but sleep overtook him quickly instead. His last thoughts before drifting off were of rolling seas, stinking fish, and hard mattresses.

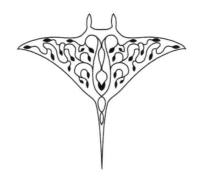

Chapter 13

Life was different, and not in Timothy's favor. The rest of the day and all the next day were a bore to him, and the new captain was taking far longer than he needed to make ready, surely to spite him. He could barely believe Isaiah's account of how the people regarded lords, how a person was simply a person until proving otherwise, but after seeing for himself the way people expected him to do many things on his own, he could believe it. *I am nothing here,* he moaned to himself. *I wish I were home. I need to be home.*

The following morning at the docks, the salty air was filled with the voices of people going about their work. Some were those of older youths doing their jobs and enjoying camaraderie. Others were of those much younger. Still others were the voices of patient but firm teachers, guiding others as they did their various tasks. But there was laughter, too, lots of laughter, as if the people genuinely enjoyed what they were doing. It was depressing. *Why should they be having fun?*

"Excuse me, sir," the youth named Dayved said, walking up between himself and Isaiah. "Mind if I take your things and bring them onboard?"

"Yes, finally," Timothy said exasperated. "Quite frankly, I've been standing here for a few minutes now and I'm appalled it's taken this long for me to be acknowledged. Furthermore, if you would address me as 'my lord,' that would be…"

"Um, I'm not sure what you're talking about," Dayved said with a chuckle. "And I'm going to stop you right there." He turned to Isaiah. "I meant for you, sir. I know your leg is still on the mend."

"Him?" Timothy asked, his eyes widening. "What about me?"

"What about you?" Dayved asked, laughing outright. Timothy's fists clenched. "You have two legs, working perfectly well last I checked, and you'll be expected to use them. We won't be pulling the weight of those who can pull it themselves, no discussion."

"You'd best watch your tone," Timothy growled as Dayved grabbed the bundle of clothes that had been found to fit Isaiah. He threw the clothes over his shoulder without so much as a second glance and turned to walk off. "I'll take you up with the captain, and he'll have you… scrubbing the deck the entire trip!"

"Yeah, I don't see that happening," Dayved said over his shoulder. Timothy watched him walk off, and it was only when Dayved stepped on deck that he could come up with a response, but by then it was too late. With a sigh, he turned to Isaiah.

"Well, I should hope you know your proper role and how to show proper respect," Timothy said. "Enough so that I don't need to tell you your job."

"Aye, my lord," Isaiah said, bowing, and Timothy turned away. He felt footsteps behind him before he was rudely shoved and the one named Calian pushed past, carrying the load Isaiah was about to carry. *These people will know their place*, Timothy thought. *I will see to it.*

Calian glided up the ramp and paused on the deck as he looked around. He found one of the boys standing around the deck, but looking eager. "Chase," he called to the boy. "Want something to do?"

"Yeah!" the boy of twelve said, excited. He bounded over. "What do you need?"

"These two bundles," Calian said, grinning, indicating the one he held and the one Dayved had set down earlier. "Take them down to the guests' cabin and make sure they're stored securely, but carefully. After that, come back up, and I should have more for ya."

"Will do," the boy said, taking the bundle and moving quickly and carefully down below deck.

"You're good with kids," Seth said when Calian walked up to where Seth was talking with Sailis and Dayved. "Then again, you technically were one a month ago, so I guess it makes sense."

"You wanna go?" Calian laughed. "I'll take you down, right now. Oh, Dayved, you best watch out, that lord kid looked like he wanted to take a piece of you himself."

"Yeah, what was he upset about?" Seth asked. "Was he upset you showed respect to the old man, or that you wouldn't bow to him, or what? I'm confused about that kid."

"Honestly, I'm not sure," Dayved said, shrugging, pausing to hand Chase the other bag. "I'm confused too, but I've got a bad feeling this trip won't be clear sailing."

"I feel it, too," Sailis said, his normal grin absent. "Cap's going to clash with him, that's for sure, but as for the end result, well, I can't say."

"Might be worth watching," Seth added, giving a half smile. "But I don't want blood on this ship yet. It's still clean."

"If it does come to blows," Calian added. "My money's on the captain."

"Darn, I was hoping you'd bet on the boy," Sailis said with a chuckle, his grin returning. "I would have taken you up on it."

"You kidding?" Calian said, laughing. "Who would bet on the kid?"

"Regardless of how you feel," Joshian said, walking up from behind them, his boots drumming on the deck. "They are still sailing with us. Timothy is young, true, but by their standards, which I found out after talking to Isaiah, he is considered an adult, so we will treat him as such. Any problems that come up, pass them to me and I will deal with them. Apparently, they prefer chains of command. I'll not have you turning into his enemies or anything like that." He pulled Calian away with him, then bent closer. "That being said," he whispered. "Remember what we talked about."

"Not a problem, Captain," Calian whispered back. "I got your back, always have."

"Didn't I tell you to just call me Joshian," Joshian whispered back, giving a short laugh.

"Only when we're not around the crew," Calian laughed back.

"You're a good man," Joshian said and smiled. "I'm very glad you're here."

"Wouldn't miss it for the world," Calian answered.

"Let's do it, then," Joshian sighed. He let Calian go, straightened, adjusted his belt, and then walked up to Isaiah and Timothy as the two came on deck. Timothy appeared disgusted by his surroundings, but Isaiah appeared to observe everything with a strange familiarity. Joshian stored the info away.

"Welcome, you two, to *Courageous Heart*," he said. "And welcome, also, to my ship's maiden voyage. Your personals have already been stored, so we'll complete our pre-voyage checklist and then be off."

"Thank you, Captain," Isaiah said. "It is our pleasure. Thank you for being willing to service this trip."

"Of course," Joshian answered. "I've been fascinated by the seas beyond the islands for some time now, so I'm glad to have the opportunity to see them. Now, if you have any concerns or issues, bring them to me and I will see what I can do. Otherwise, if you follow me, I'll show you to your cabin."

"Perfect," Timothy said, gesturing for Joshian to lead. "On that note, I have a complaint about one of your crewmen. His complete lack of respect was deeply offensive, and I would see him punished."

"What did he do?" Joshian asked, groaning inwardly as he made his way below deck. The darker interior exuded the smell of fresh wood and pitch, and a small jolt of satisfaction ran through him when he saw the boy's discomfort before he could stop it. *I know he's a man, but if I see him as a kid, I can ignore his attitude.* "What was his name?"

"I believe you call him Dayved," Timothy answered, and Joshian could hear easily the smugness laced through the words. *What did you do, mate?* "He refused to carry my baggage, taking that of my servant instead. In fact, I don't believe anyone would have taken my baggage, had Isaiah not grabbed it first."

"So?" Joshian said, sighing. "Isaiah has a leg on the mend. You, however, have no broken bones, no major injuries, and your recovery after the initial scare has been going perfectly. I don't see why you can't carry your own. Now, here we are."

"Excuse me?" Timothy asked, crossing his arms, and leaning against the wall. "What is the meaning of this?"

"Which part?" Joshian asked.

"This room," Timothy said. "What is this?"

"Your cabin," Joshian answered. Timothy laughed.

"Since you're new to the whole 'captain business' I'll be generous this time. After all, my father did say a good leader must be generous, and ignorance can be forgiven. The proper procedure for sailing includes giving the lord the best cabin, among other things, which this clearly falls short of being, and that you should sleep among the crew yourself. Furthermore, I shall require one of your men as a manservant, since as you've pointed out Isaiah is not in the best physical condition."

"Look," Joshian said, working to keep his voice patient, but feeling the strain. "I'm going to keep this simple. You sail on my ship, you do your own work, not have someone else do it for you."

"But…"

"If you work, good, we have no problems, but if not then you become a problem. We don't like problems, so you will work."

"But I…"

"As for cabin space, you're lucky this ship has cabins, because if it were one of our fishing vessels there wouldn't be enough space for beds, let alone rooms."

"But your…"

"Finally, I don't have time to deal with petty squabbles. If you have a serious problem, as in an actual concern, then bring it to me. Otherwise, deal with it yourself. But if I hear weapons have been drawn against another then there will be disciplinary action. Do you understand me?"

"I… understand," Timothy growled. "But you will know your place, Captain." Joshian shrugged.

"Do as you will. I keep my word." Joshian left, leaving Timothy and Isaiah alone.

Joshian's footsteps faded, and with his face hidden by the darkened interior, Isaiah allowed himself to smile. In his mind he knew Timothy would be furious, but he also knew Timothy would be powerless, and in this instance, it would not be a terrible thing.

I love you like a son, he thought. *But your head has grown far too big for the crown you will one day inherit. You understand a leader must be strong, forceful, someone to be listened to, but the crown will not grow bigger. Is this what I was feeling when I thought the trip would do the boy good? Do these men mean the end I've long awaited for, when I may finally return home? Master, I wait, but I do long for home, however long I can stay.*

"Of all the things," Timothy roared, dragging Isaiah away from his thoughts. "I do believe he sees me as an equal, completely ignoring my birthright. To think, doing meaningless labor as 'one of the crew' as these simpletons would put it. Pathetic. And these beds are so poor, I do believe he's giving me the worst conditions he can think of!"

"If I may say so, my lord," Isaiah said, testing one of the beds. "Our accommodations could be much worse. The room is dry, and at sea it'll be warm. The beds are not the feather mattresses you're used to, true, but they're sturdy, and they are ideal for the tighter space. Furthermore, our journey is also this ship's maiden voyage, so by right the captain deserves his cabin, but even he is sharing with his brother.

"Remember," Isaiah added. "There were no other ships available. Had you been willing to wait a week or two there would have been more ships to choose from. As is, there is only this one."

"Are you for me or against me?" Timothy demanded, raising his voice. "I did not ask your opinion, unless it's to make things better here, and I will not have you contradicting me. That behavior I would easily associate with these… swine, but certainly not you!"

"My lord," Isaiah said. "I have only ever been loyal, to your father and to you, and I will continue to be. But the only fault I perceive you having over these people is that they and their lives are simple. Why should we fight that? The captain asks little for what he gives; passage of this nature could run for hundreds of silver, and he offers it freely. His only request is we help with the tasks onboard the ship."

"You had best stop now before I decide to lump you in with the rest of them." Timothy said gravely, rising to his feet but falling back down to the bed as the ship swayed beneath him. He sighed and raised his hand dismissingly. "Now, find a way to make yourself useful and get out of my sight."

"Yes, my lord," Isaiah answered, making an awkward bow before hobbling out. He paused outside the door, breathing in the smell of the ship to collect his thoughts. Salt, pitch, wood, fish. The sea was another home. He felt strength returning to his limbs, a stirring in his heart and the clarity of mind often left distant. And he felt peace, peace he hadn't known for a long time.

His steps felt lighter, surer. The stairs themselves did not give his knees the strain they usually did. On deck, the sway of the ship felt natural, pleasant. His feet remembered.

"Hello, Master Isaiah," a voice called out in greeting. "You're just in time, we're about to set out. Is the boy... I mean Timothy, going to be joining us?"

"He will not, no," Isaiah answered, turning to find Sailis hauling on one of the ropes to raise the sails, eyes bright and hair blowing in the breeze. "He's not as accustomed to sailing yet, so he'll be down there until he can find his feet."

He set down his cane and moved next to Sailis. He grabbed the rope Sailis held and pulled with him. Old muscles strained joyfully, and he fastened the knots with old fingers that remembered the weaves before he did. Sailis, grinning, held the rope enough to give him tension. Then they joined Seth and Dayved in pulling up the last sail, secured the lines and at last rested against the masts.

"Ah, that felt good," Isaiah sighed.

"Were you a fisherman or something?" Sailis asked, wiping his brow, and looking over the ropes. "That's some good knot-work there."

"Courier," he answered absently, lost in his thoughts as he watched a gull fly past. "I used to sail between Kellivar and the cape back when marauders were still present. Fought off a few in my day, too, but that's ancient history."

"History worth hearing, though," Andrius said, walking up with a barrel over his shoulder. "You'll have to forgive us if we seem overeager, but you're some of the first contact from far outside we've had that wasn't a deep-sea fisher, and we love stories. If you have any tales to share, you will not find a deaf ear."

"I'd be honored to share them," Isaiah said, standing taller and grinning broadly. He felt his leg twinge, forcing him to lean against the mast. "I'm sorry. My leg hasn't quite healed completely, so I'm afraid I'm not going to be able to do much on it for a while... ah, thank you, Calian, correct?"

"Yep, that's me," Calian answered, walking up from behind them and handing Isaiah his cane.

"Yes, as I was saying," he continued, accepting the cane, and leaning on it. "I don't want to be a burden on anyone. I heard you don't have a cook, though. I'm not bad, and I would like to offer my services, provided the captain allows it."

"He does," Joshian said, walking up from the bow of the ship, passing a word off to the first mate before striding over to them. His posture was relaxed but sure, and when he came closer the four with Isaiah suddenly seemed... more, was the best way he could put it. They stood a little straighter, a little more alert, but not out of fear, or even respect, just readiness. Isaiah found his own back straightening, felt his heart growing bolder. Yes, here was a man that was good to know.

"I appreciate your offer," Joshian said, his smile casual and light. "And I am glad to see your leg is doing better, just, don't push yourself too hard. I am surprised by how fast it has recovered, though. Mistress Leanne never ceases to amaze me. But I'm letting myself get distracted. If you'll wait a moment, we will be underway, and I'll give you a tour of the galley. It's not very big, so the tour should be short, but I'll answer any questions you have."

The last lines holding the ship to the dock were released, and with Joshian drawing his sword to cut free the final one ceremonially, *Courageous Heart*'s maiden voyage was underway. The ship left the harbor slowly, navigating the channels carefully, but soon with sails snapping in the wind they broke through the islands to the Grygor Sea and built up speed. Once they were in open water, Joshian released the helm to Jemas and went up to Isaiah.

"Now then," Joshian said, heaving a deep sigh but grinning broadly. "While I have a few minutes of breathing room, let me show you to our galley. As I said earlier, it is small, but we have the basic necessities so it should do. If you'll follow me, please."

"Aye, sir," Isaiah said, the two descending. "Though I'm surprised you're the one showing me. Most would have had another crewman or the first officer lead guests on tours." Joshian shrugged.

"It's my ship," Joshian smiled, patting the walls tenderly. "And if that's the case, then we're not like most captains."

The mess hall was clean and orderly with a long table and small benches secured to the floor. The galley was at the end of the room, separated by a small wall with an open window. Small slats could also be opened to let in light or let out smoke, and Joshian opened a few.

"I'm sure I don't need to mention the rule of open flames while at sea," Joshian said, laughing. "Seeing as you know your way around a ship already. The crew all takes a hand at kitchen duty... oh, that's right, I don't have kitchen duty any more..."

Joshian's voice trailed off before he shook himself, but Isaiah sensed either sadness or regret in that tone.

"Sorry," Joshian said, shaking his head. "As I was saying, the crew shares kitchen duty, so depending on what you need and how many you feel can work here at one time, you'll have that many hands helping you." Joshian leaned in closer, and Isaiah steeled himself. "Now, while we're alone, there's something I need to talk to you about."

"Timothy, I take it?" Isaiah asked, giving a knowing nod which Joshian acknowledged with a slight smile. "Yes, I had a feeling he would be brought up at some point. Well, ask me your questions and I'll clarify what I can."

"I've heard rumors," Joshian began. "Stories, rather, about how royalty behaves in other lands. I do feel the need to clarify that even the concept of nobles has no place in our lives, so everything I'm going to say is based on presupposed ideas, should I cause any sort of offense. From what we've heard, nobles consider themselves far above everyone else and everything people do. They believe themselves above day-to-day work, and that those jobs are for people 'beneath' them. They believe it is the responsibility of those people to serve and obey them in all things. Would that describe your society, and more importantly, Timothy?"

"First," Isaiah began. "Thank you for explaining your position and giving me an opportunity to defend him. Unfortunately, everything you have said describes Timothy's mindset completely." Joshian nodded.

"Then this is going to be interesting," Joshian began. "For here, we have a pretty strict policy. In all my years out on the ships I've never seen it enforced, and for the most part it's remained largely forgotten. The policy is this: if a man does not work, then he does not eat. Exceptions were made for boys, but since Timothy insists on being a man he will be held to the same standards. As I told my crew, since he is a man, he will be treated as one. Furthermore, out on the open water, supplies aren't coming in, so there cannot be a distribution of additional food outside of the designated allotments.

"I know you are loyal to your country, loyal to your lord and loyal to the boy. I respect that, even if I don't understand it, but I'm loyal to everyone on my ship, whether passenger or crewman. I know the issue of you contributing isn't a problem…"

"Captain, if I may," Isaiah began. "You will have no trouble from me. To be honest, I look forward to seeing him in a situation where he has no power, where others consider him an equal. Yes, I am loyal to him. I love the boy as a son, but he has a long way to go, and much more that he needs to grow. I trust you and your men in this.

"We have a little bit of room in our laws for circumstances such as these, and through them an argument could be made that in order to ensure his safe arrival, I had to join your crew, thus joining your crew saved his life. It is understood as well that while under a captain's orders my actions are excusable so I will be free from repercussions. I look forward to seeing what comes of this trip, provided, of course, he doesn't perish."

"I can't say I look forward to the process, though," Joshian sighed, extending his hand. "But it does make me curious, to say the least. And I assure you, the boy won't die, not on my watch, so, welcome to my crew."

"A pleasure, Captain," Isaiah answered, grasping his hand. "A pleasure, to be sure."

Chapter 14

Two days into the voyage, Isaiah knew he was happier and more at peace than he had been for years. Everyone around him laughed as they went about their daily tasks, finding ways to turn chores into play, yet at no time did their work falter. The crew was a family, simple as that, and if you were on the ship, you were a part of the family. Even Timothy was included in that statement, though Isaiah noted a cloud fell any time one of them looked over at the boy, who had taken to sitting alone at the bow as the ship plodded on.

From the first day, Timothy rebelled against the captain, but the captain maneuvered skillfully with him. To no surprise, the main issue was over food; Timothy had given in on the cabin easily, but the "no outside meal" policy was a matter of contention. The first time he had tried to enter the galley outside of an allowed time, a few hours into the journey no less, one of the crew blocked his path. "Captain's orders," they said, and Timothy went back to sulk in his cabin. When he tried to push his way forward for additional rations that night, the captain himself blocked his path and imposed a one-day half-rations punishment. The two stared each other down, but the captain's will was stronger, so Timothy backed down.

However, when he tried to sneak in that very night of all things, he was banned from the galley until further notice.

During the day, Timothy would talk little and work none, shunning all contact except to try to order someone around, but all responded the same way, with a definitive no. The delivery of the responses varied, with the men either laughing or tensing with anger, but all still denied him, and eventually they just left him be. Strangely, Isaiah admitted to himself, he wasn't sure how he felt. He had told the captain that he looked forward to their results but seeing Timothy as miserable as he was made him consider changing his mind.

What amazed Isaiah the most, though, was that the rest of the crew treated himself as if he had nothing to do with Timothy. They laughed with him, told him their stories, called for his in return, and shared their songs freely. Some of songs he knew, some he knew just with different words, and through them he was able to piece together bits of their community. They were much more open than he believed they would be, freely discussing their views of life and how a ship or a village should be run, and when he presented counter opinions, they were free with their discussion which led to him agreeing with them far more than he thought he would. Things were simple for them. Things made sense.

Nights were the most entertaining, for when the ship was anchored and the men settled in, the stories would truly start. Their stories ranged from everything involving past runs to epic battles with great beasts and creatures that had been caught, to the point they became wonderful fantasies far beyond reality, but nobody minded. Other stories had to do with history, and there was a great amount of fascination with Adonar and its people, as well as a man called Grichmal, who appeared to be a legendary lord. Some of the crew, he saw, had some natural storytelling ability; their thoughts flowed easily, and the stories were consistent, but for the ones less so, the others chimed in with details, so none felt they needed to be silent.

"It was a dark night," Seth was saying as the others reclined around him. "The darkest Ebaven had known, despite the full moon and glowing stars above."

The captain stood back, leaning against the mast, but the others had seats on the sides or against propped-up boxes or barrels. Even Timothy peaked out from the stairs, though it was obvious he was trying not to look interested.

"The bodies of men and monster covered the ground, the moon's light reflecting on blackened plate and silver mail," Seth continued, his voice tense. "The kythraul advanced with no care as to which corpses they desecrated beneath their feet, their iron boots crushing bone like dried twigs. The soldiers of the queen retreated with as much dignity as they could muster, for they could not die here, not before word could be passed to the remaining nation to muster their forces… but Aureliun remained. Aureliun the Stalwart, a single Adonari scout, stood upon the green hill with his bow drawn and he let fly his fury!

"Arrow after arrow sprung from his bow, scoring marks for the retreat as every bolt brought down terror after terror. Even to this day, neither enemy nor hero has brought down as many foes as Aureliun did that night, and it's doubtful any ever will, for his kills they say were in the hundreds!

"See, during the battle," Seth continued, his tone changing again. "Aureliun danced with the blade, sometimes picking up a second as the fight warranted. He was a blur, a wind, a fluid river of death... until that first arrow pierced his leg. Moving to higher ground, he drew his bow and cleared a path for the Ebaven soldiers to retreat. When his arrows were spent, he drew from the quivers of the fallen soldiers, until they too ran out. The kythraul scaled the hill, and still he fought! With his bare hands, he struck, killing even more, the stories say, though this is only rumor, for this last act was witnessed by a lone retreating soldier as he looked back before his horse bore him away.

"The army went back to bury the bodies," Seth said in a low voice, all crew now leaning forward to catch every word. "To give the men their proper burials, that was their final task, and so regain some of the honor lost. The soldiers from the retreat went up onto the hill of the last stand, aptly named Final Hill, to bury Aureliun personally. Yet of Aureliun, nothing remained, neither bow, blade, nor body. They scoured the battlefield, searched the plains thoroughly for hours, until they found a single arrow shaft that was not theirs, buried up to the feathers in the chest of a kythraul commander. That was all, nothing else remained to suggest he was there, but nothing else was needed, for the men spread his story through all the nation.

"The arrow became the symbol for a new company," Seth said with an air of finality. "They called themselves the Green Hills, and in the battles to come they were known as the ones that never retreated until the last of their men were covered. It is said that when the Green Hills finally fell, the enemy's general was found with that single arrow shaft buried in his chest. However, it is also said that Aureliun returned to them, and after loosening the arrow himself, disappearing once more into legend."

At Seth's final words, the crew shook themselves from their trance and left silently, but there was a fire in their eyes that stirred Isaiah's heart almost as much as the story had, and though a story like that would generate applause in any tavern, here, the silence felt proper. Seth in the meantime had climbed up the mast, and as he sat up there and looked out across the waves, steady and watchful, Isaiah saw not a sailor, but an Adonari prince, and felt a new hope kindle.

"You spoke well tonight," Isaiah praised. "Elegant, articulate, just enough color to make it lively but not so much as to detract from the story. I take it you've been crafting and learning tales for some time now?"

"Oh, um, thank you sir," Seth said, giving a half laugh. "It's just something fun, nothing serious. I hear a story I like and remember it so I can tell it, that's all."

"That's a unique gift, though," Isaiah replied. "Especially that it comes so naturally. I was curious about your choice of telling Aureliun's story. I've heard that one before, almost exactly the same as far as details are concerned. Where did you learn it?"

"That one," Seth said, scratching his chin and cocking his head. "That one I learned from my grandfather. I think I made him tell me that one every night for a month, once, but he never seemed to mind. Now my grandfather, he was the real storyteller. He knew exactly how to control a crowd."

"What's your favorite story?" Isaiah asked, taking a seat at the base of the mast. "Or what are your favorite kinds of stories, if you don't have a specific one?"

"There's always something about a last stand," Seth replied after thinking a moment. "The one person, or group of people, would be willing to stay behind so either the others can live, or a runner can go for aid, or even just buy time for the rest of the forces to get there, because the people in those stories are, well, they're just really amazing to me, I can't explain it."

"Maybe not," Isaiah agreed. "But I understand it, and I agree. Well, since you fancy the story of Aureliun, are you familiar with Thremlin, Heornith, and Onesh?"

"I am not," Seth replied, his voice rising in interest. Isaiah chuckled.

"Then I shall be the storyteller for a time," Isaiah answered. "But when it is light, as sleep calls to me for now. Farewell."

The third day began in the same pattern on Timothy's part as the previous days had, and Isaiah worried more. Weariness showed clearly now; his face was strained, his eyes were heavy, and his limbs hung almost lifelessly. The crew stopped trying to engage him in conversation, leaving him alone to his misery, but he was not forgotten. The looks they gave were not ones of contempt as Isaiah expected, but more of pity, and after a crewman looked at Timothy, they would then look to the captain with the same kind of pity.

"Is there anything that can be done?" Isaiah asked Jemas. "I won't believe your captain has a mind to let him starve himself."

"Captain's put in a tough spot," Jemas said, clenching his fists when he looked at Timothy. "It's not right to put him through that."

"Are you saying... Joshian is wrong?" Isaiah asked. Jemas shook his head.

"No, it's that boy, being too selfish for his own good. Can't you see the captain? It kills him, looking over at that kid. Cap's just too believing in people, wants to see the best in people, and so he does. He beats himself up over it, too, because believe me, he's looking for every possible solution to the bloody problem, but he's bound by rules like every other captain. If he caves, he'll give up his sword, that's the man he is."

"Captain's pride?" Isaiah asked. "Not the first time I've seen it."

"No, Joshian's been like this for years," Jemas said. "It's Firebrand pride, well, it's his Firebrand pride. He sees a person in need and won't stop until they're good. Honestly, that's why so many of us follow him. He's been that for us. He calls it being a friend, but that man is stubborn. Joshian won't give up, not when he sees a mission of some kind."

"Do you see a way out?" Isaiah asked.

"The kid's fate is his own," Jemas sighed. "He'd have no trouble if he gave in, and just accepted that there are rules. Surely, he must have the foresight to see his selfishness would affect everyone. Surely, he understands that were he to ask the captain's forgiveness, he would have it."

"I don't know that he does," Isaiah admitted, hanging his head. "I don't believe he sees anything he's done as wrong."

Jemas put a comforting hand on his shoulder. He started to walk off, but paused to add, "We believe in helping those in need, but not necessarily those in want."

Isaiah shook his head, making his way over to where Timothy sat at the bow. Timothy glared when Isaiah sat next to him, but otherwise made no comment.

"I'm sorry to see you like this, my lord," Isaiah said. Timothy raised himself up slightly but then fell back to the deck.

"So, the traitor graces me with his presence," Timothy spat. "If you truly were sorry, you would do something about it. Instead, you ally yourself with them, turning against your country, myself, and my father your lord."

"I am under orders," Isaiah answered. "Under the Military Code of Conduct, article five, section three, 'in the event a member of the royal lines goes beyond the nation's borders…'"

"I know the code," Timothy grumbled. " 'In the event a member of the royal line goes beyond the nation's borders, a citizen of Ildice who joins a foreign crew or country in order to guarantee the safe return of said royal member shall be forgiven and pardoned for any tasks and orders he performs while under the new authority,' etcetera, etcetera."

"It's a very old law," Isaiah remarked. "And I'm certain it will be revised one day, but for the moment stop and think, and listen. For all the years your father has been in power I've served him, and many years before that I served your grandfather. Yes, I am old, no need to remind me. Your grandfather made me a captain, though, and when your father reached an age old enough to sail, I was charged with protecting him. I loved your father like he was my own son, and I protected him until he was old enough to protect himself, and then I walked beside him.

"When the demand to command left me, he asked that I join him in the palace to continue to guide him, and for many years life was peaceful. Your grandfather and I would pass our time playing chess and stones. Your father married your mother and life was filled with another warmth, and then a short time later, you were born. Life was good then, everything was good, but then your grandfather passed, and your father put you directly under my care. The only order he's ever given me was that should he fall then I would be there to take care of you, and that I would do everything I could to ensure you were ready for the throne. I still hold to that, out here, so listen to my advice.

"In the short time I've been with these people I've learned a few things. I've learned how they run a village, I've learned the roles the people have and how they are performed, and I've learned about their leadership, especially their captains. The position of Captain is a very unique role, in that it does not just mean one who leads a ship, but rather one who leads the village. See, a captain is responsible for leading his crew to do what they can to the best of their ability. They are meant to guide and drive them, to push them to the very limits of their ability, and to know what that limit is so as not to push too far. However young that man is, he is a captain because he can do that, and is willing to do it."

"It's all stupid," Timothy grumbled. "I saw how he was elected, too, just people giving support and that was that. Stupid."

"But full of meaning," Isaiah commented. "The seven to stand for him stand for people willing to serve under him. The three captains giving support stand for the acknowledgment of his skill by more than just one. The sword stands for being willing to defend his crew, even if he stands alone. Yes, that was that, but there was far more than just ritual. Think about your father's captains, and now think about the more successful ones among them. I know a few names came to your mind. Now think about the captains that men would die for. I don't mean die *because* of, but those who were willing to lay down their lives for their captain. When you put the two lists together, you'll find they overlap a lot. See, men will follow those whom they must, but they'll die for those they love. If you watch the crew with this captain, you'll come to realize any one of them would gladly lay down their life for him."

"Well, at least all of this will change when we get back home," Timothy said, crossing his arms. "As you said, people will follow those whom they must, and my people know me. They'll listen to me."

"What if they weren't your people?" Isaiah asked. Timothy looked up, alarmed. "If Kellivar was taken, overrun, and new leadership put in place, what then?"

"Kellivar did fall," Timothy said, his eyes and voice hard. "During the Adonarian War."

"But that was a thousand years ago," Isaiah pointed out. "There are none alive in Kellivar to remember those days, only the stories and legends left behind. The man they did rally behind, who saved all Ildice for that matter, nearly died in the process. He gave up everything to unite the people. Can you say the same about yourself?"

When Timothy would not answer, Isaiah rose and walked away. A few gave him sympathetic smiles or pats on the back as he passed, but for the most part he kept his shoulders hunched and his head down. Before he could go below deck, though, Jemas stopped him.

"The kid's stubborn, no question there," Jemas said, shaking his head. "But Cap's a good man. It'll work itself out."

That night, when the crew ate their evening meal, Joshian took his separately. The air was heavy. Jokes and songs could not be roused, even from Sailis, and the evening passed in near silence. Some picked at their food, but most sat with their heads in their hands.

"I gotta hand it to the kid," Joshian said, suddenly appearing. The captain started laughing, quietly, enough so that the crew started looking at him strangely. "Three days," Joshian said, recovering his breath. "Three days. I have never seen anyone so stubborn, and I must say, I am kind of impressed. We have reached an understanding for now, though, so Calian, remember that thing we talked about? If you would do the honors."

"Gladly," Calian said, standing up and stretching. Paul poured him a cup of coffee and extended it towards him.

"Here, you might want a cup for later or so," Paul said, chuckling. "No sense in falling asleep and dozing off on us."

"Can't argue with that," Calian laughed, reaching for the cup. He turned, raising his hand, as out of the corner of his eye a roll came flying from Seth's direction, and caught it before it could hit his head.

"Nice catch," Seth laughed. "I will get you one of these days, mark my words."

"You almost made me spill my drink," Calian shot. "Not cool, mate. Ok, see that cheese in front of you, the was Sailis' earlier that you then claimed? Yeah, that's mine now."

"On your life," Seth countered. "I swear by the heroes Aureliun, Kalsior, and…" but paused when Sailis reached over, grabbed the cheese, and tossed it to Calian. "Oi, you get back here!"

"Nope, mine now," Calian laughed. Seth rose from the table.

"Run, we got him," Andrius laughed, coming behind Seth to hold him down. Calian, laughing, ducked out as Seth and Andrius struggled, the dining room erupting in laughter. Isaiah, watching everything and feeling a peace settle, turned to Dayved, who was helping with the kitchen clean-up.

"Cap's a good man," Dayved said with a smile. "Longer than I thought, but I figured he'd win."

Isaiah started to speak, but then just shook his head and went back to work. A half hour later, when the evening duties were finished and Dayved had excused himself for the night, Isaiah poured the rest of the coffee in a couple of mugs and went out onto the deck. The night was dark, but the sky was fresh and clear, and the stars shone brilliantly. The crescent moon cast a pale white light to the deck, just enough to make out the figure of a man holding a three-pronged spear.

"I thought you'd be asleep, sir," the figure said when Isaiah walked up.

"Sleep doesn't seem to find me at the moment," Isaiah said, shrugging. "Or, if it has, it felt I wasn't attractive enough company to keep yet. Thought you might like some coffee, though."

"Gladly," Calian said, putting down his spear and accepting the still hot cup from Isaiah. "Feel free to stay up here if you'd like. We're all in this together, after all."

"Thank you," he said after a bit. "I don't like being alone, if you know what I mean."

"You're not alone," Calian said quietly. Louder, he directed his attention outward. "We may be in for an interesting day tomorrow."

"How do you figure?" Isaiah asked, taking a drink. Calian gestured out over the horizon.

"Those clouds over there," Calian said between drinks, pointing towards the mainland a little over a mile off. "Depending on whether the wind shifts or not, we may be racing a storm."

"I'm impressed you can think like that," Isaiah said with a nod, but Calian shrugged.

"From an early age, we're taught weather can change at a moment's notice. Knowing what to look for can make the difference between a crew coming home or not, so if someone doesn't have a basic knowledge of reading the weather, well, let's just say they're not encouraged to come on some of the runs. Seth's one of our best; that's why he's up top more than not."

"I know something happened down in the galley," Isaiah said, changing the subject. "Something strange with the captain and some understanding…"

"Whatever Captain decided is his business," Calian said, holding up his hand. "I don't know exactly what happened, but if he's satisfied, then that's it."

"You would do well in Kellivar," Isaiah said. "You're a good sailor, all of you are. You could be an officer, maybe even command your own ship, or just sail to distant ports as a daring trader. Even a typical crew member in our merchant fleet can live without wanting and have some to spare. I have heard you play your flute, too; court bards and songspinners can make a name and earn a fortune among everyone. I have enough sway that I could take you on as an apprentice in the palace, if you wanted."

"Ah, my life is the sea," Calian answered with a smile, shrugging. "The sea is what I know, and in my experience, at sea I'm safe. On land is where I get myself into trouble."

"Well, I can't confirm the second part of your statement," Isaiah chuckled. "But as to your first, that's partly why I offer. The sea is all you have known, and only a bit of sea at that. Why, when I was your age… ah, I swore to never use that phrase, else I would have to consider myself old. When I was your age, though, I did not know much, so when I stepped out into the wide world, it was exciting. It was terrifying, too, but it opened my eyes. I saw things I hated, but other things I loved, and I know you must have asked yourself the question of "what if" in regard to leaving your home, if only for a time. Therefore, I ask you to stay for a while, if only to visit. Even a week will show you a world far different than the one you know. If you decide to go home for good after, that is well. I've seen too many people not go and experience a different world, just staying at home, and they always longed for outside."

"That is fair, and I'll think about it," Calian answered. "I can promise you that much at least. Beyond that, well…"

"That's all I ask," Isaiah said, raising his hands. "Nothing more, just that you consider."

The rest of the shift passed quietly and peacefully. When Andrius came up to relieve Calian, Isaiah stayed up a little while longer to talk, leaving only when his yawns made up more of his speech than his words. He went below to the cabin, slowly navigating the hall despite his carried light which illuminated the cramped passage easily and found Timothy sleeping soundly. The boy wore a contented smile, which made Isaiah smile in turn. *You stand on a ship of giants,* he thought to himself. *You'll either rise with them or be crushed beneath them. Where will destiny take you, my boy? Where will it take them all?*

Chapter 15

The dawn shown bright and clear, and the sky was a brilliant pale blue, the morning *Courageous Heart* sailed into Kellivar. A steady breeze ruffled the sails, and the seas rolled as gulls cried out above the crew's heads, some flying circles while others perched on the masts. Off to their left, the sea was open, the rising sun coming up from an empty horizon, while off to their right, the cliffs of Ildice's mainland reflected the golden morning light.

"Oh, Captain, look out there, if you would," Isaiah said, pointing to a tall white tower on the edge of the cliff off their port bow. "That's the watch tower of Borran, built about three hundred years ago, to guard our northern border and coast."

"It's also the edge of the great wall," Timothy added, coming up from behind him. The boy looked much better since the first night Calian began slipping him food. He walked straighter and was more cheerful, at least around Isaiah. Now when the crew tried to engage him, not all his answers were condescending. "My father's father of my father's father completed that wall, surrounding the entire city."

"Why not just say great-great grandfather..." Jemas mumbled.

"The north," Joshian said, absently, scratching his chin. He stared out, lost in thought. "If I'm not mistaken, that area is mostly empty."

"It didn't used to be," Isaiah replied. "The kingdom of Ilshan stood there for many years and was opposed to Ildice for a long time, but it was decimated by Mahlen's forces when they crossed over from Ebaven's coast. Out of necessity, the survivors slowly became part of Ildice, and the area has yet to be rebuilt. If you are interested in ancient ruins, the cities are still in explorable condition."

"Ancient ruins?" Jhonas interjected. "Did you say ancient ruins? Are there still things undiscovered, like ancient treasures, or old artifacts... or treasure?"

"Most of the items of value were carried out by the old inhabitants," Isaiah replied. "And various archaeological teams have undertaken expeditions in the past, though it's very doubtful everything was taken. Any treasure I expect to be left, however, would be more for historical value, rather than monetary."

"The east is ocean," Joshian added, speaking to himself. "And the west is the rest of Ildice, but what's to the south...?"

"Well, that area is mostly forgotten," Timothy answered, grudgingly, for Isaiah knew Timothy couldn't resist giving an answer he knew. "The people haven't given us trouble for a couple of generations, but only because they must have known how foolish it was to try. As for who they are, they're just nomads, said to have settled when the Great War ended. There were even rumors they were part of the lost Adonarian fleet, but then, people do like to talk."

"People need hope," Joshian said. "That's why they talk. Maybe they are the Adonari, maybe they're enemies, maybe they're just nomads. If they're enemy, though, what are they waiting for, and if they're Ildician, why the separation?"

"Old wounds take time to heal," Timothy replied. "There's much distrust between the middle Ildicians and the outliers… even now."

"As you've said, they haven't acted," Joshian answered. "It's possible they aren't the threat previously thought. I don't doubt the necessity of the walls, even just as a symbol. However, the separation may not be necessary. That old distrust may be wrong."

"I… don't like that thinking," Timothy mumbled. He turned to stalk away. "Isaiah," he called over his shoulder. "See that our things are properly packed for when we arrive home. Although these… garments… are suitable for life on board this vessel, I expect to be in something more to my proper station when I see my people."

"As you wish, my lord," Isaiah answered, bowing slightly. *I hope this trip has been good for you.* He sighed, then straightened up and turned towards Joshian. "For what it's worth, Captain, it has been a genuine pleasure being on this ship. Though young, your crew does well, and I look forward to the stories I hope to hear about them. As for you, your skill is far greater than your age suggests. I'd be honored to stay on longer, but my path goes a different way."

"I understand, and respect that," Joshian answered. "Still, the honor would be mine, and should our paths cross again, my ship will always be welcome to you."

Isaiah straightened formally and brought his fist to his chest, then inclined his head in a salute. Turning swiftly, he descended below deck.

Joshian watched Isaiah follow Timothy, then turned back to the landscape before him. The old man would be missed by all, even if the boy would not, but looking back on the voyage Joshian was not sorry to have taken them on.

"Everyone's ready to make shore, Captain," Jemas said coming up next to him, excitement leaking through his voice though he tried holding it in. "Based on our speed, we should make port in about half an hour."

"No need to rush things," Joshian said lightly. "Wouldn't do to crash into their docks on our first voyage. I'd never hear the end of it."

"Oh, I'm not the one in a hurry," Jemas chuckled. "That role has been taken by our guest down below. The sooner he's off the ship, the happier he'll be, but between you and me, I think I'm going to miss the little mate. This is going to sound strange, but…"

"You have a feeling about him," Joshian finished.

"Exactly," Jemas said. "Can't give more than that, though. Don't quite understand it."

"I'm in the same boat myself," Joshian agreed. "Oddly, it feels weird to think about going home, too."

"Have you thought about what you'll do when you get home?" Jemas asked. "I mean, you may be the youngest captain, but you're still a captain, and you're still Joshian. I guess I haven't really thought about what all that means until now."

"I don't know," Joshian confessed. "Oddly, I don't know anything right now. I always saw the captainship as the end goal, never really saw beyond that, but now that it's here, it's like my path is no longer clear… maybe that's why I didn't pursue it before, now that I think about it more, because while that goal existed, and as long as I was going toward it, the path was clear, and the future was known…"

"Your future is going to be bright for a while, my friend," Jemas assured him. "You're going to get old after sailing for years, retire with your wife, kids, twenty some grandkids…"

"Yeah, speaking of that," Joshian added. "Calian said the other day that girls have been asking about me… why are you agreeing like that?" he asked hastily when he saw Jemas nodding and smiling. "What have you heard?"

"Oh man, it's bad," Jemas chuckled. "Your sister's been leading the organization, running tests and trials to find the perfect girl for you, judging all of them based on height, hair color, eyes – you do like red hair, right – and then figuring out which would be the best sister for her… dude, I'm completely joking. Oh man, you should see your face right now!"

"I really wish I hated you," Joshian growled. "Seriously, I would chain you below deck, right now. I totally would."

"You would try," Jemas laughed. "But seriously, I've heard idle chat, people talk about you. It's all good stuff, mind, but people chat. If it makes you feel any better, no one is sure what your life is going to look like, so no one is really sure how they fit with it. All the captains talk about your potential, well, they talk about ours too, and how things are meant to be great for us. Andrius and Petorius are the only two anyone has any clear thought about, so a lot of people have just been watching. I think a lot of people are just waiting for what you're going to do. Also, I'm not sure how much of that I was meant to tell you…"

"Captain!" Seth called out, causing both to look up. "I can see the whole port and the main city! Oh, wow is it amazing! And the port isn't full of too many ships, looks like most are gone, but wow they are beautiful!"

"Excellent," Joshian called back, shouting over the noise of excited crewmen. "Keep an eye out for anything troublesome and I'll call you down when we need you here. Otherwise, keep watching to your heart's content!"

"Aye Captain!" Seth answered, turning his elated face back to the harbor. Joshian turned back to Jemas.

"Like I said, I'll deal with all of that at home. For now, one quest at a time."

Joshian guided the ship into the harbor. Off to their right was a flat wall of sharp cliff that tapered down to a sandy beach further down, and to their left the ocean stood open. Schools of fish and the occasional shark passed through the transparent water beneath, of colors and patterns far different from those at home. Though the show of dolphins running in front of the bow was a familiar sight, he had assumed the fish would be the same, but even the few he recognized had slight variations.

Closer to the docks, marine life decreased as mariner life appeared, but here was the greater change from their norm. The dock workers were all older men in their early thirties for the most part, with even older ones giving the orders. Women stood further out but none were on the docks, and no children were to be seen at all, not even young men. The atmosphere was serious, business like, and though functional, there was life missing.

When Joshian docked the ship, the reactions of the Ildician men were mixed. Some looked curious, giving polite smiles and waves, going through the motions but hiding any other feelings. A few showed outright distrust, even hints of anger or fear. Nevertheless, enough were willing to overcome their initial emotions to catch the ropes tossed to secure the ship, and Joshian sent Dayved down to let his guests know. Once the gangplank settled in place, Timothy came onto deck.

"Well, captain," Timothy said to Joshian, scowling. He took a deep breath, and a peace seemed to settle in him. "I had my doubts, but you actually made it, so, I'll give you that. You know what you're doing."

"Thank you, Timothy," Joshian answered, inclining his head. "I must say, you have a surprising inner strength, one that should do you well when you're ruling this nation. I'll see you again, one day."

"Hmm," Timothy mumbled. "You were planning on staying for a few days?"

"Ideally, but only with your permission," Joshian answered. Timothy paused before nodding.

"You may stay," Timothy answered, moving away. Isaiah stepped in to take his place.

"Farewell, Captain," Isaiah said, inclining his head and extending his hand. "Clear skies and calm seas on your journey back, should I not see you before."

"And may the wind be in your favor, wherever your travels take you," Joshian answered warmly, receiving the hand firmly. "I'll at least hope to see you before I leave, but after that, well, we shall see."

Isaiah picked up their bags and the two left down the ramp, greeted by a throng of people bowing and saluting. As they moved away, the crowd moved with them, and soon the ship grew quiet.

"Come on down, Seth," Joshian called up. "When everyone is together, we'll go over the guidelines."

"Aye, Cap," Seth called back, dropping down and tumbling his way down the lines, landing with a flourish on the deck. Everyone laughed but grew quiet when Joshian raised his hand.

"It's been exciting," Joshian began, smiling broadly once the noise had died enough to be heard. "Our first leg, together, as a crew. And now, when we step off this ship, we'll be stepping out into a whole different world, with different customs, different laws. We have all talked with Isaiah. He's explained much of their customs, but where you are not sure, just do as the people do. Above all else, keep to the oaths we swore.

"Now, go out, explore, and see what the city has to offer. The food vendors and taverns sound quite appealing. If you choose to stay a night or so in an inn, by all means. I will stay with the ship, so don't worry about me leaving you out to dry. I plan to stay no longer than a week, maybe more, if necessary, but if you decide to remain longer, then I'll wish you well and do what I can to get back here soon. Jemas, anything you want to add?"

"Nothing I can think of," Jemas replied. "Now come on, Cap, drinks are on me tonight."

"In a minute," Joshian assured him. "I think that's really everything, unless I missed something."

"You have, actually," Timothy announced, coming up from the crowd. Behind him, a score of armed and uniformed soldiers marched, halting when Timothy stopped. "You neglected the part about having a ship to sail with. See, you came to this port unmarked and unaffiliated, which means you have no proof of ownership, no nation of origin. Therefore, you cannot necessarily claim this ship as yours. However, in the name of the High Lord, and as heir to the stewardship, I claim this vessel as property of Kellivar and of Ildice, and I declare you under arrest for trespassing. Furthermore, as you are carrying a weapon, I declare you to be a threat, and therefore under arrest for threatening the heir to the throne. Finally, you are under arrest because I just don't like you. Guards, if you will."

Roars of protest rose from the crew, but Joshian stayed silent. Inwardly, he fumed, but at the same time he laughed to himself. *Well played, Timothy. You get this round.* Outwardly grinning, he watched as the guards boarded his ship and surrounded his crew, but he stayed where he was. His men were tense, fists clenched, but all standing ready. Jemas, looking ready to tear the ship apart should the situation call for it, leaned in.

"Captain," he whispered, his eyes following everyone. "If we go all at once, we could stand a chance. Our numbers aren't too few, so even if we were taken, we'd put up a fight..."

"A fight we wouldn't be able to win, period," Joshian answered, sighing, loud enough for everyone to hear. The guards had spears pointed towards them now. "Or rather, a fight we wouldn't win without serious casualties. We are outnumbered, out trained, and they have more experience fighting with those weapons than we do. Even if we did win, we would still have to sail away, and I cannot guarantee that will easily happen. Our only choice is to go along with them for now. Besides that, we have our oaths. This falls under them, I'm afraid. Everyone, stand down, and give them no trouble."

The guards moved forward, threateningly, and commanded their surrender. The crew stood casually, and accepted the guards with a casual ease as their hands and feet were bound. One guard unbuckled Joshian's sword belt, and Joshian heard a barely audible, "apologies, captain," before the crew was herded down to the dock. They were met by the captain of the guards, and without a word, he turned and marched into the city. Joshian and his crew followed.

Under other circumstances, Joshian thought, amused, the city would have been impressive. The sights, sounds, and smells, though foreign, held a note of familiarity, but if he tried to stare, or even look longer than a glance, then a jab of the spear would always bring his eyes back to the front. If one of the crew lagged, they would get a prod. If they looked around too much, they would get a prod. Sometimes it almost seemed the guards prodded if they felt they went too long in-between prods. The one thing that kept the crew's attention, though, was the mob of people that currently surrounded them, and then the many small objects that came from said crowd.

At first, the guards paid the crowd and their projectiles little to no mind, even laughing at the assault on their prisoners. They stepped in to block the crowd's attempts, however, when they noticed how the way the crew protected each other drew admiration from the masses. Joshian noticed how they then worked to disperse the crowd futilely, as the mass struggled to push through, but at Joshian's slight gesture, they yielded. Progress was still slow, but it gave his crew the chance to catch longer glimpses of the shops, bakeries, inns, and venders selling their wares.

When they broke free of the mob and Joshian had some time to send his glances outward, he saw the city had changed considerably. Their path was now steady white cobblestone, where before it had been gravel or hard packed dirt. The buildings, too, went from being single story or having a top porch to now being two or three stories tall, built with polished stone rather than just worn wood. He looked behind him to see where the change happened, noticing now a tall wall they had passed through, nearly as thick as the road they were on was wide, and portioned off with guard towers at irregular intervals. He felt a jab from one of the spears and continued forward.

They entered a second walled-off area, and the differences here were almost as great as when they passed through that first gate. Leaving the higher end commercial district, they now entered what he figured was the royal district, where groomed lawns and artistic architecture adorned all the homes. Some of the homes were simple in construction, but even they were surrounded by open space, a luxury the middle and outer city could not enjoy. The shops were nicer, as well, with wares far costlier than in the other districts – a gold coin for a vase! I could make that – but they were sparser and looked to be more controlled. Another change was that there were weapons shops in this area, while the only metal working seen previously were blacksmiths. Finally, though, and this was the part most foreign to him, there were no fish markets in this area of town, and everything smelled less of the sea.

Another guard intercepted their party and exchanged words with their captain escort. The escort passed some papers to the second who then gestured onward, and the party was shuffled off to a run-down corner of the city. It was only after Joshian saw bars on the buildings' windows did he realize there would be no trial. They were simply going to prison, to a cage, to a hole.

Inside the prison, the air was cooler and damper than he preferred, but then again, prison was never the preferred inn of choice. The walls were gray stone, the ceiling was gray stone, and the doors were gray iron bars touched with rust. All in all, everything was drab and unappealing. Ushered into a cell, their door was locked, and they were forced simply to wait.

Standing on the deck of *Courageous Heart* and fingering the new sword at his side, Timothy smiled. With a curved blade, sharpened on one side, and a handle small in diameter but long enough for a two-handed grip, it was a very good sword, one he looked forward to testing in combat. *Made for me*, he thought. *Your earlier owner, that wretch of a captain, was not worthy of something of your quality, but I am. Yes, I am, and you, sword, are worthy of me.*

"My lord," Isaiah said from his side. The man had hidden his eyes as the crew passed him by on their way to the prison, and received light salutes, kind farewells and easy smiles, which Timothy could hardly understand since they had ignored him completely. "My lord, I must question your judgement in this matter. I'm not denying your right to declare such laws, merely the wisdom behind it, for I fear you have made enemies of some powerful men."

"Be at peace, Isaiah," Timothy assured him. "I have no intention of keeping them there long, at least, not all of them.

Calian, for example, showed great daring doing what he did, and that courage will not go unrewarded. I intend to bring him into the palace, to work with you under your guidance. He has some useful skills. They all do, to be fair. Most of them will go to the ships, for they seem to enjoy the work, but not that filth of a captain. He will rot until he acknowledges that I am the one who truly holds the power, and then he will spend his days kneeling at my feet."

"I hear what you say," Isaiah answered, but when he hesitated, Timothy's smile faltered. "And had they been normal men, I believe things would go as you said, but these men are not like normal men. They will not give in the way you hope. If anything, it may harden their feelings further.

"As I said before, you may have made yourself a terribly dangerous enemy, and you are only saved because of rules they have imposed. As your adviser, please listen when I say that the man you hate so much is the kind of man who can do great things and will do great things when directed in the right way."

"He will obey, or he won't," Timothy said, shrugging. "Either way, I still win."

"My lord," a guard called, coming from below deck. "I have their weapons."

"Ah, excellent," Timothy answered. "Isaiah, look, every spear has a different etching and different form. Every spear is unique, and their weight is… far greater than I expected. I like these. I shall keep them too. Now, come Isaiah. Father will have no doubt heard of our arrival by now and will expect our return to the palace promptly."

"Yes, my lord," Isaiah said, bowing, but Timothy had already turned and moved into the city, a company of armsmen at his back.

When Timothy reached the palace and stepped through the gate, he had the herald pause in his loud proclamation of arrival and allowed for only a messenger to go to the main hall to announce him. He, along with Isaiah and his company of guards, walked the halls in silence, and then Timothy stopped at a vase of small blue flowers, one of many that lined the hallway.

"Schuylarks," Timothy said quietly, running his hand over the delicate petals. "These are new." He smiled, but his lip quivered. "They were mother's favorite."

"Yes, they were," Isaiah said, laying a hand on Timothy's shoulder.

"These, um, these pots aren't good enough," Timothy said, brushing Isaiah's hand off. "We have better ones somewhere. I think we do."

"We'll ask your father about it," Isaiah said. "Or I'll summon a servant…"

"No," Timothy said abruptly. "I mean, no, I'll do it myself. Has to be done right."

"Of course, my lord," Isaiah answered, a sad smile touching his face when Timothy had turned back. "Should you need any assistance, though, I am at your service."

Composing himself, Timothy continued on, and at the doors of the Great Hall, the sound of the herald caused all eyes to turn. Advisors and servants stood off to the sides and lined the walls, ready to act as their station required, and some servants weaved their way through soldiers and other nobles that were spread out on the floor.

Smooth white stone covered with blue carpet rugs made up the floor of the Great Hall, and the high walls surrounding the room held banners and tapestries in the blue and white of Ildice. At different points throughout were a few banners in the red and gold of Ebaven, in honor of the friendship between the two nations, standing out clearly but providing a regal accent to the noble blues. Light streaming through large windows reflected keenly off the arms and armor of the guardsmen, nobles' jewelry, and the cups and plates the servants carried.

"Timothy, my son!" the High Lord, Kevian Ephaestus cried, rising from his seat in the center of the room and rushing forward to greet him. By dress alone, of all the people in the room, the High Lord was the only one who looked to not belong.

Well, Timothy thought with a chuckle. *Neither I nor Isaiah look our parts either.*

The servants were dressed in flashy outfits of blue and white, the advisors and councilmen were adorned in longer robes in different shades of blue, and the guards wore crisp uniforms of the blue and black. The High Lord, on the other hand, wore simple black boots, a black belt with an ornate buckle, and his tunic and pants were pure white. His long coat of deep blue with white and silver embroidery was draped unceremoniously over the armrest of his gilded chair.

He's in his negotiator outfit, Timothy noted. *For when he needs to sit through hours of debate. I do not envy that role.*

The two embraced warmly, though Timothy could feel some exhaustion and tension in his father's hug. At length, the High Lord stepped back, and concern crossed his face.

"My son, you do not look well. Shall I send for the physician?"

"A chef, rather, my lord," Timothy answered, grinning. "For I am more famished than I am sick, and a poor cook would do more for me than the best physician ever could. Fortunately, our chefs are not poor in skill."

"Well, a warm meal you shall have, then," his father said, laughing deeply. He gave orders to the servants and brushed aside the questions of the lords and advisors, and then turned back to Timothy. "In the meantime, let us retire, and you can tell me all about your journey. Master Isaiah, thank you for keeping him safe. Please come as well."

The three of them left the Great Hall with a score of armsmen behind them and entered into a smaller council room. The room was decorated similarly to the throne room, but it was far shorter, barely half the height, and furnished with padded couches arranged in a small circle around a short table and a few desks along the walls.

"I must dispense with the pleasantries for now, and jump straight to business," the High Lord said, shaking his head. "How did the queen and first prince receive the letter? Will they take action?"

"Father, forgive me," Timothy said, hanging his head. "Halfway through my journey, our vessel struck the rocks inside the Shield Archipelago, and crashed. Isaiah cared for me until help could come, but when it did, they kept me for another couple of weeks before returning me home. When they finally did send me home, they assigned their youngest, most inexperienced captain to do so. Along the way, I was neglected, ignored, treated like baggage, and nearly starved! That later bit was only remedied because one of the crewmen passed me food when he could. Aside from Isaiah, he was the only decent man of the group."

"Then blessings upon the man who showed you kindness," the High Lord said, smiling, but then quickly frowned. "And wrath and punishment to those who showed you evil and ill will. I will look into that personally."

"I've already handled that," Timothy assured him. "I had the guards send them to the prison for an unspecified time."

"Hmm," the High Lord answered, contemplating. "That will do for now. Still, those who show kindness and loyalty I like to reward quickly. What is the man's name? I will have him brought in immediately."

"His name is Calian," Timothy answered. "That was my thought as well. He's a gentler one, nothing like his brother, and it's not right he be lumped in with that crew. I believe some hope resides in the others though. After all, they were just following orders. I hope to give them a chance to rethink the error of their ways."

"Hmm," the High Lord said, scratching his beard. "Curious people… Come, let us go meet with our people again and prepare to greet Calian. We will get you that hot meal, my son, and Isaiah, please find an officer to bring me the one named Calian. Make sure the guards treat him well."

"Yes, my lord," Isaiah answered, bowing, and then leaving.

Captain Cornell listened to Master Isaiah as the wizened advisor gave him instructions regarding the prisoners, and then with a nod, took the company of men under his command and marched for the prisons. "Treat them well, for the High Lord's sake and for Timothy's," the old adviser had said, but it was the added, "and for my sake as well," that gave him the pause. Sentimentalities had never meant much to Cornell, but Isaiah was not an ordinary man. He was a military man, like himself, with an honorable record, and if he cared about something then it was worth taking note of. Still, prison duty was never enjoyable. Far too dirty...

His men kept march in orderly rows behind him, and as they passed through the crowded streets, people stepped aside and nodded respectfully. He smiled at them, acknowledging them graciously, but a sudden thought crossed his mind. Isaiah had mentioned an entire crew had been imprisoned, and as he looked at the men he had brought, it struck him that there would be trouble. Crews had loyalty to each other, both on duty and off, and friendship could be more dangerous than duty.

A quarter of an hour later, after pulling in some additional men to his patrol, his guards passed through the gates into the prison, and the guards there saluted him. He saluted back and took the keys to the prisoners' cell, then gave orders for some of his men to secure the exit while the rest of them went to the cell. Steeling himself, he walked down a long hallway, then descended the stairs to the lower level.

Strange that one of honor will come from the worst cells we offer, he thought. *Master Isaiah, what a curiosity you've given me.*

As he walked, he heard laughter and conversation, sounds that only grew louder the further in he went. He checked the cells, but they held just what he expected to see – dirty prisoners who barely looked up as he passed and didn't even have the strength or inclination to scowl. When he came to the cell that held the crew, the conversation and laughter stopped.

The faces in this cell were not those of criminals. They were young and strong sailors, possibly warriors, but not criminals. They didn't look at him the way a criminal would, with anger or fear, but rather curiosity. Even stranger, they looked to be waiting for him to get done with his business so they could go back to theirs. Though he was the guard with the power and authority, and the men were the prisoners, he felt that he was interrupting, that he was an uninvited guest. He spoke out, shaking the feeling off.

"The one known as Calian," he announced. "Stand and come with me. The High Lord has taken interest in you, and you have been summoned to appear before the throne. Come quickly."

"Go on, Calian," one of the men in the room said, laughing. "I promise, we'll wait here for ya until you get back." The rest of the men echoed his laugh, and Cornell felt a smile tug at his mouth before he was able to catch himself.

"Yeah, I might as well see what he wants," answered one of the men, rising to his feet. *This is Calian,* Cornell thought. *Strange response…* "Alright, then, Captain, is it?"

"Yes, Captain," Cornell answered crisply.

"Captain what?"

Taken aback, though managing to keep it under control, Cornell straightened himself. "I fail to see the importance," he answered, though a note of frustration did manage to leak into his voice. Behind him, his men watched the rest of the crew, and their hands tightened on their weapons.

"It's just that I'll feel more comfortable knowing who I'm following, it all," Calian said lightly, shrugging. "Or rather, I'll follow someone I know, unless you want to throw another set of chains on me."

"Cornell," he answered, chuckling quietly at the realization of what he'd done. *It's nothing drastic,* he thought. *It's just a name and if it makes him come along easier, there's no harm.* However, when the words, "Captain Cornelius, of the one hundredth battalion, at your service, though you may call me Cornell," escaped his lips, he realized also that he meant the words. *Yes, Calian,* he thought, *my heart gladdens that you'll be in the palace. The High Lord and his son could use a man like you, and you'll do well for Isaiah as well.*

"Calian Farstrid, at yours," Calian said in turn, inclining his head. "And now that we're acquainted, it wouldn't do too good for you to be in trouble on my account, so we had best be moving. After all, you are a man under authority, doing your job, and I cannot fault you for it. I will however need you to lead the way, as this is my first time in the city, and I don't know my way around."

"We shall gladly show you," Cornell chuckled, and his men grinned, giving light laughs to mask their surprise. They opened the prison door and Calian stepped out, holding his arms casually despite the metal chains. Cornell almost unfastened them, but after a pause apologetically explained that he was required to keep them on for the time being. Calian shrugged as if they were no trouble, and then followed Cornell as he led the way out of the prison.

Chapter 16

Seated on his throne, the High Lord Kevian looked up as the great doors opened and Captain Cornell led his prisoner in. Though the man wore chains, he walked with such a confidence and surety that the guards appeared more as an escort of honor than as a prevention of escape. He was tall and strong, and in proper clothes would strike a very convincing figure of a lord or a knight, but he was surprisingly young, and that made him very curious. For one willing to defy a captain, he had expected someone older, with far more experience and far more leverage. This man could have had his entire career jeopardized. *Daring, I can admire that.*

When the group stopped before him and the captain and his men saluted, the prisoner kept his hands clapped casually in front of him. *The chains, of course,* Kevian thought after the initial irritation settled. *Understandable he wouldn't salute.* He rose from his seat and walked towards the group.

"So, you are the one known as Calian," the High Lord said, smiling, feeling genuine joy at meeting him. "Servants, please bring food and drink for our honored guest, and let us remove these chains."

"I'd rather not," Calian answered, giving Kevian pause. "Not while my captain and fellow crewmen have nothing."

Kevian looked over at Isaiah, who sat at a small table off to the side, looking over documents, maps, and other messages. His old adviser gave an amused grin before turning back, but otherwise said nothing, which sparked Kevian's curiosity even more. Though the old man appeared focused, years of meetings gave Kevian the insight to know his ear was completely tuned to the conversation.

"Your crewmen are in there for what they've done," Kevian answered him, forcing patience into his tone to cover his curiosity. "It will be some time before they're released. As far as conveniences, it will be a while before those are delivered."

"Then it will be some time before I eat or drink, I suppose," Calian answered, sitting on the plush carpet and crossing his arms. "I won't abandon them, in this life or the next."

He must know what is happening, Kevian thought. *He must know the position he's in. Or... perhaps not. Very well.*

"So be it, then," Kevian answered, sitting back down on his throne again. He frowned. "You are aware that your friends are in prison for various crimes, crimes for which you are, in fact, being pardoned, correct?"

"We have committed no crimes on your soil," Calian answered defiantly, his voice taking on a dangerous edge, and Kevian was taken aback. Isaiah laughed silently out of the corner of his eye, though he had the decency to keep quiet. Around him, everyone gasped, but Calian continued. "If anything, you are the ones who should be in our debt, unless my understanding of your laws is incorrect, and if I may be so bold, you are the criminals. We hold no debt against you, however, though that can be changed. That being said, where we come from, if someone is accused of a crime, the accused has a right to know what crime he's committed, and he has a right to defend himself. So, let us speak simply, and please just tell me what crimes were committed."

"The crimes are simple," Kevian answered, annoyed and seeing no reason to hold back his feelings. "You are accused of trespassing on royal property, threatening the life of one part of the royal household, showing disrespect to a member of the royal household, and willingly endangering the life of the same member by starvation. Those are the crimes with which you have been charged."

Calian laughed, and everyone looked at him with horror. Kevian clenched his fists tightly, and his mind warred between feelings of anger and amazement at the man's courage. Did the man truly not understand that he had the power to either keep him locked up or to set him free? That he alone could raise him to a position of power or just order his death in the same pen stroke? Or did the man simply not care?

"Wow," Calian answered, looking around. "That is the biggest load of, well, I won't say in front of the ladies, and unfortunately that's the second time I've heard it. Alright, well, since we're all on the same page with that, tell me why I've been summoned."

"It appears that no one has taught you proper respect," Kevian growled, trying to get a hold of his anger. "Nevertheless, Master Isaiah, who has been a long-time adviser to me, says that you are one who can be trusted, and both he and my son,

Timothy, said you showed him kindness by keeping him alive. I wanted to repay that kindness, and still do, by making you my son's servant and letting you live in the palace under Isaiah's guidance and tutelage. You will be paid, of course, have free reign of the city, and shall enjoy the privileges of the throne."

"Then let me simplify things to put things into perspective for you," Calian announced, standing fully erect and narrowing his eyes. "I have never been more insulted in my life. I am a free man who serves no one save those who serve me in turn. The kindness you spoke of was nothing more than the mercy of a captain for a lazy, selfish, spoiled brat with no consideration for anyone but himself. I take it he never mentioned that the "starvation" was punishment for trying to steal from the galley multiple times, something even you should understand? No, I supposed not. If you want to talk about respect, then you have failed, because your son has none!

"And another thing... no, you sit down," Calian demanded in rage, and against his will, Kevian found himself obeying, lowering himself back to his seat. "By your leave or not, I really don't care, because I'll defend myself anyway. To start with, if we are charged with trespassing, then you are charged with thievery and piracy, as you have stolen *our* ship, and our captain's honor, all in the worse way possible. To the claim of threatening his life, that's a flat out lie. As for showing Timothy disrespect and starving him, we treated him exactly as we would one of our own, demanding nothing less, and we informed him of our expectations beforehand, too.

"What's funny, though, is that since he didn't pay, oh yeah, that's right,' Calian added. "We didn't require payment for this trip. The only thing asked was that he pull his weight and help out. Since he didn't fulfil that part of the bargain, then that makes him little more than baggage, which in my experience you just strap down and ignore.

"However, if you are anything like your son, which it seems like you are, then none of this reasoning matters, and this entire conversation has been pointless. Therefore, I decline your offer, and I am going back to join the rest of my crew. As a word of advice, the next time you want to talk to one of us, talk to the captain. You'll have better luck with him."

The room was completely silent. Kevian fumed and Isaiah, bless that man, ceased his laughter, but kept the smile. *You know something, old man. We will have words later. Now how am I going to salvage this…?*

"Captain, get this man out of my sight," Kevian ordered, and the guards came forward to hold Calian. "If he wants the same treatment as his crew then he shall have it. Throw him with the others, and as a bit of poetic justice, hold off on food for as long as it was withheld from my son. Let them starve. Now get him out of here!"

The doors closed behind Captain Cornell and his prisoner with a mournful creak, followed by a deafening clang, and then there was silence. Kevian looked around at the chaos of reactions that had risen in Calian's wake as the light buzz of murmurs began to rise… *Calian's wake,* he thought with disgust. *Calian, who had controlled the encounter, Calian who had made a fool of him, and Calian who ordered without thought it would be obeyed. How that man was possible…*

He rose to his feet slowly, and the buzz of conversation died down almost instantly. Signaling to Isaiah, the old man rose graciously and followed him from the throne room to Kevian's private conference room. When the door shut behind them, leaving him and Isaiah alone, Kevian sat on one of the couches and hung his head in his hands. After a few minutes of grateful silence, Kevian looked up at Isaiah.

"As usual," Kevian began. "I suppose I need not say that you are no longer a servant, nor I should not be treated as a lord?"

"You need not," Isaiah answered, warmly. "And I'll say again, as with your father and all times before, I shall continue to serve you any way I can in any way you'll listen."

"I'll always listen to you, Master Isaiah," Kevian said. "Your wisdom has never been deserved, and I've always appreciated it, even the words I've hated receiving. I need your guidance now."

"Then once again," Isaiah chuckled. "This will be wisdom you will not enjoy. Not only did Calian control the interaction between you two in there, but you let him do so. Furthermore, everything he said was unfortunately correct."

"Surely you exaggerate, old man," Kevian protested, but Isaiah shook his head.

"I rarely if ever exaggerate," Isaiah laughed. "You should know by now I may even play down things should I see the need. One thing I did enjoy, though, was the interaction between the two of you. I knew that Calian was strong, but it helped answer a few other questions I had about them."

Kevian groaned. "I heard the short version from Timothy and you already," Kevian sighed. "I leaned heavier on my son's words than I believe I should have, though, so if you please, tell me everything about this village and this trip."

For the next hour, Isaiah spoke, detailing all that had happened since his and Timothy's departure just over two months prior. Kevian listened painfully, but also amazed, as Isaiah detailed the crash, the rescue, Timothy's care, and the actions of Joshian throughout. He also spoke of the journey back to Kellivar, as well as all his conversations with the crew. When Isaiah came to the interaction that had just taken place, he also explained the meaning behind Calian's responses. Kevian sighed and pondered.

"So, in your opinion," Kevian asked. "Are the rest of the crew all like him?"

"They are all like him, and they are nothing like him," Isaiah answered. "They are independent, willful, but deeply compassionate and deeply loyal. They will do what they feel to be right, so if your goals align with theirs, you will be unstoppable, but in some ways their views of right and wrong differ from ours. For example, all men are equal, and all men deserve equal treatment. Titles of any kind are given to those who show the right skill, not necessarily those with the right connections or the right birth. Everyone looks out for each other, and everyone works to build each other up to be the strongest they can be."

"Titles," Kevian contemplated. "He said they treated Timothy like any one of their own, not as a lord. What does the title of 'lord' mean to them?"

"Absolutely nothing," Isaiah chuckled. "And that's at best. As of now, I expect the title 'lord' probably has a terribly negative taste in their mouths."

"I assume I'll have to pay for that later," Kevian said, letting his shoulders slump.

"Young Master Kevian," Isaiah laughed. "How quickly you've forgotten your own history. Do you remember when you were eighteen, and you joined the royal navy, you told me something important. What were your words?"

"I don't remember them, honestly," Kevian answered. Isaiah nodded.

"Fortunately, I do," Isaiah said. "You told me that a leader should understand the people and should know the people he's with. When you were even younger, you would run into the village and play with the other boys because you wanted to see how they were different. But when you joined the navy, you told me that if a lord was going to order people to fight or sail then you should understand what they went through. I still remember how furious your father was when he found I had created a false identity for you, and that you were in fact not studying in Vandor as he had thought. I also remember how proud of you he was that you did that.

"You went through the ranks and became an officer, by your own merits," Isaiah continued. "You learned how to sail, and to fight, but you also learned how to take orders and how to properly give them. Those skills made you a great commander and a great leader, but somewhere between then and the past few years you've forgotten that. You've forgotten you are also just a man, but then who can blame you. No commoner has stood up to you since you inherited your father's title, save for myself, because for too long you've hid behind the title. Calian showed you who you are without it."

"I can't be a man right now," Kevian lamented. "You know all of the struggles we've been facing right now. The Western Road is closed to us, Isaiah, and Maltis is still recovering.

Yes, we have the carrier birds, but Ebaven is becoming closed. The traditional passages are being blocked, more people are needing aid, and so new paths need to be opened. Even worse, your Captain was my friend, one of my few friends left, and now he's gone. As a lord, I've lost an option, but as a man I've lost a friend, a comrade in arms, and the nation doesn't need a grieving man. That ship you were on was one I had designed for that very purpose, and that captain was one of my last truly experienced ones. I don't have time to grieve."

"If I may," Isaiah consoled him. "You are not out of options, not yet."

"I know, I still have some time," Kevian said. "Time to build, time to redesign, but training will be another issue… My captains are either too old or too new, none with the experience and daring to sail at this time of year."

"You have a ship in the harbor that has made the journey already," Isaiah answered. "And you have a captain locked securely in your prison."

"We both know he won't listen to a High Lord," Kevian answered, shaking his head.

"He might listen to Kevian though," Isaiah said. "If he met him."

"I see your heart," Kevian said, smiling. "Being completely truthful, what other options do you see available?"

"Just the ones that you stated," Isaiah answered. "*Courageous Heart* is strong and fast, and with training a captain could learn how to handle her, but that will take time. The later we wait, the worse the weather will be, and men's courage falters when that happens. Our forces are spread thin, so we need

Ebaven's army to clear out the road and keep forces posted to prevent them from coming back. Our main enemy is time."

"So, my options are either fail or trust a captain who already hates us," Kevian sighed. "I can't stake the fate of everything on just anyone."

"Then test him," Isaiah said. "Use whatever tests you want but do it quickly."

Kevian leaned back against his couch, resting his head on the backrest as he closed his eyes. *Father, I miss you. I wish you were here now, but I've said that more times than I can remember. And my dear Kalina, my love, I wish you hadn't been taken from us so soon. What was it you said in these times, said you read it in a book once... time to take a chance, time to roll the dice...* "Isaiah, I have a plan. I don't like it because I don't like to gamble, but I have a plan."

"Sometimes great rewards come with great risks," Isaiah nodded. "As always, I will do what I can to support you."

"Then why will you not accept my wish that you formally be my chief adviser? You've earned that title multiple times over, and you deserve the respect that goes with it."

"If I may," Isaiah said. "A servant can go places an adviser cannot."

"True," Kevian said, smiling. "And a criminal can go elsewhere. Let us have some fun, then, and I will tell you the start of my plan."

Seth's eyes could spot a raft in the middle of the sea on a new moon, but even he had trouble adjusting to the darkness inside and outside their cell, despite having the entire wall to the outer corridor be nothing but bars. The torches down here were carried, not lining the walls like in the upper level, so the little bit of light that did come in was through the open window that seemed to serve only as a vent for their warm air to escape through. The stone corridors echoed well, however, and the sound of heavy footsteps reached his ears long before the glow of a torch came down the hallway. No voices went with the footsteps, but he figured Calian had returned. His suspicions proved correct when three guards came into view, escorting him in, and when the door to their cell opened on creaking hinges, Calian was thrown in without ceremony and the door bolted behind him. He picked himself up and leaned against the cell wall, and there was silence as the guards' footsteps faded.

"So, how was it out there, mate?" Seth asked through the silence, Calian chuckled.

"Complete waste of time," Calian answered. "As a reward for what all I did, I was to be the kid's servant, to wait on him personally. Sure, I'd be with Isaiah, but small compromise. These people have a strange idea of rewards and all, seriously. There was no listening to reason from them."

"There never is, to be fair," a different voice called out from one of the cells. "Those in power are the ones that are right, and the weaker ones are wrong. But then, that's the same as everywhere in this hope forsaken world."

"Not that we were aware," Dayved answered back. "We always figured leaders looked out for the good of everyone under them."

"Oh, they do, to a degree," the voice answered. "But they make sure to look after themselves and their friends first. After that, they do enough that we can't complain too loudly, and if we do complain they find a way to silence us."

"Not like home at all," Petorius said, sadly.

"Where you all from?" the voice asked.

"We come from a village called Firebrand," Paul answered. "On an island of the same name between Ildice and Ebaven."

"I thought those islands were uninhabited?" the voice said, curiously. "And I thought that area was too dangerous to sail?"

"Only to those untrained," Jemas laughed. "We've made do over the years."

"Interesting," the voice replied. "What brought you up here… and in here?"

"The High Lord's son, Timothy, crashed near our island so we brought him home," Joshian answered. "The plan was to return him here, stay for a bit, and then return home. Unfortunately, Timothy decided we needed to spend our stay in here."

"Messing with the High Lord's son, I love it!" the voice laughed. "What did you do? Did you try asking for ransom, rough him up, or torture him for secrets or something? I'm personally not a supporter of the torture part, but the roughing up plan on the other hand…"

"It's somewhat complicated," Calian answered, detailing their trip with the others chiming in, as necessary. When they concluded their story, the other prisoner laughed openly, as well as a few others in the neighboring cells.

"I'm amazed that anyone would dare to do what you just said," the stranger said, gleefully. "That people like you exist out here… I think I like you guys, but I'm going to go to sleep. Prison takes a lot out of you, as you'll see. Sleep well, and I'll hear you guys more tomorrow."

The night passed by uneventfully. The crew talked for a while, but all conversation led back to home, which drove them to silence. Sleep eventually came, and when they awoke, the morning was much like the evening.

Aside from their neighbor, who called herself Adi, the wing of their prison held very few others, and they generally stayed quiet. To Seth, this place was the furthest away from home he'd ever been, both in distance and in strangeness. The sounds that struck his ears were completely foreign; formal military commands and crisp responses were far from the jolly cries around even Captain Malrig. There were no waves, no sound of water, even though a lone gull would occasionally fly close enough to be heard. The air weighed heavier on him as well, though from the looks of the group it weighed on everyone. The captain was deep in thought. Jemas and Jhonas were subdued.

"Seth," Joshian's voice cut through the gloom. "We were a bit disposed last night, but I don't suppose you've got a story on hand?"

"Always," Seth answered, feeling his mind swirling. "Any one in particular?"

"Not this time," Joshian replied. "You've always had a good feel for crowds, though, so I know you've got one in mind."

"Alright, then," Seth said, rubbing his hands together. "Here's one I've always liked. This is the story of Heimaer, the golden-haired spy, and the only known Adonari to venture to Mahlen's capital and return…"

Around midday, right when Seth finished, guards came to transfer some of the crew to a separate cell across the hall. They could still hear one another's voices, but the lack of light prevented them from seeing each other clearly, turning them into mere shadows. "Divide the enemy's forces" was whispered a few times, and Seth wondered at this, whether it was tactics or practicality. The small cell had far more room, now, though that was a poor consolation for the lack of life.

By the third day of captivity, food still had not been delivered, the same as the days prior. Calian had long confessed this would be expected and the crew had immediately excused him for it, but now a few complained openly. Some turned their anger toward Calian, some turned it toward Joshian, but when Joshian asked if any of the crew would have responded differently, none could deny it. Just as quickly as the potential for division could start, it ceased, and they were once more a crew.

"Everyone is at each other's throats by the third day," Adi commented. "Some break sooner, but three days is usually enough for the anger to set in. Just... just fight through it though. Now's not the time to learn how strong of a crew you are... or aren't."

That night, she was taken from her cell, and did not return. The darkness closed in around the crew.

When the sun rose on the fourth morning of captivity, heavy clouds blanketed the sky and the wind blew the falling rain into their cell, making everything cold and muggy. The complaints had risen with the cold but subsided only because complaining had grown too tiresome.

Joshian took to making rounds, checking in with everyone in the cell. From time to time, he would discuss various improvements that could be made to the ship with Petorius and

Andrius, who in a matter of hours figured they had found the cell's weak spots and were otherwise bored. Paul and Sailis were engaged in a very… interesting debate about the nature of whether laws or morality governed the way people acted, and thus were left alone. Jemas and Jhonas swapped a few stories, but the others were mostly silent.

Mew

"Hey, you guys hear that?" Andrius asked, looking around.

"I heard something," Jhonas confirmed. "Not sure where it's coming from…"

Mew

"Oh, hello there, kitty," Andrius said, looking towards the open window. He stood and brushed himself off, then walked to where, silhouetted in the window, a small cat looked in, curious.

"Where'd you come from?" Jhonas asked walking over as Andrius pet the cat, who was now purring contentedly.

"We call him Skritches," a voice called from out of view.

"Why Skritches?" Calian asked.

"Well, he loves skritches," the voice said, laughing, and then stepping into view. "Doesn't have an owner that we know of, but he just comes around and gets loves from whoever likes him. He helped me get through some of those more difficult times in there."

"Wait," Seth said, scratching his chin and cocking his head to the side. "Adi?"

"Oh, that's right, we haven't been properly introduced before," Adi laughed, her voice having a clear ring. "Some call me Adelina, others just Adi, but it's still me. I've got a few other names floating around, too, for good measure."

"Adi, hi, nice to finally see you," Seth said. "How did you get out? We didn't know what happened to you, getting taken away like that."

"I was let out early," Adi answered. "The High Lord had need of my… services, you could say."

"Yeah, what do you do exactly" Calian added. "And why did you get tossed in here in the first place?"

"It's pretty simple, actually," Adi said, shrugging. "I'm a thief."

"Ok," Andrius said in between pets. "So… why?"

Adi burst out laughing, but quickly muffled her laugh as she looked around quickly. After composing herself, she continued. "Honestly, that was the response I expected the least. Well, let's see, I guess I'll just start at the beginning. My story is much like any other tragic back story, kid has parents that don't want her, grows up trying to figure out where she fits in everything, blah blah blah, learned to swipe food to stay alive, then learned to swipe enough to make a profit. I got better; people hired me to steal other things. I kept doing it. Beat doing other things… That's the short version."

"Crime is difficult to justify," Paul said, frowning. "How did you get caught?"

"My last crew sold me out," Adi said, shrugging. "Big bust, too. Can't say I didn't expect it, no honor among thieves and all. It was a tricky one, though, I mean, we had to beat a vault and then get out with the gold, which weighs a lot, mind. When it came time to scatter and meet up later, I found the city guard at our rendezvous. Not fun."

"Are there a lot of thieves around?" Sailis asked.

"Um, to be honest," Adi said, scratching her head. "I don't really know. I mean, I guess there are, more thieves, I mean. Wherever the rich are getting richer, the poor are getting poorer. It's just the cycle of things."

"Sounds like things got messed up somewhere," Petorius said, and the others nodded. Adi cocked her head to the side.

"Why?" Adi asked. "You ain't got thieves where you come from?"

"We don't, really," Joshian said. "There's not any reason. People live, things need to be done and get done, and if someone has a need then others help them out. Those who can do the work will do the work, and those who can't will do something else. As for 'distribution of wealth,' well, those who have the wealth pay us to do the work, so it all works."

"If only life really worked like that," Adi said, shaking her head. "Hey, I gotta run, this rain is seeping in everywhere. I probably won't be back before night falls completely, so sleep well and may your fortunes fare better in the future."

"Fare well, Adi," Seth answered. "Come back tomorrow and tell us about the outside world that we aren't seeing."

"Oh, I've got a few stories," Adi said, laughing. "Though I don't think you'll have time for them all."

"Well at the moment, we have nothing but time," Calian answered. "Tell us what you will, and we'll try to figure out the rest."

"Then I shall entertain you until your ears bleed," Adi answered, tossing up a salute. "But that's for tomorrow." Her figure disappeared from the window, and her footsteps faded away.

Chapter 17

Strolling along the streets of Kellivar, Adi was free. *And home, for now, I guess,* she thought, though that thought held its own pain. What was freedom, really? Was she really free if she could go anywhere that she wanted except the one place she wanted? Was she free if wherever she went, she was always looking over her shoulder for who could come? True, she wasn't in prison, but in a way, she was in her own kind of prison. *I miss home.*

Kellivar was decent, as far as cities went, with all styles of living she could wish for. It had those who had money to spend and lose, and it had those just trying to scrape by. There were people who would give her a hot meal or a warm bed some nights, and there were those who kicked her to the gutter as soon as she came around. There were people who worked hard for their living, and others who hardly worked at all. To put it simply, there were… people.

There was a lot of skill to walking properly, she thought to herself as she walked. The way you walked said something about who you were, and people noticed it whether they knew it or not, so she had practiced in many different ways. Some days she walked to earn sympathy. Most times she walked to not be seen. Today, however, she walked like someone with a purpose, keeping her posture erect and gaze steady so people who looked at her would see someone confident but simple. She glanced around casually, stopping on store products so people would see a curious customer, and she wore a bright friendly smile, because if nothing else, people said hi to a friendly girl.

Her clothing was practical today, neither of high quality nor shabby, of dark pants, short leather boots, and a hooded jacket covering a long form-fitting white tunic. They were the clothes of one who belonged in society but nothing more. *Dress to look like you belong,* her old mentor had said, *but not like you barely got there or have been there for too long to count, for then people will take notice of you and try to remember you.* Sometimes being remembered was good, but not when one needed to run. *Take the person following me, for example,* she thought to herself, shaking her head. *If he wasn't after me, I might be willing to give a few pointers.*

For about an hour now, ever since Adi left the prison, the man had followed her. At first, she used basic evasion techniques, like doubling back a few times or pausing at a booth and seeing if the figure paused as well. *A smart shadow would have recognized I was onto him,* Adi thought. *But this one clearly does not.* Even more interesting was the way the shadow moved, awkwardly, like he feared something or someone, though he didn't look encumbered in any way. That was a sure sign the man was used to wearing armor and not wearing any now, which also implied they had either served in the guard or were currently enlisted. *And a black cloak, really? And he was hooded? Does he really not understand how obvious he makes himself?* Then Adi had another thought that made her smile. *What if he does know how obvious he appears, and he does this all on purpose? Well now, the game just became far more interesting.*

She bit into an apple, suddenly realizing that she didn't remember where it had come from, only that she didn't have it earlier, but continued on. *Stealing comes so naturally now. I don't even think about the small grabs. I just walk, and things happen. Even some of the larger plans I don't think about. Oh well, I am who I am, taking any grab, any lock, any vault, any time. Well, maybe not from where those guys come from. Maybe I won't steal from there, or at least not from them... wait a second Adi,* she said to herself. *I don't know them, not enough to trust them. Enough to kind-of like them, sure, but they're outsiders, and outsiders can't be trusted. I would know, I am one, a fact people love reminding me of.*

Another thought struck her. *Bloody thinking, but nothing for it.* At no point in their conversation did the crew mention anything about either her skin or looks, and despite her unwillingness to trust anyone at once, she had to give them that much. Around Ildice in general, there were many who had given her trouble for being as much Larian as she was, and she'd received many unwanted advances. Compared to an average Ildician, she was smaller, shorter, and her skin was honey in color rather than pale. Her shoulder-length hair was dark and kept tied in the back, and her eyes were bright sapphire blue, starkly contrasted to the steel blue of typical Ildicians. Her smaller size did make for better quickness, thankfully, and her eyes and flirty smile did have a knack for getting herself out of situations most thieves would get stuck in. It helped make her the best at what she did. *I was built to be a thief, and a flirt. But those people don't see me as such. Ain't that something?*

She thought more about the assignment the High Lord had given her, an assignment she thought nothing of before, other than a chance to get free sooner. *Watch the crew, get to know them, and learn about their lives. Report back what you hear, and that will do for now.* "For now," was always a phrase used when something bigger was in the works. Any one of the interrogators would be able to do the same job and far quicker. A fellow criminal and a girl, however, would be received friendlier. *The High Lord wants me to gain their trust, not just the information, so he's looking for something else… What does he want…?*

"Hey, Olive!" a harsh voice behind her called, interrupting her thoughts. "What are you doing out so late?"

Yep, gotta love being me, she thought as she turned around. *And my skin really isn't that dark, either. Granted, if they called me 'honey' I'd probably hate that more…*

"Evening, good sirs," she said, attempting to sound meek as she turned around and bowed with her fist across her breast. "How may I be of service?" She sized up the three guards before her, making quick note of their stances, insignias, and weapons, and decided the one on the far right was the leader of this particular group. *Thank you, Deven, for all those tips years ago.*

"Well, see," the leader said casually, stretching, and flexing arms about as big around as Adi' body. "We just got off duty and we're mighty hungry, so you wouldn't mind sharing that food of yours with us, would you? Be a good girl, now, and help a few of your defenders out, eh?" The three laughed, and beneath her fixed smile Adi growled.

"You are in luck," she answered, pulling a second apple and a bit of cheese from her pockets. "I'm afraid it isn't much, but I offer all I have." *And if I hadn't passed that food cart a bit ago, I wouldn't even have this.*

"Well, this looks enough for one," the soldier on the far left said, shaking his head and looking down at the food. *Lieutenant Bareth, and the first is a lieutenant as well. The middle one was the only regular soldier, but two officers… that's so bloody perfect.* "But now that leaves two of us out. Say, how 'bout you spot us a bit of coin, eh? You know, something for a bit of drink to end our day. Surely you couldn't say no to that now?"

"Haven't any coin to spare, my good sirs, I'm afraid," Adi said, bowing her head and turning away. *Not like I'd give it to you anyway.* "Now, if you'll excuse me, it's late and I must be getting home."

"Hold a moment," Lieutenant Bareth said, holding up his hand. "You still haven't said what you were out so late for. The way you've avoided answering the question makes me wonder if I should press you more, take you in personally."

I was bloody occupied having a bribe stolen from me you half-baked, fish-headed, insult to humans everywhere. Outwardly, she answered, "I was visiting the prison, sirs. I have some friends in there, and they were downhearted." *Wow,* she thought to herself. *Telling the truth to a guard feels strange. If only that High Lord hadn't said that part about not telling anyone else about what was going on, my life would be easier. Then again, I doubt these guards would believe me.*

"That's funny," Lieutenant Bareth said. "I was stationed in the prison, and I don't remember you coming in."

"I stayed outside," Adi answered. "By the window. That one," she added, pointing to the middle guard. "He saw me."

"I don't recall seeing you," the guard answered in a dull monotone, and sighing, Adi thought, *of course you don't, because you could never have a story that would make mine believable.*

"I think you had better come with us," the first one said, pulling a set of chains from his belt. "We've gotten reports of suspicious behavior lately, by a character matching your description." *A weak excuse for a weak mind, of course. Oh well, time for some fun.*

"Actually, I've got a better idea," Adi said, laughing. "How about I race you there and meet you on the steps, alright? Later!"

Turning, she fled into the crowd, and grinned as she heard heavy boots on the stone street announcing their chase. She looked back and saw that Bareth had pulled ahead of the others and was fighting to gain on her. Though the man had been smiling through the whole exchange, his face was now full of fury and his eyes raged. *Lieutenant Bareth,* Adi thought, shaking her head. *Maybe one day, I'll find out why you hate me so much. Until then, we shall continue our little game of you chasing me and you always failing. Let's see if you've learned anything.*

Adi ducked into a dark side street, filled with clutter. A map of the city formed in her mind, and dodging random buckets, barrels, and other odds and ends, she planned her route quickly. Shouts rang out from the guards behind her and answering shouts from citizens trying to earn a good mark called out as Adi passed them. This wasn't the first time the citizens of this town proved not to be her friends, but at least it made the chase more fun.

She followed the road until it looped back to the main street and faded into the crowd of people. She saw the three guards come out of the back alley, looking confused, so she let the crowd part around her long enough for the three to catch a glimpse of her again before taking off. She ducked into the dark alley once more, laughing at the thought of leading them in circles, but made it only a few steps in before another figure had an arm around her waist. She was forced hard to the ground, a hand pushing her cheek into the dirt, and somehow another had wrapped securely around her wrist. *Brilliant.*

"Royal guard," a deep voice growled, and the cheers and chaos of citizens who felt they had taken part in the arrest fell silent. "You are now in my custody, and I would recommend that you keep quiet. For your own sake, I would keep struggling to a minimum."

"Yeah, or what?" Adi asked, struggling against grips that tightened slightly more. "Ow, easy!"

"Or you'll find I can apply more pressure," the man responded in the same, almost casual voice. "If you understand my meaning."

"Yeah, I hear ya," Adi said, resigning, and she felt the pressure in her neck decrease enough so she could turn to look up at her captor. The man wore a dark cloak with the hood up, but it was open to reveal a captain's uniform and a short sword buckled to his belt. Adi could only imagine the thoughts of the people around them, this dark cloaked figure catching a criminal. People would talk. "By the way," she added to the cloaked figure. "Nice eye patch, Eli. It looks like it's almost as dangerous working for the law as against it, eh?"

"You have no idea," the man chuckled. The three other guards marched up, breathing heavily but trying to hide it. "At ease, gentlemen, I'm taking this one myself."

"Identify yourself, citizen," Bareth demanded. "And release this girl to us."

"Captain Spencer Eli," the hooded man replied, taking off the hood. The three guards quickly stood at attention. "At ease lieutenants, sergeant."

"Sir," Bareth said, taking control. "We have this one for evading arrest and for reported suspicious activity. We were going to question her down at the guard house."

"And what suspicious activity is she being questioned for?" the captain asked, staring down the men with his good eye.

"Well, sir, she claimed she was visiting the prison," the other lieutenant, Carby, answered. "And her story doesn't match with that of the guards stationed there."

"I was visiting my friends, you bloody..." Adi began before the captain cut her off.

"Be quiet," he said. "You'll get your chance to talk. Now, lieutenant, you remember everyone that enters the prison, correct?"

"Yes, sir," Bareth answered crisply. "Everyone registers at the front gate, when they enter and when they leave."

"Good," the captain said, nodding. "Now, do you remember everyone that goes past the prison?"

"No, sir," Bareth answered. "I'm stationed inside, and when I'm relieved, I'm stationed by the palace gates."

"As I thought," the captain answered. "But you," he added, gesturing to the sergeant. "You were on guard outside the prison gates, were you not?"

"Yes, sir," the guard answered, swallowing. "When I'm not on patrol."

"And could you explain to me," the captain continued. "What is your job outside the prison and what does it entail?"

"I prevent people from entering without permission, sir," the sergeant answered.

"Ah, I see," the captain answered, and Adi felt the grips and pressure lighten a little more. "So as far as you're concerned, the only people you need to worry about are those coming in, or trying to come in, not those simply walking around?"

"Well, yes, sir," the sergeant said, looking slightly relieved. "Yes, that is correct."

"So," the captain continued, and Adi bit her lip to prevent herself from smiling. "It would make sense, then, that in the interest of protecting your fellow guards and citizen, you would have no reason to suspect someone not showing suspicious behavior, thus you would have no reason to remember them?"

"Well, yes, that would be true..."

"As I thought," the captain said, in a tone that said the conversation was finished, then lowered his voice to a near whisper. "I will deal with her myself. You three are dismissed."

"Yes, sir," they said, saluting. They turned briskly and marched away, and the crowd dispersed, leaving Adi and Eli alone.

The captain pulled Adi to her feet, but kept her arm pinned behind her back and held a tight hold on her collar. "Wait until we're away from everyone," he whispered. Adi nodded.

"There was another on my tail," Adi whispered back. "Another cloaked figure." The captain shook his head.

"I saw him when you were first stopped," he answered. "I'm not sure who he's with, but he's not one of ours, or at least, he's not one of mine. He could be the High Lord's personal guard, or part of a smaller branch, but I've heard nothing from my superiors. Now, start drifting off to your right."

"Slumville, seriously?" Adi asked, groaning.

"Can you think of a city guard of any kind who would go in there without a platoon?" the captain asked, then chuckled when Adi merely shrugged and grumbled. When they entered one of the back alleys, the change in scenery was instant. Clean roads became muddied, dirty paths, and polished walls of stone became run-down cracked buildings with rotting wood and rudimentary repairs. Where the main road was open and well-lit by the setting sun, these alleys were covered, and light was scarce.

The first couple of passages revealed a few questionable characters, characters that grinned at the two of them threateningly as they passed by. By herself, Adi wouldn't have thought much of them. They wouldn't have even seen her, for that matter, for darkness and dark alleys were her friends. Her six-and-a-half-foot tall friend, however, stood out very easily, but once one caught a look from his eye that glowed like liquid fire in torchlight, he was just as quickly avoided. The few daring enough to come close enough to see the scar under his eye patch shied away.

Adi and the captain came back to the main road and followed it until they reached the officer's district. Homes here were simple and efficient, neat, and pleasant to look at. There were small strips of grass out front, some having a couple flowers or other plants, but this captain's place was minimal. The home was made of stone, with two floors, and a roof of black slate.

They entered the house and Adi flopped down into one of Eli's large, padded chairs. The main room was sparely furnished, having a few armchairs and some tables, but the walls held a couple of paintings and hand-drawn maps, which Adi let her eyes linger on.

"Nice place, Eli," Adi said, and the captain bowed his head in thanks. "Gotta say, though, for someone like you, it's not nearly as nice as it should be."

"Honest life isn't always the wealthy life," Eli said, taking off his cloak and sitting down in the chair across from Adi. "At least it's stable."

"Still, I can't believe you went and chose the colors, though," Adi said, shaking her head. "What happened?"

"You know how things go," Eli said, sighing. "The old team breaks up, we go our separate ways. I decided to go with a more stable life, which isn't easy for someone of my particular skill set, except of course for the military. There were some openings, so I enlisted, rising quickly, though, to become an officer."

"You don't sound too happy about it," Adi said. Eli shook his head.

"Even stable life isn't very stable," Eli said. "A year back, some people were arrested and then died resisting, and a lot of citizens were outraged. Tensions grew between the guards and civilians, with many civilians ambushing guards on patrol. A few of my friends in the force have been stabbed in the back and then left to bleed out. Rioting rose in other areas, to the point that we ended up having to withdraw our presence when it became too dangerous to remain, leaving the army to move in and subdue them. Entire villages, mind, entire villages have had to be subdued… and there are rumors that people may try to destroy even this city.

"Between you and me, Ildice is threatened by outside forces, but I fear internal forces will tear us apart sooner. It pains me to say, but yes, our own people are more of a threat than those beyond our borders."

"Is that what happened to your eye?" Adi asked. "Some hoodlum decided to go at you…" She paused as Eli removed the patch, revealing a perfectly functioning bronze colored eye underneath.

"It wasn't me that lost an eye," Eli said, looking at the patch. "My brother… I just received word that he fell, when stationed out at Tilgal. He was a lieutenant, though he deserved more, wanting to be stationed around Chanost, I believe. The details of his death are withheld, but I know. Things are about to get far more terrible."

"I'm sorry," Adi said. "Why don't you quit, then? You've got more skill than most people, far more than just your martial ability. Why put yourself through the trouble? You don't deserve that."

"Call it duty," Eli sighed. "Too much hope in people, I guess, too much desire to make amends, maybe. I don't know, but I just think if enough of us decide to leave, then it's the average citizen, the innocent citizen, who gets hurt the most, and I don't want that on my conscience. What about you? What happened to you?"

"Similar to your story, just less honorable," Adi answered. "The team breaks up and we go our separate ways, but with me I had a pretty solid reputation among the underground, so I found a few other crews to run with from time to time. My face was too well known among the respectable crowd, mind, so any honest work was out. Not too long ago, one of the crews felt I was expendable which got me tossed in prison."

"That's rough," Eli said, shaking his head. "I heard about that, though."

"Could have been worse," Adi said. "I met some interesting people while I was there, a ship's crew from up north. Odd people, lots of honor, you'd like 'em. They got thrown in for making the High Lord's kid mad or something. I was freed a few days after they were thrown in, under the condition I spy on them. So yeah, interesting."

"Who are you spying for?" Eli asked, opening a bottle, and taking a drink. "I have some resources, now. I might be able to get you away from them."

"Not likely," Adi said, shaking her head and reaching for the drink. "Not unless you've got sway with the High Lord. He's the one who requested my services." Eli passed the bottle to her, and she took a drink which left her coughing. Eli laughed and took the bottle back. "Wow, that stuff could burn through stone, let alone my throat."

"What does the High Lord want with them?" Eli asked, taking another drink, the spirits leaving no noticeable effects.

"That's the thing," Adi said, leaning forward. "I don't know. He didn't say, and I didn't quite feel right asking at the time. What's even stranger, though, is that he threw them in the lower prisons."

"I haven't heard of any terrible crimes, not of that nature," Eli said, scratching at his beard. "In fact, as I recall, yours was the worst lately."

"As I thought, which means something else is going on here," Adi said, excitedly. "To be held in the lower prisons, there has to be more to this than just making some royal kid angry. Or, possibly, they pulled off the greatest heist the city has ever seen, but it's so big the higher ups cannot let anyone know about it. Or maybe they are preparing for some great conquest and they're from far across the ocean, like the dark continent..."

"Or something else entirely," Eli interrupted.

"Yes, or that," Adi agreed. "And I want to know what that something is."

Eli laughed. "Adi, I know that look. There's no way we could pull it off, not nearly as quickly as you're wanting."

"You don't even know what I'm planning," Adi said, but Eli raised a hand.

"You're planning to steal prisoners from a royal prison, and steal information from a High Lord, mind, having only a city guard and a thief."

Mew

"And a cat, apparently," Eli laughed, shaking his head at the cat that appeared on his windowsill. "Hello, Skritches."

Mew

"Ok, so you do know what I'm thinking," Adi admitted, giving a half smile and a shrug as Skritches jumped into her lap and purred at her petting. "Still, a part of you knows you're curious."

"Except we won't be getting paid," Eli pointed out. "Unless, of course, you have buyers for this information?"

"No, no buyers," Adi confessed. "But that's a minor detail. Besides, it won't be too much, just a basic smuggling plan."

"Smuggling?" Eli asked. "How do you figure?"

"Oh, well, we'll be bringing them food, too," Adi said sheepishly, shrugging. Eli burst out laughing.

"Let me see if I'm following correctly," Eli said, catching his breath. "This big plan of yours involves not only getting a few things but also giving a few others as well. The information we get stays with us, so we get no profit other than satisfying curiosity, and the risks are far greater than any plan we've done before because we'll be doing this all under a High Lord's nose. Does that sound about right?"

"Well, um, I guess so," Adi answered. "So, are you in or not?"

"Adi, my old friend, you knew I was in since I started asking questions," Eli answered, resigned. "It's making it work that gives me concern, and don't ask about what part, because you know bloody well what part I'm talking about. But back in the 'old times' we had a plan before we did something. Do you have one now, or do we need to make that, too?"

"Ok, maybe I haven't thought this out completely," Adi admitted. "Still, I can't trust my old team to make this happen, which is a shame because they were good. Let's start with the guards; do you know any that would be sympathetic to them?"

"No," Eli said. "Or rather, I doubt any would. It will be strangers and foreigners we'll be dealing with, and Ildicians have never taken too well to any kind of stranger, not unless they've been decorated with ribbons and rank first. If they had been citizens, though, it might be a different story."

"What about the old team, then?" Adi asked. "Do you keep contact with any of them?"

"Nathaniel finally got married," Eli said, then laughed at Adi' surprised look. "I know. He and Sophia finally did something. They took their share of our takes and started their own business up in Vandor. They have a couple of kids, and she spends time painting. They're legit now."

"What about Alex or Deven, then?" Adi asked. "What are they up to?"

"Who knows," Eli said, shaking his head. "You're asking what a professional forgery artist with a perfect memory, and a con artist who can change his appearance in seconds and mimic any accent, are doing right now? Anything they want. If they are working together still, finding them could be near impossible."

"So, we're on our own then," Adi said, gloomily. "At least for the time being."

"For the time being, yes," Eli agreed. "But for your plan to work, as much as I understand it, that will have to change. Whether you see it now or not, we will need a team, and equipment, and added clearance to the various layers of the city. That is just on the surface of my thoughts, though. Come back tomorrow so we can figure out all the details to your plan."

"Just so long as we can make it fast," Adi said. "They weren't doing so well when I saw them last."

Eli looked at Adi, curious. "My friend, you've made this personal. I thought you always tried to keep that out of the job."

"It's strange," Adi said, shaking his head. "But something about these guys hits me, something I can't place or put a finger on... oh, I almost forgot, these are yours." She reached into her pocket and pulled out a small bag of coins. "I swiped it earlier, when I thought you were, well, someone else."

Eli shook his head, grinning as he caught the bag Adi tossed to him. He counted out a few coins and passed them back. "Here, the first part of our plan can at least be legal. Get some food, for yourself and your friends. I'll get you a schedule of the guards' shifts so you can sneak it in. Remember, bars are about as far apart as your hand so keep the items small. I will do what I can to keep attention from you, but I won't be working at the prison for a month so I can't distribute. I will let you know when I hear anything else. Where are you staying, so I can get a hold of you again?"

"Oh, well, I jump around," Adi shrugged. "Lately I've been in prison, so… yeah."

"I'll keep a window open," Eli said. "Just don't make too much noise, I start when the sun rises. The guest bed upstairs is made if you'd like to stay here."

"Thanks," Adi said, graciously. "Almost like old times, us under one roof and all."

"Those were good times," Eli agreed. "That was too long ago, and times aren't what they used to be. Rest well, little friend. You too, Adi."

"Rest well, Eli," Adi called after him. Night fell, but her mind refused her sleep. Eli's words played in her mind, about why she was doing this. *Why do I want to do this? There's not much that would be gained from helping this crew, not proportional to the risk taken. They aren't getting out and I think they know that, but trying to get them out could cause serious problems later on. Am I crazy for considering it? Or am I crazy because this actually feels right? Adi, you know what you're supposed to do, why you're here. What is going on?*

Skritches purred on her lap, asleep.

Chapter 18

The air was cold, and the sky was colored a bleak gray on the morning of the fifth day of Calian's imprisonment. The cell was dreary as well, with the crew subdued and alone with their thoughts, but some like Seth and Paul seemed at peace about the quiet. Joshian sat in the corner with Jemas, the two discussing the state of the crew and which ones were having the hardest time of it all, and it struck Calian that Jemas really was the perfect first officer. Not only did he have a solid understanding of the crew, but he had a solid understanding of Joshian. It was a side of Jemas he had never seen before, and had no idea even existed.

"Rise and shine, sleepy heads," called a cheerful voice from the other side of the barred window. "Up you get. The sun is, well, it's somewhere behind the clouds, and the weather is, well at least it would be warm if the clouds went away, and, um, okay, the weather stinks and it'll probably rain, but get up quick anyway." The voice giggled, and Calian smiled in recognition of Adi' voice.

"Too tired," Seth said in a groggy voice. "Wake me tomorrow."

"You'll never get up then," Andrius mumbled back.

Calian heard Adi sigh, amused, and then a wrapped bundle flew through the bars and hit Seth on the cheek.

"Ow," Seth grumbled, opening his eyes, weakly. His eyes widened when he spotted what had hit him and unwrapped the cloth. "Wake up, there's food!"

"Keep it down," Adi whispered, laughing quietly. "But yes. I've got some bites to hold you over for a bit, but I need you to move quickly before I'm caught."

All were up now, and the subdued atmosphere was replaced with lightness once more. Joshian stepped forward and extended his hand through the bars.

"Many blessings to you, my friend," Joshian said. "We cannot give anything in return, but if we can find a way to repay your kindness, we will."

Adi gripped his hand, and something crossed over her face before she released Joshian's hand and ran off. She didn't return for the rest of the day.

Though the food was little, consisting of some apples, bread, and cheese, it gave them all new strength, new life, and a new hope. Jemas and Joshian collected everything and began to divvy it up, and Petorius and Andrius passed over the share to the other cell. Seth and Sailis told a few jokes, and then Dayved started a song that most joined in with. As Calian talked with Jhonas, Joshian stood up, and conversations stopped.

"My friends," Joshian began, standing by the door to their cell so those across the hall could hear easily. "My crew, hear me. I know our time here has not been ideal, not by any stretch of the mind, but we are still here. We are still alive, and we are still Firebrands. This is just another trial we're facing, nothing more, and we have faced trials before."

"Easy to say, mate," one of the crewmen from across the hall, Thom, said. "Now that we have food, anyways. And since we have food and strength returning, I think it's time to plan how we're going to escape from here."

"Thom's right," another of Thom's cell mates, Jadas, said. "Does anyone have any sort of plan for getting out of here?"

"I have one," Joshian said. "It will the end of our crew, though, and not everyone will be out…"

"Yeah, not worth it," Sailis said. "Sorry, Captain, but that's not going to happen."

"Even if it means freedom?" Joshian asked. "This is more than just my pride. The kid has his issues with me, and if my staying in here means you all can get out, I have to consider it."

"We are who we are," Jemas said, shrugging. "You said it yourself, we're Firebrands. We don't like the situation, sure, but I think I speak for everyone when I say how can I accept freedom knowing it's cost you yours?"

"We could try to break out," Jadas answered. "We could overpower a guard when they open our cell next."

"It's the end result that's important," Thom countered. "If we get free, it doesn't matter how. Sure, I'd like them to come to their senses, but if that's not going to happen, then we need to do something about it."

"I won't support a break-out," Paul declared, adamantly. "We could try reasoning with them, though, and I'm sure if an audience were requested then it'll be granted."

"Cap doesn't negotiate with men like him, though," Jhonas countered.

"Well, I wouldn't go that far," Joshian said. "I'm not opposed to talking. Still, we do have to ask, and answer, do we stand together in this, accepting our fates together or individually?"

"Cap, forgive me for being cliché," Jemas said. "But sitting in prison, thrown in by a high lord's son, this feels like something out of a story, so I'm going to just say it. Follow your heart, mate, and just do what you feel called to do. We're all with you, whatever you decide."

"Are we?" Joshian asked. He looked around the cell and saw everyone's determined affirmation. "Jadas?"

"We're with you," Jadas answered after a pause. "Whatever your decision, we're behind you."

Though Adi had walked the halls of the palace many times before, she still felt uneasy. There was power here, in the walls, in the floor, in the tapestries, a power of history, stories, and generations. She was familiar with people having power over her, or thinking they had power over her, and she was familiar with how to take as much advantage of those situations as possible, but this power settled heavily upon her, permeated her, and elated her. Her footsteps had echoed off the walls, but on the softer carpet the sound was silenced. The eeriness was only offset by the pair of guards sent to escort her, though they talked none, not even with each other, so Adi' mind wandered to the events of the past few days.

"Hello, Dec," the High Lord said, breaking into her thoughts. Recovering quickly, she saw she had entered the throne room and was now before the High Lord. "How are the prisoners faring?" She gulped.

"They are as well as they can be, I suppose," Adi answered, swaying awkwardly on the balls of her feet, and cringing at the name. "But your majesty, if you don't mind, I prefer going by Adi. I used to go by Dec, but that brings up too many bad memories."

"Alright, Adi," the High Lord acknowledged, nodding his head. "I think I like that better, actually. Now, tell me about our guests."

Adi looked around at the various robed advisors and armed guards. She looked at the High Lord and his son, who watched her carefully. She looked each person in the eye, met their accusatory or judgmental stares evenly, and sighed. Gathering her thoughts, she told them the stories the crew had shared with her, adding details about the village they were from, as well as the crew's thoughts and opinions about Kellivar, and about Ildice in general. She also shared her own thoughts and opinions of the crew, and every positive comment earned a look of scorn for the High Lord's son. She added, finally, the details about the city and the nation she had shared. The High Lord listened closely and nodded thoughtfully as she spoke.

"Sir," Adi said, hesitantly, after finishing her report. "I fear the little I learn is not much use, mostly because I'm not sure what to ask. Are there any details you want to know specifically, any direction of information you would like me to go down? It helps gathering information when I know what questions to ask."

"No, all you've shared has satisfied my curiosity," the High Lord said, dismissingly. "Well done, you are free to go for now."

"Thank you, my lord," Adi said, bowing awkwardly. She left the High Lord's presence, followed by the escort guards, out of the palace. As she walked, her mind worked frantically, wondering about what she had said, wondering how it had helped the High Lord, wondering what she had given. She sifted through the information but came to no conclusion. Frustrated, she kept walking out the front gate, and the guards let her be.

Sitting at Eli's place with a plate of steak, potatoes, light greens, and a cup of ale before her, Adi massaged her temples. The few days of playing a street urchin that Eli had taken in meant she could come and go freely from Eli's place, even during the daytime, and some of the neighbor officers had even been friendly. Bareth, now, gave her a berth, either ignoring her completely or just brushing by without a word, but both were improvements. Around town, too, after trying to appear as if her time in prison had changed her, shop keepers regarded her as a regular customer.

"That's all that happened, I tell you," Adi said, taking a large bite of steak and then setting her fork down. "The High Lord, he asks me to spy on them, but he never says what I'm spying for. He never asks for specific information, just more of the same general questions about their lives and stories of growing up. It doesn't make any sense."

"Maybe not on the surface," Eli agreed, nodding before taking a gulp of his drink. "But the High Lord is not a man to be trifled with. Underestimate him, and you may find yourself trapped."

"That's the problem," Adi answered. "I've looked, I've thought, I've analyzed, but I'm not seeing anything."

"What if we look at it from another direction," Eli pondered aloud. "What does the High Lord learn about them through your stories and conversation?"

"Their daily lives, I told you," Adi said, chewing.

"You've told me many things so far," Eli chuckled. "Now let me tell you one interpretation of what you've told me. They come from a small island, staying apart from most people. They're given spears at a young age for some reason, and their leaders are called 'captains.' This captain is supposed to be one of the youngest captains to be raised and his men think very highly of his skills, thus implying the others are equally or more skilled. Now the High Lord has a chance to see how the crew and captain interact with each other and with others, to see who they trust. Quite simply, the High Lord is looking at whether they are a threat to his nation or whether they will be in the future, and also how he can use that information to his advantage."

"Then they have to get free immediately," Adi said. "They're going to be killed, or worse, used…"

"Calm down," Eli said. "Don't jump to conclusions yet. I simply named possibilities, based on one interpretation. There are probably many more that I don't know about, and those only because of the information you've told me. The high lord may be receiving other information from other sources so no one source knows everything. We've had jobs like this in the past."

"That's true," Adi agreed.

"One thing I've been thinking about a lot, though," Eli said, scratching his chin. "You've mentioned getting them out a lot. Well, how do you plan to do it?"

"We'll need to steal the key, naturally," Adi said, counting off her fingers. "Then, well, it would have to be at night, where there's lighter duty on the prison. We would have to take out the guards, too, and we can't use the windows, so it'd have to be through the front door…"

"Ok, stop," Eli said, holding up his hand. "Ignoring the obvious problem with the plan, let us start with the biggest one. What are we going to do with them once they are out? There would be about twenty foreigners loose in a city that believes them to be criminals. Where do we put them, or take them?"

"Well, I haven't thought about that part yet," Adi admitted. "I'm not sure, but I know we have to get them out."

"Look, I'm not trying to discourage you," Eli said, seeing Adi' disappointment. "I like this side of you, this compassion and desire to help others. It reminds me of the days we were working together. I am just saying you are still lacking the ability to see the bigger picture. Now, do I know the bigger picture? No, I do not, but if we can't see it then there's no way to know if we're just being pulled along with it. So, let's turn this around. We will start by targeting the High Lord himself. You already have his trust, and you already have a role to play, and yes, I have a feeling Adi is still an alias. You've done the hardest part, now, we just play for time. Also, learn more from the crew, learn everything you can. Then hold back the knowledge you need to."

"What are you going to be doing?" Adi asked.

"Trying to use that time," Eli chuckled. "Like I said, we need more hands, more people we can trust."

"Well then, good luck to you," Adi said. "Also, you were right, Adi being an alias and all. It's Cesilia. That's my real name, though I'd prefer none to know. I'm not sure who I can trust anymore."

"Thank you for trusting me, then," Eli said.

Sunlight poked through the clouds to cast beams of treasured light upon the city, but the ground still took its time in drying. The air was warmer and less muggy, but a week in the prisons was still far more than Seth cared for, and no improvement of the conditions would change that. The crew was far happier and joyful, complaining had decreased, and their bellies were content; since Adi had first brought them their first meal, guards had begun bringing them food regularly. The fact that Timothy had gone without for only three days while they endured five did not escape any of them, but they had endured worse.

A shadow crossed the window's light, and Seth looked up to see Adi by the bars.

"Welcome back," Seth said, standing up as Adi sat down.

"Good to be back," she said, smiling. "Sorry I don't have anything for you guys today."

"Don't worry about it," he said. "The guards have started bringing us meals, now, so we're surviving. It's just good to see you."

"I wish I could do more, though," she said, tucking a strand of hair behind her ear.

"We'll be alright," Seth assured her. "We've been through worse."

"Really?" she asked, skeptical, raising an eyebrow.

"Sure," Seth said. "Out at sea, we've had storms that have broken our ships, forcing us to rebuild right there in the middle of nowhere. We've had other times where we've had to throw out food that molded. We've had times where half the crew came down with some kind of sickness and we had to care for them and get the ship home. Sometimes we had help, but most of the time it was us. Here we've got at least some help, and we're all together. We are Firebrands, after all."

"You people are strange," Adi said, laughing. "Most people, by now, would be trying to make a deal with the jailer or the High Lord, or somebody. Most would have sold out even their friends, but you guys…"

"We're family," Seth shrugged. "And we're a crew. You don't sell out your crew."

"When the price is right, it happens," Adi mumbled. "Still, your place sounds nice. Your people, too. I wish it were my home."

"When we get out, we'll find a way to get you over there," Seth said.

"Yeah, good luck with that," Adi said, shaking her head.

"We will," Seth laughed. "One day, we'll get out, and then we'll go home. At the least, they must do something with us if we die in here. Well, I hope they do something with us, otherwise the next person who gets thrown in here will be seriously creeped out, and after a bit we'll start to smell…"

"I get the picture, thank you for that image," Adi said, shaking her head. "I really don't like that kind of talk."

"I'm sorry," Seth said. "I didn't mean anything by it."

"I hope not," Adi said. "I've seen too many give up in here, too many who felt that this was their end and did something about it."

"We're not going to give up," Seth assured her, reaching his hand through the bars, which she took. "We've got each other, and we've got family waiting for us. I'd say don't worry, but I get the feeling that won't help."

"No, not really," Adi answered, squeezing his hand before letting go. "Well, maybe a little."

The palace felt almost like a second home to Adi, now, with the amount of time she spent visiting and walking the halls. The guards accepted her and now smiled in a friendly manner, and the Captain, Cornell, became a fun conversationalist, to the point she looked forward to coming to these meetings. She shook her head and tried to think. She was not just here to give the High Lord her report. She was here to try to get her friends free. Things would need to be delicate.

She walked up to the throne as she had done many times before and bowed. "My Lord," she began. "I'm here to give my report."

"Very good, Adi," the High Lord said, smiling, though his face looked weary. "Come, come, and tell me what you've learned today."

"Well, my lord," Adi began, carefully. "They have… changed."

"Changed?" the High Lord asked, tilting his head. "If you would kindly explain, I am not in a mood to puzzle out that which I don't understand right now."

"If you recall, sir," Adi said. "In my earlier reports, I told you they were subdued, and I felt they were nearly at the point of breaking. Well, instead of breaking, there is now a peace about them, a new determination. I've seen people in prison, I've seen people give up, but when I've seen people get like this, they don't break, and may fight harder to keep going, if you know what I mean, my lord."

"I do," the High Lord said, nodding. "Well, that is enough, then. Thank you, Adi, but this will also be the last I need of your services, at least for this task, though I hope to call on you at some point in the future. When people cannot be turned and broken, I cannot use them, so they shall be disposed of.

"I can tell you, now, that was what I looked for, and now that they are of no use or can be of use to me, well, they are still criminals. I have prepared a stipend for your services, as well as a bonus that I believe will be acceptable, and I hope that you cause no more problems to my streets.

"Captain Cornell," the High Lord added, turning his attention away from Adi, his words faded and muffled from the shock she felt. "Inform the prisoners that they will be taken to the gallows and hung on the sixth hour, tomorrow, and then send word to the executioners."

"Begging your pardon, my lord," the captain said, bowing. Adi allowed herself a moment of hope. "The Sarrath happens tomorrow, and the priests do not like anyone killed on their most holy of days. I am assuming, of course, you'll have the execution held in the palace gallows?"

"Yes, I shall," the High Lord answered. "And thank you for that reminder. No, we won't do it on that day… and I don't care for the day after, either. The day after that will be better, with larger crowds. Thank you for that, Captain."

"Yes, sir," Captain Cornell said, bowing his head, and Adi thought she heard the man's voice shaking, and a look of pain crossed his face. "Shall I inform them now, then?"

"Yes, you are dismissed," the High Lord said. "Thank you. The both of you are free to go."

Adi and the captain bowed their heads and left, though once outside of the throne room they both shared a look of regret. The captain put a comforting hand on her shoulder before taking his platoon of guards and marching to the prison. Adi waited until they were out of sight, and then turned towards the officers' quarters and ran.

Pacing back and forth across the floor of Eli's home, Adi fumed openly while Eli sat quietly, smoking a pipe.

"Eli, they're sentenced to death!" Adi said again. "Are you not listening to me? Time has run out, completely. Three days, that's all. Worse, I hastened this. I shouldn't have been so dense, saying their spirits wouldn't break. This is my fault. I must do something. I have to do this."

"It's a fool's mission," Eli said from his chair. "We don't have nearly the resources, the people, not to mention the time to make it work."

"I've been talking with some of the smaller crews around town," Adi said. "I'll finalize things later, but most of the work will be done by them, so we won't need to worry about that. We don't need much in the way of equipment, because again, everyone will take care of their own parts. Look, I know even then it'll be a fool's chance, at best, and I've been a fool before, but for some reason I feel like being a fool rather than a coward."

"You don't have to be either, though," Eli said, sighing. "Whether you know it or not, I've always been watching you from the shadows, especially when you started running with that other group, and when you were with them, you stopped thinking, started making moves that didn't make any sense, almost like you wanted to get caught. You were one of the best thieves out there, legendary among anyone who had tried to pull anything. Captain Tolmey, a junior lieutenant at the time, called you his most worthy of adversaries. Yes, capturing you was the foremost event that led to his promotion."

"The game wasn't any fun anymore," Adi shrugged. "Honestly, it was like it didn't matter anymore. Nothing really mattered, for that matter. Now, I'm not doing it for the game. It's like when we were working together, back when we were helping people. I like doing that kind of work. That work mattered, and these people matter. It feels important again."

"So, when do we enact the final stage?" Eli asked.

"Does this mean you're in?" Adi asked, grinning.

"I've always been in," Eli said, giving a slight smile. "Ever since you first started, I've been in."

"That's something I wanted to ask you about, also," Adi said. "All this talk about going straight and working with the colors and being legal... why are you helping me?"

"You are my friend, and always have been," Eli said. "Like a little sister, and I don't want to see anything bad happen to you."

"Yeah, bad stuff isn't much fun," Adi laughed. "Alright, now, our part will be the simplest. We don't need to get them out immediately. All we must do is make the guards think they got out, by sneaking them into another cell and then making it look like they left in a hurry. I'll alert the guard and lead them on a mighty good chase, and then in all the chaos, while the guards are away and occupied, they can leave on their own. We'll get a few uniforms to some of them, too, and they can lead small groups out at a time. No bloodshed, no harm to anyone, yes, I've thought this out a lot. The unfortunate part is they won't be able to get to their ship, but done right, we can get the groups to the Western Gate and then they'll at least be able to survive in the wild until they can get to a village."

"So, you are speaking sense," Eli said, approvingly. "Then go take care of the rest of your part. I have a few more things to do today, but I'll meet you back here later tonight. Good luck."

"Won't need it," Adi chuckled. "We've got skill, that's better than luck."

Chapter 19

Silence fell over the two cells after Captain Cornell pronounced their sentence. Joshian heard the words, but it took a while to fully process them.

Death comes to us all, he thought. *We all know that it will happen eventually. Every day we step onto a ship knowing it could be our last... but I never thought it would come this way. At least I don't have to be the one telling this to my crew, but in a way, I wish it were. Still, something feels off about all this, but I can't quite place it.*

"So," Paul said, breaking the silence. "I guess this really is our end."

"Not the end I would have preferred," Joshian said. "But it is what it is."

"At least we're in it together, sir," Seth said. "Firebrands to the end."

"Not sir," Joshian said, shaking his head. "Not in my last days. I'm just Joshian, the same as I was before I became a captain and got everyone into this mess. If I'm going to die here, I want to die as me, as just a man."

"Begging your pardon," Andrius said. "But you're not just a man. You are our captain, and we made a pledge to follow you. Seth is right, we're Firebrands to the end, and part of that means as a crew standing behind their captain. Then again, you always were a captain long before you were raised officially, so I'm sorry, but I will not deny what you are. None of us will."

"Fair enough," Joshian acknowledged. "Very well. Captain Cornell, thank you for informing us. I am glad it was you, as you're one of the few to show us genuine friendship, and I'm comforted by the regret I hear in your voice. I do have one request, though, if possible, and if it may be allowed."

"Name it," the captain said. "I will do everything in my power to honor it."

"Our families deserve to know what happened to us," Joshian said. "If you could bring parchment, ink, and some pens, then that would be greatly appreciated. Also, a last meal wouldn't be frowned upon."

"I can make that happen," Cornell said. "I'll even make sure whatever you write is delivered, whatever it takes." He started to leave but paused. "For what it's worth, Captain, I don't agree with what was done to you, nor do I really understand why it was. I do truly regret that a man like you will find his end like this, because if your crew can find faith in you here, then you must be a truly remarkable man. I wish I had known you longer."

"You're a good man, Cornell," Joshian responded. "Farewell, Captain."

"Farewell, Captain," Cornell said in turn. He stepped away, and soon his footsteps faded to silence.

An unnatural weight of oppression hung around Isaiah, who confined himself to his room to think. The proclamation of the impending death of the crew had been made a while ago, but still, Isaiah could not bring himself to believe it. He paced, he thought, he remembered the boy he had helped raise, and wept. *Oh, Kevian, why of all times do you choose now to be such a fool! Why do you choose to dishonor the memory of your father in this way?*

He left his room and made for the throne room, but finding it empty, went ahead to the council chamber. The guards admitted him, and he entered to find the High Lord writing a letter, while Timothy sat studying. The High Lord looked up when he entered and smiled.

"Master Isaiah," Kevian greeted him. "I wondered how long it would take."

"My lord," Isaiah said, trying to balance tact with the need to speak openly. "Far be it for me to speak against a judgement or ruling of yours."

"And yet I ask for it," Kevian said. "As we are in this room, now, speak as you always have."

"My lord," Isaiah began, but Kevian interrupted him.

"Kevian," he said. "Speak as you always have in here."

"Alright, Kevian," Isaiah began. "I do not feel your judgement in all matters concerning these crewmen has been right. In fact, I don't believe your judgement in any matter concerning these crewmen has been right, from their imprisonment, their treatment, and now their death. You have fallen far from the man you were, and I am here to inform you that should they die, I will not remain by your side."

"This is an outrage!" Timothy declared, rising from his place. "How dare you speak that way against my father? Beg your forgiveness now or accept what comes!"

"Be silent!" Isaiah ordered, straightening to his full height nearly a head above Timothy, who visibly recoiled. "And I will speak that way to you as well since you clearly need to hear it. I speak the way I do because it is right. I speak the way I do because innocent men were not allowed to speak and defend themselves. I speak this way because you yourself are in the wrong, and if you continue throwing into prison anyone who challenges you, you will be left alone. Finally, I speak the way I do, because I serve a higher power, a greater master. I will not beg forgiveness!"

"Nor will you have to, thank you Isaiah," the High Lord said calmly. Both Isaiah and Timothy turned to look at him, and Timothy's mouth was open wide in shock.

"But father," Timothy began, but the High Lord raised his hand.

"Timothy," the High Lord began. "I would like you to meet Isaiah, the man who has been my advisor and teacher since I was born, the one man whose voice I've come to respect above any other. Out in front of the people, he lets me be the High Lord." At that, he chuckled. "But in here, he lets me be just a man, especially when he needs to tell me where I go wrong. I have made many wrong decisions in the past, and he has been there to correct me. Sometimes he's been gentle, but other times, like now, he's needed to be a bit more forceful.

"You're going to be the High Lord one day, and when you do, you're going to find you make many more mistakes than you thought you would. When that happens, you are going to need someone next to you whom you can trust to tell you when you are wrong, so you don't stay being wrong. It is not a weakness surrounding yourself with people who know more than you. Now, I must speak with Isaiah alone."

"Yes, father," Timothy said, and with a sigh, left.

Isaiah watched Timothy go, letting a slight smile play on his face. *Kevian expected me to come.*

"I wasn't wrong about the prisoners," the High Lord said, once the door closed, and Isaiah let his smile drop. "Or at least, I wasn't completely wrong. It's an unfortunate world, indeed, where one must do wrong in order to do right."

"I must confess I do not understand," Isaiah admitted. "Tell me, what's on your mind right now?"

"Far too much," Kevian sighed. "The first thing involves why you and my son were sent off to begin with, the issue of raiding parties along the Western Road. Those attacks are still happening, even with armed guards, so I'm closing the road at the Gangburg crossroads. I have sent a patrol to secure the boarder, but something will have to be done on Ebaven's end. Also, I have reason to suspect they are more than just bandits."

Shuffling in the pile of papers on the table before him, Kevian pulled out a small strip of paper and handed it to Isaiah.

"The shadow has taken on shape," Isaiah read aloud. "Nightmares are in the waking world. Darkness approaches."

"It's quite poetic," Kevian commented. "I might be able to appreciate it and then disregard it, if this was the only such note of these I've seen. Unfortunately, it is not, for I have received many rumors, but nothing I've been able to prove until a sergeant came riding in and presented this message to my gate."

He pulled from another box a black clawed hand and a curved dagger of foreign design.

"When did the sergeant arrive?" Isaiah asked in a tight voice.

"As timing would have it," Kevian replied. "It was a few days before you arrived back."

"Kythraul," Isaiah mumbled.

"So, they do have a name, Lord Adonari," Kevian acknowledged. "Be at peace, Master Isaiah," he added quickly in response to Isaiah's inquisitive look. "I've suspected you to be much more than you seem for a long time, and I'm honored that one such as you have been by my side all these years. I've only heard the name kythraul a few times, though, so for you to say it with certainty... you encountered them before, I take it?"

"I have," Isaiah replied. "Long ago."

"Then let us hope their name is recollected again," Kevian said. "For asking men to fight that which is called 'the shadow' creates fear where it cannot be afforded. At least a name gives a form to the enemy."

"The people trust you," Isaiah assured him, his hand subconsciously reaching for a sword he no longer carried. "And thank you for your silence concerning my origins. Far too often, what people expect of us is based on stories that have long been exaggerated. Therefore, I will speak plainly. Does your son know about this yet?"

"He does not," Kevian said. "And the reason for it is I have not thought about how to tell him."

"He will find out in time," Isaiah nodded. "I'll let you decide how. One thing that does need to be addressed, though, is our ally situation."

"Ebaven and Sanasis are at the front of my concern," Kevian said. "We at least have the comfort of being on the coast, and even Asard is protected by rivers and mountains, but Vandor will likely be the first to fall, so they must be warned. Sanasis is more desert than anything, so that will protect them, but the great forest could lead to them being the next to be attacked."

"Have you given thought to Rikaere or Laria?" Isaiah asked.

"They're fighting their own war," Kevian said, shaking his head. "Also, they are far from the fighting, protected by oceans and mountains, so far removed from us. Still, perhaps their war can be put on hold for a time. We both know it will be needed."

"You've said what needs to be done," Isaiah said. "How do you plan to make it happen?"

"You were right about that captain in my prison," Kevian smiled, shaking his head. "He seems to be a good man, but there's something at the back of my mind I just can't place, something I'm still waiting for. He's not going to die, either; that was never the intention, but I needed to know if he would break, and now that I know he won't, I have hope where there wasn't any before."

"So, the sentence remains for now, then," Isaiah said, and Kevian nodded.

"Now just to see how long it takes."

"Then if you'll excuse me," Isaiah said. "I must see to this messenger."

"I can summon him if you prefer," Kevian said. Isaiah shook his head.

"No, that won't be necessary," Isaiah replied. "In fact, for the time, I would prefer this meeting to be not made known."

The putrid smell of rotting plants and human waste hung in the air of the streets of Slumville, leaving little question as to why the streets were mostly empty. Adi covered her mouth with the edge of the dark brown cloak she wore to try to cut the smell, while at the same time being careful to avoid the small rivers of sludge winding across the ground. She knew something had already gotten on her shoes and the hem of the cloak, unfortunately, so she already had plans to burn all items.

The disgust was shared among everyone gathered, from the crew of younger men, around fifteen years of age, to the crew of older men led by a lanky man with a long face, to one elder gentleman who leaned on a cane. It wasn't the kind of crew Adi preferred, with only a few of them being people she would regularly work with, but they made up the numbers she needed, and time was short.

"I like it," the youth across from Adi said, his mouth twisted in a lopsided grin. He was young, but energetic, and his crew had a habit of taking jobs that let them run wild. "It's simple."

"But it's logical," the older gray-haired man said from his place on the wall, keeping away from the water as much he could while avoiding leaning on the wall. "And all we have to do is what we normally do? That sounds far too simple."

"The trick is having everything happen at once," Adi said, gaging a little when she accidentally breathed through her nose. "Up till now, you did your work on your own. If everything happens at once, the guards will be spread thin. One group goes for the moneychangers, one group goes for the minor lord's manor, and one group will go for the royal mint. By themselves, they aren't too special, but they're all located in such a way as to pull guards from the barracks, which will then require the guards to run past the royal palace."

"If enough talk in the right ears about a change of government were to happen," the lanky man added. "Then the guards might start to get suspicious as they run by, which may cause a fair number to abandon our targets and converge on the palace itself."

"Which would conveniently be the one place we don't care about," Adi continued. "Payment wise, I figure we make it simple. Everyone keeps what they take, I get ten percent of what you take."

"Well now, hold on," the youth said. "Our crews will be doing all the work, here. What makes you think you have a right to our take…?"

"Be quiet," the lanky man sighed. "That's more than fair and you know it."

"It also sounds low," the old man added.

"My main goal is my friends," Adi said. "A ten percent take from the money changers and the mint will be enough to get them outside the city and for me to get a little place of my own. My crew will take the prison. Only a small crew can get in, mind, and there wouldn't be any take for anyone, so only I'm taking this one. My part has less risk, so I'm taking less cut, simple as that."

"I like simple," the lanky man said, nodding. "But it sounds challenging enough to make it fun."

"My team will be ready," the older man said.

"Us too," the youth said, shrugging, then grinned in a mischievous way. "And maybe after this, you and I Adi can do another thing together…"

"Go away," the lanky man said, grabbing the youth by the collar and throwing him down the road. "We'll be ready, as well, Adi. Good luck."

"Do you trust them?" the old man asked, after the two other groups had walked off.

"I trust them as far as I can throw them," Adi chuckled. "Do I trust you? No offense, but no, not really. I trust that none of the crews are stupid, and I trust everyone will see sense. I trust you want to make money, and if everyone does their part then we'll all score."

"Fair enough," the old man laughed. "If this works, look for me and my crew again." He tossed Adi a salute and walked away, his cane sounding as if it were trying to crack the few bits of good ground. Adi watched him go, but kept a watchful eye around her, and once the old man turned a corner, Adi took off. Tracking these crews down had been harder than she thought; the guards had apparently been getting better at discouraging her line of work, but she knew the city.

She checked her sleeves again, relishing the familiar feel of the throwing knives strapped to her wrists and belt. No, she didn't completely trust them, but a few knives made for adequate security. Times were different, and in some ways, things were safer, but just in case... Out of habit, she slid one of the daggers from its sheath and threw it into an old barrel at the end of the road where it stuck securely. In another motion, she was beside the barrel and the knife was sheathed.

The only part left would be Eli and making sure he was in place. Every plan needed a way out in case things went bad, and Eli could always be counted on to take care of that. In terms of people she could trust, Eli was one of the very few she could really count on, and while that made her smile, it made her sad as well. Trust was one luxury she couldn't afford, but at the same time one luxury she really wanted. *When you guys get free, maybe I can come back with you to your home. Maybe there's a place for me there.*

Though the news had fallen heavily, Joshian had peace. As if a weight had been lifted, he sat with his back against the wall and let the frustration come out as laughter. *We're always laughing,* he thought. *Even when we shouldn't, we do.* He held a sheet of parchment in his hands, but the only words he could write were, *Dad, I'm sorry.* He let his thoughts drift, settling on his father and mother, and resigning himself to never seeing them again. *I'm sorry you're going to be losing two sons. I'm sorry you're going to be the mother and father of the captain that lost his entire crew. I'm sorry, Firebrand, that I'm taking your sons with me. I'm sorry you can't even hold me accountable. I'm sorry, Marianne, that you won't have your brothers to look after you. And I'm sorry, Captain Malrig, Captain Ryken, Captain Zebahd, that I wasn't the captain you stood behind.*

"So," he heard Jhonas say to Jemas off to the side. "Death. Weird."

"I hear you brother," Jemas chuckled, shaking his head. "Haven't quite wrapped my head around it yet."

"Poor pop, too," Jhonas sighed. "Lots of plans in store."

"I know," Jemas echoed, his voice choking. "He planned to take you out by Long-Tooth Island, now that you're old enough. We were going to go out earlier, too, but then this trip came up. Some of the best shark fishing around is out there."

"I remember the stories you used to tell," Jhonas said, his voice cracking. "They were good stories."

"They're still good stories," Jemas said, laughing. "Oh, you haven't heard this one, but there was this one time, a couple years ago…"

Sorry Jemas, Jhonas, you were the best of us all when it came to fighting until the end, and if even you can crack… you would have gone so much further than anyone.

"How can they laugh like that?" Joshian heard Dayved say in amazement to Seth. "Doesn't anything affect them?"

"They laugh because they can," Seth answered, smiling. "And they laugh so we can have a little bit of laughter if nothing else. Andrius was right, that if we die, then we die as Firebrands, but those two will be Stormwinds to the end. I'm not going to lie, mate, I'm scared. I'm really scared of what's going to happen, but it's going to happen. We can't change that part, but we can stay true to who we are."

"What about your family, though?" Dayved asked. "For mine, I've got seven other brothers and sisters, but in yours, there's only you."

"I know my family will mourn," Seth said, his voice trailing off. "Don't think I haven't thought of them. I think about them every day. But I remember something Captain Aydle used to say. 'The storm will hit whether we like it or not. We can fight it, fear it, yell at it all we want, but it's still going to be there. All we can do is surrender to it, ride it, and then we might make it out.' Granted, accepting it won't make the act any better, but if we feel different about it, then that helps."

"You know," Dayved said, shaking his head. "Sometimes you sound so much older than your years, but other times, you're so much like a kid."

"Yeah, well, gotta balance it out like that," Seth said, grinning. "Otherwise, people might expect me to be mature or something, and where's the fun in that?"

Oh Seth, Joshian thought. *Where would I be without you, you or Dayved? You're two of the youngest, yet you're able to carry us along, push us at just the right moments, and keep us going. I may lead this crew, but you're what keeps it moving, keeps us moving.*

"You know what the worst part of this is, Pete," he heard Andrius say.

"What's that, little bro?" Petorius answered.

"I am so bored!" Andrius said, laughing. "Forget the hunger, forget the conditions, forget even the death sentence. There has been nothing to do but think on things I won't be able to make or build or see… and I am losing my mind!"

"I hear you, Andy," Petorius agreed. "I'm starting to see why we didn't leave the islands. I used to think pa was just exaggerating things when he talked about how terrible the mainland was, but now I'm thinking he got it just about right."

"I agree with you there," Andrius answered, and then the two of them started discussing new ways to heat treat metal and Joshian tuned them out.

I agree with you both, Joshian thought. *I see why a lot of our policies are in place, too, but it's a bloody shame I won't be able to do anything about them.* He shook his head. *No, the problem isn't with the mainland or even the mainlanders. It's with certain mainlanders. Some people could see sense, some people had compassion and other general human natures, while other individuals had the problem. Individuals could be dealt with, and even systems could be changed.*

Chapter 20

On the day of their execution, the morning dawned bright and sunny with hardly a cloud in the sky. The air was warm and dry, and songbirds had come out, filling the air with song. There were the sounds of people laughing, children playing, neighbors greeting each other with enthusiasm... so Joshian laughed.

Of all the days, he thought. *Of all the days for things to be nice and everything to be perfect, it has to be this day. I thought it was supposed to be all gray and dreary on people's last days in the stories. With weather like this... so bloody perfect.*

"Joshian, Calian, Seth, everyone! Get up now!" a breathless Adi yelled from outside their cell door in the main corridor. The crew rose to their feet. "Everyone needs to move, now!"

"Adi, what's going on?" Joshian asked as Adi looked uneasily around outside their cell. "What's wrong, and how did you get in?"

"Nothing's wrong," Adi answered, sounding giddy as she dug through her pockets. "In fact, everything is good, very, very good. I'm breaking you out, all of you. It's a pretty impressive plan, if I do say so myself, but if everyone does their part it should go quite simply."

"Adi," Joshian began, but Adi stopped him.

"No time for that," Adi continued, still searching. "I have three other groups doing their parts in different areas of the city. Our goal is to distract the guards enough to make it so we can escort you guys out. Now, here's the key, and I do mean the actual, literal key," she added, giggling, pulling out the keys to their cells from her pocket. She passed one to the other cell and then held out one to Joshian. "Wait until I talk to you again, which should be in a few hours, and then you'll be free, simple as that."

"No, Adi," Joshian said. "It's not as simple as that. See, we can't leave."

"What are you talking about?" Adi asked. "Of course, you can!"

"Don't think we don't appreciate it," Joshian said, the words getting caught in his throat a bit. "We really do, but do you remember how we said we took oaths before sailing? Part of those oaths include obeying the laws of the land we step upon, and as terrible as this is, we cannot escape without becoming criminals. They may call us criminals now, but if we escape now, we would be, by our standards and theirs. We must be better."

"Speak for yourself," Thom said from the other cell, walking towards the bars. "We have a chance to be free, and I mean to take the opportunity while it's here!"

"Wait a second, Thom," Sailis cautioned.

"No, Thom's right," Jadas added, jumping in as Thom took the key and opened the cell. "Why die here when we don't have to?"

"But mate…" Calian began.

"Oh, burn the oaths!" Thom said, angrily, coming up to Joshian's cell and unlocking the door. "What good is an oath if it costs you everything when you gain nothing?"

"I cannot hold you here," Joshian said, simply. "Nor can I hold you to them. That is for you to decide amongst yourselves, but just know you cannot call yourself my crew outside of them."

"Then this is goodbye," Thom said, holding out his hand to Joshian. Joshian looked at it, and then after a pause, clasped it firmly.

"Wait a moment," Adi said. "I still need time to finish everything."

"There's less of us, now," Jadas said, joining Thom in the corridor. "And they sound like they're not going to be looking for us anyway. Is anyone else joining us?" he called out to the rest of the crew.

Two came forward at once, and two others with their heads bowed moved to join them, none making eye contact with the other crewmen. As the group turned to walk away, three others shared looks before rushing out. Adi started to close the second door.

"Wait," a voice said, coming forward to the bars to reveal Efrain's face. "One question, first, Captain!"

"You'll either stay or you'll go, Efrain," Joshian said, sighing.

"Begging your pardon, sir," Efrain said. "But if this is going to be our end, do we have to stay separated?"

"He has a point," Seth chuckled. "If we're going to stay here anyway, why not stay here together?"

Joshian laughed. "Get over here, then. You're all welcome."

After the two cells merged, Adi shut the empty door, locked it, and then went over to the door with the rest of the crew. Though nine men less, all stood together more as brothers than they had before, even when they first set out, and looking around at all of them, Joshian saw peace on all their faces. He turned back to Adi as she shut the door, and after it was locked, she held out the key once more.

"Here," Adi said, placing the key in his hand. "I know you won't use it for yourself, but I can't be found with it on me, not unless I want the headsman's axe to fall. I know I'm not going to be able to convince you to go against your beliefs, and in a way, I hope you don't; that's one thing I've admired about you all. I'm going to miss you guys."

"Fare well, Adi," Joshian said. "I wish I could have made good on our debt, but all I can do is thank you and ask your forgiveness."

"You have it," Adi answered, turning before she could cry. "Many times over. Goodbye." Her footsteps joined those of the others who left. Joshian rested his head against the bars.

Eli stood casually in the entry to the prison. His armor gleamed with fresh polishing, and the spear in his hand and the sword at his side were freshly oiled and sharpened. Though it was true he wouldn't be stationed in the prison for a while more, exchanging guard duty had been simple. All the guards knew about the strange group of prisoners by now, so all of them freely talked, and Eli had quickly learned the respect Cornell had developed for the crew, as well as how hard informing them of their deaths had been. The palace duty was always more preferable to all the guards, anyway, but Cornell was a friend, one of the few he had, and keeping him out of more trouble than he would need to be put his heart at ease.

Shouts rose at the end of the hall, and Eli sighed. It wouldn't be the first time Adi had gotten herself into a situation and needed a way out, but with this one, she was a lot earlier than she was supposed to be. He looked around at the guards gathered; two were specifically his, while two were regular guards assigned there normally. He had done all he could to change the schedules of any he considered close to a friend at the least, but the ones left behind would be troublesome.

Rounding the corner, though, were only nine individuals, not the twenty-some Adi had said there would be, and Adi was not among them. They held up, seeing the six guards blocking the exit, and for a moment, everyone looked at each other and paused. Then, as a mass, the nine all turned and ran back the way they came.

"Lieutenant Bareth," Eli said, looking over at the man as he rose. "Take Argen and Garit and give chase. Run them down before they can reach the south exit and then force them back this way. Hopefully, they'll see our spears and surrender without a fight, but if not, you're one of the best at navigating these tighter corridors. You'll bring them down easily."

"Aye, sir," Bareth answered, grinning. "Guardsmen, you're with me!" The three took off quickly and disappeared after the escapes.

"Why do I get the feeling the plan just changed?" the tall, dark-skinned guard said from Eli's side.

"Can you remember any escape plan that didn't have to be changed at the last moment?" Eli laughed, and the man chuckled. "Just like old times."

"Just like any time, Alex," the third guard added, nudging Alex with a youthful enthusiasm that used to wear on Eli. "I'm just glad I'm finally able to use this soldier identity. I've spent months getting it set up!"

"I'm just surprised it took you so long to make your soldier identity," Alex said, chuckling. "And why did you choose such a low rank, Deven, not an officer, or at least a sergeant?"

"I still look young, mate," Deven laughed. "Sergeant would have too much responsibility, and no one would believe someone of my age to be an officer. With mine, a little bit more than a private, I now look like someone with ambition, drive, and if I keep acting enthused, they'll believe I got where I am for good reason."

"You have a point," Alex said, shrugging. "Remind me to make you some papers for it when we're all done here. Who knows, we could start a new life here, same as Eli did."

Tracking the two of them down had been one of Eli's more entertaining challenges. He never even thought to look for either of them until he heard about some of the new paintings in the palace, and upon inspection, discovered the artist was one of Alex's aliases. After a few short inquiries he learned there would be a showing at one of the minor lord's manors one night and volunteering himself as security gained him entrance to the event. Though the air was stuffy, the fights were few, so he was able to enjoy himself. What made things even more convenient though was when Deven himself, dressed as a footman, came up offering a plate of appetizers before mingling with other guests. After the party, the three met up and made plans.

"Quiet, both of you," Eli ordered quietly, and the two went silent. "If Adi comes running this way things are going to be tricky as it is, and I don't want other guards to show up until then or things will be more complicated… and I don't want complicated from this."

"Oh yeah, that lieutenant guy had a thing against Adi, didn't he?" Deven asked. "Yeah, that's one guy we don't want sticking around and asking questions."

"Then stop talking," Eli said, chuckling, remembering why that enthusiasm had always irritated him. "You're just as bad as you've always been. Remember, you are a guard. Act like it!"

"Boring and stoic, mean as you." Deven said, his features deadpanning perfectly. "Got it."

Eli sighed.

Adi ran. The walls rushed by her in a gray blur as she tried to chase after the escaping crewmembers.

I'm always running, she thought. *I'm either running, sneaking, sleeping, or eating, and once in a while a few of them at once. But what's the point, anymore? I can understand why most of the crew didn't run, and hate them and love them for it, but why didn't the others listen? Why did the others have to act out, now?*

She rounded the corner and saw a guard outside of a cell midway down the hall. Cursing to herself, she pulled a dagger from her belt and threw it into the guard's unprotected leg, causing him to go down to his knees. She had enough time to run by and mumble, "It's nothing personal," before turning the corner to another section. She heard the guard calling out her position, but when she ducked down another corridor, the voice became muffled. Quickly though, the guard's voice became the least of her concerns.

Barreling down the corridor, yelling frantically, were the nine that had escaped earlier and were now retreating. Their shouts of panic were mixed with shouts from the three guards chasing them, and without thinking, Adi ducked into an empty cell to watch them pass by. *Nothing personal, but if you're going to screw up so badly that I can't help you, then I won't. You're on your own.* She must have shifted in some way, because as the group of nine passed by, one of them called out, "Adi!" and then one of the guards paused. They had just gone by her door, and she was ready to make for the entrance to the prison, but then she caught the guard's face, saw the hungry look in Bareth's eyes, and then she ran with Bareth immediately behind.

Deven put his hand up to his ear, tilting his head to the side. He held up a hand for silence. "Something changed," Deven said. "I hear footsteps coming back this way, but only a couple this time."

"Reinforcements?" Alex asked. Deven shook his head.

"One set is too soft to be a guard's boot," he said. "What? They have a very distinct sound."

"Are you saying one prisoner broke off from the others?" Eli asked.

"Most likely," Deven said. "And it sounds like one guard decided to follow. Not sure what they're thinking, I mean, the guard knows we're here blocking the exit. You really need to get on these guards about crowd tactics."

"Oh, Adi…" Eli sighed. "Bareth was in that group, and if he found Adi…"

"What is that guy's deal, anyway?" Deven asked. "He's had it out for her for a while."

"We'll probably never know," Alex shrugged. "And you just said that mate."

"How long until they get here?" Eli asked.

"Ten seconds," Deven said, moving to block the hallway. "If Bareth is behind her, we should take her into custody. We can always get her out later."

"Agreed," Eli said. "Make it look good."

Adi rounded the corner, and Eli saw Deven rest more on the heels of his feet so when Adi barreled into him, he fell sprawling back. Adi still had a solid lead on Bareth, so she had time to shove passed Alex before Bareth even came into view. Eli caught Adi' eyes, and then Adi pulled out one of her knives and lunged. Eli caught her wrist easily, flipped her around and pinned her arm behind her back.

"Good catch, sir," Bareth panted. "The other men are herding the main group in this direction, as well as the guards we've gathered along the way. When this one broke away, however, I knew I could chase them to you and your group."

"Forget the one," Eli sighed. "There was nowhere for this one to go except here. How many are still in pursuit?"

"Four," Bareth said. Eli shook his head.

"Private," Eli said to Deven. "Get manacles on this one and keep her away from her friends, lest they decide to attack and free her. Get her down to one of the single cells. Lieutenant, take up position at the entrance, and the three of us will wait for the rest of them to get here."

"Aye sir," both men answered.

Deven walked up to Adi and fastened bands on her wrists.

"Come with me," Deven said in the serious, yet somewhat shaky voice of a private making his first arrest. "Offer no resistance, and we'll make this as easy as possible."

"Yeah, I know," Adi said, letting herself be led away. The two entered a small hallway and soon they heard the two groups coming together. The ones with weapons and armor were clearly the ones with authority as evident by Eli's commanding voice and the sounds of the shouts dying down. Deven gave a little laugh.

"Hey, Adi," Deven said, quietly. "It's Deven. We're here to get you out."

"Deven, wow, I didn't recognize you," Adi smiled. "Where have you been?"

"Out, around, traveling," Deven said, leading her down the hall. "By the way, nice tackle."

"Thanks," Adi laughed. "I saw you rock back on your heels, though."

"Guilty," Deven shrugged. "So, Eli gave us the basis of the plan, and everything sounded good. What happened? All the numbers were off."

"It's a very long story," Adi answered. Deven led her into a cell and unfastened her manacles. "I'll have some time to tell it, but with Bareth moved to jail guard, I don't want to be in here longer than I have to."

"Can't blame you there," Deven laughed. "Want me to just leave the door unlocked, you can get out when you feel up to it?"

"Where would be the fun in that?" Adi laughed. "Besides, you're a guard now; it wouldn't look good on you for me to get out too soon. Na, I'll wait for a bit. I don't suppose Eli was able to grab anyone else from our old crew, was he?"

"Alex was the other guard," Deven said. "Hey, when you get out, we can get the crew back together, like old times."

"Maybe," Adi shrugged. "At least with Nate, we had a purpose. I'm tired of this life, though. I'm not sure what my plan is. I'm not sure what I want to do anymore."

Chapter 21

Having been summoned to the High Lord's council chamber almost as soon as she had been arrested, Adi stood in the grips of Eli and Alex as the High Lord paced. His steps were deliberate, but he would look over from time to time, either shaking his head or laughing quietly.

"Only a few days," he chuckled. "I must say, I would have expected you to be gone by now, but instead you get caught and I find you in the prisons helping criminals escape. Oh Adi…"

"You people are all the same," Adi snapped. "What were those people to you, anyway?"

"My prisoners," the High Lord answered. "Now, give me one reason you shouldn't be locked up and left as well?"

"Do what you will," Adi shrugged.

The High Lord sighed, shaking his head when he saw Adi would say no more. "At least give me some reason you would stick your neck out for them. Something, just… help me understand."

"They were my friends," Adi said. "I admired them. They were people not afraid to say what they believed, and not afraid to believe the way they did. They didn't look down on me for who I was, either, didn't try to take advantage of me or anything like a lot of people tend to do. I don't know if they were guilty or innocent, I just know they weren't wrong."

"Is that all, then?" the High Lord asked.

"Yep, that's it," Adi shrugged.

"I see," the High Lord sighed. "Captain Eli, while you're here, there is one other thing I want to bring up. Lieutenant Bareth brought this to my attention earlier, but he claimed you've been housing Adi for the past while. While that isn't a concern to me, he even went as far as to say you assisted with the attempted liberation of the prisoners. I've questioned many of Bareth's actions in the past, and false accusations against senior officers are easily enough for his release, but is there any truth to his words?"

"There is," Eli said.

"Which parts?" the High Lord asked.

"All of them," Eli answered. "Adi was my friend long before this, so it's only natural I'd provide her assistance in her time of need. Knowing her compassion for them, I knew it was a matter of time before she would want to help them, so naturally I aided."

"And will you do me the decency of telling me why?" the High Lord asked, taking a seat.

"I will," Eli answered. "I looked into the case of the prisoners, and quite frankly felt their sentence was unjust. I can't obey unjust orders. Furthermore, with recent events of citizens rising against fellow guards in the other cities with no noticeable action taken to help them, I see true justice must take place by individuals, and not through the organizations that claim to support them. In short, I'm just tired of seeing lives wasted anymore, and I'm tired of supporting something that treats my brothers this way."

There was a knock on the door, and a servant poked his head in. "Your pardon, sir, but the preparations you've asked for have been completed, and you wished to be informed immediately..."

"Yes, you've done well, thank you," the High Lord said. "Send the guards outside in here."

"Yes, sir," the servant answered, bowing on the way out.

"You're a woman of few words," the High Lord said to Adi, shaking his head. The two guards entered. "And you, Captain, this was one tragedy I did not expect, and it grieves me to hear. Take them away," he said to the guards. "I'll deal with them later. Also, send for Captain Cornell."

The guards, as well as Alex, took Adi and Eli and led them out. Once the door closed, the High Lord sent for Isaiah. The man arrived shortly after, followed by Captain Cornell.

"Captain, good, take Isaiah and a few guards and retrieve the prisoners that were admitted a couple of weeks ago. I know that a few of them did try to escape, and that is unfortunate, but those that did not try to break free, bring them to my personal drawing room."

"Sir?" Captain Cornell asked.

"They will be suspicious, true," Kevian continued. "Nevertheless, tell them they are to be set free. Once you've shown them to the room, have the captain come here."

"Yes, sir," Cornell said. He saluted before leaving the room.

"Of all the faces," Joshian sighed when Cornell opened the cell door. "Yours was the one I wished to see the least. I had hoped we would end only as friends, not also as our escort to death."

"Then I'm pleased to say that's not the case," Cornell said, warmly. "You've been set free."

"I sense a trap, Captain," Paul said.

"I agree," Jemas said. "Nothing against you at all," he added quickly to Cornell. "It's just tough knowing what or who to trust anymore."

"Will you trust me then?" Isaiah asked, stepping forward. "I assure you Cornell speaks true. Accommodations have been provided, and Joshian, the High Lord wished to speak to you personally."

"I would pass on the personal invitation if too much wasn't on the line," Joshian sighed. "And if it had been anyone other than you two, I would have declined." Then Joshian laughed and stepped forward, embracing Isaiah in a hug. "It is good to see you, sir."

"The pleasure is all mine," Isaiah smiled, returning the embrace. "I've seen to a few things, personally, that I think you might like."

"Perhaps we can see a bit of that city you promised," Calian said, standing up. "At least more than some basic roads and a jail cell."

"I hope we can have the time," Isaiah answered. "Though I confess I'm going to be much busier than in the past."

They were escorted out of the prison and walked down the road to the palace. Whether by orders or Cornell's kindness, none of them were chained, though the guards watched them wearily, especially given how the prisoners far outnumbered the guard. A few people stopped to stare at them, and Joshian could only imagine the thoughts running through their heads since none dared to comment. When he would make eye contact, they quickly scuttled off, looking behind them to make sure none of the crew were following. Joshian smiled.

When they entered the palace, they were joined by more guards who escorted them down seemingly endless corridors. The room they were led to was large and cozy, with couches and chairs on one end and a large banquet table set at the other. Smaller tables with wooden boxes sat along the walls, but on the main table was an assortment of food and drink; various meats and breads and fruits were arrayed in colorful patterns, hot and steamy or cold and chilled. Wines of different varieties were set aside, and on a smaller table were cakes and pastries.

"What's all this?" Seth asked, pausing to breathe in all the scents. They all looked to Joshian, who in turn looked to Isaiah.

"The High Lord wishes to… negotiate," Isaiah answered. "As I said, I looked to the presentation of these myself, and when you're all finished, he wants you, Joshian, to see him at your convenience."

"What about?" Joshian asked.

"I don't entirely know what the High Lord is planning," Isaiah confessed. "Nor what he will reveal. But I know he will answer your questions. I know what you must think about him, as well, but I would still encourage you to speak with him. That is all I can say about that. I do have one thing to give you, though, even though this was of much concern, and irritation, to Timothy." Isaiah walked to one of the boxes and upon opening it, pulled out one of their spears.

"All of your spears are here," Isaiah continued, and then opened a thinner, shorter box. "And here is your sword, Captain. Fresh clothing has also been set aside in these other boxes, and the guards outside can escort you to a washroom should you wish."

"Captain?" Jemas asked. "What's your call?"

"I hate secrecy," Joshian sighed. "I hate how they can never tell you flat out what is happening, what their plans are, have to make things all mysterious. I hate how they can never be straightforward… what could be so secret? For now, we eat, and after that I'm going to have a few words. Let's just get our answers and be done with it. I assume we can't leave until I do, correct?"

"The High Lord has given you permission to leave now, should you desire," Isaiah answered. "I can only say things are much bigger than you know, and if I have earned any favor in your eyes, then you'll trust me when I say you would be wise to speak with him."

"I trust you, Isaiah," Joshian sighed. "You are one of the few people here who hasn't lied to me yet, and for that I am grateful."

The crew ate heartily, quickly consuming the arrangement on the table and asking for seconds, which were provided, and Isaiah excused himself. Soon even thirds were asked before everyone was satisfied, and once they were done Joshian rose and walked out. A pair of guards were waiting for him, and instinctually wrinkled their noses.

"Lead me to the High Lord," he said.

"Begging your pardon," one said. "But would you not prefer to wash and present yourself in a more suitable manner?"

"This manner is the result of his accommodations," Joshian answered. "Thus, it is more than enough for seeing him in."

"As you wish," the guard sighed, directing the way down the hall. "If you will… come with me, then."

Joshian followed his two guards down more hallways much like the earlier ones, but lost track of the turns after a while, so he watched the décor instead. The halls were bright and white, and the tapestries on the wall gave them a warm feeling, so he found himself admiring the place.

The guy has good taste, I have to give him that much.

The guards stopped at a modest set of double doors, and one rapped on the door and poked his head in before signaling Joshian to enter. When he did, he found the room smaller than the drawing room with far fewer couches and tables, but the sparsity made it almost feel bigger. There was a small table set with drinks along the side, but he left that alone for the time. He was not the only one there, however; Isaiah was seated, chatting with a figure in a floor-length black cloak. Both rose when he walked over.

"Can't say I'm too surprised to see you this way," Isaiah laughed. "Still, you look better now that you've eaten."

"I feel better, too," Joshian laughed. "But then again, I haven't met the High Lord yet, so we'll see what happens. And you sir," he added to the cloaked man, extending his hand. "Are you here by summons as well, or some other purpose?"

"Oh, I'm here for my own reasons," the man chuckled, taking the hand. He removed the cape and draped it over the chair. "But I've kept up the farce for long enough. Isaiah, let us begin. Joshian, my name is Kevian, the High Lord of Ildice."

"Perfect," Joshian said, releasing his hand and instinctively going for his sword. "You owe me some answers."

"You're right, I do," Kevian agreed, gesturing toward the drink table. "Care for one?"

"I'll pass for now," Joshian said. Kevian shrugged.

Joshian took the moment that it took for the man to pour his drink to really study the High Lord. He was a proud looking man, strong and youthful, but aged and weary. Though he stood with poise and authority, he also looked to be constantly carrying a great weight. The authority gave Joshian pause, however. He could sense it, not like in Captain Malrig or Captain Ryken, but it was still there. This man's authority was his own, not just inherited.

"So, we come to it at last," Kevian said, giving a small grin.

"Indeed," Joshian stated, masking his face.

"You're an interesting man," the High Lord continued. "You came to us as one who rescued my son, for which I truly am thankful for, but due to a number of faults of my own you were charged as a criminal instead of getting the honor you deserve. While you were in prison, you could have fought, you could have tried to overpower my guards, but you chose not to, and never asked pardon for your actions. I respect that. Finally, when your death was ordered, you chose to protest peacefully, rather than try to escape.

"That time spent observing you, alone, would be interesting enough, but it's the people you've earned the support of that have me equally curious, the first of which being my advisor, the man who's word I value above all others. Then you earned the trust of a selfish, but very skilled, criminal, one who chose to sacrifice herself to save you and your friends. Finally, you earned the respect of one of my captains, to the point I could not trust him to carry out a death sentence on you. Very few men have earned the respect of noble, commoner, and criminal alike.

"I'm left with the question, now, of what to do with you. I have many saying you have earned your freedom, while some are saying forcible conscription. Many have recognized your heart, and Isaiah spoke well of your skill, leading many to want you to serve in our navy. A few fear you, and want the death sentence to hold, while some are simply saying banishment and to leave you be.

"I already gave the order that you and your crew are free. You are free to take your ship and go, with my good will. None would stop you, but what I want you to do for me pertains to everyone, I believe, whether in the immediate future or at least the near future."

"You have my attention," Joshian nodded, walking over to pour a drink. "And I applaud you for seeing to my crew, not just me. Isaiah must have told you a lot about us."

"Quite a lot," Kevian answered. "Your brother, though, said he would refuse my gifts while the rest of the crew had none, and that I would have better luck talking to you. I figured you would mirror his sentiment."

"Then can we just dispense with the pleasantries and get to business?" Joshian asked. "I hate flowery language. I feel someone is trying to hide something, manipulate me, or both."

"Fair enough," Kevian said. "Then to put it simply, Ildice is under threat from the dark powers that made war on Learsi nearly a thousand years ago. Is that simple enough?"

"Very," Joshian agreed, scratching his chin. "I will need more information, of course."

"Naturally," Kevian answered. "Isaiah, if you would be so kind as to have the maps brought in, I would appreciate it. Have the servants bring additional tables as well and have someone send for my son."

"With pleasure," Isaiah said, stepping out.

"I don't suppose now is a good enough time to speak with you about the release of my other crewmen," Joshian asked, once the door closed behind Isaiah. "Captain Cornell said under your orders that the ones who chose not to try to escape were free, but nothing of those that did try."

"They are criminals in actuality," Kevian sighed.

"I understand that," Joshian answered. "But until we return home, they are still my crew. Once home, we have our own rules they will be punished under, naturally, but I cannot leave without them."

"I'll be willing to negotiate," Kevian said. Joshian nodded.

Isaiah walked in with a handful of servants, and some set about arranging tables while others laid out the maps and other settings. After bowing, they left, and Kevian directed Isaiah and Joshian to the table.

"Isaiah knows most of what is happening," Kevian began, pausing to take a drink. "Captain, I trust you're familiar enough with the layout of the land, so I'll skip that. Now, with this map, we can see all Ildice, everything from our furthest outposts back to Kellivar. Normally, our main form of transport to Vandor is through the port city of Maltis or through the Great Western Road. Maltis is still struggling to repair itself, but the Western Road has been overcome by bandits and we cannot afford the troops to secure it now, not by ourselves. Ebaven, however, would be able to supplement our forces well enough to secure the road. That was what I sent Timothy to Vandor for in the first place.

"However, I had long heard reports from other officers, or would simply lose contact with outposts, about something else stirring in the mountains. For a long time, it was just a few reports, no tangible evidence, but while my son was gone a rider came back with the proof I dreaded. I can say with certainty now that we do not fight normal flesh and blood. But that will be my fight soon enough.

"That brings me to you and your part in all this," Kevian concluded. "Maltis is not an option anymore. The Road is not an option anymore. I considered sailing down the coast and then coming to Vandor by land, but the time it would take would be far too great for any reasonable traveling, so that leaves going through the islands you call your home."

"So, in summary, you want someone to sail?" Joshian asked. Kevian shook his head.

"I need someone to carry the fate of Ildice," Kevian answered.

"Alright, I think I follow," Joshian said. "Fine, I'll carry what you want, in exchange for the rest of my crew."

"Whom would be a better description," Kevian said. "Your crew if you carry a select group of my choosing with you. Not only items, but a diplomatic party will be necessary when you reach the capitol."

"And by select group, I assume that means Timothy will be coming as well?" Joshian speculated. Kevian nodded, and Joshian took a deep breath. After a moment, he sighed. "Things will have to be much different than our last trip."

"Not drastically, but yes, they will," Kevian answered. "To start, we'll be funding the entire voyage, so he would not be considered, how did Calian put it, 'baggage.'"

"Calian told us about your interaction," Joshian said. "Sorry about all the circumstances surrounding that conversation."

"There are some moments a man needs to be a man," Kevian said. "Other times he needs to be his position."

"I think I can understand that," Joshian nodded. "There are times I don't like the position, and just want to be like everyone else."

"But there are times it's needed, Captain," Kevian said. "Sometimes the man is enough, but at other times the title is necessary. You are young, and you will learn that sometimes for the people you love, you must become what they need. That being said, I am still trying to figure out how to recover from your brother's conversation. Now, on the note of the voyage, how soon would you be able to sail? How much time do you need?"

"Honestly," Joshian answered. "If the ship were prepped, we could sail now, if we absolutely needed to. Frankly, we just want to get home."

"I understand," Kevian said. "However, that won't be necessary. Or rather, it won't be possible on our end. None of my people will be ready by then. It's just as well, though, as there are a few other details to discuss. What do you know of Vandor?"

"Capital of Ebaven," Joshian answered. "It's a coastal city, but otherwise that's about all I know."

"That's fine," Kevian said. "Not only is it Ebaven's capital city, but it is also its most wealthy and most populated. That place is a maze if you're not careful, though being on my business there will be many people you can draw on if you need guidance through the streets. It is ruled by a queen, Queen Esthera, but her brothers and sisters have their own lands that they maintain, and while it may not be possible to gain the support of the entire nation, you may find a few lords and ladies who are sympathetic. Below them, knights are given smaller portions of land and a regiment of troops to command, so even they will be good to meet."

"Makes sense," Joshian agreed. "Then let's talk cargo. What all am I carrying?"

"A few sealed documents, mostly," Kevian answered, procuring a rolled-up scroll and a few letters, all sealed with dark red wax. "Timothy, of course, will be going, as will a few aids and a couple guards. Timothy will be doing most of the negotiating, so you will just be responsible for ensuring they get there safely, nothing more… at the moment."

"At the moment" Joshian asked, narrowing his gaze. Surprisingly, Kevian looked regretful.

"You're a piece to the puzzle I didn't realize was missing," Kevian said. "Many of my people's lives are going to be saved because of you, and now that I've found you, I intend to use you as much as I can."

"I don't like the idea," Joshian said, crossing his arms. "But I can at least see where you're coming from."

"There are many things I don't like about this job," Kevian sighed. "Sometimes after a while, you sit back, you look in a mirror, and you realize you don't know who you're seeing anymore."

The two were silent for a while, drinking their wine and staring at the walls.

"Sir," Joshian said after a bit. Isaiah coughed into his mug, and Kevian looked up with interest. "I know that there is much more going on behind all of your actions. I understand that there are some things that some people don't need to know, but where I'm from we give our crews as much as we can and let them act on it." Kevian scratched his beard, and Isaiah nodded. "If I am to do everything I can, I'll need everything you can give me. Tell me everything, and not just the part considered 'my role.'"

Surprisingly, Kevian laughed. "While you were in prison, I told Isaiah I was out of options. Maybe you can give me a few more. Alright, Captain, I will trust you. I will wait until Timothy comes and then tell you both together. I just hope you are who I think you are."

The wait was not long, for a few moments later, the door opened, and Timothy entered the room. He struck a far different figure in his finer clothes than in his travel clothing, and he walked like a man of entitlement.

"Hello, Father," Timothy said as he entered the room. Joshian watched him over his shoulder, but otherwise kept his back to the door, hovered over the table. "I received your summons…" He trailed off when he noticed Joshian. "Father, what is *he* doing here?"

"That remains to be seen," Kevian said, grinning. "At the moment, he's the captain I found for your expedition."

"Father, I beg you to reconsider," Timothy pleaded, staring now at his father. "Surely you cannot be serious?"

"Oh, I am very serious, my son," Kevian answered. "In fact, now that I have you both here, I can truly begin.

"My story starts with the Adonarian War, some thousand years ago, now. The stories are many, ranging from those about adventurers fighting giants over twice their size, men who can change into beasts, and even meeting death itself. There are tales of great winged beasts, men who wielded weapons of the gods, and tales of a dark lord to bring ruin upon the world. These stories have been expanded upon greatly, exaggerated to truly epic proportions, but what I am here to tell you, now, are that the stories are *real*.

"The Adonarian War was great and terrible. Many men gave up their lives for a cause that was just and true, but it is difficult to ever justify the loss of a life. We knew hope when the dark one was pushed back, and for the past thousand years we have known a shaky peace, but even that is ended. Our furthest western patrols have been attacked, sometimes by monstrous beasts, other times by the mindless corpses of past friends and allies. One report even claims the Necromancer walks the world again."

"The men must be crazy," Timothy declared. Kevian shook his head.

"That was my hope," Kevian answered. "However, the evidence I have here and the knowledge of them personally says otherwise. This threat is very much real, and one we very much need to act upon."

"But Father," Timothy pleaded once more. "Why must it be him who sails?"

Because I'm the only one who would accept a mission like that, probably, Joshian thought. *Because everyone you've asked turned it down already, most likely, and I'm just the sucker...*

"Because, my son, there is no one else that I'd trust with your life," Kevian answered, which brought Joshian up short. "I trust that no one else would be able to make it through, either, and I trust him for another reason I can't quite place."

"I have one," Joshian said. "I've got family, friends, and my islands to look out for, so this concerns them too. I'd be a fool to think a war involving Ildice and Ebaven wouldn't affect my people, so, I'll do it. I'll carry your message and all you've got for me."

"Big words," Timothy scoffed. "People always talk big when trying to curry favor with my father."

"Frankly, they're not," Joshian shrugged. "I'm just looking out for my own."

"Fine," Timothy said. "I'll take back my sword, then."

"Excuse me?" Joshian said, his hand dropping to grasp his sword's handle. "Nothing that we brought shall be taken from us."

"I've already taken it," Timothy laughed. "I've claimed it as property of Ildice..."

"I don't care what you do," Joshian growled. "Or claimed. Quite frankly I don't care what a thief declares. It doesn't make it his."

"You dare call me a thief!" Timothy roared.

"Yes, I do!" Joshian answered back. "I call it like it is, nothing more."

"In one word I could have you sent back to those prisons!" Timothy yelled. "I could have your crew scattered, force you to parade naked through the streets as people pelted you…"

"Because you're a coward," Joshian said, making Timothy pause. "You could absolutely do all those things because you're a spoiled, cowardly thief used to getting his own way. You may call it 'legal' but you're still taking what belongs to someone else for your own personal gain. Imagine if you didn't have a title to hide behind."

"Title or no," Timothy growled. "I will not allow a commoner to possess arms in my presence. There is a law in our nation about that, in fact."

"Then we have a very real problem," Joshian said. "And I won't budge in this."

"There is a simple solution to it all," Isaiah interjected, and all three looked over at him. "One that would solve all of our problems."

"What solution?" Timothy asked, and Joshian thought the same, partly curious, partly concerned.

"Under the nation's laws," Isaiah began. "While citizens are not allowed to bear arms in your presence, the royal military must. If Joshian were a captain in the royal navy, for example, not only would he sail under your authority, but he would also sail under your banner as well, relieving possible tension of those sailing with him. At the very least, the queen would receive him better."

"Impressive maneuvering," Joshian said, shaking his head. "I see why my village has avoided royalty."

"I do what I have to," Kevian said. "Still, I accept that condition. How long would it take you to get to Vandor?"

"One month," Joshian said. "It'll take a couple of weeks to get through the islands, and then it'll be clear sailing once we hit open water. That's at most, I should be able to cut that down further. But assuming I accept this captainship, I have some conditions. First, my crew is completely excluded from this deal. Anyone that I say is a part of my crew is part of my crew, too. If anyone wants to sign with you, then I won't stop them, but anyone who wishes to sail and still be free is under my protection. Fair?"

"Reasonable," Kevian said. "Though a bit unorthodox."

"Good," Joshian said. "Now, Timothy, the conditions of 'baring arms' I'll accept provided the spears are still on board with us."

"I accept that condition," Timothy began, but Joshian interrupted.

"And if anyone draws a weapon against any of my crew," Joshian continued. "Then they *will* be allowed to defend themselves through whatever means necessary, period."

"No," Timothy said. "I don't like it."

"You'll have to," Joshian said.

"I'll expect better living conditions than last time," Timothy countered. "I'll expect my own room..."

"You'll share a room, even the best room, with a person of your choosing," Joshian interrupted. "Space is limited, and the only other option is getting a bigger ship. But then, you would need a new captain because I will not leave mine."

"I expect full meals," Timothy added. "And unhindered access to the galley at any moment. Furthermore, you cannot 'boss around' anyone not of your crew, and I will get the respect I deserve."

"I am the captain of my ship," Joshian said. "What I say, goes, but I won't order your guard around, provided you don't give me a reason to. Galley access is just common sense. I don't see how you don't see that supplies will be limited, and precautions must be taken to ensure people don't die, but that's all there is to it, no debate. And you will get the respect you deserve, not necessarily the respect you think you deserve."

"Just be clean," Timothy grumbled, folding his arms, and slumping down in a chair. "You reek right now."

"Since that's settled," Joshian nodded. "I have a request. I want Captain Cornell to be one of the guards."

"Understandable," Kevian said. "He's a good man."

"Also, I want the thief, Adi," Joshian continued. "And yes, before you ask, I hear things."

"I can't say I'm surprised," Kevian said, scratching his head. "They're also actual criminals who have a sentence to serve out."

"Can I buy their sentence, then?" Joshian asked. "Protecting the royal son, instead of spending time in prison, would be a better use of resources, at the very least."

"Possibly," Kevian said slowly, his tone betraying his curiosity. "Why would you want to?"

"I owe a debt to Adi," Joshian said. "I pay back my debts."

"You said the journey would take about a month," Kevian said. Joshian nodded. "Fine. For three months of service, I will give you all that you've asked for. For three months, you are a captain in the royal navy, subject to my command. You are free to choose your crew as you wish, your crew is under your protection, and the men who choose to follow you are under your command. After the three months are concluded, you are free to go wherever you wish, or should you desire, you may contract longer. Furthermore, every man that came with you is free to go with you. That is my bargain."

A bargain, Joshian thought. *So, this is the cost of freedom, to a degree. I come free, stay as a prisoner, and leave employed. Could be worse, at that. I have my crew, our spears, my ship, so there's that. I free a friend, making good on a debt. And under this captainship, I'll fall under different rules. This world isn't home, but I am in the world, so time to play by their rules, so I can learn how to twist the rules to my own.*

"I agree," Joshian said, extending his hand. "I don't like all of it, but I agree. Too much is at stake."

"Good," Kevian said, accepting the handshake. Joshian nodded to Timothy, who eyed him in return. Joshian smiled. *And now, the games begin.*

Chapter 22

Joshian left the high lord's chambers and stepped into the hall, feeling his knees wanting to buckle. The guards saluted crisply, and he saluted back, steeling himself, and then gestured down the hall back the way he had come.

"If you'll be so kind as to escort me back to my crew," he said to the two guards, "I would appreciate it."

"Yes sir," the replied, and then promptly led him onward. They didn't speak but he sensed no malintent. He recalled a lack of conversation from other groups of guards that passed, a silence confined to whispers at best. It was one more thing that differed between his people and theirs. It was also one more thing he would have to change.

"You were part of the guard that brought us to the prison the first time," he said to them, and they stiffened at his words. "Unless I'm mistaken."

"You're not mistaken, sir," one of them answered, still looking forward.

"Have you been to Vandor before?" Joshian asked.

"No, sir," the guard replied. "Barely been as far as Asard, though I originally signed with the navy and had plans to sail up to Shorvall and hopefully go as far as Rikaere..." He cut off his words quickly, as if he had said more than he planned.

"You like to sail?" Joshian asked.

"Yes sir, I do sir," the guard replied after a pause.

"Would you like to come then?" Joshian asked. "Guards familiar with ship workings are preferred to those who are not, and as Timothy is already familiar with you, I don't see a reason he would object."

"I would... appreciate the opportunity, sir, thank you," the guard answered, his voice quickening for a moment.

Joshian nodded.

"And you," he said to the other guard.

"I have family there," the second guard answered. "I too have wished to go for some time."

"I shall tell the high lord, then," Joshian said. "What are your names?"

"Corporal Codi," the first guard replied.

"Corporal Caleb," the second guard answered.

"I shall remember that," Joshian affirmed.

When they came to the crew's room, he paused before entering, though he couldn't place why. He almost knocked, but then he clenched his fist, reached out, and turned the handle. The guards remained outside, though there was a noticeable stiffness gone, and the nods they gave were softer, but when he stepped in, the air felt foreign. Most of the crew were asleep. Cots and bedding had been supplied while he was gone, and any chair that provided reclining comfort was claimed, but there were still a couple sitting up by the fire, and he fell into a chair next to them. Still, for the first time, he felt like a stranger among them.

"So how bad are things?" Jemas asked after he had sat and rubbed his temples. "You've been gone a while, and you look terrible."

"They got me, mate," Joshian said, shaking his head. He got up, poured himself a mug of water and drained it. Pouring a second, he went back to his seat. "They got me, now I'm a captain under them, too."

"Hmm," Seth said from Jemas' side. "What happened? I thought we were free?"

"Some of us were," Joshian said. "Those of us who didn't run, anyway. The others…"

"No, I can see what happened," Jemas nodded. "I won't deny that I was worried about them, and I was afraid they would have to remain as a result. I know you would have been powerless, too, so for what it's worth, I'm glad you got out of that. The village will deal with them."

"Adi was caught, too," Joshian continued.

"I heard," Seth lamented. "Is she alright?"

"I think so," Joshian answered. "I didn't see her, but the high lord allowed the option of coming with us instead of serving prison. I hope she takes it, but if not, I might be able to negotiate with him when I come back."

"You did all you could," Seth replied. "And it sounds like you did as well or better than could be expected."

The three went silent, and Joshian stared into the flames, watching the wood crackle and collapse on itself. After a bit, Seth put another log on and cleared his throat.

"So, Cap, I get that you're with Ildice now, we both do, and as with home I get that there's stuff you know that average crewmen don't need to, but how much can you tell us? Why did you do it, and what are we getting into?"

"Why else do I do anything?" Joshian sighed. "Once the high lord started talking openly, I realized there was a lot more at stake than a single captain or even a single crew. I'll tell everyone later, and this is definitely something the village will be hearing about, but I'll give you the short version now."

Though he intended it to be short, and there were very few interruptions or qualifying questions, it was some time before he finished his summary. The fire, untended, had diminished to a few glowing embers and crackling flames, casting his friends' faces in a red wavy glow.

"Wow," Seth said.

"Yep," Jemas echoed.

They stared into the flames once more as time passed by.

"When do we leave here, then?" Seth asked after a while.

"Tomorrow, I hope," Joshian said. "We're sailing on Ildice's time, so it will be when they are ready and not before. My plan is to leave tomorrow, when the sun is high, take an easy first day and then push on later."

"Good plan," Jemas said, stretching. "Can't say I'm a complete fan of the 'Ildice' part, but it could be worse."

"I'll understand if you want to stay home when we get back," Joshian said. "This was as far as we planned…"

"Not a chance," Jemas said, shaking his head. "I need a good adventure, still. That's what I signed up for, and this doesn't count."

Adi stood before the high lord with Eli, and behind them other soldiers stood guard. The chains around their wrists and ankles were unnecessary; she suspected Eli could break his, and she knew she could slip hers, but she doubted that would be an acceptable justification. The High Lord sat at a table and sorted through documents, almost as if they weren't there.

"Adi," the High Lord began, reading aloud. "Short for Adelina. No last name is given, and no other information save that which is in the prison records. You were imprisoned for numerous crimes, chiefly theft, were released early on probation, but then attempted to spring other prisoners from their cells. Though arguably noble, it is still very much illegal, and you did assault a guard, though thankfully he will make a full recovery. Your sentence for your actions is one year.

"Spencer Eli, former captain of my guard," the High Lord continued, shuffling the papers. "Before the guard you were a mercenary, and before that a retrieval expert of sorts. Though you would have been in line for a promotion in another year, you chose to aid Adi in her actions with the prisoners. You stated your reasons for doing so, and I accept them. I still have the law to obey, thus you must still face the consequences for your actions. Your position as captain is officially revoked, and you will serve an added six months in prison. These are your sentences according to the law.

"Another choice has been made known to me, however. I have a captain sailing for Vandor, Adi, who believes your skills could be of use to him. He has asked that you have the choice of serving on his ship rather than staying in prison, a request I am granting. I extend that to include everyone."

"Nearly anything beats prison," Adi said, shrugging. "There's not much left for me here, anyway, so I accept."

"I've been on ships before," Eli said, nodding. "I'll serve there."

"Would it be possible to say goodbye to… a few people first?" Adi asked.

"I assume you mean the foreign crew that tried to escape?" the High Lord asked. When Adi nodded, his face softened. "The captain has negotiated their release, so they're sailing with you."

"Thank you," Adi smiled, bowing, a respect for the man growing.

"I'm not quite finished," the High Lord continued, and then chuckled. "Alex'andi Harson and Deven Soreaux."

"Shoot, he caught us," Deven said from behind Adi, dressed as one of the guards. "Alex, we gotta run."

"Deven, you idiot," Alex chuckled, wryly, who was dressed as another guard. He shook his head and sighed heavily. "Don't say anything."

"Mate, he caught us, there's no question," Deven said. "Freeing prisoners is big to them."

"Hold a moment," the High Lord said, raising a hand.

"Not yet," Deven answered, waving the High Lord off. "We can make it, mate. I've mapped out this place a dozen times, easy. There are more open passages than I think even he realizes."

"Thank you for informing me of that," the High Lord said.

"Any time," Deven said. "Now, Alex, it's simple…"

"Enough," the High Lord said, sighing. "Rumors of your crimes are far too numerous to count, not to mention the crime of impersonating guards that you are doing at this moment. Fortunate for you, said crimes have been devoid of violence, and we do not have any concrete proof connecting you with most of them. Therefore, I pronounce the sentence of one year upon each of you and will then let the matter of the rumors rest."

"That's not too bad," Deven said. "Thanks. We'll go now."

"Deven, just be quiet," Eli sighed. "Please, just, stop digging."

"You haven't changed," Adi mumbled, smiling.

"And if I offered you the same option as the other two?" the High Lord asked.

"The terms are acceptable," Alex said, covering Deven's mouth to keep him from talking more. "Deven, we're taking it."

Deven pulled Alex's hand from his mouth.

"Easy, boss man," Deven said. "You get no argument from me."

"Why, though?" Adi asked. "What's to stop us from running once we get to Vandor?"

The high lord folded his hands.

"You are free to run," he answered in an even tone that gave Adi pause. "You are free to do whatever you wish, in fact, but also know that your captain will be held responsible. The decision is yours. Are we understood?" Adi gulped but nodded.

"Then make sure you are all down at the docks tomorrow morning," the High Lord ordered. "Their ship is *Courageous Heart*. Good luck." As they were leaving, Adi thought she heard a

mumbled, "and take care of them, please," before the doors
closed behind her.

Though Joshian had said it wasn't to be until midday that
they were to depart, the last of the crew stumbled on their ship
shortly after the first light touched the sky. The harbor was quiet,
save for the creaking of swaying ships and the cries of sea birds
circling. For a while, the crew rested in the peacefulness, taking
seats on the ship's deck, or hanging from the ropes somewhere
as they watched the sky grow lighter. Platters of pastries and fruit,
and pitchers of fruit juice and milk had been waiting for them
when they had awoken, so their bellies were comfortably full.
New clothing had also been provided, so their clothes were fresh,
clean, and now had a bit of color to accent them. Though there
were some perks to being under the nation's employment, they
were not quite enough to get rid of the negative feelings
completely.

Traffic picked up after the sun had climbed further into
the sky, and then the more "important" figures made their
presences known, reveling in the gawking and adoration of their
crews and other dockhands. Carts with shipments and supplies
rolled up, deck hands moved around loading the other ships and
organizing equipment, and some started to load their own ship.

"Hey, Captain, you're doing your new position wrong,"
Seth laughed, earning the stares of some of the Ildician
deckhands. The men looked around frantically, with some
panicking as they realized they hadn't noticed an officer's
appearance. Joshian had remained quiet, but with a sigh he threw

on his jacket and allowed the salutes. "See how those captains do it? You need…"

"Just get to work," Joshian laughed. "Look at the sky, it's far too light, and I've let you slack off for much too long. I want to get home."

Dayved, Seth, and Sailis dropped to the dock and started first to unload the carts sent from the palace. Then, with the other dock workers' assistance, they brought the pieces up to the deck where Jhonas and Paul started to organize their storage.

"Worst and longest weeks of my life," Dayved said, laughing. "I swear, I will not complain about pulling anchor, ever."

"At least we're leaving," Seth said, wiping his brow. "I think I've had enough of cities for a while."

"Well, I've got news for you, mate," Sailis said, lifting a box to his shoulder. "Apparently Vandor is even bigger."

"Oh joy," Seth said wryly. "I think I'll stick to the ship when we get to port, then, if I make it down there. I might sit that leg out, though, and just stay at home for a while."

"Aw, don't say that," Sailis said, grinning his traditional grin. "I mean, sure, we were prisoners for most of our time here, but when you take that away, the city itself is pretty impressive. We'll be completely under royal protection when we visit the next, and I intend to take full advantage of that. Think about it, shops with wares completely foreign, buildings that rise hundreds of feet above the ground, streets paved with the finest of stone that fit so tightly together you can't even fit a knife blade into, and music! Think of the music, with bards competing with each other for stage space, performers coming in from all corners of the land to perform. Where's your sense of adventure? Where's your curiosity into the unknown?"

"Honestly, it's a little afraid of getting locked up again," Seth laughed. "But that could just be prison me talking, and your words have stirred me. A day out at sea will probably clear my head, and a day or two at home should help things a bit, too, and then…" Seth sighed. "Alright, I'm coming."

"Good," Sailis said. "What about you Dayved? You staying at home, or are you coming further?"

"I'm definitely going with you," Dayved grinned. "But though the city is supposed to be amazing, I'm more curious about the land outside of it, specifically the mountains. The mountains are supposed to rise high into the clouds, and in the evening, they glow with purple and pink light, and the trees catch fire with the evening sun… Adi' stories sounded pretty impressive."

"She's one of the few good things to come from this place," Seth said to himself.

Sailis laughed, nudging him good heartedly. "I heard that."

"Yes, she is pretty good, so that makes you guys fine in my book," a voice said from behind them. They turned to see a young man in loose fitting clothing of black and yellowish tan. He had on a light hooded jacket draped around his shoulders, a pair of knives of some exotic curved design secured to his belt, and a pair of black fingerless gloves on his hands. He had golden blond hair that fell to just above his eyes, dark stubble around his chin, and eyes that appeared gold but glowed with a silver light "Hey, I'm Deven. I'm part of your crew now, I guess."

"You guess?" Seth asked. "Well, I'm Seth, this is Dayved, and this is Sailis."

"Once again, my friend has jumped forward a bit as far as necessary information is concerned," another man said. He had dark brown skin over a muscular frame and towered over Deven by a good foot. He wore clothing more like the crew's, but sleeveless, exposing heavily tattooed arms of black designs. His head was bald, but he had a short thick beard of black hair, and his eyes were dark blue, almost black. On his belt, he had an odd-looking pouch and a few vials of dark liquid, and on his back, he carried a long, curved sword. "My name is Alex, and we were part of the group that tried to help with your premature release. The high lord and your captain struck a deal concerning our release and admittance to your ship."

"That makes more sense," Dayved laughed, extending his hand. "Welcome to the crew."

"Thanks mate," Deven said, taking his hand and then moving to the others. "Still can't believe you guys broke the plan. It was perfect."

"Everyone has their own reasons for acting," a third voice said, walking up. "Though after hearing about you, I think I understand why. Spencer Eli, at your service."

"Oh good, you all came," Adi said, almost skipping up the dock and embracing Seth and the others. She was in form fitting clothes of dark green and light grey and had a slender knee length tunic of darker green hung over the ensemble. Her shoulder length rich brown hair had a reddish tint in the light and was tied in the back save for a few strands that fell to her bright blue eyes.

"You're late, sis," Deven laughed.

"It's still morning, and they're still loading," Adi answered back. "Though it looks like I'm not a moment too soon. I'm just glad you didn't do something epic like 'leave at first light' like you see in all the stories."

"Cap wanted to sleep in," Seth laughed. "No 'first light' for him, and who are we to argue?"

Meow

"Well, hello there, Skritches," Adi said, bending down to pet the cat that had come up and rubbed against her leg. Skritches purred at her touch. "Are you planning on coming with us?"

"When did you get a cat," Deven laughed.

"When he adopted me," Adi laughed, picking him up. "Do you want to come with us, Skritches? You would like Vandor, yes you would. I don't know if you should, though. It might be dangerous. Yes, it probably will be."

"You appear surprisingly fit," Eli commented, staring at them, and looking them in the eye, ignoring Adi's baby talk. "Food deprivation, lethargy, darkness, despair… with little more than a day you seem to be recovered."

"Oh, we're still not all the way," Seth said. "Probably a few more days until we recover completely."

"Either way, what I want to know is did you really torture the High Lord's kid earlier?" Deven asked. "That's the word going around."

"We gave him only what he earned, nothing more," Sailis answered. "Hey, wait a second. You're here! Come on, let me take you to Cap and the others and let them know you're here."

"Too late," Joshian called from over the railing. "He's already heard. Welcome to my ship. Come on up!"

Sailis went back to the bags as Adi set Skritches down before bounding up the gangplank. "You smell better," she greeted him.

"Thank you for that," Joshian laughed. "The High Lord was more than willing to allow use of his servants to get enough water for my crew. Timothy himself demanded it. I'm glad you all decided to join us and thank you for all you did on our behalf. I only hope this will help alleviate some of the debt we have towards you."

"I'm grateful for the opportunity, Captain," Eli said, stepping forward and extending his hand. "Spencer Eli, at your service. This is Deven and Alex."

"Joshian Farstrid at yours," Joshian answered, his returning handshake of equal strength. "I trust you've been filled in already of what we're going to be doing?"

"Only that we're sailing for Vandor," Eli answered. "Beyond that, nothing more was given."

"Not surprised," Joshian nodded. "Alright, well, the ship is in fairly good order; it looks like Timothy's people didn't touch much of anything, so if you guys go help load the rest of the stuff on board, we can sail shortly. Once we're in open water, I'll explain things as well as I can, and see where you fit in best. Any questions?"

"Yeah, what are we doing?" Deven asked. "Why are we sailing?"

"As I said, I'll explain things once we get into open water," Joshian laughed. "Until then, let's just say we're going off to start a war."

"Okay, I like you guys a little more," Deven nodded.

"Glad to hear it," Joshian smiled. "Now then, let's go."

There were no dramatic speeches to send off the crew, not even a dramatic word to get everyone moving. Joshian simply looked at everyone, cracked his knuckles and smiled, and then everyone exploded into motion. Some went to the ropes to hoist the sails, others scampered to the sides to call out changes in the ocean's floor in their path, and some scampered up the masts for better vantage points. The guests, for the most part, stood around looking awkward and confused, with Timothy's party looking around in awe. After they were well underway, Joshian addressed the newcomers.

"Gentlemen," Joshian began. "And lady. Welcome, formally, to *Courageous Heart*. This voyage will be broken into four legs, the first of which will take approximately two weeks and will take us from Kellivar to our home of Firebrand. From there, it will take another couple of weeks for us to arrive in Vandor, where we'll stay until Lord Timothy feels there is nothing more to do. Once our business in Vandor is concluded, we'll return to Kellivar in the same way, taking the same amount of time. Altogether, our time on the ship will be a little more than two months, which I know can be a long time for some, so I'd like for us to all get along and keep disagreements to an absolute minimum. I will also do whatever I can, provided I feel it safe enough, to push hard and cut down the time sailing, specifically for our journey down to Vandor. Now, are there any questions about that much?" Heads shook, but Deven raised his hand.

"Um, what exactly are we supposed to do?" he asked.

"I was getting to that," Joshian answered. "Lord Timothy has his diplomatic party that he will need to prep and work with, and Captain Cornell has been placed over command of the guards. The ship shall be at your disposal, whatever training or work you need to do, provided you don't break it. I like my ship. Meals are three times a day, but beyond that, no food is to be taken, period. All of it is rationed, and if everyone keeps fair, we should be fine. If anyone has a problem with that, understand I eat the same food as my crew at the same time as my crew."

"Will we eat the same thing all the time?" Deven asked. "That really gets boring."

"This food is provided by the High Lord himself," Timothy declared. "It will not be boring."

"I'm sure I could spice it up," Deven shrugged. "Provided you have spices. Tell me you have spices, please."

"Everything food related is boring if he doesn't have a hand in it," Alex said, shaking his head. "Pay it no mind."

"That is all I have for the diplomatic party," Joshian continued. Timothy turned and walked away, but Captain Cornell smiled and nodded respectfully before following.

"Now, however, I come to you four," Joshian said, addressing Adi' group. "Adi explained a little of what you all did together, but I'm still unsure about the specifics."

"Thieves, grifters, con artists, mercs," Deven said quickly. Eli, Alex, and Adi looked over at him. "What? It's an honest question, albeit about dishonest professions, but we're here for a few months, so we might as well make the most of it. Oh, also, forgers."

"Wait, slow down," Joshian said, putting up his hands. "What do you mean by 'grifters' and 'mercs'? I'm afraid I'm unfamiliar with the terms."

"Grifters are people who pretend to be someone else as part of a con job," Alex said before Deven could speak. "Mercs is just short for mercenaries. When we ran together, Adi was our main thief; she could usually get in and out of anywhere and make off with whatever she wanted. Deven was the real artist as far as acting went. He could switch between personas like you wouldn't believe and have people believing he was whoever he wanted. His main flaw, however, is his mouth; he tended to run it off more than he should."

"Hey, I have things to say that people need to hear, whether they know it or not," Deven interjected. Alex continued as if he hadn't heard.

"I'm a scholar and an artist," Alex continued. "I made most of my living painting forgeries and passing them off as the real thing, but I'm pretty apt with graphite and regular ink. I can study handwriting and copy it pretty nearly, though a thorough inspection would reveal them to be fake, of course. Still, they were always enough to get us in and out without much trouble."

"Have you ever studied cartography?" Joshian asked. Alex smiled.

"I love maps, actually," he said. "Oh, the libraries in Vandor have some that predate the Adonarian War in case you're curious. There are maps that shift constantly the borders of Ildice and Ebaven, and by going through the records you can plot conquests of various generals or kings. The later maps show the break-ups of land by the different lords and ladies, different acquisitions of the queens… it's all exciting."

"That's three of you," Joshian said, scratching his chin. "Spencer, what was your role in the whole thing?"

"I was the muscle," Eli smiled. "I was the one who got their necks out of trouble when things became physical. I served for a while with Ebaven's army, and then hired myself out to parties of adventurers when my time was completed. Eventually I was hired to look after these guys."

"Which we're very glad of," Deven added.

"You were an officer, correct?" Joshian asked. Eli nodded.

"Led small battalions," Spencer said. "Usually just city patrols in Kellivar, but from time to time I was stationed in Asard, and other times I had escort duty for one minor lord or another."

"He taught us everything we know about fighting," Deven chimed in.

"If you call what you do *fighting*," Alex mumbled, and Eli chuckled.

"Yes, I trained them," Eli said. "Though you never showed much skill for anything besides knives and short swords."

"Everything else was too heavy," Deven mumbled.

"Or too bulky," Adi added. "The best weapons were the ones you could hide. Like me."

"And we're too weak for hand-to-hand combat," Deven said. "That was your job."

"You still needed to know," Eli said.

"Would you be interested in training my crew, then?" Joshian asked. "We have our weapons, but to be honest we don't really know how to use them. I can't use one of the guards. They are Timothy's, and he made it clear that our two parties would be separate. You, however, are not part of Timothy's party, and thus not part of his conditions."

"Yes, I am, sir," Eli answered. "Begging your pardon, but we are your crew. Why ask when you can simply tell?"

"That's not what I do, not with friends at least," Joshian said, shrugging. "If a person wants to sail, then he will because he wants to. If he doesn't want to, then I won't take them on, simple as that. I could order you, that is true, but in our experience in matters like these, a crew that doesn't have to be ordered to perform works far better than one that does. If you prefer, I can order you, but again, I prefer not."

"I think without will be fine," Eli said, smiling a little as he nodded. "When would you like me to start?"

"Once you're dismissed," Joshian said, handing Eli his spear. "We know how to throw them with decent accuracy, but when it comes to close-quarters combat, we are not adept. Once you're comfortable with it, figure out what we need to know and go from there. I'll let you come up with your own training plan, and I'll do what I can to set aside time, hopefully something consistent."

"Sounds fun," Eli said, giving another nod.

"Good," Joshian grinned. "Now, Alex, I am glad you have an interest in maps, because the ones I have now are old and torn, and I'm pretty sure have maybe one more trip left in them. What I'd like are fresh versions, as much detail as you can, and when we get to Vandor, I'd love it if you could make copies of some of the ones you mentioned. We have spare parchment and ink supplies, so we should have everything you need."

"I can do that most definitely," Alex answered.

"Perfect," Joshian said. "Deven, you made a comment earlier about the food…"

"Begging your pardon," Alex interrupted. "Do not get him started."

"I catered every one of your events," Deven said. "That food was fantastic, and you know it! The prices everyone else was charging for quality of far lower was ridiculous, too. Not only did I do you a favor, but I did a favor to everyone else there. One thing you do not mess with is the pallet of the tongue. My dishes were to die for."

"Here we go," Alex sighed. "Captain, I would like to apologize for him…"

"No need," Joshian said. "Isaiah was our chef last trip, but he's not here now…"

"I am completely in!" Deven said, clinching his hands and hopping in place. "Give me the kitchen, I will make you culinary delicacies unlike anything you've ever tasted!"

"Alright, alright," Joshian laughed. "The galley is all yours, then. Also, the crew cycles through kitchen duty, so you'll have hands for prep and clean-up."

"Even better!" Deven said, gleefully. "I'll start categorizing what all we have, then."

"Oh, I hope it's no trouble," Joshian added. "But some evenings a few cast their lines in, and we cook up what they catch later on."

"An ever-changing pallet," Deven said, rubbing his hands together and smiling. "Always being challenged for every meal…"

"You have no idea how you have made his day," Alex chuckled. "Or his next few months, at least. Hope you're ready for it."

"...And I have so many plans for spices," Deven continued. "Can I make a list?"

"You'll have plenty of time," Joshian agreed. "And we'll do what we can about getting it all together. Alex, you too, figure out if you need anything more and I will see what I can do. This brings me to my last detail, though. Adi, in all our stories, you made comments about how you were the one doing the actual grabbing. You have an eye for value and a deep knowledge about acquiring said pieces of value. Would you be interested in managing our goods?"

"Managing, as in... what?" Adi asked.

"Quartermaster," Joshian said. "Someone to keep track of all the items on my ship, all the equipment, all the food, and as we go through food to keep a careful count, so we don't run out. To be frank, I've got my people, Timothy's people, the ship, and the journey to worry about, and if I don't need to worry about keeping us stocked for anything, that's one huge problem relieved. You'll also be responsible for keeping track of what we need and then when we get into port, making sure everything is properly delivered and stored."

"You're trusting me with... everything?" Adi asked. "You're trusting a thief with..."

"No, I'm trusting a friend," Joshian answered, smiling. "Are you up to it?"

"Um, yeah, I can do it... thank you," Adi said. Joshian nodded.

"Good," he said. "So, Alex, Deven, give your lists to Adi. She's in charge of that now. And that is everybody, perfect. Anything else before you're dismissed?"

"One small thing," Spencer said, chuckling. "I prefer going by Eli, since you're asking."

"Fair enough," Joshian confirmed. "Anyone else have anything they want to go by?"

"Cesilia," Adi replied. Alex and Deven looked at her, curious, but Eli looked at Joshian with much respect. "I don't trust people with it for the most part, for reasons I can't quite get into right now, but my real name is Cesilia, and you all can call me Ces."

"I have no doubt there is much behind your name preference," Joshian answered. "Nevertheless, since you do trust us with that, my crew shall hold that secret, and I thank you. And with that…"

Mew

"Oh, no, I'm sorry Captain," Ces said, bending down to pick up Skritches. "I guess he followed me on board…" Joshian laughed.

"Well, well, well, looks like we have a little stowaway, don't we," Joshian said, reaching out to scratch behind Skritches' ears. "Do you know what we do to stowaways on my ship? We put them to work. Yes, we do, Skritches, and you are no different. Now then, I keep a clean ship, but sometimes I miss things, so I am putting you on rat duty. Keep my ship clear, alright?"

Skritches purred in affirmation.

"You're not mad, Captain?" Ces asked, a mixture of relief and worry in her voice. Joshian shook his head.

"Not in the slightest," he chuckled. "Then, unless there are any others to address," he continued, pausing to look around. "Allow me to formally say, welcome to *Courageous Heart*."

Chapter 23

In the *Grey Gull Tavern,* near Kellivar's main port, Maer sat alone. Night had fallen on Ildice, so the streets were dark and deserted, and illuminated by a few lit windows that cast their shuttered light outward, which caught the occasional rat, stray cat, or random soldier in their beams. Before him, his drink sat half empty, much like the tavern. Most of the patrons had gone home for the night or were trickling out, but he had patience. There was nowhere he needed to be tonight… not anymore.

A sheet of creased and wrinkled parchment lay on the table before him, a parchment he had kept tighter to himself even than the orders he carried to the high lord. The high lord's adviser, Isaiah, had tracked him down personally and exchanged a few words with him aside from giving him the note. The man had always felt trustworthy but looking into his eyes and knowing what they meant, Maer knew every word the man said would be worth all the gold in the treasury. He gave Maer instructions, in the form of the sheet. The instructions were simple, but they were enough, at least for him: *The darkness rises, but the light will be there to meet it. Meet at the Grey Gull after darkness has fallen for the answers you seek.*

"Maer, we're leaving," Sergeant Voss said, walking up. He and a few others of the guard had taken a table before Maer had walked in. "Coming with, or are you sticking around?"

"I'm staying," Maer answered. "As long as I have to."

"I would feel remis if I didn't point out that you're likely wasting your time tonight," Voss said.

Maer nodded, swirling the liquid in his mug before taking another drink.

"You didn't see what I did," Maer responded.

"Are you sure you saw what you did?" Voss countered. "We heard your story, Maer. We've heard it from other crackpots, too, and the soldiers are beginning to think you're a little, well…"

"Doesn't bother me," Maer said, leaning back from the table. "Few months ago, it might have, but not now. I'm used to being alone, and if that's what it takes for the truth, then so be it."

"This devotion to these… myths is going to get you in trouble. Men have been discharged for talking like this, or worse," Voss said. "You know that don't you?"

"I know there's a chance," Maer said, nodding. "But the truth is far worse."

"Come on, Sarge," Corporal Grinds said from the door. "You can't convince him, he's just like Lukas was. Just let him go."

"It's his grave," Private Drant added. "No sense in…"

"He's one of ours," Voss snapped, cutting him off. "Just like the others. Don't forget that."

"Yes, Sarge," they replied. Voss turned back to Maer.

"It's alright," Maer said, gesturing to the door. "I know what everyone's saying about me. I wouldn't want you caught up in that."

"Whatever people say, I chart my own course," Voss countered. He sighed, looking between the door and Maer. "Look, it's late, and I'm pretty sure you're being set up…"

"I'll be fine," Maer said.

"Take care of yourself, alright?" Voss said. Maer just nodded, and Voss stepped out, leaving him alone with his drink and his hopes.

The tavern emptied itself further. More tables vacated, and then more of the patrons that were sitting at the bar picked themselves or their buddies up and left. Still, Maer waited.

The tavern keep announced closing. Maer rose to leave, but then he saw a lone patron at the bar rise from their seat, put a few coins at the counter, and head for his position.

The figure was very unsuspecting, tall, but with a small frame covered by a dark blue cloak that was like those worn by soldiers. Their boots fell light and steady, but the way they moved, Maer was surprised any sound could be heard. They were strong and graceful, the walk being closer to gliding, and when they gestured for Maer to sit, he felt a strange authority behind it.

Taking a seat opposite him, they removed their hood to reveal a striking woman with pale blonde hair and piercing gray eyes. She appeared young, but her eyes were old, and her figure spoke of combat.

"Hello," she said, her voice soft and melodious.

"Hello," Maer responded, taken aback and unsure of what to say.

"I have many ears in this city," the woman said. "So, I know where you come from, and I know what you come from. Even if I didn't, I see it in your eyes. You know what I am."

Maer nodded. "They said I would find you if I looked. Their name…"

"There's no need," the woman said, raising her hand and bring Maer up short. "Sometimes having our names in the open is dangerous, especially with the ears I know in the city."

"I'm sorry," Maer said. "I have questions, though."

"As do I," the woman said. "Though mine can wait. You deserve some answers, I am glad to give them, and this place is safe enough. The tavern keep is my friend and can be trusted."

"There's really only one I want," Maer said. "O… my friend, didn't have much time before having to ride off to warn… someone else, but he mentioned one name." Here, Maer bent closer. "Emyran."

"And you wish to know Him," the woman smiled, and Maer felt a warmth flow through him.

"My friend believed in him," Maer answered. "It gave him hope, and it gives me hope, and I want to know him. I tried searching the archives. I found mention of him in the ancient histories, but there wasn't anything on who he is, or was."

"Nor would there be," the woman said, her tone saddened. "After the War, people tried to forget Him, erase Him, or change Him into nothing more than a story."

"I don't understand why," Maer said.

"People don't want a king," the woman said. "People want to be in control of their own lives, or the lives of others. They want to be the ones to rule, not to be ruled. But to accept Him, you must accept all of him, and that is difficult."

Maer mulled over her words, taking a few more drinks. Moments passed between them as the words settled, and as they settled, so did a sense of revelation. "You're right," he finally said, and she nodded. "I don't want a king… but I don't want the alternative. Please teach me what I don't know."

"Our story begins long ago," the woman began. "Thousands of years before the Adonari War, to a time beyond my memory. I will start at the beginning, where things were far different, by reciting the words as they were given to me… Before the first age of the world, there was Emyran."

Bareth sat in silence before the woman of his affection. For years he had been her confidant, her trusted eyes and hand, and though his actions remained secret to all but her, she always rewarded him fairly, though her affection was more than enough.

"Your words had better be more than you are giving, Bareth," the cloaked woman said in front of Lieutenant Bareth.

"My lady," Bareth began, sweat dripping down his back, and feeling his collar tightening. He hated displeasing her, and always sought to make amends for the few times he had, but he still had to endure her stare, her scorn, and the hurt in her voice. "Lady Dahlia, I have done everything…"

"Such a cliché," she sighed, her voice both alluring and venomous as she drew the words out. She pulled back her hood, her black hair illuminated by the tavern's low yellow light, and her golden eyes catching the flame in a way that made him feel weak in the knees and light in his head. "And such a pointless statement. You had one job, one simple job for one of your station, and you have failed. Did you not think that when I told you to keep the girl contained, I meant anything less?"

"No, no my lady," Bareth stuttered. He hated the way he could never act collected in front of her, hated the way he could never appear as strong as he knew he was, and it shamed him to his core. "Of course not. However, if I may ask as to the reason…"

"Is it not enough that it is what my master ordered?" she asked, her eyes narrowing. Then her lips curled into a sultry smile, and her voice softened. "Is it not enough that it is what I have asked, my dear?"

"My lady," Bareth said carefully. "I mean no disrespect, but I simply wanted to ask why you only wish her contained, rather than killed. For years I have followed her and pursued her as you asked, or had my men do so in my place, but would it not be easier to simply have her silenced?"

"It would if her elimination was what I desired," she answered, reaching out to stroke his cheek, sending a pleasant yet disturbing chill through his body. "But my goal is the conquest of Ildice itself."

Bareth recoiled, his eyes widening against his will, but his companion appeared unconcerned.

"Still, the fact that she is on her way to Vandor is troubling, but not terribly so," she continued, tucking a strand of her hair behind her ear, and leaning back in her bench. "I don't like pieces out of my control if I can help it."

"Begging your pardon," Bareth choked. "The conquest of Ildice?"

"I don't see why you're so concerned, my love," she said. "Once my lord has control of Ildice, we shall live as we've desired. Remember our dreams, those of our coastal home, a fleet of trade ships, and the Ildician guard under your command? All these things take time, and under the current leadership they are not possible."

Bareth shook his head, the thoughts not fully forming, but in the back of his mind, something felt off. He felt her hand play lightly against his, and it was as if the thoughts had never existed.

"We will make this work," she assured him, bringing his hand up to her lips. Tears welled up in her eyes, and she brushed them away, forcing a smile again. "Forgive me my outburst, darling."

"My lady," he said, taking her hand in his. "It is I who am sorry."

"I am tired of my life," she said softly. "I am tired of the man who is my husband and the way he treats me. I am tired of the way he sees me as little more than a servant, made to look pretty but be silent unless it is suitable for his needs. When he touches me… there is no love anymore. His grip is firm, as opposed to your gentleness, but I am his, and I am trapped as only a lady can be trapped. I just… I long for a life of just us."

"As do I, my love," Bareth replied, smiling, feeling his heart willing up with a passion that threatened to consume and burn him to his core. "Tell me what you need for me to do."

Gray clouds hovered above the Truvona Mountains as Onesh and Laehenarado rode along the desolate ridge. The wind howled as they continued, tugging at Onesh's cloak, but then a chill beyond the wind hit Onesh. Laehenarado paused in his stride, and Onesh dismounted, so Laehenarado assumed his human form, but waited for Onesh, who stood ill at ease. After sensing a measure of peace return to Onesh, Laehenarado spoke.

"You are troubled," he said. "Speak your mind, my young friend."

"And you are observant as always," Onesh acknowledged. He let out a deep breath, piercing the empty air. "And I am grateful. I confess, my heart is troubled. I feel a war like last time, but I don't have the same hope for this as I did the last."

"This will be the end of many things," Laehenarado said. "But we all know the end will come eventually."

"I feel my end approaching," Onesh sighed. "After all these years…"

"Come, my friend," Laehenarado said, gesturing onward. "We must fly now."

"Yes, you are right," Onesh said, and Laehenarado transformed himself once more into his natural form, materializing a saddle of sorts for Onesh to cling to as well. Onesh nestled himself between the wings. "I am ready, old friend."

Laehenarado leaped off the ground, spreading his wings, and climbed. They wheeled away from the mountains, plunging west, into Mahlen, where the land grew even darker. The ground disappeared as the mountain range fell away, but before them, through the clouds, a much taller peak materialized. They climbed higher, and then higher still, to where Onesh started to notice the cold, and came upon a sight Onesh had frequented many years ago, but no Learsian had seen before.

The stonework was old, but kept with care, of bright white marble columns and walls reinforced with silver steel. Towers were placed at equal intervals; one tower on each of the corners and two more on each wall, making twelve guard towers in all. There were no gates, but they needed none, and inside the city, torches burned everywhere darkness could threaten to touch. Valoria was its name, the last watch, and the city of the Vigel.

They descended to one of the towers, and a lone figure greeted them.

"Welcome, Laehenarado and Onesh."

"Thank you, Maikahael," Onesh replied to the muscular, armored figure once he dismounted and Laehenarado returned to his human form. Laehenarado placed his hand over his breast and inclined his head, which Maikahael mirrored.

"Speak freely, Adonari," Maikahael encouraged, inclining his head, and opening his hands.

"Sir," Onesh began. "Kythraul have attempted to invade the Ildician border."

"Why are you here, then?" Maikahael asked, his tone carrying concern. "Your mission should be Ildice."

"I've sent another to spread that word," Onesh answered. "Another they will listen to better. He needed the quest more than I."

"You know the ways of man better than we," Maikahael answered.

"What news have you of Ebaven and Sanasis?" Onesh asked.

"We worry about Ebaven," Maikahael answered. "They've already allowed the darkness to saturate their lives, though they refuse to see it, but there is a little truth that still clings to their hearts, so they are not lost completely. There is still hope."

"And Sanasis?" Onesh asked.

"Sanasis is lost," Maikahael answered. "Come."

Maikahael led them into the city, down crystalline roads of polished quartz and past rows of bright flowers of orange and yellow, and brought them to a center courtyard of green lawn where another ranger in dark brown and sandy garments sat in silence.

"Urlong," Onesh greeted the man.

"Onesh, my old friend," the man answered, pulling back his hood, and exposing leathery tanned skin with dark tattoos of ancient Sanatian design. His eyes glowed with pure silver and warmth upon seeing him. "Your presence is a shade upon my soul."

"Maikahael spoke of Sanasis falling," Onesh spoke. Urlong nodded but raised a hand.

"Not quite, but it is only a matter of time," Urlong answered, gesturing for Onesh to sit with him. "The nation is divided over ideals, each party desiring only their own ends and not the good of the nation. Indeed, it is difficult to speak of it even as a nation, as local lords and governors are like kings of their territories."

"War has united people together before," Onesh said.

"War will cripple them, Onesh," Urlong lamented. "The people have lost not only their will to fight... they've willingly surrendered it."

"Explain," Onesh said.

"The territories have decided their own laws," Urlong said. "Some of the interior territories, and those near the mountains and northern coast are all for rising up against the darkness, but those near the forest, and near the old City...

Onesh, they've already outlawed the existence of swords and arms. The boarder territories have outlawed going into the eastern forest to hunt and have even outlawed the trading of game, in prelude to their push to outlaw bows and spears as well."

He trailed off, and his fists clenched.

"What of their army?" Onesh asked, fearing the answer.

"Some of their new leaders have spoken of the army being the reason for war," Urlong replied. "They have raised their voices enough that the people are starting to think as they do, and some of the territories have actively disbanded their troops and are encouraging others to do the same."

"How do they not understand?" Onesh asked.

"I do not know," Urlong replied. "I can only say that the darkness has touched them far deeper than we thoughts, that even common sense is regarded as foolish."

"We cannot abandon them…" Onesh began, but then his words were abruptly cut off by a loud horn blast.

"To the walls, Adonari!" the cry rang out. "To the walls!"

Onesh and Urlong ran, joining more of their brethren as they raced through the city. The Vigel were enraged, roaring or drawing great blades, with their armor shining and glowing in response. Maikahael stood as a beacon of light and fire upon the easternmost wall, a gigantic blade as wide as a man and as long as two held in his outstretched grip.

"Cast your eyes west," Maikahael ordered, his voice like rolling thunder and a captain's horn harmonized together. "And steady your hearts."

"So, the end begins," Urlong sighed. "At least, so my end begins."

"You won't be alone," Onesh said. "I can feel my end is near as well, but I have one more journey at least still in me. Sanasis will not fall, not as long as there are those who will still fight for it."

"And when those fighters are gone?" Urlong asked.

"Then the world will be lost," a gentle voice answered. The Adonari speaker was a head shorter than Onesh with rich brown hair and cream-colored skin, and she was dressed in elegant leaf-patterned armor. "But we are not yet gone."

"Not nearly gone," another Adonari said, coming forward in heavy plate with a pair of axes strapped to his back. Scars covered his face, though much of that was covered by his long dark hair and dark full beard. "We will ride with you."

"Aliscia, Dergeron," Urlong acknowledged. "And Onesh, thank you."

"The fires of Malgalon, or worse, arise," Onesh declared, staring out westward. *Nothing out here* he thought, reflecting on the words spoken by many of the men he rode with. If only that were true. That fantasy was gone, however, as the gray sky and gray surface was now tainted with the red glow rising.… a red horizon. He closed his eyes and hung his head.

A warm, metal hand clamped hard over Onesh's shoulder. Raising his head and opening his eyes, he stared at Maikahael, and the fire of his gaze washed over him. His hand clenched around one of his knives, and he smiled. "But we will rise to meet it. In the name of Emyran, we will meet it."

Stay tuned for a scene from
the next book!

Firebrand

Book 2

Crimson Shore

Calian felt something through the ship. He couldn't place how he knew, but a moment later the ropes securing the center mast to the aft section snapped. Wood cracked and splintered as the wind caught hold of the unsecured mast. He cried out something that was lost in the wind, and then watched the mast shatter at its base as the rest of it crashed to the deck.

He heard shouts, men calling to others as to their condition, but then, somewhere off the side of the ship in the water, he heard the quieter pleas of a man calling for help. He rushed to the side, dodging broken timber, ran to where the mast had broken the railing, and stared out.

"Anyone out there?" he called, scanning the sea.

"Calian, it's me!" he heard back, and then realized he couldn't see Timothy anywhere on deck.

"Timothy! Are you alright?"

"I'm stranded in the middle of the ocean clinging to a floating plank surrounded by water! How do you think I bloody am?"

Surprised with himself, Calian laughed. "Alright, what hurts, what's broken, and are you stuck?"

"Got hit in the head when I came up, so everything's spinning. These clothes are soaked and heavy, and I'm getting tired. Can you get anything out here?"

"Not yet!" Calian answered back, scanning the sea and trying to see through the water blowing around. "Just yell out when I say, alright? We'll get ya!"

"Calian," Timothy called back, and then coughed. "Calian, I can't stay above water. Help me!"

"Timothy!" There was no answer, so Calian called again. "Timothy! Blazing water rat, answer me!" There was still silence from Timothy's last call. Calian looked down, surveying the sea before him to find a part free of debris. He kicked off his shoes and rolled up his pants. "Nathane!" he called out, who acknowledged him quickly. "Get something out to me once I surface!"

"What's happening?" Nathane asked, coming into view as Calian climbed onto the rail.

"Fishing for a lord," he answered back, and then dove into the murky black.

His hands broke the water, and then the rest of his body submerged into the murky chaos. Sounds became muffled, reducing themselves to random noise as he swam downward, his arms pulling him towards his friend and his feet pushing him away from the ship. Once in a while, his vision would catch something that looked out of place, and he would swim towards that until it disappeared.

His lungs began to ache, reminding him air would have to come soon before it was too late for him as well. *No,* he said to himself. *I can go longer, have gone longer. I have to go longer.* He pushed the pain aside.

He could see Timothy up ahead, now, held suspended in the water, as if he was just waiting for him, waiting to be rescued. His lungs screamed back in protest, telling him it was hopeless. Still, he fought on.

Can't hold out, he heard himself say, but then he heard a new voice, a strange voice, ordering, *You Must.* Darkness filled his vision, all sounds, all feelings went dead. The water no longer held the icy touch it once had. Darkness consumed him.

About the Author

Stefan Coleman is an author, a graphic designer, and substitute teacher from the frozen wilderness of Alaska. Although initially a mathematics major, a random creative writing class necessary to fill a hole in his schedule awakened his passion for writing, and the works of Tolkien, CS Lewis, and Timothy Zahn have kept it burning. In his spare time, he loves photography and sharing it with the hope people can still find the sun through whatever clouds are going on in their lives.

He'd love to connect, and he can be found on Twitter, Instagram, and Facebook at firebrand101 and on YouTube at Firebrand101author.

FOR WAYS TO CONNECT WITH THE AUTHOR,
INCLUDING BOOK PAGES, AUTHOR PAGES,
SOCIAL MEDIA LINKS, AND MERCH LINKS,
SCAN THE QR CODE BELOW

ALSO, IF YOU ENJOYED THIS BOOK OR ANY OF
MY OTHER BOOKS, PLEASE CONSIDER
LEAVING A REVIEW, AS IT HELPS MORE THAN
YOU CAN IMAGINE.

YOU CAN ALSO FOLLOW ME ON FACEBOOK,
INSTAGRAM, AND TWITTER AT
FIREBRAND101
OR ON YOUTUBE AT
FIREBRAND101AUTHOR